PLENTY
More
LOVE

BOOK YOUR PLACE ON OUR WEBSITE AND MAKE THE ARABESQUE ROMANCE CONNECTION!

We've created a customized website just for our very special Arabesque readers, where you can get the inside scoop on everything that's going on with Arabesque romance novels.

When you come online, you'll have the exciting opportunity to:

- View covers of upcoming books

- Learn about our future publishing schedule (listed by publication month and author)

- Find out when your favorite authors will be visiting a city near you

- Search for and order backlist books

- Check out author bios and background information

- Send e-mail to your favorite authors

- Join us in weekly chats with authors, readers and other guests

- Get writing guidelines

- AND MUCH MORE!

Visit our website at
http://www.arabesquebooks.com

PLENTY
More
LOVE

CHRISTINE TOWNSEND

BET Publications, LLC
http://www.bet.com
http://www.arabesquebooks.com

ARABESQUE BOOKS are published by

BET Publications, LLC
c/o BET Books
One BET Plaza
1900 W Place NE
Washington, DC 20018-1211

All Kensington Titles, Imprints, and Distributed Lines are available at special quantity discounts for bulk purchases for sales promotions, premiums, fund-raising, and educational or institutional use. Special book excerpts or customized printings can also be created to fit specific needs. For details, write or phone the office of the Kensington special sales manager: Kensington Publishing Corp., 850 Third Avenue, New York, NY 10022, attn: Special Sales Department, Phone: 1-800-221-2647.

First Printing: October 2005

10 9 8 7 6 5 4 3 2 1

Printed in the United States of America

This book is dedicated to
Mary and Charles
Alice and Asa
Earline and Sam
Vera and Rick

. . . love endureth all things.
(I Cor. 13:7)

ACKNOWLEDGMENTS

I sincerely appreciate the conversations I had with Captain Lenny Manning of the Nashville Fire Department while I was mulling around ideas for this book. His insight helped me make Jonathan's role as a firefighter more realistic.

Meals and menu items discussed in this book are from *Our Mother's Table: The Culinary Journey of Beneva Mayweather* by Emma Mayweather Lincoln and Denise Sims. For more information about this book, visit my Web site: www.ChristineTownsend.com.

CHAPTER 1

Lisa Stevens hurriedly shoved papers from her desk into her briefcase. She knew that her brother's corporate jet would wait for her; nonetheless she hated being late. With the energy of hurricane-force wind, she dashed through her office door only to encounter a hard, solid mass that sent her stumbling backward.

Jonathan Hill instinctively threw out strong hands, placing them on her arms to steady her. "Hold on a minute. What's your hurry?" he asked, smiling down at his friend. Lisa was pretty tall for a woman, about five feet nine inches, but Jonathan towered over her at six feet five.

Stunned from the impact, Lisa didn't answer for a moment. Her eyes flew from his bright smile to the blue denim shirt that fit neatly across his broad shoulders, and back to his dark, handsome face. She caught her breath, inhaling his clean, fresh scent. "Hi, what are you doing here?" she finally asked, ignoring his question. Her husky voice was seductive to him, even asking such an impersonal question.

"I was in the area and decided to stop by," he

replied, taking in her rapid breathing and dark, glowing complexion.

Lisa's eyebrows knit together as she earnestly tried to remember if they had made plans for the evening. She immediately dismissed that possibility. She would not forget any plans to be with Jonathan, even though their relationship was a casual friendship.

Seeing the puzzled expression on her face, he explained, "I thought you might want to do something? You know—it's Friday and all." He tried to sound casual. There was no way he'd admit to her that he'd spent the whole day planning to see her. When he'd left his twenty-four-hour shift at the fire department, all he could think about was spending the next forty-eight hours of leisure time with her.

"I'm sorry. I can't. Jet's plane is waiting for me. We're going to Kiawah Island for the weekend," Lisa apologized. She lifted earnest eyes to his, silently pleading for understanding. He was so filled with jealousy that he missed her plea entirely.

"I guess that includes your boyfriend, too?" Jonathan blurted out angrily before he could stop himself.

Seized by a burst of anger that matched his, Lisa looked down at her work boots for a moment to rein in her emotions. After having a long, difficult day at a construction site for one of her company's new buildings, she was in no mood to try to pacify Jonathan.

She paused, guilt pushing her anger away. Yes, she felt guilty about leaving him for the weekend. He'd grown to expect to spend his time off with her. Bringing her emotions under control, she lifted her eyes again to look into Jonathan's before saying evenly, "He's not my boyfriend. He's just a friend."

He returned her gaze. Jolted by her beauty, he almost missed the meaning of her words.

She shifted the heavy briefcase from one hand to the other so that she could put the strap of her overnight tote on her shoulder before adding, "Anyway, what does it matter to you?"

"I'm your friend, too. You need to listen to me. I know about dudes like that. He'll try to take advantage of you." His open, friendly smile had been replaced by a dark, dangerous look. He folded his muscular arms across his chest and held her in his stern glare.

"No one will do anything to me I don't let them do," she replied saucily. Even in dusty jeans and a short-sleeve shirt, she managed to give him an imperious glare. Her ponytail, which had been sleek that morning, now hung low on her neck. She tossed her head and the ponytail fell over one shoulder. Strands of hair fanned around her face. Her checkered shirt was soiled and no longer tucked into her jeans.

"Are you sure about that?" he asked in a deep, challenging voice. He refused to let his desire to pull her into his arms, or her attitude, deter him from his cautions. After all, he thought, it was for her own good.

"I'm positive," she replied, holding his gaze. The tall, slender woman was un-self-conscious about her disheveled appearance. Having grown up with three brothers, Lisa had been called a tomboy most of her life. Now that she was nearly thirty, that term no longer applied. However, she still lacked many of the feminine graces. A busy executive, she could not be strapped to a desk for long periods. Educated as a mechanical engineer, the dirty profession, she didn't mind getting in the trenches with her construction crews. Stopping to primp was a waste of time with so many other things to do.

That was precisely why she was so appealing to Jonathan. She was totally without vanity and eagerly threw herself into sports or any other activity without concern for how she looked. Somehow he knew that she would make love with unleashed passion.

Seeing the stubborn look on her face, he realized that she would leave now just because he'd warned her not to. He looked at her intently another moment, his scowl firmly in place, before saying, "I see I'm holding you up." He turned away without saying another word.

Her anger, always quick to dissipate, had already abandoned her by the time Jonathan moved away. "Wait a second," she called to his back. But his long, determined steps had taken him too far away to hear her.

She cursed herself for not explaining things to him. But what could she have said to make things better? That she would rather be with him? That his touch set her on fire? She could still feel the warm imprint on her arms where he had steadied her. All he needed to do was say he cared about her and she would have canceled the trip in a heartbeat.

But she knew she was not likely to hear any words of endearment from him. They had tried dating when they first met, but he'd decided a romantic relationship wasn't right for them. Jonathan had been put off by the difference in their incomes. She was part owner of a multibillion-dollar corporation and he was a firefighter, a simple city employee. He'd insisted that he wasn't the man for her. Yet their friendship remained strong.

Shaking her head as if to get rid of problems that seemed to have no resolution, Lisa moved into action. Rushing toward the elevator, she reached it seconds before the doors closed. Already filled with weary workers eager for the weekend, it stopped on each of the eight floors below hers before releasing its passengers into the lobby.

The Sand Castles corporate car waited patiently for her at the curb. As she exited the revolving doors, the driver, Matt, met her and relieved her of her burdens. When they arrived at the late-model Lincoln Town Car, he opened one of the back doors for her.

Settling into the plush leather seat, she inhaled deeply. Matt closed the door and deposited her bags in the trunk. After he'd taken his place behind the steering wheel, he asked, "Are you ready, Lisa?"

"Yes, finally. Do you know that I'm flying out of Cornelia Fort Airpark in east Nashville?"

"Yes, I've already talked with one of the pilots. They were wondering what the holdup is. They should be in Miami picking up Cara and Jet about now."

"I know. It took me forever to get out of the office. It was one thing after another," she said tiredly, relaxing her head on the headrest.

"Maybe you'll be able to forget about work and enjoy your weekend," Matt commented.

"That's my intention."

Leaving the Sand Castles offices in downtown Nashville, Jonathan was at loose ends. He didn't have to work again until Sunday, but he had absolutely no one to spend his time with. Winding his way through one-way streets, he thought briefly of stopping by the firehouse as he passed. Something was always going on there. The guys would be cooking, playing cards, video games, or table tennis.

But he dreaded the surprised looks that would be

on the firefighters' faces if he were to drop in just
to socialize. He almost always kept to himself, even
when he was on duty. His friends could be counted
on one hand and that number included Lisa Stevens.

Jonathan continued driving aimlessly through
city streets until he found himself on I-65 North. He
took the I-24 juncture, subconsciously making the
decision to head home. Within minutes he was at the
Ashland City exit. His low-slung 1978 red Corvette
raced down the highway, taking him even farther
from civilization. Feeling free from the restraints of
inner-city traffic, Jonathan pressed the gas pedal
and watched the needle on his speedometer move
to the right. As his speed increased, his spirits soared.

Approaching the gravel path that led to his large,
two-story farmhouse, he reduced his speed to a
crawl, carefully climbing the steep hill. He parked at
one end of the long, wraparound porch and quickly
entered the house. Once inside he took the stairs to
his bedroom two at a time and changed into one of
the gray jumpsuits he wore when he worked on cars.
Without looking around his spacious bedroom or the
tidy rooms of his newly renovated home, he headed
out to the barn in back of the house.

His barn was not home to horses and cows, but to
an array of Corvettes that were in various stages
of repair. They lined one side of the meticulous structure that was as sterile as a medical laboratory. The
concrete floor was washed down regularly and the
walls of the old barn had been replaced with Sheet-
rock and painted white. There was a place for everything in this work space.

At an early age, Jonathan had discovered his passion for all things mechanical. Quite by accident, he
had built a small side business restoring old
Corvettes. It had begun with an old car his father had

given him even before he was old enough to drive. He still had that car, refusing to part with it under any circumstances. Convinced his car had a female's temperament, he had named her Zora.

Immediately after flipping the switch that lighted up the barn, he moved to his CD player and pressed the button that filled the voluminous space with zydeco music. As the Cajun music with its curious mixture of guitars, accordions, and washboards lifted his spirits, Jonathan rolled his tool bench over to the 1969 Stingray he was refurbishing for his friend and mentor, Alan Mueller.

Once his hands were busy, his mind returned to Lisa. Of course, he couldn't admit that he thought about her all the time. He rationalized that she was on his mind because she frequently worked on cars with him in this barn. And if he admired her, it was only because she had such an analytical mind. At least that's what he tried to convince himself. Lisa could break down an engine and put it back together as well as he could. Who wouldn't admire a woman who could figure out why an engine sputtered quicker than most experienced mechanics?

After thinking about her for a while, he had to be honest with himself. Lisa's analytical mind wasn't the only reason he enjoyed being with her. She was touchable, she was real and she was honest about her emotions. Lisa didn't hold anything back. And that was what made the thought of making love to her so enticing.

They had dated briefly, but it hadn't taken him long to realize that friendship was all there could be between them—ever. That's the way it had to be. He had no right to expect more from a woman like Lisa Stevens. She was privileged and accustomed to the high life. Her whole life had been lived before TV cameras and news reporters. The last thing a man with Jonathan's background needed was a nosy investigative reporter.

Around midnight, Jonathan looked at his handiwork and decided he'd done enough for one day. After cleaning his hands with degreaser, he carefully wiped down the car and his tools as he put them in place. He cleaned his hands again and headed inside.

After a brief stop in Miami to board Lisa's brother, Jet, and his wife, Cara, the plane had headed north again to a small island off the South Carolina coast. When they arrived at the resort, Rodney, Lisa's friend, was already waiting anxiously for them.

He looked Lisa over appreciatively as she approached him. Although she was in disarray, she exuded vitality and exuberance that attracted people to her. "Let me guess, you got held up at work," he teased Lisa after greeting her. That was her usual excuse.

"It couldn't be helped," she said quickly. "I was at a construction site for a new building all day and you know how it is with construction—the unpredictable can always be expected."

"That's true," Jet agreed, coming alongside Lisa as they crossed the lobby.

"Maybe you should have taken the day off like I did," Rodney suggested.

"Next time," Lisa said without giving the suggestion any consideration.

"Let me take that bag for you," Rodney offered, reaching for the tote bag slung over her shoulder.

"It's not heavy. I'm okay," she responded, rejecting his offer.

In moments the group was checked into the hotel. Before parting to their separate rooms, they agreed to meet in the lobby for dinner.

Sitting on the side of the bed in her hotel room, Lisa was relieved to finally remove her heavy work boots, jeans, and shirt. She had wanted to change before leaving her office, but had run out of time.

Stretching to get the kinks out of her joints from sitting too long, she caught a glimpse of herself in the full-length mirror. She saw a tall, slender, pecan-brown woman. The white cotton tank top that she'd worn under her work shirt had just a bit of lace around the scooped neck. Her white cotton panties were French-cut bikinis. Some people might have been surprised at Lisa's closet femininity.

There were no bulges on her body anywhere. Her shoulders were well defined and hips were slim. She straightened her shoulders and tried to make her small breasts protrude. Laughing at herself, she felt like a teenager again.

Maybe her boyish body was why Jonathan still saw her as just one of the guys, somebody to hang with when no one else was around. If she were curvier, maybe he'd be more interested in her. For a moment she wished her body were different, but quickly banished the thought. An extreme makeover was definitely not in her future.

Stripping away her remaining clothes, Lisa stepped into the shower and lathered up quickly before rinsing off and stepping out just as quickly. She never spent more than a few minutes grooming. She considered spending any more time than that a waste.

Knowing that it would take the others a lot longer to get dressed, she lay on the bed and relaxed for the first time since she'd gotten out of bed before daylight that morning. Closing her eyes, she let her mind drift back to Jonathan. Why was he always at the top of her mind? She thought she'd accepted the fact that he'd rather be her friend than lover. They got along just fine and had a lot in common.

But sometimes the way he looked at her made her think he wanted more. When he didn't know she noticed, she felt his eyes following her and they burned intensely hot, to her very soul.

When he'd first come to her with the mess about being just friends, she thought he was giving her a line, a way of letting her down easy. She'd been about to tell him to go get lost, until she realized he was sincere. He really did want a friendship with her. And for some reason, Lisa had felt that Jonathan really needed a friend much more than he needed a lover. The problem for her was that his touch still set her on fire.

Without realizing it, Lisa drifted off to sleep and was awakened by the ringing phone. "We're waiting for you. Are you about ready?" Rodney asked when she answered the phone.

"No, go ahead and get a table. I'm not dressed yet," she hurriedly explained.

"You're not dressed?" Rodney repeated. He was totally surprised because more often than not, Lisa had to wait for him.

After dressing in an island-print wraparound skirt with a matching halter, she stepped into gold low-heel sandals. When she finished dressing, she fastened the clasp on her diamond tennis bracelet. It had been a gift to herself for making all of her business goals last year.

As she fumbled with the catch of the bracelet, she noticed that the safety chain was broken. She made a mental note to have it repaired when she returned home. Before heading for the door, she grabbed a long gold shawl from the bed.

As she entered the dining room, her bouncy walk conveyed her high energy, causing quite a few heads to turn. When she made her way to the table where Rodney, Jet, and Cara were seated, both men stood. Rodney held a seat out for her. "Are you all right?" Jet asked as soon as they were all seated again.

"Yes, why are you looking at me so funny?" She looked around the table at the concerned eyes turned on her.

"You're never late for anything," Cara explained. "Do you feel okay?"

"Are you using your inhalers?" Jet asked anxiously.

"Please don't start nagging me about that now," Lisa said, rolling her eyes.

"You need to take care of yourself," Jet said gently.

"Look, I haven't had an asthma attack for ages. I don't need to walk around sucking on inhalers anymore. I'm just fine." She spread the large, pale blue napkin across her lap. "In fact, I'm hungry enough to eat a goat."

"They don't have goat here, but they have delicious she-crab soup," Rodney suggested.

The appetizing soup was followed by jumbo shrimp grilled on skewers with cherry tomatoes, pearl onions, chunks of pineapple, and yellow peppers served on a bed of wild rice. While feasting on the succulent meal, they engaged in light conversation. Their words floated around Lisa, but she never felt involved. Her mind kept drifting back to Jonathan. She wondered how he was spending the evening.

As the server removed empty platters from the table, Rodney casually mentioned, "Since we handle security for Sand Castles throughout Europe, I'm thinking of opening offices to handle security for

other U.S. corporations doing business abroad."
He leaned back in his chair, not looking directly at
Jet, but waiting for his response.

He didn't have to wait long. Jet responded enthusiastically, "That's a good idea. If there's anything that I can do to help, let me know."

"Maybe you could introduce me to Carl Timeon.
I understand he has a home in France. I'd like to get
his business." Rodney was referring to the president of one of the largest hotel and resort chains in
the world. He was confident Jet would help him.
They'd been friends since they'd played football
for the Tampa Bay Buccaneers. Having retired from
the NFL when his father had died suddenly, Jet had
taken the reins of his father's company, Sand Castles. When Rodney had retired and started Grimes
and Associates Security and Protection Agency a
few years later, Jet had not hesitated in turning over
the responsibility of his firm's security to him.

The only time Rodney and Jet had disagreed over
the years was when Rodney had begun wooing Lisa.
Knowing Rodney's promiscuous past, Jet had warned
him to stay away from his little sister. He quickly discovered the more he protested, the more the two of
them seemed to enjoy thwarting his attempts to control their lives. When he ended his attempts at block-
ing the romance, it had cooled down considerably.
From the looks of things, the budding romance had
ended. Too bad Lisa and Rodney didn't know it.

After the table was cleared a final time, a reggae
band struck up a familiar beat. Without much encouragement from Jet, Cara followed him to the
dance floor.

"Would you like to dance?" Rodney asked Lisa,
who was absently keeping time to the music with her
fingertips.

"No, I don't much feel like dancing tonight."

"What do you feel like doing? You don't seem like yourself."

"I'm just a little distracted. I have a lot on my mind," Lisa admitted.

"Do you want to talk it over with me? Sometimes having someone to tell your troubles helps," Rodney offered, putting an arm around her shoulders.

Lisa shifted in her seat slightly so that his arm was on the back of the chair instead of her shoulders. "No, it wouldn't help me to talk to you," she said honestly, hoping that she didn't sound unkind. She couldn't help but notice his hurt expression when she moved away from him. She certainly didn't want to compound that hurt.

Unable to think of anything else to say, he remained quiet.

"Why aren't you two dancing?" Cara asked when she and Jet returned to the table.

"She doesn't feel like it," Rodney said, nodding toward Lisa.

"You know, I'm real tired," Lisa said, standing. "I think I'll call it a night."

Rodney stood with her. "I'll walk you to your room," he offered.

"No, I'm cool. Stay and enjoy the music," Lisa said over her shoulder before picking up her pace to be sure no one tried to stop her.

In her room, Lisa stripped away her clothes and climbed into bed. Only she wasn't tired enough to sleep. Her mind returned to Jonathan. She wanted to call him, but knew that wouldn't help. He'd just play off his earlier disappointment and pretend everything was okay between them.

When he'd decided that dating wasn't working for him, it had seemed so easy to remain his friend. But over time, pretending to be just a friend had become increasingly difficult. Her heart pounded just seeing his smile. Something had to give. What if he started dating again? The thought of him with someone else made her angry.

When the sun rose, she had not slept and she still had not decided what to do about Jonathan. She stole down to the pool early and swam lap after lap, hoping exercise would give her clarity.

Swimming at a frenzied pace, she didn't stop until her arms could not make another stroke. As she pulled her tired body from the pool, she looked up to see her sister-in-law slipping out of the long, white gauzy wrap that covered her bathing suit.

"Good morning. What brings you down so early?" Cara asked as she sat on the edge of the pool, dropping her feet and legs into the warm water.

"I couldn't stay inside a moment longer. I was feeling rather restless." Lisa emerged from the pool and began swabbing her body with a towel. She mischievously dripped water down Cara's back.

Swatting at her and moving slightly, Cara looked up at Lisa. "Now, that's the Lisa I know and love, the one full of pranks. What was wrong with you last night?"

"I don't know. I guess I was still wound up from work. I had things on my mind." She hoped she'd said enough to assuage Cara's concern.

"You had someone with you who was eager to put something else on your mind," Cara teased.

"Rub it in. Everyone's not happily married like you and Jet. Maybe one day," she added wistfully, then looked at Cara quickly, hoping Cara hadn't heard the longing in her voice. Lisa didn't know where that sound had come from and certainly could not explain it.

"You could be. With a little encouragement, Rodney

could be the one. You hardly talked to him at all last night," Cara said, feeling safe since her last remark had not been rebuffed. "Are you upset with him?"

"No. It's not him." Lisa felt obligated to make some kind of explanation, but actually did not know what to say.

"Are you working too hard?" Cara asked, seeking to eliminate the most obvious explanation first.

"It's not work," Lisa admitted, walking over to the chaise where her beach robe lay. Cara followed her and sat at the foot of the chaise, while Lisa covered her pale blue two-piece bathing suit with the robe.

Taking a seat on the same chaise, Lisa asked, "Aren't you going to swim?"

"I just wanted a dip to cool off, but you've already gotten me wet," Cara answered, moving away from Lisa. "Let's order something to drink."

"Where's Jet?" Lisa asked curiously, looking around.

"He met Rodney after his morning jog. They're playing tennis."

They moved to seats at one of the round tables sheltered from the sun by a large, colorful umbrella and placed their order. As they sipped their fresh papaya juice that was brought promptly to them, Cara began, "Speaking of Rodney—"

"I don't believe we were," Lisa interrupted drolly.

"Yes, we were. I told you Jet's playing tennis with him." Cara continued, "You wasted a beautiful island moon last night. We saw Rodney sitting out on the terrace alone. Weren't you supposed to be getting together for a romantic weekend?"

"I enjoy being with Rodney, but there's no chemistry. Being with him is like being with one of my brothers," Lisa said, surprising herself to finally put into words what had been bothering her.

"Wow! That's deep. Does he know that?" Cara hadn't seen that one coming and doubted if Rodney would either.

"No, he doesn't know because I didn't know until now. I knew it was something, but I just couldn't put my finger on it," Lisa said slowly. "I enjoy being with Rodney. He's a fun guy and always has interesting things to do. But we never have any time just for us. It's always about the next party or getting introductions to people he needs to know for business," she added in a fit of honesty.

"But that's what this weekend is about. I thought if the two of you got away from business obligations you could have some time to focus on your love life. Maybe move your relationship to the next level," Cara explained, looking at Lisa anxiously.

"I always heard that happily married people were incurable matchmakers. Now I'm a living witness that it's true," Lisa teased.

"I've always heard that some people won't give love a chance," Cara returned. She hoped that Lisa wasn't dismissing her chance to be with a really great guy for the wrong reasons.

"Isn't it odd the way the pool and the ocean blend together? From here you can't tell they're separate," Lisa said, changing the subject and inhaling deeply. She had turned away from Cara and was staring out at the horizon.

Lisa said no more and Cara looked at her closely. They sat silently, each deep in her own thoughts. For the life of her, Lisa couldn't figure out how she would get through the next few hours. She knew that Jet would gloat when Cara told him how she felt about Rodney, and she knew for certain that Cara would tell him. But worst of all, she was worried about hurting Rodney's feelings.

"Hot damn! I thought I'd never see the day," Jet called out as he approached the two women.

"What is it?" Rodney asked.

"My wife and my sister are sitting side by side and neither is speaking. Are we about to have a lunar eclipse?" Jet asked, dramatically shading his eyes and looking up at the clear morning sky. "This is a supernatural phenomenon."

"Leave us alone," Cara said, smiling up at her tall, handsome husband. "How was your tennis match?"

Before he answered, he leaned over to kiss her on the forehead. "We beat those chumps so bad they were afraid to play another set."

"We had them running over each other trying to get our returns," Rodney bragged, going around the table to sit next to Lisa.

"When they did happen to be where the ball was, it came at them so hard they ran from it." Jet laughed as he dropped into the remaining chair.

"You'll have to play us," Cara challenged, looking from one powerfully built man to the other.

"You would want to take us on after we're exhausted," Rodney answered.

"The offer is open. We'll take you two on any time before the weekend is over," Cara returned. "You don't have to be tired for us to beat you down."

When Rodney didn't return the teasing, Cara and Jet noticed that he was totally focused on Lisa. Her hair was wrapped in a towel, but that only served to emphasize the delicate features of her face. Her usually bright eyes seemed to have dimmed and her lips looked strange without their usual smile. He wanted to get her away from the others so they could talk. He knew things would be much better between them after tonight.

"I need a swim to cool off," Rodney said. "Come into the water with me." He reached for Lisa's hand.

"I just got out of the water. I'll be in later," she answered quickly, ignoring his proffered hand.

Rodney dropped his hand and turned away. As he headed toward the edge of the pool, she stole a look at his impressive physique. He had been in business for only a few years, yet his business already grossed several million a year. Lisa had no doubt that Rodney would achieve all the goals he'd set for himself. But he didn't have her heart.

In a few moments his large, dark body was slicing the aquamarine water. "Lisa, what's wrong with you? Did you have to cut my man like that?" Jet asked, interrupting her thoughts.

"Mind your own business," Lisa replied without looking up.

"I just think—" Jet began.

Cara stood and put a hand on his large biceps. "I bet I can beat you into the water," she challenged and raced toward the pool. "The last one in has to pay for dinner."

Watching the three adults frolic in the pool, Lisa couldn't help but feel she was in the wrong place. Try as she might, she couldn't get the look of disappointment that was on Jonathan's face out of her mind. What had she done wrong? Why did she feel guilty? Now she'd upset Rodney too. It seemed she couldn't get anything right.

Sleep deprivation mixed with the vigorous swim and hot sun worked together to make her drowsy. When the others came out of the pool, they found Lisa sound asleep on the chaise. Jet touched her shoulder lightly and she jumped. "Wake up, sleepyhead. It's time to go up and get dressed."

"Get dressed for what?" she asked, stretching.

Rodney looked at her long, slender limbs and pushed his lust aside. She obviously wasn't into him today. Maybe the surprise he had for her later would make everything all right.

"We're going to get on the trolley and go sightseeing," Cara explained, rubbing a towel through her short hair.

"Count me out. I'm too tired to spend the day in the hot sun. I'll see you guys when you get back," Lisa said, rising from the chaise.

"We're going up, too," Rodney responded, leading the others as they joined Lisa. The group boarded the elevator and parted company on the third floor.

Lisa slept solidly throughout the day. Perhaps her melancholy mood was the result of exhaustion. She had been working extremely hard, barely giving herself time off. When she awakened, she felt much better, ready to face her family and friend.

She washed her hair in the shower and blew it dry. Standing in the mirror, she did the best she could with a curling iron. Long, hot curls dropped to her shoulders one by one as she worked methodically across her head.

While she worked, she thought over her predicament. She realized she'd need to explain things to Rodney real soon. He looked at her like a hurt puppy each time she rejected him. She didn't like to think she'd used him. But when she needed an escort or a dance partner, Rodney had been there for her, and she'd served the same role for him. Everyone expected them to deepen their relationship. Maybe it was time to end it.

Her hair done, she dressed quickly in a floor-length, black, jersey-knit dress that slid softly over her gentle curves. She casually tossed a matching, sequined shawl over one shoulder. Looking over her attire, she was satisfied that she was dressed well enough for an elegant dinner while being casual enough for the island. She added her diamond tennis bracelet and headed to meet the others.

After they were seated, Rodney leaned close to her. "Did you have lunch?" Looking at her tenderly, he placed his arm on the back of her chair.

She felt guilty accepting his solicitous behavior, but was reluctant to move outside his loose embrace. She dreaded seeing the hurt show up on his face again. Instead she gave him a wan smile. "No, I slept straight through lunch. What did you guys do?"

"Mr. I-know-my-way-around wanted to have an authentic low-country meal. He took us to this little restaurant that had three other customers and no air-conditioning," Rodney teased.

"I bet you've never had shrimp potato salad like that," Jet tossed back.

"And those collards were good," Cara added. "Not too many people can make collards that good without meat in them."

"I wonder if the health department knows about that place," Rodney retorted.

The group joked and teased as they always did when they were together. Lisa made a sincere effort to contribute to the conversation, but her mind drifted back to Jonathan. She wondered if he had replaced the engine in Zora. She imagined the changes she wanted to make to the 1969 Stingray. She hoped he didn't start on it until she returned.

"Remember how much pain Jet was in when he danced for me at the Caxambu in Tampa?" Cara was asking Lisa. She was referring to a time when Jet had taken dance lessons to perform with Cara at a big, community-wide event.

"Yes, he was in worse condition than I was and I'd run a ten-K that day," Lisa added, ashamed to admit she'd missed the first part of the conversation, but hoping her answer was appropriate.

"And your friend Jonathan came across the finish line as if he hadn't even run. He was barely breathing heavily," Cara related. Her bright eyes were full of laughter.

"I didn't know Jonathan had come to Tampa for the Caxambu," Rodney interjected, drawing Lisa's attention away from Cara.

"Oh yes, he likes to compete in short races and triathlons," Lisa explained eagerly. "Last year he won the Music City Marathon. People from all over the world come to compete and Jonathan came in third. He finished in two hours, forty-four minutes, and forty-eight seconds." She stopped, realizing everyone was staring at her. Her voice had not been that animated the entire weekend.

"And you say he's just a friend?" Rodney questioned her. It was something about the way her face lit up when she talked about Jonathan that bothered him.

"Yes, that's what I said," Lisa said brazenly. She looked at Rodney unflinchingly. Silence hovered over the table.

"Lisa ran track in high school and college," Jet said, coming to her aid. "She's always gotten a little carried away with the statistics. Have you run lately?"

"Seldom. I don't seem to have the time anymore," Lisa replied.

"You have to make the time," Jet reminded her firmly. "It's good for your lungs. With your asthma, you need to stay in shape."

"Maybe you can hire someone to take on half my workload," Lisa returned. She hated the way her family was always on her about her health; she preferred to forget she had asthma. And usually she could.

"Having Bryce take on daily operations has freed me up to do some of the things I've always wanted to do. Is that what you'd like?" Jet asked his sister, looking at her intently.

"I'm not sure if I can let go of any of my responsibilities," she answered.

"Sure you can," Rodney assured her. "Just look at the things that can be systematized and turn those over to someone else."

By that time, the table was clear and the band was in place. The reggae band of the night before had been replaced by an old-school rhythm-and-blues group. As usual, Cara and Jet joined the crowd on the dance floor immediately.

"Do you want to dance?" Rodney asked, half standing. Ordinarily, he would not have thought twice about asking Lisa to dance, but she'd been so strange all weekend, he couldn't be certain.

"No, I think we should talk. Let's go for a walk," Lisa suggested, standing with Rodney. They walked through the double doors that led to the terrace and followed a path through the tropical gardens. She allowed Rodney to hold her hand. He led, taking charge as if walking had been his idea.

"Let's sit here," he suggested when they approached a green-painted wooden bench in the middle of one of the gardens. They faced a lighted pond and could see the flashes of brightly colored fish.

"Rodney, I need to tell you—" Lisa began, turning in her seat to look at his profile.

"I know, I know. You're wondering where our relationship is going. I noticed how restless you've been this weekend. You're probably wondering if I'm serious about us. Before you toss out any ultimatums—" He sounded breathless and stared straight ahead.

"Rodney, I don't—" Lisa tried, touching the sleeve of his jacket slightly.

"Let me finish, please, Lisa. I know Jet told you I was a womanizer when we played football—"

"You still are," Lisa interrupted, giggling slightly.

"I'm ready to change all that," he said in one breath. Perspiration was beading on his forehead.

"But—" Lisa tried one more time, leaning forward to see his face better.

"Let me talk while I have this together in my head," Rodney persisted, staring straight ahead. "I'm thirty-six years old now and my business is going well. Better than I expected it would at this point. I'm doing well, but people don't trust a single businessman. It's time for me to settle down. You're the only woman I can get along with for any length of time. I'll be good to you, Lisa. I need to focus on my business expansion and you can help me with that. Lisa, will you marry me?" At that point he turned to look at her expectantly.

As he waited, he took out a handkerchief and wiped the perspiration from his face. The night was mild, cooled with a balmy breeze from the ocean, but his speech had caused him a great deal of stress. He put the handkerchief back in his pocket and felt around in another until he fished out a small black velvet box. He opened it and held it out to her. When she didn't reach for it, he tried to place it in her hand.

"What is this?" Lisa asked, staring at the diamond ring.

"It's a ring," Rodney said, surprised that she didn't get it.

"Rodney, are you talking about a business deal or

marriage?" Lisa asked. Their eyes met and he looked away.

"I just popped the question, didn't I?" He couldn't quite fathom her strange behavior. She hadn't thrown her arms around his neck, nor had she burst into tears of joy. This wasn't the scene he'd envisioned. This was what he thought she'd been waiting for. Wasn't this why she'd been edgy all weekend? Hadn't she thrown Jonathan up in his face just to let him know if he didn't make a move, she had someone else waiting?

"Rodney, the growth of your business is not a good reason to marry," she said gently, touching his cheek lightly.

"I didn't expect you to analyze my proposal. I thought our getting together was what this weekend was supposed to be about." He rose from the bench and stood over her.

"For you to propose to me?" Lisa asked incredulously, leaning back to look up at him.

"Yes. I thought you were being distant because I've dragged my feet so long," Rodney explained.

"No, I'm not ready," she said, glancing down at her feet. She took a deep breath and wondered what would come next.

"But I am. I've grown my business and now I need a family. I need to show my clients that I'm stable. Everyone still remembers me as the NFL playboy I used to be." Rodney talked and walked a small path around the bench.

"I think you should marry for love," Lisa stated, folding her arms across her chest and stretching her legs out in front of her.

"I could fall in love with you," he said, returning to the seat he'd just vacated. He took both of her hands into his.

"Maybe you could," she agreed, looking down at

their hands. His touch was warm and comfortable. Rodney was a good friend and she wanted him to stay that way.

"My mother was real happy when I told her I was going to propose to you," he added for good measure. He knew Lisa and his mother got along well.

"If I had a mother-in-law, Mrs. Grimes would be ideal. You have a sweet mother and she has a wonderful son," Lisa said, freeing a hand to gently stroke Rodney's arm.

"If you are about to tell me how great I'll be for some other woman, please don't," he said, looking directly into her face.

"You will be," she replied, giving him a sincere smile.

"I've been with a lot of women, but none of them met my requirements. We may not be in love right now, but you meet all those requirements," he explained, trying once again to help Lisa understand where he was coming from.

"Don't you want to be in love when you marry?"

"It's not all that important," he said and shrugged. "I've never been in love with any of the women I've run around with. When I played football I worried that they were with me only because I was a celebrity. Now I wonder if they're with me because I have money. With you I don't have to worry. You have your own money and your brother was more famous than I ever was, so my celebrity doesn't impress you."

"You deserve love," she said gently.

"Love is not everything What if I fall in love with someone who has no sense of business? Who can't entertain my clients with me?" he asked, truly concerned.

"You have to trust yourself. If you fall in love and

she loves you, she'll learn what it takes to keep you happy," Lisa advised.

He looked at her skeptically. "Do you want to keep the ring just in case you change your mind?" he offered.

"I won't," Lisa said with finality. "This is something I may live to regret, but I want to have a great love like Cara and Jet's. I'm looking for my soul mate."

"Okay, little girl. But if your biological clock starts ticking and you need someone to help you out, you know where to find me," Rodney said, stroking her cheek.

"I won't count on that. Someone will have you snatched up before the year is out. You're ripe for the picking now," Lisa replied, smiling up into Rodney's eyes. This was the first time she'd seriously thought of marriage and she liked the idea. Only not to this man.

"Okay, don't say I didn't try. You're going to be heartbroken when I marry some other woman," Rodney said, helping Lisa to her feet.

"I may be, but I'll always remember you asked *me* first."

CHAPTER 2

After leaving Rodney in the tropical gardens, Lisa spent another restless night in her room alone. As she prepared for bed, she couldn't figure out what to do about Jonathan. They'd dated sporadically for about six months. And then, out of the blue, he had told her she was a great friend. There could never be anything more between them, he had said, because he was a public servant—a firefighter—and she was a high-powered executive—part owner of a multibillion-dollar corporation.

At first she'd been flabbergasted. Then she realized she should have seen it coming. During the entire time they were dating, he had been rather noncommittal. She'd never been sure of his feelings toward her. So she had accepted his friendship.

She moved to the bed, pulling back the covers, but knew there was no need to get in. Too much was on her mind. Pacing the room, she thought about Jonathan. She felt real chemistry with him and she believed he did too. It was in his eyes—eyes that followed her whenever he thought she wouldn't notice. When she looked at him, he always looked away, but not before she saw the longing. It was in his touch—why did she feel a hot rush each time he touched her? And the way he acted—he was always attentive to her, anticipating her needs before she even thought of them, like keeping her gas tank full. He knew that she had a tendency to wait until the gas gauge registered empty before stopping for gas.

One good thing had come about as a result of talking to Rodney. She'd found out something about herself that she didn't know. Having never considered herself a romantic, she had found Rodney's practical reasons for marriage very unappealing. And if he thought she'd buy into that reasoning, she'd better take another look at herself. Did people see her as the practical, unlovable type? She now knew that the only reason she'd marry would be for love. Anything less would be unacceptable.

The source of her quandary came to her like a kick in the brain. Growing up she had watched girls, and later women, throw themselves at her brothers. She had felt pity for those poor females. And she had despised their desperate attempts to get with men who had no interest in them. Her brothers did very little to earn their women's undying devotion, but they had it anyway.

On the other hand, she had always believed in going after what she wanted. And if she did, she would be just like those desperate females she'd grown to feel sorry for. If she told Jonathan how she felt about him, she'd be no better than all the other women in the world who threw themselves at the men they wanted. *If he doesn't feel the same way I do, I will feel like a complete idiot. But worse than that, I'll lose my best friend. Hasn't he already told me he wants nothing more than a friendship? Why do I still think he has some kind of romantic interest in me?*

Climbing into the king-size bed, she lay flat on her back, uninvited thoughts swirling in her mind. *The look on his face when I told him that I was going away for the weekend with Rodney was sheer jealousy. I know he wants me.* Lisa pulled the pillow from beneath her head and put it over her ears, hoping to silence the raging arguments. But the thought that she wanted Jonathan and he wanted her was clear to her.

By morning, the practical side of Lisa had won out, just as it did every day in business. She had decided to take a giant risk to get what she wanted. She would face Jonathan with the truth. He could accept her or push her away again. It would be his decision to make.

The early morning sun found her throwing her things back into her bag. Certain that the others would be at breakfast, she left her luggage with a bellman and headed for the dining room. She spotted her brother and sister-in-law at a small, round table near the French doors that led to the terrace. It did not surprise her that Rodney was not with them.

Nor were they surprised with the announcement Lisa made as she pulled out a chair. "I've decided to cut this trip short. I've sent for the Gulfstream." She referred to the Sand Castles private airplane.

"What about Rodney? Did you tell him you're leaving?" Cara asked.

"I don't think he'll be very concerned about where I go. I won't be seeing him anymore," Lisa replied, leaning across the table to eat from Jet's plate of fresh fruit and assorted breads.

"No joke!" Jet exclaimed with a smile on his face, at the same time swatting at Lisa's hand as she reached for a bunch of grapes.

"Don't be so smug," the younger sister said, redirecting the grape that was headed toward her mouth and tossing it at the man who considered himself her adviser.

Jet caught the grape easily and smiled at Lisa. "I tried to warn you about Rodney."

"There was nothing for you to warn me about. He's been a perfect gentleman. The problem is all mine," she said, standing, obviously growing impatient with her delay. "I'll talk to you later."

"Call me," Cara called after her. They watched the proud woman stroll through the tables that were still sparsely filled in the early morning hours.

After a quick flight, Lisa was back at her small cottage in the Historic Edgefield District in Nashville. Nervously pacing from the living room through the dining room and back to the kitchen, she rehearsed her pitch. She realized she was about to make the most important sales call of her life. She had to get it just right.

For a conversation this important, she wouldn't trust a phone call. For one thing, Jonathan was too miserly with his words and emotions. She needed to see his face to gauge his reactions.

With her pitch firmly in mind, she headed toward her bedroom closet. "Okay, Lisa," she said, giving herself a pep talk, "you can do this." Now what should she wear? Not her usual navy suit. She pushed through the khakis, jeans, and business suits in her closet, trying to figure out what to wear. *What kind of woman am I?* she wondered. *I can't get a man's attention with these unisex outfits.* She was referring to a wardrobe that represented the focus of her life, clothes that took her from the boardroom to construction sites.

Shifting through the contents of her closet, she finally settled on a pale blue sundress made of a soft, sheer fabric that her mother had sent her. She

slipped the dress over her head and was pleased with
the fit. Her mother was right on target again. The
dress lifted her breasts and hugged her torso before
flaring slightly from the waist and lightly skimming
her hips. It stopped at midthigh. She was uncomfortable with the length of the dress. But what did
she expect? Her mother still wore her skirts above
her knees.

When she'd first received the dress, she'd rejected
it as another of her mother's attempts to make her
more feminine. It was perfect for today. She wanted
to remind Jonathan that she was a woman. After fid-
geting with the dress for a moment, Lisa returned to
her closet to find the right shoes to wear with it. Too
bad her mother hadn't thought to send shoes too. She
pulled out a pair of silver sandals from last summer
or the summer before. They would have to do.

Sitting on the side of the bed to put on hose, she
wrestled with it several minutes before giving up in
frustration. She balled it up and made a three-point
shot across the room to the wastebasket. Putting on
hose was beyond her ability and today she didn't
have the patience to struggle with it anymore.

Not wanting to spend another moment thinking
about what she was about to do, Lisa rushed from
the house. Without much more thought her big
pickup truck was speeding down a main thoroughfare through the city. She became impatient with the
multitude of traffic lights on Gallatin Pike and opted
for Ellington Parkway, a wide highway that traversed
the northern part of the city. The Sunday traffic was
light and it wasn't long before she had cut a path to
Ashland City Highway.

At the turnoff to Jonathan's farm, she slowed
down to avoid bouncing around on the gravel road.
Braking in front of the large two-story house, she was

immediately disappointed. Jonathan's car was
nowhere in sight. In all her planning, she'd never
considered that he might not be at home. Then she
remembered that when she'd seen him on Friday,
he'd told her he was off until Sunday morning.

After coming so far, she refused to let her plans
be derailed. Determined to complete her mission,
she jumped back into the Ford F-250 and headed
back to the Ashland City Highway. Traffic was light
as she neared the city. In what seemed like no time
at all, she had arrived in downtown Nashville. She
parked the truck and marched through the doors
of the fire hall.

Normally the men on Jonathan's shift would not
have paid much attention to Lisa's arrival. They all
knew she was the captain's friend; she was one of the
guys. In fact, the three men watching a sports show
on a floor-model TV barely looked up when she
entered the room.

Two other men were playing Ping-Pong at the
table on the other side of the large hall. As she
crossed the floor, the game stopped. The shorter of
the two men, Vaughn, had become distracted when
he took a second look at her. He let his gaze slide
leisurely up her body.

"Hey, where did you get those legs from?" he
called out as he sidled up to her. "We've never seen
them before. Are you going somewhere special?"

"No, Vaughn, I just came to make your eyes pop
out," Lisa joked, looking at the man who was practically drooling.

"Down, boy," the second Ping-Pong player, Foster,
warned. Turning his attention to Lisa, he asked,
"Hey, Lisa. Are you looking for Jonathan?"

"Hi, Foster. Yes, I am," she replied, smiling at the
man she considered a friend. Although Vaughn's

comments were embarrassing, they were also reassuring. Not accustomed to dressing in such obviously feminine attire, she had felt uncertain of how she looked until Vaughn had given her his appreciative stares.

"I'll get him," Vaughn said, anxious to get away from the stern look Foster was giving him. Vaughn had thought he'd have a chance to make his moves on Lisa, but maybe she was more than just a friend to Captain Hill. He sure wouldn't settle for being a *friend* to someone with legs like that.

Lisa followed Foster toward one of the tables where the men often played cards. It was away from the TV area and the Ping-Pong table. "Do you want to sit down?"

"No, I'll stand."

Foster gave her a questioning look, but kept his thoughts to himself. He wasn't as bold as Vaughn. There was no way he would ask her why she looked so fine. Nor would he comment on her nervous pacing. Instead he asked, "Where have you been keeping yourself?"

"I've been pretty busy. Work, work, work. You know how that goes," she said nervously. "How is Mia?" she asked about his wife, who was a registered nurse.

"Just great. We'll have to get together some time soon," he answered.

"We've had a hard time catching up since she changed hospitals. Does she still work days?"

"She does, but she works twelve hours a day for three days, and then she's off four. Her schedule changes all the time and they don't always coincide with my off days," Foster explained.

* * *

Down the hall several feet, Vaughn burst into the captain's bunk. In his excitement he had forgotten to knock. Few men would dare do that. Vaughn also missed the cold stares Jonathan stabbed him with.

"Captain, you've got to get up front. Your friend is here and you've got to see her."

"What are you talking about?" Jonathan asked, laying his magazine across his lap and folding his arms across his chest.

"I can't tell you. This is something you've got to see for yourself." Amazement was evident in Vaughn's voice.

"You need to tell me what this is about now," Jonathan said in a low, commanding voice. Normally Jonathan's demeanor would have stopped Vaughn short, but the firefighter was sure his behavior would be exonerated once the captain got a look at Lisa.

Vaughn looked at him and said, "Just come to the front. You'll see." Turning to leave, he took several steps before checking over his shoulder to be sure the big man was following him.

In a couple of seconds, Jonathan saw Lisa standing at the other end of the lounge. His heart started beating wildly when he saw her. She was talking to Foster, but Jonathan could tell she was distracted. She stopped pacing and fidgeted with the bracelet she constantly wore. He approached her swiftly, wondering at her surprise visit.

"I didn't expect to see you any time soon," he said when he stood before her. He was totally unaware of the smoldering desire that leaped into his eyes as he took in her appearance. She looked softer, more vulnerable than he'd seen her in a long time.

"Well, I'm here," Lisa said, looking up at Jonathan

and feeling pleased with herself. She recognized the desire in his eyes.

"What's up?" he asked, folding his arms across his chest, but still unable to remove his eyes from her.

"I've got errands to take care of," Foster said, retreating hastily. Neither Lisa nor Jonathan seemed to hear him.

Jonathan was having a hard time keeping his excitement under control. Why was she dolled up like this? Surely it wasn't for him. He pulled together every ounce of willpower he could muster to keep from pulling her to his bunk and ravishing her.

Both feminine and sexy, the pale blue sundress exposed her well-toned arms and shoulders. It contrasted beautifully against her rich brown complexion. The fitted short skirt gently hugged her tight, ripe bottom and stopped midthigh, flattering her long, gorgeous legs. The girl had no right coming to him looking like that.

He was so entranced by her appearance that he totally forgot he was staring at her. She stood uncomfortably before him, no longer able to read his expression. She had no way of knowing that his fingers itched to touch her delicate brown face. Her coal-black hair, hanging long and loose over her shoulders, begged him to wrap his fingers in it. She looked accessible and attractive. She was totally appealing.

The intensity of his gaze was unnerving. She tried to swallow before she spoke, but her mouth was dry. This was what she'd hoped for, wasn't it? Wasn't that why women dressed up and put on makeup? She'd never felt this power before and it scared her. She didn't understand it and she wasn't sure how to use it.

The men were ogling her like fools. As many

times as Lisa had visited the fire hall, the men had never acted the way they were today. Usually it was no big deal when she grabbed a beer and sat down to watch a basketball game with them. All it took was taking off jeans and putting on a short skirt to make them notice she was a woman.

In a voice uncharacteristically soft, she said, "We need to talk."

Despite her lowered voice, one of the men in the hall said, "Uh-oh. We know what that means. Captain's in trouble." And they all slapped each other high fives.

"Don't you all have something else to do?" Jonathan growled at the men. "Jefferson, did you gas up the trucks? What about you, Peyton? Is the lawn mowed?" Before they answered, Jonathan had taken Lisa's hand.

"Come with me," he said in a gentler voice, leading her down the long hallway. In all the times she'd visited him, he'd never invited her to his bunk room. He wouldn't dare. That would be asking for trouble. He could handle her when they were at a ballpark, in the gym, or even in his barn, but never in a room with a bed in it. That would be entirely too tempting. But he didn't like the way his crew was ogling her.

After they entered the neat room that apparently served as his bedroom and lounge, Jonathan closed the door for privacy. The only items in the sparsely furnished room were a single bed, a desk and chair, and a small table holding a television.

"Have a seat," he said, pulling the chair away from the desk and turning it toward the bed.

Lisa carefully smoothed her dress before she sat on it. As she crossed and uncrossed her legs, he realized that she was nervous. He was totally confused now. She had never—ever—been nervous about anything. Who was this woman and what had happened to his Lisa?

If resisting the old Lisa had been nearly impossible, this woman before him would be his undoing. Did she have any idea crossing and uncrossing those long, gorgeous legs in that short dress was doing for him? One thing was for certain, if he were less of a gentleman, his gaze would not be on her face.

Friday, when he'd found her glowing with excitement at the prospect of spending the weekend with another man, he'd once again sworn he'd stay away from her. But staying away was actually the last thing in the world he wanted and would probably prove to be the most difficult thing he'd ever tried in his life. She had gotten under his skin the first time he'd set eyes on her and had proven to be an itch he couldn't scratch.

He wasn't aware that all the time he'd been assessing her, she'd been giving him a careful appraisal as well. His navy T-shirt, stamped in white with the Nashville Fire Department logo, stretched across his muscles and hung long, over creased navy slacks. He was a gorgeous hunk of pure masculinity even though he was not as immaculately groomed as usual. When Vaughn had summoned him to the front hall, he hadn't had time to tidy his appearance.

She looked from his freshly shaved head to the muscular arms that were once again folded across his broad chest. She'd identified that as his protective gesture, a move he used when he wanted no emotions to breach his defense. None could get into him, nor could any get out. He sat on the bed and rested his back against the wall as if to move away from her.

"Lisa, what is this visit about?" he asked when her

silence stretched into minutes. His deep voice was filled with patience and curiosity.

She looked up and their eyes met. It was all he could do to keep from pulling her into his arms. There it was again, the vulnerability that made him want to protect her. Yet he knew that he was the only person she needed protection from. He was the one most likely to hurt her. He had to keep his focus or he would forget his resolve. She cleared her throat but didn't speak.

"Would you like something to drink?" he asked in spite of his sudden need to get her out as quickly as possible. He was too weak to keep her around much longer.

"I'll have a Coke if you have any." She cleared her throat, her husky voice barely a whisper.

While he was gone, she took a moment to look at her surroundings. This room was just as neat as his home. His books were placed carefully on a small five-shelf bookcase. Recent issues of *Popular Mechanics, Motor Trend,* and *Car and Driver* magazines were in an orderly stack on one side of the desk.

Okay, she reminded herself, *this is all or nothing. This is where the rubber meets the road. I have to tell him why I'm here and give him a chance to say he feels the same way too.*

"Here you are," he said, returning with a canned soda and a glass of ice.

She accepted the offering and watched the fizz as she poured soda over ice. Finally she spoke. "Before I met you, I had never been in a fire station before. Well, once when I was in the second grade, but I don't remember it well. It was two stories. The firemen had a pole to slide down in emergencies, just like in the movies. This one is all on one level. It must be fairly modern. It's a well-constructed, solid building. It looks like you have everything you need in here. A nice little home away from home." Realizing she was rambling, she stopped to take a sip of soda.

"Lisa, why are you here?" Jonathan asked pleasantly. He was sitting on the bed again, this time bending toward her with his forearms resting on his thighs. He looked at her intently, sympathizing with her nervousness.

"I want to—need to—talk to you."

"About our fire-hall architecture?" he joked, trying to help her relax.

"No." She laughed and paused, gathering her resolve. "I need to know something. I'd like to know why you became upset Friday."

"I told you. I thought we could hang out together. I was just disappointed, that's all." He tried to modulate his voice to sound casual.

"But you asked me if I was going to be with my boyfriend like it made a difference to you. Does it bother you when I'm with Rodney?" she persisted. This was a conversation she would not have a second time. This was her one chance.

"Like I told you, I don't think he's your type." In his typical fashion of not revealing his emotions, Jonathan shut down and let the silence grow.

Lisa rushed to fill it. "You told me I need a rich man. Rodney is wealthy. Why is it you think I shouldn't be with him?" Lisa asked again, trying to keep her voice steady.

"That's right, he is. But he's not right for you," Jonathan replied plainly.

"Why do you say that?"

"He has a reputation with women. You're not the only woman he's seeing, you know," he said as if his statement was common knowledge.

"You don't even know Rodney. You can't believe everything you read in the tabloids." Of course, she did know Rodney dated other women. Jet had made it a point to let her know.

Lisa looked at Jonathan steadily. Knowing that he was an expert at schooling his face to hide his emotions, she watched him carefully. She was almost certain he was jealous of Rodney, but she needed him to face it before she could go on to help him realize how deeply he cared for her.

"I guess it wouldn't bother you that he sees a lot of women. After all, didn't you tell me he's just a friend?"

"He asked *me* to marry him," she blurted out and waited for Jonathan's reaction.

Jonathan felt a sharp pain in his heart, but it never showed in his face. "Congratulations," he managed to say. "But I do think you could do better."

"The only way I could do better is if I were with you," she said boldly, finally getting to the point of her visit. She leaned forward in her chair and looked directly in Jonathan's eyes.

"No, Lisa. We've already been there. You can definitely do better than me."

"How can you say that?" she asked incredulously. "Don't you care for me?"

"I do. You are a good *friend.* But your world is so different from mine. I can't go to an island for the weekend on a whim. I don't fly around in a private jet." He rose from the bed and moved to stand before the bookcase, placing himself farther from her.

"You know those things don't matter to me. I'm just as happy when we're in your garage breaking down an engine or watching a game on pay-per-view," she said softly, feeling frustration and defeat. Too late she realized that the difference between this sales pitch and one she might do for her job was that this time the answer really mattered. She couldn't bear losing.

"Lisa, things change. I know money doesn't mean a lot to you now, but as you grow older it will."

"And how do you know this? You're trying to sound like a wise old man, but you're not much older than I am. At the ripe old age of thirty you're trying to play the role of a sage." She turned in her seat to look up at him.

Jonathan saw the tears welling in her eyes and felt his resolve weakening. But he reminded himself that whatever he did, he could never allow Lisa Stevens to get caught up with him. With her prominent family, his past would surely be dredged up sooner than later. He knew he should not even have tried to remain her friend. She was looking sorrowful now, but if she knew the truth about him, he definitely wouldn't be able to stand the look in her eyes.

"Look, Lisa, I like you a lot. That's why I encouraged you to do what's best for you. Like I told you before, I don't see our relationship going anywhere."

Lisa remained in her seat and looked up at the most stubborn man she'd ever met. Taking a long shot, she said, "I don't want your friendship, Jonathan. Either you see me as a woman or not at all. Call me within five days and let me know what you decide. I'm not going to grovel and I'm not going to have any more discussions about this." Without giving Jonathan a second glance, she tossed her long black hair behind a shoulder, held her head high, and exited the room. She moved swiftly through the hall, taking long, athletic strides, refusing to make eye contact with anyone. Her springy steps set her hair to bouncing wildly around her, drawing the appreciative attention of the men as she passed.

Jonathan watched them, jealousy growing hot in the pit of his stomach. It was not the result of men doing what came naturally when Lisa walked by. No, it was knowing she'd spend her life with another man. If not Rodney, then someone like him, someone who could give her the kind of life she deserved. That's what he wished for her.

He stood in the doorway to his bunk room and continued watching through the long floor-to-ceiling windows until he saw her cross the parking lot and climb into her pickup. He grimaced when the gravel spun around her wheels from her rapid acceleration. And she was gone in a cloud of dust.

It was for the best, he assured himself. Lisa was a wealthy woman. She probably earned multiples of his income and she shared ownership in her family's business. He was just a firefighter and that was the fulfillment of his career goal.

With the heavy baggage he carried with him, there was absolutely no need to hope that they could have a long-lasting relationship. If the truth about his past came out, she might become repulsed by him, or even worse, afraid of him.

He flopped carelessly onto his bunk without turning back the blanket and closed his eyes against the hopelessness of his situation. Trying to think of anything other than Lisa was out of the question. Her intoxicating fragrance lingered in the air and the grim look on her face before she turned away was emblazoned on his mind.

Jonathan thought he knew what was best for Lisa, but being without her certainly wasn't best for him. Being self-sacrificing wasn't easy at all, and at the moment he didn't even *feel* noble.

CHAPTER 3

The next morning Lisa sat at the desk in her bedroom. Her meeting with Jonathan was still on her mind. Heaving a deep sigh, she studied the calendar on her Blackberry. Viewing her appointments for the day, she decided on her attire. This was part of her morning routine.

Seeing that she would be inside all day in appointments with two of her property managers, she dressed in a no-nonsense gray pin-striped suit and a pale gray shirt with pearl-gray buttons and cuff links. Without as much as a second glance in the mirror, Lisa headed for her first meeting. It was with Jennifer Malone on Church Street.

Jennifer had come to Sand Castles with sterling references and a platinum transcript from the Olin School of Business MBA program. Yet she'd somehow managed to fall short of expectations. This was a meeting that was long overdue and one Lisa did not look forward to.

Arriving shortly before their scheduled eight o'clock meeting, Lisa went straight to Jennifer's office. When the manager still had not arrived by 8:15, Lisa began pacing.

Thirty minutes later, Jennifer rushed to her office door and paused when she saw Lisa was already there. "I'm sorry I'm late," she apologized, entering the office. "The traffic coming out of Antioch was horrendous this morning."

"It is *every* morning," Lisa said pointedly. After letting her remark sink in, she continued, "We have quite a bit to cover today. Let's begin with a tour of the building."

As they walked through the building, Lisa commented on details that Jennifer had overlooked. "It's the small things that count. If we overlook the small things, we are only a second-rate property with high rent."

When the tour was over, they went to a small conference room adjacent to Jennifer's office. After they were seated in burgundy leather chairs opposite each other at the long, mahogany table, Lisa took an employee performance evaluation form from her briefcase.

"This is a follow-up to your evaluation we conducted last year," she began, to signal the beginning of the interview portion of the assessment. "Of course, we weren't able to do your follow-up on time because of the fire in this building. In fact, we've been extremely lenient with you because of the related extenuating circumstances. However, some things can't be overlooked."

"Like what?" Jennifer challenged, turning in her chair to face Lisa.

"Your consistently low occupancy rate and—" Lisa began, resting her arms on the table before her. She was prepared to read from the list before her.

"You know the low occupancy rate is not my fault," Jennifer interrupted impatiently.

"Your occupancy rate was low prior to the fire, which was your responsibility. When you were hired this building was usually occupied at ninety-six percent. We have asked you to work to return to that level. What have you done?" Lisa asked, her pen poised over the form.

"We've only been back in this building six months," Jennifer replied sullenly, looking away. She couldn't believe Lisa would have the audacity to complain about her work after all she'd done for the company. After the fire she'd worked night and day to make the building operational again.

"You've had enough time to reach at least the eighty-five percent goal. You're only at sixty percent. That's unacceptable," Lisa said firmly, making notes on the form before continuing. "Although this building has new floors, they are scuffed and dull. Do you have the janitorial service on a regular buffing schedule?"

"No, they told me our contract only requires them to buff monthly."

"Read the contract, Jennifer. *You* should be telling them what it says. Not the other way around." Lisa paused, marking additional notations on the form.

Throughout their session, Jennifer continued making excuses. Lisa could feel a headache coming on, but resisted the impulse to rub her temples. Instead she continued marking the form as the interview continued.

As they ended, Lisa said, "I will review your work again in three months. If the needed improvements have not been made, we'll have to assume this building is too much for you."

"Do you mean I'll have to relocate?" Jennifer asked, alarm clear in her voice.

"I mean you'll have to find another job. Sand Castles will no longer need your services. This is one of our premier buildings. If you can't handle this one, we don't have anything for you." Lisa looked steadily at her employee before directing her attention to the papers before her. It was plain to see that Jennifer was perturbed, but Lisa had no more patience for the woman's excuses.

She gave Jennifer a copy of the evaluation form after they'd both signed it. As she stood, Lisa said, "Please call the corporate office if you have questions. We're there to help you. And I mean that."

"Thank you," Jennifer replied absently. It appeared that she'd already dismissed Lisa.

On the way out the door, Lisa stopped in mid-stride. "Oh, Jennifer, don't forget the mandatory meeting in Human Resources next week. I expect you to be there on time."

Jennifer's performance evaluation had taken longer than expected. Without stopping for lunch, Lisa drove to the meeting with Bruce Whitten in Brentwood, a community south of Nashville. As she drove, she didn't try to suppress thoughts of Jonathan. They were preferable to dwelling on the unpleasantness with Jennifer Malone.

Lisa was still replaying her encounter with Jonathan in her mind. Frustration filled her as she wondered for the hundredth time what she could have done or said to bring about different results. But to be perfectly honest, there was absolutely nothing she could have done differently. She refused to believe that she would have to live her life without Jonathan's love.

She had wallowed so completely in her thoughts

of Jonathan that she was totally unaware of her location until she pulled into her parking spot at the Brentwood building. She exited the truck and followed the long hallway to the administrative suite.

"Hello, Lisa. I have everything you need in the conference room," Bruce, the building manager, greeted her. "Would you like to start there?"

She followed him into the richly appointed conference room. The furnishings were dark shining cherry wood. The chairs were upholstered in a flame stitch in deep shades of green and blue. The beautiful, rich green-blue wallpaper had streaks of metallic gold that blended perfectly with the surroundings.

A long elliptical-shaped table surrounded by twelve chairs sat in the center of the room. Linen place mats and sparkling place settings were at two positions. As they entered the room on one end, a caterer appeared, as if by magic, through the doorway at the other end with a cart of food.

"I assume you skipped lunch as usual," Bruce explained.

"You're right, I didn't eat and this smells delicious. What are we having?" she asked, anxiously peering onto the serving cart.

"It's a surprise, but I assure you it's something you'll like," Bruce teased, pulling a chair out for her. "Have a seat."

"You can be assured it's something I'll like, because I like everything." Lisa laughed.

"That's true. Feeding you is so easy, but this is superb. Mr. George, will you tell her what we're having? She's not going to let us wait before eating." Bruce leaned back in the big upholstered chair and waited expectantly.

"Ma'am, this is called voodoo pasta. It is made with

shrimp, scallops, and lobster in a Cajun sauce," the caterer said, scooping up a lavish portion onto a white china plate and placing it before Lisa with a flourish. "We also have green salad with a raspberry vinaigrette dressing." After filling a bowl with the greens, he put it next to the plate.

"You sure do know what I like." She looked hungrily at the meal before her, smiling at Bruce.

"That's the easy part," he teased her, lifting a fork. They had an easy friendship, having worked together since she'd first taken over the region, and he was one of her most dependable employees.

She sampled a mouthful of the spicy dish. "Umm, this is as good as it smells," she moaned, closing her eyes in ecstasy.

"Yes, it is and you'll never guess what we have for dessert." Bruce paused in wrapping pasta around his fork and made a grand gesture toward a domed silver dish on the serving cart.

"Don't make me guess. What is it?" Lisa asked between bites of salad.

"Chocolate cheesecake," Bruce announced gleefully.

"Dang, Bruce. You don't play fair at all. I know you're trying to bribe me into not cutting your budget. I wasn't going to take all your money away. I just need to snip it here and there." Lisa put her fork down and tried to look stern.

"I can't stand even one little snip," Bruce said. Seeing that the food had not completely seduced her, he added, "Let's save the budget talk until later. Tell me what's going on in your life."

"Not a thing. I must be the most boring creature alive," Lisa complained with a little pout.

"As outgoing and smart as you are, you could have something going on if you wanted. What happened to Sir Rodney? I thought he'd swept you off your feet."

"We had fun for a minute. But partying and rushing here and there gets old," Lisa explained, bringing another forkful of pasta to her mouth.

"Tell me about it. I went dancing with Jay-Z and Usher again last night. It does get old," Bruce joked.

"You're funny, but I'm very serious. Rushing from one party to the next was fun in the beginning, but sometimes I want to just stay in with my big fluffy house shoes on. With Rodney that's not an option. He says that he's trying to build a business and he has to network."

"Isn't that what your brother and his wife do?" Bruce asked.

"They network, but they know when to quit. The only reason Rodney was interested in me is that I fit in well with his plans for the future. He considered me another business asset. At best I could introduce him to the right people, and at worst I wouldn't cost him anything. He's real particular about how much he spends on a woman. I was surprised he had a ring for me. I should have looked at it to see if it had a diamond."

"He proposed?" Bruce exclaimed. He leaned forward in his seat, practically drooling. "Give me the details. You've been holding back."

"He proposed. He needed a permanent date. I wasn't up for it. He's moved on. That's all there was to it," Lisa said in a staccato voice.

"You sound like it's over," Bruce noted.

"It is."

"Okay, that's one down. Now what about Jonathan?"

"Why did you bring him up?" Lisa asked, surprised that Bruce even remembered Jonathan.

"Because you're always with him. Don't try to tell me you're just friends," Bruce said, giving her a look that dared her to refute him. "I see how you look at him. You've got serious lust for him."

"I gave him an ultimatum yesterday," she said and burst out laughing at the look on Bruce's face. She knew she had shocked him. Heck, she'd shocked herself with her brazen act.

"You what?" Bruce shrieked.

"I got the idea when Rodney proposed. He thought I was about to give him an ultimatum. I figured if I was going to give anybody one it would be Jonathan. So I did. I told him this friendship thing is not working for me and he'd better declare himself." She was putting on a sassy act with one hand on her hip and waving the other hand about as she talked.

"Girl, no, you've got to be kidding," Bruce said, enjoying the drama of it all.

"Yes, I did. I know I'm risking our friendship, but the friendship was getting to be too much of a strain for me. I want him for myself and if I saw him with somebody else I'd have a fit," Lisa said, no longer putting on the sassy sister-girl act for Bruce.

"How did he take it?" Bruce asked sympathetically, sensing her change of mood.

"I left him speechless," she said, trying to be light, but she looked as if she was about to break into tears.

"Do you think you've given him enough time to get over his I'm-not good-enough-for-you complex?" Bruce asked, propping an elbow on the table and resting his head in his hands. He looked at Lisa with tender, caring eyes.

"His self-confidence is too strong for that. It was a problem initially, but he's come to realize that the things really important to me don't cost money," she said contemplatively, mirroring Bruce's pose with her head resting in the palm of her hands.

"What do you think is holding him back, if it's not the money issue?"

"I have no idea," Lisa said with a deep sigh. "He can be so private sometimes. There are some things he just won't talk about."

"For what it's worth, I wouldn't have a problem with you earning more. I've always dreamed of being a kept man. In fact, if I didn't work for you, I'd proposition you," Bruce said playfully, hoping to hear her laugh again.

"Proposition me to do what?" Lisa asked. "We both know I'm not your type."

"But you're the type of woman my mother wants me to have. She's absolutely crazy about you."

"Tell your mother I said hey and if she needs someone over to taste her pot roast, I'm available."

"I'll let her know. She loves having people around who want to eat her cooking and who aren't counting calories."

"That's me. Now let's look at your numbers before I fall asleep," Lisa said, standing and stretching her long, lean body.

"Don't you want your cheesecake first?" Bruce asked, still stalling.

"No, not now. Maybe later."

They moved to the other end of the table with a stack of printouts and their notebook computers while the caterer cleared away the soiled dishes.

"See, Bruce, I thought we could cut ninety-five thousand dollars here," she said, pointing to a column of numbers under the heading *Maintenance*.

"Actually, I was going to ask you to increase that by two hundred thousand dollars," he answered.

"Come with me." He stood suddenly and motioned for her to follow him.

Giving her a detailed tour of the building, he pointed out worn carpeting in the hallways on the third and seventh floors. In several of the restrooms, he showed her slightly chipped countertops. "Besides," he said, "these pale colors are so 1990s. We need rich, dark colors that denote wealth."

When they returned to the conference room, Lisa said, "I'm ready for my cheesecake now. You've walked off every bit of that pasta."

"So what do you say about my budget request?" Bruce asked anxiously.

"You've made a very strong case and I also agree that it would look tacky to replace the carpet only where it is obviously needed. Let's replace the carpet in all the hallways."

"And paint the common areas forest green," Bruce prompted.

"And paint the common areas forest green," she repeated dutifully. "Now, is that all for you, Mr. Whitten?"

"Thanks, Lisa. That's more than I expected," Bruce said happily.

"I know you have the best interest of the company at heart," Lisa explained. "We'll cut some from William's budget." She referred to the manager of the Cool Springs property.

They both laughed. "Did you remember that we have a meeting with Human Resources next week?" Lisa asked.

"Yeah, I did. What is that all about?"

"They want to be sure all our managers understand the Americans with Disabilities Act. We've made all our building accessible to those with disabilities, but our property managers don't always follow our corporate guidelines when hiring," Lisa explained.

"It's a long drive into the city for me, but I'll be there with bells on."

"We'll start promptly at eight-thirty," Lisa emphasized, ignoring Bruce's play for sympathy.

"You don't ever have to worry that I'll be late," Bruce reminded her.

"You're right, I don't worry about you. But some of your counterparts . . ." Lisa began and stopped herself.

"You don't even have to tell me. I know. I don't mean to gossip, but you need to keep your eyes on Miss Jennifer," Bruce warned, leaning forward in his chair with concern in his eyes.

"Bruce, you know I'm uncomfortable discussing another employee with you—" Lisa began.

Bruce held up a hand to stop her. "All I'm saying is there's something not quite right about that one. Don't ever let her stand behind you. You could end up with a knife in your back."

Lisa felt a chill down her spine but said nothing more.

CHAPTER 4

When Jonathan's shift ended Thursday morning, he was overcome with an undeniable urge to call Lisa. Since they'd first met, he'd seldom gone so long without talking with her. Their instantaneous attraction had been followed by several months of dating. During that period they'd discovered all the mutual interests they shared. In the beginning he had found it unbelievable that she enjoyed NASCAR races, basketball, and football as much as he did. But she'd explained that growing up with three brothers, she had not had much choice. It was either go along with them or be left at home with her mother. As much as she loved her mother, she just knew the boys were having more fun out with their father.

Things had come to a halt when their relationship had begun to become more physical. He knew that if they had become lovers, he would never have been able to let her go. And if she lost respect for him after discovering his past, he would have been destroyed. It was best to stop things before they went too far.

But even after six months, he could still feel the

softness of her hair on his fingertips and taste the sweetness of her lips. When he closed his eyes, he could smell her scent as she leaned into him to accept his kiss.

Being around her without having the right to touch her had been difficult, but not as difficult as it would have been not to see her at all. And now this was the threat she was making. How could he live without Lisa in his life? He missed her so much that his resolve to do what was best for her was growing weak.

Wheeling his red Corvette into the left lane on the highway, he pressed the accelerator while berating himself for letting his thoughts dwell on Lisa so long. But he'd done nothing else since she'd stopped by the fire hall.

He recognized and respected the tremendous courage it had taken for her to come to him. What no one knew of was the self-control and strong willpower it had taken for him not to pull her into his arms and never let her go. It had been painful to see her walk away from him.

The only pleasant memory of that day was the way she was dressed. Lisa, who usually wore jeans or sweats, had actually put on a dress for him. Good Lord, her legs were gorgeous. He grew hot just thinking about her long legs. She certainly hadn't tried to be subtle coming on his job looking so soft and pretty.

Her questions to make him confess his jealousy had been anything but subtle. She had wanted to know if he was jealous of Rodney. *Yes. Hell yes!* he thought emphatically. The mere thought of her being with someone else was enough to send him into a rage.

Yet the only thing he'd wanted to do was pull her

into his arms and shower her with kisses. She'd looked so determined and nervous sitting across from him in her dainty little sundress and sexy slippers. In spite of her nervousness, she had said what she came to say.

To think she'd done all that for him. Not just the outfit or subjecting herself to his crew's gawking. She had also risked his rejection. The thought hit so suddenly, he almost came to a complete stop in the fast lane on I-24.

He slapped himself on the forehead. She had shown him once again that Lisa Stevens had more balls than most men. This girl was not afraid to go after what she wanted, even if it meant suffering humiliation and rejection. She just wasn't willing to let their relationship remain in limbo. She'd told him she wanted all or nothing, and like a fool, he'd let her walk away. If he didn't speak up quickly, he'd lose her forever. She'd be free to live her life with some other man. Was that what he wanted? Could he bear that?

He'd better stop her before it was too late. If it wasn't already too late. What did he have to lose? So what if she found out about his past? There was a slim chance that his secret would remain buried forever. Perhaps she'd fall in love with him before she discovered his past. Maybe she'd love him so much that it wouldn't matter anymore. That was a risk he was willing to take for just a little more time with her. If she was willing to risk rejection and humiliation, surely he could take a risk too.

Relieved to have finally made a decision, he took his exit off the interstate and zoomed down the long, isolated stretch of highway to his house. Once there he rushed inside and dialed her number. He had a sense of urgency, feeling that he'd wasted too much time already.

"Hello," she answered, her throaty voice sexy, even at 6:00 a.m.

"Hi, uh, Lisa, this is Jonathan." He was more nervous than he'd expected to be. Anxiously, he began pacing the length of his living room.

"Yes, it is," she replied with a sexy giggle. She was so surprised and relieved to hear from him that she wanted to throw the phone down and yell with joy. But she tried to contain herself. He had not stated the purpose of his call yet. Did he want to try to renegotiate her offer or to tell her that he accepted her as a woman?

"I've been thinking over your—uh—offer." He wasn't sure those were the right words. Was it an offer or a proposal? Now he understood why she had been so nervous when she came to see him. If she was brave enough to confront him, then surely he could do the same. "Maybe we could get together and talk things out."

"That sounds like a good idea. What do you have in mind?" She tried to control her voice, but she was anything but calm.

"Tonight or tomorrow night—or whenever it'll work for you—I thought we could go out. Maybe have dinner or something," Jonathan offered awkwardly.

"Okay. Tonight will work for me. I'll meet you at seven." She wanted more information, but decided to be patient.

"No, I'll pick you up at home," he interjected quickly. He wanted her to understand that this was different, it was a date.

"I won't have time to go home. I'll be coming in from Cookeville. I'll meet you at Amerghetti's. Is that okay?" she asked briskly. She wasn't going to make it too easy for him until she knew what was on his mind.

"Sure, that's fine," he accepted solemnly.

"Good. See you tonight." She hung up before curiosity got the best of her and she started seeking clues to figure out what he had decided.

He stared at the buzzing phone for several minutes. That hadn't gone well. He hadn't sounded sure and confident at all. Here he was, a big old man, feeling as nervous as a virgin on prom night.

Shaking off his mood, he went upstairs to his bedroom and changed into one of his old jumpsuits that he wore when he worked on cars. Alan Mueller was coming soon to pick up the 1969 Corvette. Jonathan hurried to the barn to put the finishing touches on the customized automobile.

A short time later, Jonathan heard Alan Mueller before he saw him. "Wow! Is that my ride?" the middle-aged attorney called out, trying to sound hip.

Jonathan turned toward the older man as he approached. "It sure is," Jonathan said, smiling. "Are you ready for a test drive?"

"Yes, I am," Alan replied enthusiastically. He walked around the car, lovingly touching each surface as he looked it over. "Look at these bumpers. They're something else."

Stepping away from the car to allow Alan Mueller full access, Jonathan put his hands in his pockets. His pride in the car wouldn't allow him to remain quiet. Jonathan cataloged custom features of the car for his customer. "The bumpers are completely chrome, just like you asked for. And they're molded in so there's no seam. Don't those chrome bumpers look sharp with the chrome side pipes? We also put in chrome headers."

"This is better than I expected," the attorney said in a voice usually reserved for someone falling in love. "The color is perfect and this gold flame work is exactly as I described it to you."

"Take a look at this engine. It's all chrome too." Jonathan raised the hood and the older man rushed to look inside. "It's so fast, the cops will never see you coming. All they'll feel is the wind after you've blown by them. You'll be way down the road before they realize they should be chasing you," he added with a chuckle. Alan joined him.

"Let's blow her out. I don't mind getting a ticket today," Mr. Mueller said excitedly. "Jump in."

Jonathan got in on the passenger side and tossed the keys to Mr. Mueller. They went down the gravel road leading from the farm at about fifteen miles an hour. But as soon as they were out on the highway, the law-abiding attorney pressed the accelerator to the floor. Jonathan tightened his seat belt and smiled. Fast was the only way to drive such a mean machine.

An hour later they returned to the barn without being stopped by the police in any of the counties they'd raced through. Alan sat at the round table near an area that also contained an old soda machine and stereo.

"What is my total?" he asked, his hand paused over his blank check.

"Fifty-five thousand dollars," Jonathan said quickly.

"No, that can't be right. All that custom work you did has to cost more than that," Alan protested.

"I'm only charging you for the cost of the accessories I had to buy," Jonathan explained.

"No, I want to pay fair market value. What would

you charge any other customer?" Alan asked, tapping his pen with each word.

"I don't want to charge you the same as any other customer. You're a good friend and I owe you a lot," Jonathan said, leaning against the old Coke machine with his hand thrust deeply into the pockets of the jumpsuit.

"Boy, you don't owe me anything. This is business. Now tell me the truth. What does a job like this cost?" Alan looked up at the tall young man who made him so proud.

"I would charge anyone else seventy-five thousand dollars," Jonathan admitted, taking a Coke from the machine and opening it.

"Is that right?"

"Yes, it is," Jonathan said, taking a long swallow of his Coke.

"Okay, then, I'll pay sixty." Alan began writing and then paused, saying, "I'll accept the friendship discount."

He tore off the check and Jonathan accepted it, sticking it into his pocket. "Thank you."

"You know," Alan said, "I think it's time for you to give consideration to taking this restoration business to the next level." He leaned back in his chair and looked at Jonathan fondly. "You have the brains and the skills to make your business a success."

"I don't want to leave the fire department. This is just something I do to pass the time since we have so many consecutive days off," Jonathan responded, taking a seat across from Alan.

"Sure."

Jonathan set the Coke before Alan and took his seat again. "My job is more important than anything else I do. I thought you understood that."

They had had this conversation so many times before, Jonathan hated repeating himself.

"You don't have to keep that job anymore. I believe you've paid your debt to society twenty times over," Alan said gravely, his voice growing deeper with emotion. "You've more than made up for your past mistakes. Besides, it wasn't your fault."

"I do my job well and I like what I do," Jonathan returned, becoming impatient.

"You also restore old cars extremely well. You could make a mint doing this. I'd be willing to help you with start-up capital," Alan offered tentatively, knowing the young man would not likely accept his offer of money. He never had, not even to go to college. Jonathan had allowed Alan to pull a few strings to get him into North Carolina A&T. But that was all the young man had accepted. He had gotten scholarships and worked, but that was the extent of his dependence on the older man.

Jonathan organized his thoughts before he spoke. "I've saved quite a bit of money. But I don't have very many expenses. You helped me figure out how to buy this property so that I don't even have a mortgage. I enjoy working on the cars, but I wouldn't if I did it just for the money. I'll work for the fire department and work on cars as a hobby." He folded his arms across his chest.

"What about Lisa? You always say she's too rich for you. At least if you started you own business, you'd have the potential to become wealthy, too," Alan pushed on, knowing that he didn't have long before Jonathan shut down.

"Lisa will accept me the way I am," Jonathan said with a certainty that surprised even him. But once he'd said it, he knew it to be true.

"Of course she will. She's smart. But she's a beautiful woman. You're going to want to buy her pretty things." His opportunity to make his points was almost gone.

"I'll keep doing what I'm doing," Jonathan said succinctly and walked over to the red Corvette that he called Zora. It was now hoisted with a series of pulleys so that he could work under it while standing.

Alan followed him, knowing that his time for pushing and probing was over. He gracefully changed the subject. "Once my friends see my car, you'll have more business than you can handle. I'm going to tell all of them about you." He smiled really big, thinking of how his cronies would envy him.

"Thank you. I appreciate that. But it'll be about six months before I can get to anything else. Look at the cars I have lined up now."

"No one will mind the wait. What are you doing to her now?" Alan asked, standing next to Jonathan beneath the 1978 Corvette.

"I've decided to take out the 350 and put in that 548-cid monster that I was saving for another customer. He changed his mind, so I'm putting it into Zora."

"Are you crazy? What are you going to do with an engine that big?"

"Exactly what you just did. Let the top town and speed like crazy." Jonathan laughed.

"I might take a look at it after you're finished," Alan Mueller offered.

"No, I'd never sell Zora. She and I've been together a long time. I could never part with her," Jonathan said adamantly.

"Well, if you ever want some quick cash, give me a call," Alan said, moving around the bright red Corvette.

"I'll never need money that badly," Jonathan said firmly.

That night Jonathan waited anxiously for Lisa to arrive at the restaurant. Surely he was at the right place. The server came to refill his water glass for the third time and replaced the empty bread basket.

When the server moved out of his line of vision, Jonathan saw Lisa walking toward him. Her athletic past was evident in her long-legged stride. As usual her hair was in disarray and her blouse was no longer tucked neatly into her slacks. This was the Lisa he knew.

Relieved to see her, he stood and smiled while she approached the table. He had begun to think that she would stand him up and he knew that it would be exactly what he deserved.

Her breath caught in her throat when he stood. Tall and lanky, he looked wickedly masculine in a navy silk T-shirt underneath a navy blazer and navy slacks. He had the attitude of someone who'd faced death and lived to tell about it. She had no idea how she identified that attitude. She'd certainly known no one that fit that description before.

"I hope you weren't about to give up on me," Lisa said in a breathless voice.

"No, I'd never do that," Jonathan replied, giving her a dynamic smile. "But I did wonder if you'd forgotten about our date."

Heat began at Lisa's cheeks and spread over her body. Jonathan's smile always wrapped her in warmth. Was she reading too much into him calling this a date?

"No, I didn't forget. I made the mistake of stopping by the office and the human resource director caught me. She wanted my input on training she's doing for us next week. I'm starved. Have you ordered?"

"No, but the server is hovering nearby. He's been very attentive. Would you like bread? It's excellent." He poured olive oil on her bread plate and added parmesan cheese. Tearing off a piece of the fresh bread from the basket, he dipped it into the mixture before feeding it to her.

"Umm, this is delicious," Lisa moaned softly after taking a bite. "And it's still warm." Some of the olive oil dripped to her chin and Jonathan carefully wiped it away with his napkin. His touch had her suffused in warmth again. She'd better watch herself or she'd have a meltdown before the evening was over.

"Thank you. I'm so hungry. This has been one of those days. You know I never eat breakfast and I didn't have time for lunch. I was just at the Church Street building Monday and thought I'd seen everything that was wrong over there. Today while I was in Cookeville, I got a call from one of our anchor tenants in that building. He was irate because three weeks ago he had made a simple request for lightbulbs to be changed in the ceiling and the property manager still has not responded. When I called her about it, she said she just hadn't gotten around to it yet. She told me that she had more important things to do. Can you believe that?"

Jonathan nodded but didn't say a word. He was used to Lisa's need to unwind after a stressful day at work. It was okay with him because he never wanted to talk about his work. Some of it was too horrible to repeat.

The server interrupted to take their orders. When he left, Lisa continued, "I told her she'd better take care of the small things, as well as the big ones. I had just gotten to Cookeville, but decided to rush through my inspection there to go appease the tenant. So I rode three hours back. While I was there I checked to see if there were other maintenance issues. Now, mind you, when I was there Monday we had not discussed the manager's relationship with her clients. We shouldn't have to spend time on something that basic. Today I discovered she has a stack of maintenance requests about six inches thick. Of course, most of them were from the same tenants who have called two and three times. All she could say is they weren't high priority for her."

While their food was served, Lisa stopped talking but resumed her story as soon as the server departed. "I thought about sending Bruce to Jennifer's property. He could have things straightened out in a few months. But I decided that wouldn't be fair to the tenants in Brentwood. Maybe I could send the manager from the Cool Springs building out there. Let him see how the other half lives." She stopped and chuckled at the thought before taking another bite of her veal marsala.

"Do you like that?" Jonathan asked.

"Yes, it's delicious. Do you want a taste?" Before he answered, she cut a small portion and fed it to him.

"That is good. I'll have to order it next time. Have some of my seafood pasta," he offered.

She tasted it gingerly. "That's not as good as the voodoo pasta I had Monday when I had lunch with Bruce," she said after tasting it.

"How is Bruce?"

"He's fantastic. Of course, he asked about you. By the way, the insurance company finally sent a check for the Church Street building fire. Can you believe it's been a year?" Lisa asked.

"Yes," Jonathan said softly. "That's when I first met you."

"You remember?" Lisa asked softly. She set her fork down and looked at him intently. He sounded as if meeting her was a special memory.

"I'll never forget," he replied in a voice filled with emotion. He paused as if trying to find the right words to go on. "I saw you when I first arrived at the scene. I asked one of the investigators why you had been allowed behind the yellow tape and she told me you owned the building. You seemed so young and helpless to have to handle so much alone. I decided to help you and when I finally caught up with you, you were panting and your chest was visibly heaving. At first I thought you were overcome with desire for me," Jonathan joked.

"Yeah, right. And you thought I was whistling at you when you heard my wheezing across the room," Lisa joined in self-deprecatingly.

"It did take me a couple of minutes to realize you were having an asthma attack. Your eyes were as big as saucers and you couldn't say a word," Jonathan remembered.

"As usual, I didn't have an inhaler with me. I would have passed out if you hadn't given me that air mask. I hadn't thought about how smoky the building would be, and smoke is one of my triggers," Lisa said. "I hate feeling that helpless."

"Since that episode, you've shown me over and over that you can handle anything. That's why I'm in such awe of you," Jonathan said, knowing that she hated to be reminded of her weaknesses. He took one of her hands in his and was surprised to find it cold and shaking.

"Lisa, what's wrong? Why are you shaking?" he asked, concerned.

"I like the way you take care of me, Jonathan," she replied simply. "I'm just a woman, Jonathan, and sometimes I'm weak. But I know what I want."

"What do you want, Lisa?" he asked.

"I think I've made that perfectly clear. Remember when you brought me the insurance papers after the fire? *I* asked *you* out," Lisa reminded him, pointing at her chest with her free hand.

"That was to repay my kindness," Jonathan said, still holding one of her hands between his.

"No, that was because I wanted to get with you. When I was looking at the fire damage that night, I noticed you even before you came over and introduced yourself. You were all smudged with soot and dripping with water, but you stood out. It was obvious you were in charge. It was in your walk and the way the others responded to you. If I hadn't been in the throes of an asthma attack, it would have been all over for you that night," Lisa said saucily. She tossed her head to the side and her ponytail fell over her shoulder.

"It *was* all over for me that night. You captured my heart and I don't want it back," Jonathan confessed. He lifted her hand and pressed it to his lips.

"You too?" Lisa asked in a wonder-filled voice. Before she could say more, the server interrupted to ask if they were finished with their half-eaten food. When he had cleared the table, they continued their conversation.

"Yes. Lisa, I want to be with you in the worst way. I want to have the right to caress you, to kiss you, and to hear you moan my name. Can we go back to that?"

"Let's not go back. Let's move forward," she suggested, gently stroking Jonathan's lean, freshly shaved cheek.

The restaurant staff began putting chairs on the

table and the server again asked if they cared for anything else. "Sir, we're about to close. May I settle your check now?"

Jonathan absently took a credit card from his wallet and gave it to the server. When he returned with a receipt, Jonathan led Lisa out the door. Although it was late September, it had gotten cooler outside. Refreshed by the chilled air after the cozy atmosphere of the restaurant, they stood at her truck to talk for several minutes longer.

"I forgot to tell you how pretty you look tonight," he said, before leaning down to kiss her. It was not like the tentative kisses of the past. This kiss was filled with urgency and raw need. Without restraint, she wrapped her arms around his neck and clung to him. He held her tightly and drank in as much of her sweetness as he could.

When he finally raised his head, they were both breathless. Afraid to risk speaking, Lisa turned **toward her truc**k. Jonathan quickly reached around **her and open**ed the door. As she stepped onto the running board, he put his hands around her long, slim waist and lifted her into the seat.

When her round, feminine backside was at his eye level, he was too much of a man and not enough of a gentleman to look away. While he was still gaping at the view, she turned to slide into the seat. He automatically gave her a hand to steady herself and he let the other rest comfortably at the base of her spine.

She wiggled around to get comfortable in her seat. "Thank you, Jonathan. This is a little high, but you know I'm in and out of this thing by myself all day," she reminded him.

"I'm here now. You shouldn't have to strain to climb up there when I'm around." She opened her

mouth to speak and he uncharacteristically interrupted her. "It looked like a strain to me."

She laughed then. Her laughter was always unre-
served and filled with pure joy. He loved the sound
of it, but wondered how it flowed from her so freely.
That kind of easy happiness was foreign to him.

CHAPTER 5

A short time after leaving Jonathan in the restaurant parking lot, Lisa entered her house. Leaning against the closed door, she released a long sigh to relieve built-up tension. Since Jonathan's call that morning, she had felt as if she were holding her breath, waiting to see him. All day long she'd reminded herself not to read too much into his call. One date—that's all he'd asked for. He'd given her no indication that things would be any different than they had been in the past. But the evening had been much better than anything she'd hoped for. Things had changed between them.

Licking her lips, she savored his taste. Inhaling deeply, she breathed in the manly scent of his soap. This was the man who drove her mad with desire and crazy with confusion.

Pulling herself together, she made her way to the bedroom on the other side of the house. She was no longer tired, but energized with thoughts of Jonathan. Stripping off her work attire, she replayed the evening in her mind frame by frame.

The phone rang and, thinking it was Jonathan

checking to see that she'd made it home safely, she dropped to the bed and lifted the phone from its base. Prepared to settle in for a sweet good-night chat, she was slightly disappointed, but not surprised, to hear her brother Melvin's voice come through the receiver.

"Hey, sis, where have you been?" he greeted her.

"I went out to dinner," she replied.

"You had a date on a work night?" he asked.

"Yes, Melvin. Grown-ups can do that," she replied.

"Yes, other grown-ups can, but not you. You are a workaholic. Who did you go with?"

"Jonathan," she said quickly.

"Oh, are you still hanging out with him? I thought you had a date," Melvin said.

"What's up with you?" Lisa said, changing the subject. Her new relationship was too undefined for her to tell her brothers about it yet.

Easing her feet from her low-heel pumps, she rubbed her toes, then flexed her feet as they talked. She'd been in the dress shoes all day and her feet were still feeling cramped.

They chatted for several moments. Melvin didn't want anything in particular, but since being released from a psychiatric hospital earlier that year, he had made an effort to stay in touch with his family. They'd surrounded him and supported him through his struggle with bipolar disorder.

When their conversation ended, her mind immediately went back to thoughts of Jonathan. An image of the way he was smiling when she entered the restaurant popped into her head. She wished she could keep him smiling that way always. Laughter and happiness seemed to have eluded him most of his life. He acted as if he was always surprised by joy, but grateful for its arrival. An easy man to please, he was appreciative of even the smallest things she did. Sometimes he acted as if he didn't deserve joy.

She thought of the desire written all over his face as he took her hands into his, and she instantly experienced a heat wave. She headed to her bathroom for a cooling shower.

While toweling dry, she heard the phone ring and dived across the bed to reach it before it went into voice mail. "Hi, Lisa. This is Jonathan." He identified himself as if his deep, inviting voice wasn't imprinted on her brain. "Did I wake you up?" he asked hesitantly.

"No, I was—I was getting ready for bed," she answered, not willing to tell him that she was just coming out of the shower and was now stretched across her bed naked.

"I wanted to tell you that I had a wonderful evening. Thank you for giving me another chance." Jonathan's deep voice wrapped her in a blanket of warmth.

"I had a good time too." She wondered what she'd given him another chance to do. Break her heart? Or to leave her wanting more from him?

"When I go in tomorrow, I won't be free again until Sunday. Do you have plans for Sunday?" he asked.

"No, I don't. What do you have in mind?"

"Would you like to go to the races with me?"

"Yes, I would. You know how much I like going," she exclaimed enthusiastically. "What time will you pick me up?"

"I'll be there as soon as my shift ends. Let's say six forty-five," he suggested, pausing to look out his bedroom window.

"Why so early?" Lisa asked. "We usually don't go until noon."

"This is going to be a big one. We've got to get there early if we want a good spot for the tailgate party. I'll smoke my world-famous ribs and Artis claims his deep-fried Cornish game hens are the best. His lady is making potato salad and who knows what the others will bring," Jonathan related.

"Oh, I didn't realize we'd be with a group," Lisa said, trying not to let her disappointment show in her voice. They had been alone together for the first time in ages tonight. Now he was back to going out with a group.

"The only others besides Artis and Raquel will be Foster and Mia." He turned away from the window and leaned against the sill.

"Okay," she responded dryly, rolling to her back and laying the damp towel over her body.

Sensing her lack of enthusiasm, he asked, "Is there something you'd rather do?"

"No, you know how much I like going to the races. It's just that we had so much fun alone together tonight. I'm a little disappointed, that's all." She stood and wrapped herself in the towel.

Her words brought a smile to his face. "I'll have to keep that in mind," he replied thoughtfully. "I just thought you enjoyed being around Mia and Raquel."

"I do. That's not the problem. It's just that you and I need to spend some time together. Getting to know each other," she explained. She sat on the side of the bed and studied her short, broken fingernails.

"Don't you think we know each other pretty well?" he asked.

"I may not be the person you think I am. There's a lot you don't know about me," she replied.

"I guess that's why people date. We'll take our time this time," he promised. Did she realize how much she did not know about him? Was she waiting for him to confess his past? Did she suspect? Would she still be talking to him if she knew?

"That's a deal," she replied. "What do you want me to bring Sunday?"

"I'll take care of our contribution this time," he replied.

The good thing about a date at the speedway for Lisa was that she had plenty of appropriate outfits. The sport fit perfectly with her casual wardrobe. However, nothing she would have worn before was fit for her new relationship with Jonathan. No longer willing to be one of the guys, she went shopping for an outfit that would make him remember she was a woman. While she was in the mall, she got in the spirit and decided to buy several new outfits.

All the time she was shopping she thought of her sister-in-law, who had a unique sense of style. Cara knew exactly what looked right on Lisa, always encouraging her to wear clothes that accentuated her long, slender figure. She took into consideration Lisa's fast-paced lifestyle and desire for a look that didn't require a lot of maintenance. Lisa tried to remember that as she selected several carefree outfits that were soft and feminine.

On Sunday morning, she answered the door wearing pink shorts that fit low on her hips and a pink tank top that exposed a sliver of her well-toned midriff. Jonathan gulped twice and gave her a big smile that clearly told her he liked what he saw. "Hi, Jonathan, I'm ready. I'll get my purse."

As he watched her walk away, his eyes followed her long slender legs up to her derrière that was riding snug in the shorts. When she returned, he was still standing in the same spot. He'd been unable to think of anything but the way she'd looked walking away from him.

"Did you get another new outfit?" Jonathan asked when she returned.

"Yes, I still have my old baggy jeans, but I'll save them for work. I'm almost thirty years old and was still dressing like a tomboy. I've decided those days are over," she confessed.

"You always look good to me, Lisa. But I do like the outfits you've been wearing," he said after swallowing hard.

She smiled, enjoying the effect she was having on him. Since she'd returned to the room, he had looked at her as if he'd never seen her before. "Are you ready to go?" she asked.

He smiled at her curiously and replied, "Yes, sure, I'm ready. Oh, I forgot. I have something for you." He reached into a bag and pulled out a pink, long-bib baseball cap with *Race Girl* embroidered in white across the front.

"Thank you. You must have known I was going to wear this today. It's the perfect shade of pink. This is so sweet," she gushed. She raised her arms to put the cap on and he caught a glimpse of her perfect little navel. His instant arousal surprised him, but there was something so personal, so intimate about seeing a part of her that was usually covered. He was still struggling to breathe when she asked, "Do I look like a real NASCAR fan now?"

"You sure do, you'll fit in well," Jonathan answered. He bent down and pushed the hat back to kiss her lips. He held her firmly against his body and kissed her until he thought he'd drown in her warmth. She didn't protest, but luxuriated in the delicious sensations racing through her body.

Completely relaxed in his arms, she gently stroked his back.

"You're too much. Do you know that?" Jonathan asked when he could speak again.

"Am I enough for you?" Lisa asked lightly.

"You're more than that," he replied, opening the door before he was tempted to take her into his arms again.

When they got into the Corvette, she adjusted her cap and fastened the new five-point harness. "Would you like the top up?" he asked, glancing at her.

"No, leave it down. Isn't that why you gave me the cap?" she teased.

"I didn't have an ulterior motive for the hat. I saw it and picked it up for you, knowing how much you like NASCAR," he answered seriously.

"I know you gave me the cap because you're so sweet. I was just joking." She chuckled softly.

"Good. I didn't want to get into another debate with you about gifts." He glanced at her to be sure she wasn't offended.

"We won't. Remember, we decided not to go back to where we were before. We're moving forward." She was not going to ruin the day getting into a discussion about the difference in their incomes.

Looking around the interior of the car, Lisa asked, "What's different in here? Oh, the dash. You got rid of that old cracked-up wood. What is this metal? It's not chrome, is it?"

"No, it's aluminum," he replied, shifting the car from third to fourth as he took his place in the fast lane on the interstate.

"What are these things?" Lisa asked, pointing at a series of dials on the dash.

"Those are my new AutoMeter Ultra Lite gauges. And if you look down here," he said, pointing to a place above the steering column between the seats, "I've also added a Sony CD player."

Touching the dashboard that looked like an airplane's control panel, he continued, "Here you have the AC controls, power window switches, and a toggle switch for the fuel pump. How do you like me now?" he asked, stealing a glance at her.

"I'm impressed! You have more high-tech stuff than a cockpit," Lisa gushed. "How did you do all this without me?"

"It was hard. I ended up getting Artis to help," he answered. "I thought it would be trial and error, but it all went in perfectly the first time. All I had to do was follow the instructions."

"It looks like you're finished," she said, sounding disappointed. Lisa, a mechanical engineer, was what other engineers called a gearhead. She loved working on cars.

"Yeah, I wanted you to help me, but you've been working so hard lately, I didn't know when you'd have the time," he replied. He didn't tell her he'd only done it the past weekend when she'd gone off with Rodney.

She didn't respond, but looked out the window as the green countryside gave way to the steel and glass buildings downtown. How could she tell him that she'd thought about him and that car the entire weekend with Rodney? That car had been their connection, their common ground.

Sensing her disappointment, Jonathan tried to make amends. He reached across the gear stick and lifted her hand to his lips. "Okay, little gearhead, I promise I won't work on another car without you. In fact, I need you to help me with my newest car. I just found a pewter Corvette. Do you know how rare that car is?"

Lisa turned toward him. He had captured her interest. "No, I don't. What's so special about it?"

"That color is unique. It was used only in 1972. There are no others."

"Where did you find it?" Lisa stopped the CD player so that she could hear him better.

"I was on my way home, taking back roads instead of the highway. As I approached the old barn, I spotted the car sitting beside it. I had passed it before I realized what I'd seen. I slammed on my brakes and made a U-turn right in the middle of the road. Almost as soon as I knocked, the farmer answered the door. He acted as if he knew why I'd stopped. He already had his cap in his hand. He put it on and walked out to the barn with me. He told me that the car had been his son's. But his son had never come back for it. I asked him how much he wanted for it and he told me to pay whatever I thought it was worth." Jonathan related the story the way a woman does when she's found a good sale on designer shoes.

"What did you end up paying for it?" Lisa asked, absorbed in the story.

"Five thousand dollars," Jonathan replied, unable to suppress his excitement.

"Is five thousand dollars a good deal for a car that old?" It was clear she thought five thousand dollars was too much to pay for the car.

"Yes, it is," he assured her. "There are so few of them out there. When I get this car all fixed up I can easily sell it for ten times what I paid. First I've got to order matching paint."

Knowing the lengths Jonathan went to to keep his cars authentic, Lisa asked, "How are you going to find the original paint if they only used it one year?"

"I scraped some paint from the car and sent it to a design firm. They'll have to custom-make the color."

Jonathan's voice had an energy that fascinated Lisa. His depth of knowledge was impressive, but she was even more excited by his passion for the topic. His enthusiasm for cars matched her own. She knew that if she did not work in the family business, she would have sought a job with one of the major automobile manufacturers.

The sun was high in the sky by the time they reached the speedway forty-five minutes later. Jonathan's friend Artis had already set up a gas grill and was working on assembling the deep fryer.

"Hey, Lisa, good to see you and I see you looking good," Artis said, giving Lisa a flirtatious once-over.

"Good to see you too," Lisa replied. "Where's Raquel?"

"She's coming later. Her mother's babysitting today and told her not to bring the kids before sunup. I had to get out here to get everything started," Artis explained.

It wasn't long before the grill had red-hot charcoal glowing in it and oil was bubbling in the fryer. "What smells so good?" Jonathan asked, taking slabs of ribs from the ice chest and placing them across the red charcoals.

"That's the maestro's baked beans, but you have to wait for them. Until it's ready I've got you covered, brother. Biscuits are wrapped in the foil back here," Artis said, pointing to a bundle on the back of the long grill. "Can you fry the sausage and scramble eggs?"

"Sure, we'll take care of it," Jonathan said agreeably. "Do you want some too?" He was ready to eat and didn't mind cooking.

Food was ready in a very short while. The three of

them sat down to eat together. By the time they'd eaten and cleared away the breakfast food, Raquel showed up. Barely five feet tall, the medium-brown woman wore her hair in a short style becoming to her round face. Her shorts and matching top flattered her hippy figure. Lisa always enjoyed Raquel's company because of her quick sense of humor.

"Hey, babe," Artis called out. Raquel raised her hand as if waving him away, but didn't respond.

"Hi, Raquel, how's it going?" Lisa asked. The men had returned to the grills and Lisa had begun the task of organizing the serving tables.

"Can you believe that man left me before sunrise and I had to get three kids up and to my mother's all by myself?" Raquel looked tired already and quickly lowered herself into one of the folding chairs.

"Do you want me to cook something for you? We just ate."

"No, I had breakfast with the kids. My mother told me they had to be clean and fed before they arrived. Let me tell you, girl, if it's not one thing it's another. What's with that outfit? Who're you trying to impress?" Raquel's disposition brightened. There was more to the outfit than just a change of clothes. You could actually see Lisa's figure. Something was up and Raquel wanted to hear the story.

"Guess," Lisa demanded with one hand on her hip.

Raquel looked from Lisa to Jonathan, who stood on the other side of the tables at the grill. "No, you're not. You two are going for a second round. Is that it?" she squealed, unable to contain her delight.

"Yes," Lisa said, returning Raquel's big smile.

"Good. He's been looking so sad and lonely lately. When he came by last Saturday to get Artis to go over to his place to play with his cars, I had to let Artis go. We wondered why he was so sad, but he keeps everything to himself. You know how Jonathan is. He doesn't tell anyone anything. One day he's going to explode keeping everything all bottled up like that," Raquel predicted, leaning forward in her chair so that her voice wouldn't carry to the men.

"Yes, he can be pretty private," Lisa agreed neutrally.

"Private nothing!" Raquel exclaimed in a loud whisper. "He's downright mute most of the time. I've known the man all these years and can count on one hand the conversations he's started with me."

"He'll talk forever about things he's interested in," Lisa said in his defense.

"Yeah, he does manage to work your name into most of our conversations," Raquel allowed with a sly smile.

"Woman, please!" Lisa said, though secretly pleased.

"Oh yeah, he does," Raquel insisted.

"If he does, it's just because we do so many things together," Lisa conceded.

"Whatever. He's your man. I guess you're not going to let me say too much. Now that he's got you, maybe he'll keep his butt out of my kitchen," Raquel joked. She knew there was no way she could keep Jonathan and Artis apart. They had been best friends forever.

Looking past the two women, Jonathan called out, "Look who's coming just in time to eat!"

"Oh, Mia and Foster are here," Raquel said, turning around.

Lisa hurried toward the latest couple to arrive. "Girl, I'm glad you're here. It's been too long. Did Foster tell you I ask about you all the time?" Mia asked, struggling to hug Lisa around the packages in her arms.

"Here, let me take some of your load," Lisa offered after Mia's warm embrace.

They set everything down on the table near Raquel. "Did you know that those two are an item again?" Raquel couldn't wait to ask.

"Yes, Foster told me about them Sun—"

Foster quickly interrupted his wife. "Lisa, I'm glad you and Captain are seeing each other again. Maybe he won't make me wash trucks every day if you soften him up a little. You think you can get him in a better mood?" he asked playfully.

"Foster told you about them sunning what?" Raquel asked, not missing anything.

"I didn't say that," Mia replied, spreading cloths on the tables Lisa had just lined up for serving.

"What were you about to say then?" Raquel persisted. She was not about to let anything just drop if she smelled good gossip in it.

"What did Foster say about me coming to the fire hall on Sunday?" Lisa prompted. She should have guessed her visit would be the subject of firehouse gossip.

Mia's hands became still for several moments and she looked across the table at Foster. He had moved away to chat with the men. "Yes, he told me you'd come to the firehouse Sunday."

Lisa had to know the details. "What else did he say?"

"He said that you looked real good. In fact he said you were dressed to seduce. He didn't know how Jonathan could let you leave so quickly," Mia said, trying to think of the positive things to tell her friend.

But Lisa wanted to hear everything—good and bad. "And what else did he say?" she prompted.

"Let's see. Look, Lisa, I can't remember the whole conversation word for word. Girl, you look real good today."

"Go on, Mia," Lisa insisted, not willing to be distracted.

"Okay, okay, he said all eyes were on you when you strutted out of there with that tight little dress on. Jonathan gave all the men another chore after you left. Said they didn't have enough to do if they had time to sit around getting into other people's business."

"I'm sorry," Lisa said, embarrassed. "That's not what I went up there for."

"Well, what did you expect?" Raquel asked. "Some of those men haven't had any in ages."

"And some of them are horny even if they had some right before they left home. And there's nothing you can do to help them. There's no need for you to apologize, girl. You did what you had to do. You had to get your man's attention. At least it's better than hitting him in the back of the head with a two-by-four," Mia joked.

"Uh-huh, I'm glad Artis is not a fireman. I couldn't stand for him to sleep away from home all that time. I hear some of them slip women into their bunks," Raquel said, ready to go on with the least bit of encouragement.

"Come on, help me put the serving pieces on these tables," Mia said as she finished covering the tables. Raquel remained seated, while Lisa and Mia went to work.

At Mia's insistence, the table where they'd have their meal was covered with elegant lacy cloths. The other tables, which would hold the buffet, were covered with plastic-coated paper. After they'd placed chairs about the dining table, they set it with Lenox china plates and crystal. That was one area where NASCAR tailgate parties differed from football. NASCAR fans tended to be formal when it came to meals. Some of the groups served shrimp cocktail, lobster bisque, and filet mignon. Champagne was always a staple. Paper plates and plastic utensils were never used.

Mia discovered she'd left the serving dishes in her car and demanded that Raquel, who'd done nothing, go with her. When they were gone Lisa continued arranging the tables. Jonathan walked up behind her and wrapped his arms around her waist. His touch on her bare skin flooded her with warmth. When he bent his head and kissed her on the neck, the desire that washed over her was tangible.

"What's that all about?" she asked, relaxing against his hard chest.

"Can't I kiss my lady if I like?" he whispered into her neck. No longer able to resist temptation, he caressed her warm brown skin, leisurely stroking her navel.

"Yes, but you're not prone to public displays of affection," she reminded him, all the while enjoying the combination of spine-tingling kisses on her neck and his gentle touch on her skin.

"I heard Mia giving you the skinny on the latest rumors," he said in between nibbles on her neck. "You know those men always have to have some kinds of tales to tell. It's the nature of the job. We are in close quarters for long periods of time. Everyone is always in each other's business. Don't let it embarrass you," he said softly, still holding her against his chest.

"I'm not embarrassed. You know it would take a lot to embarrass me. I just wondered how you felt being the subject of gossip." She turned to look into his eyes and was warmed by the concern she saw there.

"It didn't bother me. After all, you're the most beautiful woman that's walked through there in a long time. Of course they also think I'm stupid because I let you walk out on me. But I'm trying my best to rectify that act of stupidity." He kissed her lightly on the lips and she tightened her arms around his neck.

"Okay, folks, break it up. You know NASCAR doesn't allow that kind of stuff. These are family-friendly grounds," Foster called out as he and Artis approached them.

Jonathan scowled at his friends, but didn't remove his arms from Lisa's waist. He warned, "You need to check your meat to be sure we don't have to eat burned steaks again."

A short time later, the meal was prepared and the group was sitting around the table. Their first helping was eaten in near silence as everyone enjoyed the smoked, grilled, and deep-fried foods. After they finished their first helping, Jonathan was set for more. Standing, he asked, "Lisa, want more ribs? I'm going for seconds."

"Yeah, you know I do. They're delicious," she said, setting down a corncob and licking her fingers before rubbing them on a napkin.

"Does anyone else want anything?" Jonathan called out.

"I want more but I wouldn't dare eat any more. How do you stay so slim?" Mia, who was as tall as Lisa and almost as slender, asked. "I have to cut down on what I eat because I don't have time to go to the gym anymore."

"I guess it's my metabolism," Lisa replied. She had grown accustomed to comments about her appetite and wasn't offended.

"I know I shouldn't eat more, but this food is too good to let go to waste," Raquel interjected as she held out her plate for another steak. "Seriously, girl, how can you eat so much?"

"I grew up playing sports with my three brothers. I ate whatever they ate," she answered, beginning to feel guilty about her healthy appetite. She looked at the plate of meat and potato salad Jonathan had just handed her and considered not eating another bite.

"Don't let them slow you down, girl. You know my grilling is addictive. Remember that big pile of bones left on your brother's table after they'd devoured all those ribs? It looked like they hadn't eaten for weeks," Jonathan said, smiling.

"When did that happen?" Raquel asked, probing for more information as usual.

"When we went to Miami for her mother's wedding," Jonathan explained as he returned to the grill to fill his plate after giving Lisa hers. "We had a cookout and I was in charge of the grills."

"But you weren't her date. I mean, you were still doing that 'best friends' thing until a day or so ago," Raquel suggested, to see if they'd agree or disagree. While she waited she took a bite from her corn on the cob.

"That's right," Lisa replied for Jonathan. She fixed Raquel with a glare that dared her to say more, but that didn't stop her.

"So, you're already in with the in-laws," Raquel teased.

"I've met Lisa's family," Jonathan responded dryly, not taking well to Raquel's teasing.

"Well, tell us how the other half lives," Raquel said.

"The other half of what?" Jonathan asked indignantly.

"Raquel, you'd better leave Jonathan alone," Artis warned her.

"You know Jonathan. When I've said enough, he'll just stop talking." Turning to Lisa, she asked, "I heard on CNN that your family is one of the wealthiest in America. Do you have more than Bill Gates?"

"I don't know," Lisa answered honestly.

"If your family is all that rich, why do you still go to work every day?" Raquel persisted.

This wasn't the first time Lisa had been asked that question, but she always answered patiently. "Bill goes to work every day. Why shouldn't I? Do you think his job is more important than mine?" She put her corn cob down and fixed her attention on Raquel, waiting for a response.

Put on the defensive, Raquel opened her mouth and closed it without speaking.

"I'd like to have the choice," Mia said, sighing. Raquel raised her hand, testifying her agreement.

"What would you do if you won the lottery?" Foster questioned the group in general.

Silenced for only a moment, Raquel was ready to talk again. She closed her eyes as if she could see visions of how she would spend leisure time. "I would stay in bed until three in the afternoon and when I got up, it would be time to go shopping."

"Every day?" Mia asked.

"Yes, *every day*." Raquel emphasized each word.

"Wouldn't you eventually run out of things to buy?" Artis asked, although he knew how much Raquel loved shopping.

"No, never. First I'd be sure we had all the basics. And with three kids, that would take a while. Then I'd get luxuries," Raquel dreamed aloud.

"Like what?" Lisa asked, wondering what Raquel considered a luxury.

"Your bracelet, for one. Let me see it closer. This may not have enough diamonds for me," Raquel joked, holding a hand out.

Lisa dropped her bracelet into the shorter

woman's outstretched hand and watched her eyes gleam with delight. "This is really beautiful. I haven't seen this many diamonds outside of Kay's," Raquel exclaimed.

"Does that one have enough diamonds for you?" Artis asked.

"Yeah, but they're not big enough." Raquel laughed.

"I hate to end the fun, gang, but if we're going to make it to our seats in time, we'd better start cleaning up," Jonathan interrupted after taking a final bite of potato salad.

Raquel gave the bracelet back to Lisa after one more longing look. Having decided to eat in spite of the teasing, Lisa hurried through her last few bites and joined the others in cleaning up and packing away the remaining food.

As the group entered the high-octane arena, the million-dollar cars were just beginning their laps. The excitement was palpable as spectators spotted their favorite drivers. "There's Dale Earnhardt Jr. coming around the bank now." Jonathan pointed out the number 8 Budweiser Chevy.

"How does he win anything in a Chevy? Where are the Fords?" Lisa asked, putting binoculars to her eyes.

"You'll have to wait a while before you see a Ford," Jonathan teased. "They're usually the last thing around the track."

"It looks like number seventeen is leading the pack. What is it?" Lisa asked, feigning ignorance. "Oh my, I see an F. Now there's an O and an R. What could it be?"

"That's a Ford," Jonathan admitted.

"Ohh—I can't watch. It's taking that curve so fast

it's going to run into that Chevy. No, it just left the Chevy in its dust," Lisa joked.

"That was Matt Kenseth. He's the defending champion," Jonathan explained.

"If I remember correctly, he was driving a Ford when he won the championship last year, wasn't he?" she asked casually.

"Yes," Jonathan answered, seeing himself about to fall into her trap and hating it.

"I rest my case," Lisa said triumphantly, lightly punching Jonathan's hard biceps.

Their conversation ended when the green flag signaled the start of the race. Lap after lap they watched the strategies and maneuvers with growing excitement, riveted to their seats. Lisa loved the noise of the roaring engines, the tight synchronousness of the pit crews. Although she would never admit it aloud, she enjoyed the crashes and near misses most of all. They added excitement to the sport.

"It's amazing how each team member knows exactly what to do," Lisa commented as Sterling Marlin's Coors Light car made a pit stop.

"And they have to do it with precision timing," Jonathan added. "Races can be won and lost in the pit."

"That's so true. There's nothing like having a good mechanic," Lisa commented before her attention was drawn to a car that had lost control, spun three times, and headed in the wrong direction. Five other cars crashed or wrecked, trying to avoid the first car.

When the final flag signaled the end of the race, they stood and cheered with the rest of the audience while the winner performed his celebratory burnouts, spinning circles to produce a pillar of white smoke.

As the smoke cleared and car number 6 moved toward the winner's circle, Lisa and Jonathan took their seats again. It would be a while before the crowd would thin out.

"That was a good race, wasn't it?"

"Yes, and with the season ending in a few weeks, it'll be good to see how fast the winners have to go to set records. I would give anything to drive two hundred miles an hour just once. Can you imagine speeding around a racetrack going as fast as you possibly can?"

"It gives you a feeling of freedom. It's great to feel so liberated," Jonathan said, smiling peacefully.

"So you've gone that fast before?" Lisa asked, looking at Jonathan quizzically.

"Yes, I have—a time or two. It feels like flying," he related.

"I'd like to do that. But first I'd have to check the car out myself. I wouldn't want to get up to two hundred miles an hour and have a wheel fly off," she said thoughtfully.

Impulsively, Jonathan said, "Would you like to go backstage, to one of the garages?"

"Yes, can we do that?" Lisa asked. In all the years she'd gone to races with her father, she'd never been to one of the garages.

"Hey, guys, we'll catch up with you later," he called out to the others as he led Lisa away.

Although the race was over, the crowd was not thinning. Some people were milling around, engaged in leisurely conversations, and others seemed to be rushing away on personal missions. Jonathan held her hand and guided her through the thick crowd, past the autograph booths and concession stands.

They stopped in front of a nondescript-looking building that Lisa immediately noticed had no windows and four sets of oversize doors. As they approached the door, they were stopped by a menacing-looking security guard.

"May I help you?" he asked, scrutinizing Lisa and Jonathan as if to see if they were crazed fans. Two other guards left their posts to assist the first guard.

"I'm here to see Tuck Lane," Jonathan replied. Lisa inched closer to him, feeling intimidated by the defensive stance of the men surrounding them.

One of the guards talked to someone on a walkie-talkie and in moments a young man came to the door to meet them. While he greeted Jonathan, Lisa looked him over. Wearing the racing team colors, he was quite thin and slightly taller than Lisa. A boyish face made him appear to be young, but Lisa wasn't sure about his age. What surprised her was his brown skin.

"Come on in—come on in," the young man said enthusiastically. They followed him into the cool, fluorescent-lighted garage. The area looked like a cross between a biology lab and a computer lab.

"I'd like you to meet my lady. This is Lisa Stevens," Jonathan said as soon as they'd entered the building. He looked at Lisa proudly and presented his friend. "Lisa, this is Tuck Lane."

"I'm so pleased to meet you," Lisa said. "I have to admit, I was pleasantly surprised when I first saw you."

"Let me guess. I look too young to drive?" Tuck joked.

"Yes, you do, but that's not it. I didn't know any African-Americans were involved in NASCAR," Lisa admitted.

"I'm one of the first," Tuck said modestly. "But now NASCAR has a diversity council to try to recruit more African-Americans and other people of color."

As he talked, they followed him through a maze of computers and machinery.

They stopped walking and Tuck said proudly, "This is my work area."

"You have the latest in technology here," Lisa noted, staring at all the instruments in the area that was more of a control room. "What is your role in the pit crew?"

"I'm just the tire changer," Tuck said.

"That doesn't begin to explain what you do," Jonathan interjected. "Tell her what all you do."

"On race day, we have to be in the pit ready to change tires. This instrument helps us determine the inflation rate we need," he said, pointing at a computerized panel. "We have to be sure we have just enough air, not too much, nor too little. After tires are used we analyze them for wear to be sure we're getting the most effective speed for the wear," Tuck explained.

"This looks like a computerized tread meter," Lisa said. She was mesmerized by the variety of instruments.

"It is. Those modifications are mine," Tuck said.

"We were in school together at North Carolina A and T. He was at the top of the class though. He was always inventing prototypes for new instruments. Tuck, Lisa is a mechanical engineer, too."

"Oh, another gearhead. I should have known, if you were with Jonathan." Tuck gave her a warm smile.

"Would you like to look around?" Tuck asked when he realized Lisa would be interested in the machinery. As they walked deeper into the garage, Lisa was surprised to see several engines hoisted up and ready to serve as a replacement at a moment's notice. As they returned to the spot where they'd started, Tuck said, "Well, what do you think, Miss Lisa? Is it what you expected?"

"Not quite," she said. "But I'd love to spend some time on your computers."

"Any time I'm in town, just stop by," he said as they parted.

After visiting with Tuck, they walked hand in hand to find their group. When they neared the booths that sold fan memorabilia, Lisa wanted to stop and shop. She picked up Nick Staunton jackets for her brothers and added a fourth for Jonathan.

"Lisa, those jackets are expensive. You don't have to buy one for me," Jonathan protested.

"I know I don't have to, but I want to. I'm a real generous person. Please don't make me suppress my natural inclinations," she pleaded quietly. One of their ongoing issues in their income difference was her ability to afford things he couldn't.

"No, I don't want you to suppress anything. You are who you are," Jonathan said gently, stroking her cheek.

"See, we've come a long way." She grinned up at him.

"Yeah, we've matured since the night you threw a fit because I brought you roses and champagne," he said.

"That was two dozen roses and Cristal champagne," she corrected.

"Which you thought was too extravagant for my budget," he added.

"Yes, I did. I had invited you over for dinner to repay you for all the money you'd already spent on me and you still spent more," she argued.

"That's because I'm so crazy about you," he said, pulling her close to him and kissing her on the nose.

"I never knew that. I thought you were extravagant with all your women," Lisa admitted.

"All what women?" he asked, taking a step away from her.

"We didn't see each other much, so I figured you were seeing someone else. That's why I started seeing Rodney," Lisa explained.

"No, Lisa, after I met you, there was never anyone else," Jonathan said quietly.

Lisa looked at him in amazement before stepping into his embrace and kissing him lightly on the lips. He became embarrassed and said, "I guess we'd better find our gang." His voice was hoarse with emotion. What he wanted to do with this woman was not for public attention.

The two couples were already making plans for the next race when Lisa and Jonathan joined them. "We'll grill catfish," Artis decided.

"And I'll fix wild rice," Mia offered.

"What are you bringing?" Raquel asked Jonathan.

"The usual." Jonathan smiled.

"That would be nothing," Artis said.

"Why do we always have to lug everything for you?" Raquel asked.

"You know I can't carry much in my 'Vette," Jonathan reminded her.

"Man, you can't carry anything in that car. You can barely fold your long legs up enough to get in it. Why don't you get a real car that will carry something other than your big head?" Artis teased.

"A 'Vette is the only real car. If I need something, I'll buy it when I get there," Jonathan answered.

The group parted company, promising to complete their plans later.

When they were in the car and headed home, Jonathan asked, "Do you really want to go? We could do something else—without the others, I mean."

"No, it wasn't so bad. In fact, it wasn't bad at all. I've had a lot of fun," Lisa enthused.

"You know you want to get me alone," Jonathan teased.

"Oh, we'll be alone all right. I've got plans for you," she replied provocatively.

"Is that a promise?" Jonathan asked, feeling his desire for her building.

"You can bet on it," Lisa said, looking up at him with the meaning clear in her eyes.

CHAPTER 6

After their speedway date, Jonathan was on duty at the firehouse for twenty-four hours. Although they had several telephone conversations, they weren't enough for Lisa. She missed his touch, and, most of all, she wanted to see his handsome, rugged face.

Jonathan missed Lisa just as much. As soon as he finished his shift, he headed for her offices on Broadway Boulevard. Sitting in front of the tall downtown landmark, Jonathan berated himself for not thinking clearly. But he never did when it came to Lisa. It was only 6:30 and the doors to the skyscraper would not be unlocked for at least another hour.

Not sure what to do next, he was still in front of the building when his cell phone rang. "Are you headed home yet?" Lisa's energetic voice asked him.

"No, I'm downtown," he admitted, not being more specific on purpose. If she knew he was sitting in front of her building at dawn, she'd know the power she had over him. He wasn't ready to reveal that just yet.

"Come over and have breakfast with me," she invited him. She tried to sound casual, although the effort she'd put into preparing the food was very purposeful. She had stayed up late watching her yeast rolls rise three times, kneading them to perfection after each rise.

He swallowed his surprise at her suggestion and headed for her place. The early morning streets were nearly deserted, allowing him to get there in fifteen minutes. She greeted him at the door wearing a simple little white silk slip dress that stopped midthigh. Even though the dress was plain, Lisa's body made it special. It gently flowed over her soft curves and outlined her perfect breasts. It hinted at hidden treasures that he had yet to explore.

Following her into the foyer, he found himself becoming nervous. She had cooked for him before, but that was before. They both knew their agreement to move forward had changed everything. Since verbalizing their desire to be together, they had moved to unchartered territory. Each explored the parameters of the relationship tentatively, testing the terms and boundaries.

As if she'd read his thoughts and sought to reinforce them, she put her arms around his neck and kissed him thoroughly. Enjoying the fresh, minty taste of her mouth, he let his tongue play with hers and sank into her warm embrace.

Before relinquishing herself completely to the pleasure overwhelming her, she pulled back and took a good look at him. He looked tired, yet relaxed. His eyes were warm and inviting, beckoning her to kiss him a second time. He put his big hands on her back to draw her nearer. She shivered slightly. "Are my hands too cold?" he asked huskily, ending the kiss.

"No, Jonathan, your hands feel good." She sighed, snuggling against him.

Her soft breasts against his chest and her thighs against his legs were all he'd longed for. He was back where he belonged. He kissed her lightly to honor that thought. Then he kissed her a second time, deeply, because he couldn't help himself.

As she relinquished herself totally to the ecstasy she felt whenever she was in his arms, cooking was the furthest thing from her mind. She was brutally tugged back to earth when Jonathan asked, "What's burning?"

"Oh no!" Lisa exclaimed, dashing into the kitchen that was filled with smoke.

He followed close behind her and as she opened the oven, he stepped around her to take out the flaming pan. "Don't stay in here. Go get your inhaler and stay outside until this smoke clears," he ordered in a low, urgent voice.

She left the room without argument. He looked around for a fire extinguisher, and not finding one, he quickly smothered the flames with a box of baking soda.

He turned on the stove fan and opened a window to clear the room of smoke before he allowed Lisa back into her kitchen.

"I hope that wasn't my breakfast," he said, looking at the charred mass.

"That was your bacon, but I also cooked salmon croquettes. See what you get for distracting me like that?" she said, looking pretty shaken up in spite of her teasing words.

"It's all right, Lisa. I'll eat whatever you have," Jonathan promised, looking around the messy kitchen. "What did you do in here?"

"I wanted to fix something special for you. The

table is set in the dining room. Will you take these in there?" she said, giving him a basket of rolls and a dish of fried apples.

Picking up the grits casserole and a bowl of scrambled eggs, she led the way into the dining room.

Her hair hung loosely down her back and bounced lightly as she strode through the room. Of their own volition, his eyes dropped from the blunt ends of her hair to her softly curving hips. The silk dress that she wore hung loosely, caressing her hips as she moved about the rooms. His eyes automatically drifted to her long, slender legs, leading him to wonder how it would be to have them wrapped around his waist.

After she'd set her load down, she turned to take the food from him. "Uh-uh, you'd better stop that," she said, chastising him. "I know where your mind is."

"You caught me," he admitted without any regret in his voice. Suddenly he needed a few minutes of refuge to rearrange himself. "Do you mind if I wash my hands?"

She pointed him to the small powder room next to the kitchen. By the time he returned, he was okay until he saw her soft hair gleaming in the early morning sunlight as it streamed through the window. His hands were itching to sink into her soft hair and to feel her body beneath his. She looked too good to be real this morning.

She looked up at him, giving him an angelic smile, and said, "Everything's here. Have a seat." When he'd done as he was told, she directed, "Pass your plate and tell me what you want."

"Is that sausage?" he asked, looking over the spread of mouthwatering food.

"No, those are the salmon croquettes I told you about," she said, stabbing a patty with a serving fork. She followed that one with three more. "That's the grits casserole. That dish has fried apples and there are the scrambled eggs. In that bowl are hash browns, and homemade rolls are in the basket."

"Did you make the rolls?" he asked, doubt clear in his voice.

"Yes, of course I did," she replied indignantly.

"I'd like some of everything," he said, realizing how much trouble she'd gone through to prepare so much for him.

She passed the food-laden plate to him and prepared one with almost as much food for herself. "I don't usually eat breakfast," she explained. "But when I do, I want it to be worth the calories."

He looked at the plate, clearly hesitant about taking his first bite. Pausing with the fork halfway to her mouth, she saw him staring at the food. "What's wrong? Did I fix something you don't like?"

"After that episode with the bacon, I'm afraid to eat." He tried to make it sound like a joke, but she could see he had serious doubts about her ability. Although the food smelled good, he couldn't help but wonder if she could really cook. He was preparing himself to fake it if the food was tasteless. Seeing her stern look, he reluctantly took a bite. "This food *is* good," he said after several mouthfuls.

"I can't believe you doubted my ability," she said, watching his doubt turn into delight as he chewed. For a minute there, she'd thought she was going to have to tell him a thing or two. After all the time she'd put into preparing the meal, he'd better eat every bite and enjoy himself. After watching him for another minute or two, she smiled, revealing perfect, even white teeth as he rapidly followed one bite with another.

When he was nearly stuffed, he put his fork down.

"I can't believe my baby can throw down in the kitchen like that." He gave her a big apologetic grin.

She certainly had not overestimated the amount of food she needed to cook. When his plate was polished clean, he reached over and took another roll from the basket. One by one he buttered and ate the remaining rolls.

Catching her watching him as he broke off a piece of the last roll, he paused before popping it into his mouth. "What's wrong? Were you saving these rolls?" he asked.

"No, they were made just for you. I was just fascinated with the systematic way you finished them off. Would you like more coffee?" she asked, reaching for the electric coffeepot. When he nodded, she walked around the table to refill his cup.

"You can actually cook," he said, pushing his chair away from the table and lounging in a comfortable position.

"I've cooked for you before," she reminded him, reaching for him empty plate.

"No, leave that. You cooked, I'll clean," he ordered. Pulling her to sit into his lap, he gave in to his desire to stroke her soft hair. "The last time you cooked, it was some of that light gourmet stuff. And besides, we argued that night. I couldn't digest anything."

"I know. I shouldn't have been so upset with you for bringing me all those roses and Cristal," she demurred, enjoying the feel of his hands burrowing deep into her hair. It was relaxing, yet sensuous.

She almost protested when he moved away from her to look into her face. He asked with mock surprise in his voice, "Are you apologizing to me?"

"Yes, I am. Will this meal make up for that fight?" She tried to rise from her comfortable seat on his lap, but he wrapped an arm loosely around her waist to hold her still.

"Wait a minute. I don't know if I should let you off so easily. Maybe I should give you a penalty."

"What kind of penalty?" she asked suspiciously.

"You have to cook for me every morning," Jonathan teased, stroking her hair again.

"Don't press your luck. This was a lot of work," she warned him, at the same time rising to her feet and picking up their plates.

"It's worth it. Now this is what I call real food. Who taught you how to cook like this?" he asked, picking up the now empty platters and following her into the kitchen.

"My mother," Lisa answered, feeling pleased with Jonathan's lavish praise.

"I just never expected you or your mother to be able to cook. I mean, you're both high-powered career women. I figured you'd leave the cooking to somebody else." Jonathan looked around for some place to set the soiled dishes. The countertops were cluttered.

"We cook when we can," Lisa explained as she pushed a pot to the side and set down the plates.

"So someone else does your cooking most of the time," Jonathan said in an accusatory tone.

"Surely you don't begrudge my mother and me a little domestic assistance?" Lisa questioned, pausing as she loaded the dishwasher.

"No, I don't. Your mother has worked hard. She told me how she worked beside your father to establish the company and I admire her for that. She's a real tough woman." Jonathan filled the sink with warm sudsy water to wash the pots and pans that had been scattered over the kitchen when he arrived.

"Do you think being wealthy makes us weak?"

Lisa asked, ready to attack if he gave the wrong answer.

"To the contrary. It's not every day that you find a family with a company number one on the *Black Enterprise* Top 100 and also listed on the *Fortune* 500 list," Jonathan replied.

"We don't let those accolades go to our heads. We know the hard work that goes into staying at the top," Lisa replied.

"Is that why you work so hard?" Jonathan rinsed a skillet and set it on the drying rack.

"That's part of it. My parents built the company when they had nothing. It was given to Jet and me and we don't want to lose it," Lisa explained.

"Do you think Melvin will ever be in business again?" Jonathan asked, knowing that Melvin had attempted a hostile takeover of Sand Castles from Jet a while back.

"No, I don't. Jet would probably welcome him now that he's had treatment for his bipolar disorder. But Melvin seems to be real content doing his own thing. He likes being a professor because he's the center of attention at least five hours a day and his audience has to hang on to his every word. They even take notes on what he says."

"I can see where Melvin would enjoy that. What is Kevin into these days?" Jonathan referred to the youngest of the Stevenses.

"His music career has taken off and his group is about to go into the studio to record a CD. It's just Jet and me to keep the family business going," she said neutrally. It was just a fact to her. She felt no pressure to keep the business going, but she knew she would do what it took.

"Do you think you'll ever move to Miami to work

at corporate headquarters?" Jonathan asked, setting another clean pot on the rack.

"No, I don't. Jet asked me to take over as president a few months ago, but I didn't think I was the best person for the job. He hired someone outside the family." Lisa had finished loading the dishwasher and began wiping off the cleared countertops.

"You never told me about that," Jonathan said, amazed that she'd turn down such an opportunity.

"I didn't mention it because it wasn't that important to me." Lisa folded her dish towel and said, "It looks like we're finished in here. I'm going to go get dressed."

"I thought you were dressed. You look real good," Jonathan commented, looking at her with lust-filled eyes again.

"I can't wear this to work. I'll be back in a minute. Make yourself at home." When she left, Jonathan finished tidying the kitchen. His mind was on the amazing Lisa Stevens. She could throw down in the kitchen, read blueprints, and put cars together too. What were the odds that a woman like that would want him too? How could he be so lucky?

When she returned from her bedroom, she found Jonathan in the kitchen putting away pots and pans that had been sitting out on the drying rack for weeks. "Wow! My kitchen looks better than it did before I started cooking. If you don't watch it, you're going to be detailed to the kitchen permanently."

"You know how I hate clutter," he replied, turning to look at her. She was fully dressed in her work attire. A big smile lighted Jonathan's face as he took in her hair pulled back tightly with a plain black elastic band. She was wearing a familiar-looking gray T-shirt that was tucked into loose-fitting denim jeans, and steel-toe work boots completed her ensemble.

"Now this is the Lisa I know and love," he said, opening his arms to her.

"Well, I can't walk around a construction site in those short little outfits that make your eyes bulge, as much as I enjoy seeing your reaction." She stepped into his arms.

"You're mistaken, Lisa. You look good to me regardless of what you wear. If I stare a lot, it's because I'm not used to seeing you in those girly-looking outfits," he said, giving her a reassuring embrace.

"Yeah, right. So you're saying I look good to you right now?" she asked, stepping back and walking around in a circle before him.

"You'd better believe it," he said, taking her hand and pulling her back into his arms. After giving her a light kiss, he said, "I guess I'd better let you get moving."

"I guess," she said wistfully and moved toward the living room.

"What do you want to do this evening?" he asked, following her through the house.

"I'd like to see the new pewter car. I want to know what's so special about it," she said, gathering up her briefcase and a tube containing blueprints.

"Call me as soon as you get in this evening and I'll come get you," Jonathan promised, giving her a final brush of the lips before they parted.

After working at the construction site all day, Lisa returned to her office late that afternoon. As she exited the elevator and rushed toward her suite, she almost missed seeing Artis. "Hey, Miss Lady, what's shaking?" Artis greeted her.

"Hello, Artis," she said, focusing her attention on

him and juggling her hard hat, blueprints, and briefcase. "I didn't recognize you."

"Well, I recognized you. You look more like your old self today. Have you been playing in dirt?" he asked, looking at her drooping ponytail from which strands of hair had broken loose. His eyes drifted to the T-shirt and jeans that were now stained with red clay and her ankle-high boots caked with the same.

"I've been at a construction site all day. What are you doing in this building? Did you come to see me?" she asked curiously. The tube of blueprints slipped from her hand.

Artis stooped to pick it up for her. "No, I've been transferred over here. Someone named Kita called for me to empty one of the big paper shredders."

"When did you move down here?" Lisa asked, walking with Artis.

"I haven't been in this building that long. I used to work in the Church Street building, but the woman who runs it renegotiated the contract with American Building Services. She said she had to cut back on the cleaning staff. Said she didn't have enough money in the budget this year," he explained as they walked through the suite and headed toward her private offices.

That was strange information to Lisa, when in fact Jennifer Malone's budget had been increased because of her staggering need after the fire. She made a mental note to look into that.

Inside her office, Lisa dumped everything on her desk. "You can put my blueprints right here," she told Artis, indicating a credenza behind her desk.

"Well, I've got to run. The boss man will be looking for me." He turned to leave, then stopped. "Is this yours?" he asked, picking up her tennis bracelet from the floor.

"Yes, it is. I've got to remember to get this catch repaired. Thanks so much."

"No problem," Artis muttered, handing the bracelet to her. "You need to be careful. Someone less honest would have taken that bracelet and run."

"You're right. I'll get this taken care of. See you around," she called out as he left her office. She had taken a seat behind her desk and was already shaking the mouse to clear the screen saver from her computer monitor.

After she completed entering her construction notes into the project file on her computer, she shut down and hurried home. She was looking forward to spending the rest of the evening with Jonathan.

Once at home, she considered leaving on the dirty jeans and T-shirt she wore. After all, she was anxious to get under the hood of the pewter-colored Corvette. But she reconsidered. It was worth the extra effort to see Jonathan's admiring gazes.

She took a quick shower and called Jonathan before she dressed. By the time he arrived, she was wearing a cream and tan floral-print circle skirt with a tan blouse that snugly fit her petite bust and slim waist. Quickly discarding the sandals that she'd planned to wear with the skirt, she pulled a pair of brown ballet slippers from the closet. They would be easier to walk in from the barn to the house. Slipping her feet into them, she raced to the front of the house as soon as she heard the doorbell ring.

Taking a quick look through the curtained sidelight at her door, she saw Jonathan standing on her porch. He was dressed casually in a black zipper-front sweater and black jeans. As usual, he was unsmiling and his face bore a look of danger, as if he dared anyone to approach him. She wondered what was on his mind.

As Jonathan reached to ring the bell again, Lisa threw the door open. "Hi, come on in," she welcomed him.

"Hi, yourself," he replied, giving her a fire extinguisher.

"Oh, how lovely," she said, looking at the red cylinder blankly.

"You need to place that in your kitchen. I couldn't find one in there," he explained.

"This is so thoughtful," she said sincerely as she walked into the kitchen. He followed her.

"There's a bracket in there for you to attach it to the wall," he noted.

"I'll take care of it. And to think you used to waste money on roses." She turned to tease him after placing the fire extinguisher on the countertop.

"You didn't appreciate my sensitive little gestures. I thought I'd go for the practical," he said, slipping his arms around her waist and drawing her to him. Before their lips met, she noted that his face had relaxed into a smile.

He released her after a thorough kiss that left her warm and breathless. He spun her away from him and looked at her from head to toe. Her hair was hanging loosely about her shoulders again and now she wore the dazed look of a woman who'd just been kissed passionately. He gave her an admiring assessment before saying, "I thought you wanted to work on my new car tonight."

"I do," she answered, smiling at him sweetly.

"You can't in that getup."

"Maybe I'll just look it over tonight. Then we'll plan what we're going to do to her. How's that?" she asked as they walked back into the living room. She grabbed a sweater and her purse from the sofa.

Tonight the top was up on Zora and Lisa was glad she didn't have to ask him to raise it. She knew he was being considerate of her because he would ride with the top down in the dead of winter.

As they approached Jonathan's property, she admired the still darkness. "When we're out here, I feel like we're on a planet all alone." The only light was that cast by the moon. The trees that surrounded them were mere shadows.

"It's easy to forget that I have neighbors, but I never knew you to be so whimsical," Jonathan commented.

"Like I said, Jonathan, there's a lot you don't know about me," Lisa said, giving him a sideways glance from her seat next to him. The car's interior was so dark she could only make out his profile, but she knew he was smiling.

"Are you going to give me time to discover all I want to know about you?" he asked.

"I'll give you all the time you want," she replied, her breath catching in her throat. It had not occurred to her before that there might be a time limit on their relationship.

Once on the gravel road, he drove past the house, all the way back to the barn. Believing that her thin little slippers would not be enough for the rocky, muddy climb from the house, he parked right in front of the barn. He threw the huge sliding doors open and stood back to let her step inside first.

"There she is," he said proudly, referring to the small rusty-looking car that was now center stage.

"She has nice lines, but I can't imagine how she'll look when you're finished. What have you done so far?" Lisa asked. Seeing this car as anything desirable was beyond her imagination.

Jonathan's enthusiasm was undeterred by Lisa's lack of vision for the dream car. "I've spent days removing the old paint. What you see now is the primer—" he began.

"I can't believe this car was ever pewter," she said, trying to hide her disappointment.

"It was and it will be again. She'll be fast and beautiful when I finish with her. I'm going to put a 528 engine in her—" he said, talking fast and passionately.

"I don't think you need an engine that powerful," Lisa interrupted.

"Yeah, I do. I'm fixing her up to sell, remember. Mr. Mueller said his friends want a car like his. They like the possibility of going that fast, even if they never go beyond seventy," Jonathan argued. "It gives them bragging rights."

"Do you really think you'll be able to sell her?" Lisa asked, standing back and looking at the car from various angles, trying to see beyond its obvious flaws.

"After I get this car all tricked out, I'll let Mr. Mueller know and have her sold like this," he said, snapping his finger

"You're probably right," she answered with doubt in her voice.

"What's wrong? Don't you think I can pull it together?" Jonathan asked. He was ready to argue with her if she thought he wasn't up to the challenge.

"You haven't had one in such poor condition before. This car has no redeeming value. The seats are torn and sprung. The exterior is rusted. It needs new bumpers," she said, listing the car's faults.

"But the frame is good. There are no dents. It's never been in an accident and is perfectly aligned.

There's nothing wrong with it that I can't fix," he said enthusiastically. He stepped back to let Lisa have complete access to the car.

She moved closer and opened the doors to peer inside. "Black velour upholstery would look real good with the pewter exterior," she said as she leaned into the car. "You could use that on the seats and the headliner. Why don't you pull out the door panels and use black tweed there? It'll give the car a real plush look."

When she turned around, Jonathan was beaming with satisfaction. "What's wrong with you?" she asked.

"I knew you'd get it and it didn't take long. You see what I saw in the car." He couldn't believe how many times they had come up with the same ideas for restoring the cars.

"Yes, I can see it now—the new paint, the luxurious black interior. It will be so sexy," she said, stretching out on the hood of the car, her long, lean lines matching those of the sports car.

"Now that's sexy," Jonathan said, looking at her pose. "You look just like one of those models at the auto show."

"Uh-huh. Do I make you want this car?" Lisa turned and propped up on one elbow. Posing, she smiled at him.

"Not as much as I want you," Jonathan answered, inching her over so that he could sit on the hood next to where she reclined.

"You can have me any time you want," she whispered, now sitting up with her back against the windshield.

He rested a cheek against her hair and stroked her back. "Girl, you're going to get into trouble saying things like that. You'll have me believing you."

"You'd better believe me," she said, resting her head on his shoulder. "Because I'm going to get you."

"Why do you want me?" he asked, incredulously, wondering if she realized what she was doing to him with her seductive voice. He still found it hard to believe she was serious about being with him.

She sensed that he was seeking reassurance. "You make me feel the way no other man's ever made me feel." She stopped to gauge his reaction to her testament before she continued. "From the day we met, you've made me feel safe and secure. I believe you always have my best interest at heart. What I feel when I'm with you is unbelievable."

They stared into each other's eyes. He knew without a doubt that he had fallen deeply in love with this woman. But could he be enough for her? Would love be all they would need? Lord help him. He loved her so much. He leaned forward until he was practically lying on her, pressing her back against the windshield again. He forgot everything when his lips found hers. He kissed her deeply, finding delight in the texture of her tongue, the warmth of her mouth, and her eager response.

Pulling himself from the center of pleasure, he managed to raise his mouth from hers. "How does that make you feel?" he asked huskily.

"Divine, hot, and sexy," she answered, her arms entwined around his neck.

"Do you feel loved?" he asked.

"Should I?"

"Yes. I love you with all my heart," he declared.

"When did you decide that?" she asked, amazed.

"It wasn't a decision. I've loved you since the first time I saw you. You were standing in the middle of that steaming rubbish looking all lost and confused at that fire in your Church Street building." He smiled at the memory.

"You saved my life that night. My asthma attack came on so suddenly. I was sucking air and couldn't even ask for help. I was sinking fast. You still had on all your heavy firefighting gear, but you came over to see what I needed. You were so kind and gentle. Luckily, you recognized my symptoms and put the air mask on me. That was the first time I'd had an asthma attack and didn't feel embarrassed for needing help. You took charge and knew just what to do," she answered, smiling softly with the memory.

"You were brave and beautiful. I fell in love with you that night. After I took you home from the emergency room, I was afraid I'd never see you again. That's why I went and asked for that insurance information. So I'd have a reason to come to your office," he confessed, touching one of the soft curls that tumbled over her shoulder.

"You couldn't have fallen in love that night," Lisa said incredulously.

"Why not?" he asked, moving back only slightly so that he could see her face.

"Because I looked awful," she replied. "I had thrown on the first thing I could get my hands on when the security company called."

"And you hadn't bothered to comb your hair. But you still looked good to me. You looked good until I noticed your mouth was hanging open like a fish out of water," he teased.

"Don't make fun of me. I was sick," she scolded, with one hand on her hip.

"You always look good to me," he said softly. "I want to be with you always."

"I'm with you now," Lisa offered seductively, looking at him invitingly.

He gathered her in his arms again with the intention of kissing her lightly to acknowledge that she was indeed with him. But when their lips touched, he couldn't pull away. His tongue found its way inside her delicious mouth. He was flooded with emotions that he knew he had no right to enjoy, but for now he would. And he vowed that he would as long as he could. Finally he pulled away to look into her kiss-dazed face again.

"I love you, Lisa Stevens," he whispered in her ear, trying to get even closer to her.

"I love you too," she said sincerely, molding her upper body against his.

His kisses and frantic caresses were driving her out of her mind. Breathless with her fever for him, she stroked his back through the soft fabric of his sweater. Anxious to taste more of him, she broke the kiss and moved her mouth to nuzzle his neck.

When she began planting kisses from his neck to his ear, he almost erupted with passion. Cuddling her head with one hand, he unbuttoned her blouse with the other. When her blouse fell open, her firm round breasts were exposed to his surprise and delight. She had worn nothing beneath the blouse. He cupped one in each hand, overjoyed to finally touch them. The nipples became hard instantly as she gasped from his warm touch.

Unzipping his sweater a little more, she placed small kisses on the smooth skin of his chest. While he fondled her breast, rolling the hard nipple between his fingers, she leaned back on the windshield again.

In the throes of ecstasy, she stroked the back of his head with one hand and his back with the other. She hoped the sensual heat flowing through her would never stop.

Cradling her in his arms, he was beyond bliss. He wanted her so badly. If they didn't stop now, they would make love right here, right now. He needed to pull himself together. This was Lisa Stevens, his Lisa, his love. He wanted her right now, but not on the hood of a car.

"Lisa," he said softly.

"Yes," she cooed.

"We need to stop."

"What?" she asked, pausing in her random sampling of his salty skin.

"We can't make love out here," he said softly.

"Why not? We're alone," she said, finally paying attention to what he was saying.

"I can't treat you like this. Not out here on top of a car. You're too special," he said, resolutely rebuttoning her blouse. "We're not lusty teenagers. Our first time together should be special, something we'll want to remember always."

She looked flustered for a moment. He stroked her cheek, looking at her with lust-filled eyes. "You know how much I want you, don't you?"

"Yes, I think I do," she said, looking at the obvious proof before her. With shaky fingers she zipped his sweater to cover the hard muscles of his chest. Although she had not wanted it, she accepted the end to their lovemaking session.

He kissed her lightly before asking, "And you know how much I love you?"

"I'm beginning to figure it out," she said.

He held her in his arms for a few moments until they could breathe again. "I promise you, our time will come," he said.

"You've got that right," she said, quickly recovering. "Look, I'm starving. Let's go inside and eat our dinner."

Inside they took boxed dinners Jonathan had picked up at Kijiji's deli into the living room. Lisa put place mats and plastic utensils on the coffee table while Jonathan turned on the CD player. Keb' Mo's voice filled the house with the up-tempo beat of zydeco music. Jonathan sang "You Are My Sunshine" with his favorite artist.

"I can't believe you're so corny," Lisa laughed.

"You can't say you didn't already know that," Jonathan said, laughing, too. "But you *are* my sunshine. I was facing some very dark days all alone until you came into my life."

"But you don't have to be alone anymore," Lisa answered, flashing him a big one-thousand-watt smile before taking a bite of the Southern fried chicken. "Umm, this fried chicken is so good. What kind of dark days were you facing?" she asked, returning her focus to him.

"Sometimes it seemed like I couldn't rise above my past," he began and paused.

"What is so bad about your past that you needed to rise above it?" she prompted.

"I need to tell you everything. But I don't want to start tonight. We need more time. Once we begin we'll have to finish it up. Do you know what I'm saying?"

Lisa looked at him for a moment, considering his response. "Okay. Let's set aside a day to do it. When you get off duty Saturday, come get me. I'll spend the day with you or as much time as you need to say what you've got to say. Deal?"

He reached over and touched her cheek. "You are a beautiful person, Lisa Stevens. I hope I can be half as good to you as you have been to me."

"The feeling is mutual," she said, pausing to look at him with tender, love-filled eyes.

They ate a few moments in silence. Lisa pushed her plate aside and dug in the box until she found the dessert. "Oh, goody, lookie, you got my cheesecake," she said gleefully. "What do you have?" she asked, peering into his box.

"Red velvet cake with cream cheese frosting. But don't you want to walk first?" Jonathan asked.

"No, I'll walk after I eat this," Lisa said. Jonathan looked on as she devoured the rich creamy dessert, closing her eyes after each bite.

When she was finished she stood and said, "Let's go."

"You're not going to be able to go far in those thin shoes," he commented.

"It will be difficult, but I need to walk off that fried chicken and all those greens I ate. We should stay on the level ground close to the house," she suggested.

When he opened the door, she said, "Ewww, it's gotten chilly since we came in." She rubbed her hands over her arms.

"Wait a sec," he said and reached around her to the closet under the stairs. Pulling out a jacket, he said, "Here's a jacket for you." He kept the other for himself.

They walked out into the still darkness of the hillside. The only illumination was from the full moon. As they approached the edge of the property that overlooked the river, Lisa said, "Can you imagine how old this land is? I always think of how it must have been before the land was settled. A time when only Native Americans roamed the land."

"Can't you just imagine the young braves paddling a canoe up the river?" Jonathan joined her flight of fantasy.

"See there, you can be whimsical too," she accused, looking up at him.

"I guess it's contagious. I feel so light and carefree when I'm with you," he said jovially. They stopped walking to stare at the moon's reflection on the water. He placed her body in front of his and wrapped his arms around her. She leaned against his solid strength.

"We're going to be so good together," he whispered into her hair.

"We *are* so good together," she corrected. "There's just one thing I need you to know." She stepped away from him and turned to look at him.

"And what is that?" He was curious because her voice had taken on such a serious tone.

"Stop treating me like I'm fragile. A bed is not the only place to make love, Jonathan." She folded her arms across her torso and looked defiantly at him.

"Thank you for setting me straight," he said, trying to match her serious tone. But the twinkle in his eyes gave him away. "If you felt that way, why did you let me stop us?"

"Because I couldn't figure out how to get this out of my pocket," she said, taking a small, square foil packet from the pocket of her skirt.

"So, I see you came prepared tonight. Miss Lisa, were you trying to seduce me?"

"You've got it, buddy. That was my plan," she replied, smiling up at him.

He laughed loudly and pulled her back into his arms. "All you had to do is ask. Do you want to go upstairs and go to bed now?"

"No, you ruined it. You plan the next seduction scene." She laughed, looking up at him.

CHAPTER 7

The next morning when Lisa arrived at her offices on Broadway Boulevard, she got off the elevator on the eighth floor. As she walked toward her suite, she thought she saw Jennifer Malone walking away from her. The woman, dressed in a short black jacket and dark print skirt, dashed through the stairwell door before Lisa could see her clearly. Almost as soon as the recognition registered, Lisa dismissed it. There was no way Jennifer would arrive at work forty-five minutes early.

Lisa walked through the entrance to the suite and headed straight to her office. Following her daily routine, she automatically reached to turn on the computer. She was about to push the Start button when she noticed the bright green light. The computer was already on. That was unusual. Since being warned by the information technology staff to always turn off the computer as a safeguard against hackers, she never forgot to turn it off. Then again, yesterday was different. Maybe she had forgotten in her haste to spend time with Jonathan. He'd been on her mind all afternoon.

Shrugging a shoulder, she rolled the mouse around on its pad to dissolve the screen saver. In a second the screen shone brightly. Her e-mail was open. That too was unusual. The last thing she'd worked on had been a contract; not e-mail. She scrolled to see if any activity had taken place that she'd not initiated. Everything looked to be in order.

By the time she'd finished responding to her e-mail, Kita knocked on her door and entered the office. "Here's your financial report. It's in early this month." The administrative assistant set the heavy, bound document on the edge of Lisa's desk.

Lisa turned around and looked at the two-inch-thick stack of computer printouts that were bound in big green ledger covers. "I thought we'd moved beyond these big awkward ledgers. Weren't we receiving these via e-mail?" Lisa asked.

"Yes, we were, but that's been ages. Do you know why they stopped sending the e-mail?" Kita asked.

"Somebody probably complained about having to use their own paper to print them out. But I liked it that way. These things are cumbersome and take up too much space. I've just pulled all of last year's off the shelf. Will you call housekeeping to have someone come up here and shred them? We don't want these reports floating around the building," Lisa instructed. When she began flipping pages, instantly becoming engrossed in the new financial report, Kita silently exited the room. She was used to the way Lisa could be animated one moment and totally engaged in her work the next.

Lisa completely lost track of time until Kita returned thirty minutes later. "Boss, it's time for your meeting. I know you don't want to be late. I hear they have hot Krispy Kreme doughnuts," Kita teased.

"Don't tell me good old Florence sprang for

doughnuts," Lisa said lightly. "I thought she was serious about her diet this time." Standing, she tucked her pink and tan pin-striped blouse into her chocolate-colored slacks.

"You know it wasn't Miss Florence Henry. The diet is not the problem. They come and go, but Miss Henry never stops being cheap, even with her departmental budget. You'd think it's coming out of her own pocket."

"She's not that bad." Lisa laughed.

"Oh yes, she is," Kita countered. "If she wanted doughnuts down there, she would have called me to pick them up. That way they'd be charged to our budget."

"So true," Lisa said, joining her assistant's laughter. "So who brought them? Bruce?"

"Believe it or not, it was Jennifer Malone," Kita said in the tone of someone with a story too good to be true. She was rewarded by Lisa's reaction.

"Jennifer? Don't tell me she's here already," Lisa said, pausing as she slipped on the jacket that completed her pantsuit. The surprise was evident in her voice.

"She is. You must have put the fear of God in her when you met with her last week. Rumor has it, she was here when the building opened," Kita declared.

"That's strange," Lisa said. "I thought I saw her leaving our suite when I arrived."

"Why would she have come to our suite? The meeting is down on the first floor," Kita commented, holding the door open wider to allow Lisa to pass her.

"Who knows?" Lisa replied absently. "Oh, by the way, I should be back before lunch."

"I'm going to lunch a little early today. My sweetie is picking me up," Kita said, smiling dreamily.

"Okay, then I'll see you after lunch." Lisa hurried through the double doors that led into the hall.

The meeting started right on time, but was boring the bejesus out of the property managers. They sat in gray leather chairs around a long marble table. The room was light and airy with ultramodern furnishings, but Florence Henry's PowerPoint presentation was mind numbing. Lisa reached for her bracelet to fidget with it, but it was not on her wrist. It must have fallen off when she removed her jacket in her office.

Bruce, who was sitting next to Lisa, scooted closer. He whispered in her ear, "Can't you stop her?"

"I don't know how," Lisa replied, looking around the table at her other twenty-two managers. Make that twenty-one. One chair was empty. Someone had slipped out already. At least it was better than seeing him or her nod off, as a couple of the others already were.

"Shoot her. Put us out of our misery. Carl is about to get whiplash." Bruce nodded toward the man across from them.

Lisa looked at the man and could barely contain her laughter. His head would fall forward, almost to the table; then he would jerk it back so hard that she thought he'd snap his neck. She decided to have mercy on her staff. While Florence was in the middle of explaining penalties for infractions against Americans with Disabilities Act regulations, Lisa slipped her a note.

The older woman stood at the head of the table. The light cast by the projector brightened her red hair, flaming it against her smooth walnut-brown skin. She looked annoyed when she read Lisa's note and glared at her. She reconsidered when she followed Lisa's nod toward the poor lifeless bodies around the table. Realizing she'd lost her audience, Florence announced a five-minute break.

As the group broke up, Jennifer was coming toward the conference room. Her nice black suit featured a full skirt with tiny white flowers. "We're taking five," Lisa said, smiling. "We decided to follow your lead."

"I needed to check on some things back at the office," Jennifer apologized. She was breathing rapidly, as if she'd run a great distance.

"Don't worry. There's no need to rush. Excuse me," Lisa said, heading for the ladies' room.

After the break, the rest of the morning moved much quicker. At the end of the meeting, the group stood around chatting while Lisa thanked Florence. She knew she needed to assuage the woman's hurt feelings.

Bruce approached Lisa after her conversation ended. "Do you care to join us for lunch?"

"I can't today. I have a report due to corporate that I need to work on," Lisa explained.

"But you've got to eat sometime," Bruce cajoled. He was surprised Lisa was turning down a meal.

"Will you bring something back for me?" she asked, glancing at her watch. It was already twelve o'clock. "It's crunch time for me."

"What do you want?" he asked, giving up on trying to persuade her to join the group.

"Whatever you have. Just order for me as you're finishing your meal. I'll be in my office all afternoon." Lisa headed for the elevator, but thought better of it. She took the back stairs that led directly to her suite.

As she passed Kita's desk, she noticed that her assistant had left already. She entered her office and saw Artis busy at work. He was taking pages of the computer printouts from the heavy green binders. As he pulled the pages apart, he fed the contents into the giant shredder that sat on a cart he'd wheeled into the office. A stack of the disemboweled binders sat on the bottom of the cart. He had apparently been at his task for a while.

"Kita told me it was all right for me to keep working. She had a hot date for lunch," Artis explained when he noticed Lisa had entered the office. "I hope it's all right."

"Go right ahead with what you're doing," Lisa said, moving to her desk chair. "How are you doing today?"

"I'm pretty good. How about yourself?" Artis asked, pausing with a sheaf of doomed papers on the shredder's edge. Once they went in, the noise would be too great to hear her response.

"I'm fine," she replied, reaching for the financial report that Kita had given her just before the meeting. However, it wasn't where she'd left it.

"Artis, did you pick up the binder that was on my desk?" Lisa asked, going through the various stacks of paper surrounding her.

"No, Kita told me to get the ones that were stacked up over here. That's all I've worked on." He looked at her, waiting to see what she needed.

"See if you have one with today's date on it," she requested, moving to join him at his cart. He looked through the stacks, while she looked through the binders that had already been emptied of their content.

After several moments of flipping through the binders he said, "It would help if you tell me what I'm looking for. Is it profit and loss statements or balance sheets?"

"Would you recognize the different financial statements?" Lisa asked and immediately regretted her words.

"I'm a janitor, Lisa. That doesn't automatically make me a dummy," he replied in a huff.

"Very few people know the difference in the financial statements by looking at them unless they work with them every day," she explained apologetically. Not knowing what else to say, she remained silent and he resumed taking the printouts from the brass slides and feeding them to the shredder.

She went to the outer office and looked around Kita's desk, bookcase, and files for the missing financial report. When she didn't find it she returned to her office.

Artis was loading his cart with plastic bags of shredded paper when she returned.

"It looks like you and my man are getting pretty close," Artis said conversationally as he worked.

"Yes, we are getting alone very nicely." Lisa couldn't help the big smile that spread across her face.

"I'm glad. He needed to get over his hang-up. If a sister's going to get a straight man who's not on drugs, he's probably going to have served time. That's where all the good brothers are. Behind bars, right?" Artis waited for her answer, then winked and said, "You know, one out of the three. All these sisters complaining they can't find a good man, but I say their standards are too high. What's wrong with getting a man that's been incarcerated? That's part of the black man's experience in America."

Lisa was so stunned she couldn't move. Her mouth was suddenly so dry she couldn't speak. She waited quietly for Artis to leave so that she could call Jonathan. She didn't like finding out about him from his friend.

"I'll see you around," Artis called out, hurrying away.

As he rushed through the door, Lisa still hadn't uttered a word. She was deep in thought. How could Jonathan have kept such important information from her all this time? Didn't he trust her? Why had he served time? When did he plan to tell her?

Without knowing when it had started, she realized she was wheezing. She smelled a faint scent of smoke in the air. It must have been coming through the HVAC. The system must have been malfunctioning. If it had been a fire, the security system would have shut down the HVAC system to prevent the spread of smoke.

She felt in her purse for an inhaler, but couldn't find one. Looking through her desk drawers, she still came up empty. Hurrying to her private restroom, she found an inhaler in her vanity. After taking two puffs, she knew that she was in a crisis. Breathing had become extremely difficult. She sat down to allow the medication time to work. Putting her face on the edge of the sink, she closed her eyes and focused on breathing normally.

The phone extension next to her rang, but she didn't answer it. She heard movement in her office, but couldn't call out. She knew she'd feel better if she rested. Rather than feel better, she began to feel worse. Going back into her office, she was alarmed by the unusual silence. Where had everyone gone so quickly?

Walking through the outer office, Lisa thought it was like a ghost town. Neither Kita nor any of the clerks were around. Lisa opened the double doors that led into the hallway and was instantly overcome with thick black smoke. She couldn't see a thing. Backing into the suite, she closed the doors and hurried to her office. Using the back stairs, she began the long descent.

Panic rose in her chest, further restricting the flow of precious oxygen through constricted vessels. Her breathing became increasingly difficult, her chest heaving with each step. She told herself that she would be all right over and over again. It became a mantra. The smoke she encountered on the fourth floor surprised her, depleting the oxygen in her burning lungs. She sat down on a step, thinking that if she rested before continuing she'd be better able to make it. Her chest burned as she tried so hard to pull in clean air. Closing her eyes, she decided to rest for just a moment.

Jonathan's engine company was the first to arrive on the scene of a major fire at the Broadway Boulevard building. He sized up the situation and called for backup, giving enough details for the dispatcher to know that a potential disaster was in progress.

With Jonathan's shouting directions to get his men into action, they were fully engaged immediately. They were intent on bringing frightened employees from the building at the same time they fought wildly leaping flames. Smoke was billowing from all sides of the building, but the fire was mainly contained on the west side. Workers had broken out windows in a panic, causing fresh air to feed the blaze.

When he looked up, Jonathan could see frightened faces in the windows. He thought of Lisa's office on the eighth floor, but pushed thoughts of her out of his mind for the millionth time since he'd gotten the call. He had to remain objective.

If he focused on saving her, he could end up endangering everyone.

He stayed outside until he'd briefed the arriving captains. They wondered why no alarm had sounded to warn the inhabitants. It should have prevented a fire of this magnitude.

There was no more time for conversation. Jonathan took a final look at the building's floor plan and pulled his Nomex hood around his neck and over his face before strapping on his helmet. As he walked toward the entrance, he strapped a self-contained breathing apparatus on his back and fastened it in place. He placed the SCBA mouthpiece between his teeth and turned the valve to start the flow of compressed air.

Feeling his way through the blackened bowels of the building, he found his crew. Grabbing a section of a hose, he helped aim the spray at flames leaping through the ceiling and fought to endure the steam that rose around them. In what seemed like a short time to those on the outside, the blaze was reduced to small embers and then to smoldering debris. When the flame died, he continued holding the hose. It was his lifeline to the outside world.

As he followed the hose to the door leading to the outside, a blaze flared up behind him. Hearing his calls for help, the men turned and joined Jonathan in battling the blaze again. This time he methodically searched for the fire's source. They chopped into walls, tearing out the plumbing for the deep mop basins in the janitor's closet. The most charred area on the first floor, this closet was obviously where the fire had started.

As the smoke cleared, Jonathan mentally noted the remains as he was trained to do. He could make out the wide metal frames that once held dust mop heads on long poles and the metal handles that were once attached to oversize mop buckets. The fire had been so intense that even the deep utility sinks had melted. They were identifiable only by the faucets that hung from the walls.

There was nothing out of the ordinary in the room until he eyed the brass clasps and long metal posts that went through data binders. He would have expected to see those items in a file room or storage closet. He couldn't imagine why anyone would have a data binder in the janitor's closet unless it had fallen out of a trash bag. But there was no other trash in the closet. All other objects that he could identify had a logical explanation for being there.

He kicked at the ashes near the binder fasteners and another shiny object caught his attention. Moving the smoldering ashes around with the toe of his boot so that he could see the metal device better, he immediately knew that it wasn't a part of the binder.

Bending over, he had picked up the familiar-looking object before he realized it was Lisa's diamond bracelet. It was covered with soot and sludge, but it was recognizable. She wore it religiously. In fact, it was the one bit of dash to her uniform-like daily ensembles.

Terror pumped through his body with each beat of his heart. He pressed the button on his walkie-talkie to find out if Lisa was one of the evacuated employees. Several minutes and an eternity later, a voice came back with dreaded information. "Lisa Stevens is not on any of the lists we have." That bit of information was like a kick in Jonathan's gut. He gathered the remains of the data binders and placed the bag in his left pocket. Lisa's bracelet was carefully placed in his right pocket.

Without a second thought, he raced through the remains of the first floor to the nearest stairwell. He had to find Lisa. He had a strong feeling she was still in the building.

He knew his air supply was low, but he couldn't take the time required to go out for another SCBA. Thick black smoke still filled the air. Sloshing through the muddy water that covered the stairs, he raced up to the eighth floor, ignoring his heavy equipment.

He knew he was out of order, but did not care to discuss his actions with anyone. He was breaking one rule by being alone and another by searching the floors out of order. He compromised by being extra careful. This was not the time to become lax about safety, because he might be her only hope. Fire could pop up in the walls, ceiling, or floors at any time. If she was not out of the building, she was probably not able to leave. She could be lying somewhere injured.

Going up the main stairway, he easily found her office. The hallway was filled with black smoke and he had to use his flashlight to find his way. He pushed his way through the double doors and felt his way to her desk. Shining his flashlight around, he saw that her purse was sitting on a credenza. If she'd had time to leave, she would have taken it with her. That led him to believe she'd left in a hurry. Papers were scattered about her desk.

Turning toward the door, he spotted an illuminated sign with the word EXIT in bright red letters. He followed it and opened the door to a stairwell. Calling her name, he got no answer.

Instinctively, he started down the steps. Barely able to see, he continued his descent until he almost tripped over an unmoving object on a step near the fourth floor. Stooping, he realized it was Lisa. Gathering her into his arms, he slipped off his air mask and placed it over her face. Her breathing was so shallow that he could barely get a pulse. Cradling her gently in his arms, he rose and rushed through the building to the nearest exit.

When he ran out of the building with her, emergency workers immediately gathered around him. They put Lisa on a gurney and loaded her into an ambulance. He gave the EMTs her name and told them to be extra careful with her. As she was whisked away to the hospital, Jonathan collapsed to the ground, overcome by bouts of nausea. A medical team gathered around him, checking his pulse and giving him oxygen.

When he saw his chief standing over him, Jonathan took the flameproof evidence bag from his pocket and gave it to his boss. He hoped they'd leave him in his turnout until he had time to conceal Lisa's bracelet. But contrary to his wishes, he was removed from his gear and taken away in an ambulance. The chief wanted him checked by a physician immediately.

Lisa regained consciousness in the emergency room and wondered how she'd gotten there. Unable to speak, she couldn't ask any questions. She wanted to tell someone that she'd only had an asthma attack, but people rushed around her. No one stopped to talk or ask her questions. She tried to remove the mask, but that only made a nurse strap her hands down.

A young doctor listened to her heartbeat and her breathing through a stethoscope. He ordered a nebulizer treatment for her, which almost im-

mediately restored the color to her cheeks. She
went from an ashen brown to her normal rich
brown coloring.

It was during this period that Lisa learned about
the fire and the number of employees from the
Broadway Boulevard building that were being treated
at various hospitals throughout the city. Filled with
grief, she felt responsible for those victims, but all
she could do was lie there incapacitated.

Lisa also heard the doctor tell a nurse to get a
room for her. But before she was taken to her room,
she had additional breathing treatments with a nebulizer. Leaving the ER, she was taken for X-rays,
then to have blood drawn. When she reached her
room, another nurse sponged the soot from her
aching body before helping her into a too-short
hospital gown that left her unnecessarily exposed.
But at that point, Lisa didn't care. When she lay on
the bed again, the nurse gave her a prednisone injection. Finally, the nurse put an oxygen mask over
Lisa's face and left the room. A combination of
relief from surviving the traumatic experience and
medications put Lisa to sleep immediately.

Jonathan was treated for smoke inhalation in the
same emergency room. After examining him a
young resident physician said, "You were deprived
of oxygen for a great deal of time. We need to find
out if there's scarring in your trachea. I'll keep you
overnight." He began writing on a pad.

"No, I can't stay. Give me whatever medication you
need to give me, but I can't stay," Jonathan insisted,
rising from the gurney.

"You can't leave," the doctor said. "We need
X-rays."

"I'll come back later," Jonathan promised, buttoning his shirt and walking away. He stopped at a desk to get the room number for Lisa Stevens and hurried to her. The nurses at the nursing station on Lisa's wing looked at Jonathan, baffled, when he demanded a report of her condition.

"How is the patient in 6314?" he asked.

"I'm sorry. Who are you? We can't tell you that," a nurse answered. She moved away, but Jonathan followed her around the long semicircle desk.

"Did you call her private physician? She has a chronic condition that could make her current crisis life-threatening. She could die on you and you'd never know why."

That captured the nurse's attention and she circled back to where Jonathan was standing. "Who *is* her physician?"

"First tell me how she is and what treatment she has received," he demanded, folding his arms as he was prepared to stay for the duration.

The nurse returned to the computer. Looking at the screen before her, she read off the information he requested. In return, he gave her the name of Lisa's doctor.

When he reached Lisa's room, she was sleeping peacefully. "It's okay. I won't leave you," Jonathan whispered from the chair he had pulled up next to the bed.

With the oxygen steadily flowing into her lungs, Lisa's breathing was less laborious. Yet Jonathan could still see that she struggled. Sitting at her bedside, he swore that he would do anything in his power to protect her. She looked so vulnerable lying there.

He must have dozed off briefly because he was startled when he heard loud voices and what seemed like a commotion outside the door. Before he could rise from his seat, one very petite woman rushed into the room, followed by three giant men and two tall women.

Jonathan stood and smiled when he saw the group. He didn't know what he'd been thinking if he had thought they weren't coming. They all started talking at once.

"How is my baby?" the petite woman asked, rushing to the patient's side and taking her hand.

"She's okay, Mary," Jonathan told Lisa's mother. "She's on oxygen and she's had several breathing treatments. That's exactly what they did when she had her last episode, and she pulled through just fine."

"When was that?" Jet asked. That bit of information was news to him.

"After the Church Street building fire," Jonathan explained, surprised Jet didn't remember.

"She never told us about that." Mary looked from Jet, her stepson, to Lisa's young man.

"Mom, if I told you—would fly here. Jonathan took me—doctor—care for me," Lisa whispered with her eyes still closed. Startled, everyone turned toward her.

Jonathan rushed to her side. "Baby, you're awake. How are you?" he asked, taking her hand in his.

"Thirsty," she replied. He filled her cup with the ice-cold water from the pitcher on her rolling tray. She took a large gulp and when he would have moved the cup away, she reached for more. Her family watched in silence.

"Is that enough?" he asked before removing the cup again.

She nodded. "Were you at the fire?" Her voice was little more than a croak.

"Yes, I was," he answered.

"Don't you know he saved your life?" Kevin, Lisa's youngest brother, asked, moving forward. "They have pictures of your rescue on the news."

"He was the first one on the scene, but you were nearly dead before he found you," Melvin, the middle brother, said. Everyone ignored him but Jonathan, who looked at him with a brutal expression on his face. Louise broke the silence.

"He found you when you were barely breathing and gave you his own air mask," Louise, Jet's mother, finished. Lisa and Jet had the same father but different mothers. However, they never referred to themselves in *halves* or *steps*. Louise pressed a button to raise the bed so that Lisa could see her guests better.

"I didn't know. How did you find me?" Lisa asked after removing her air mask. She began to cough so deeply, she immediately replaced it. Her mother placed pillows behind her back to ease her breathing.

"I followed my heart," he said, smiling at her as if no one else were in the room.

"I'm glad you did," she said and closed her eyes. "How is it?"

He knew she referred to her building and didn't try to spare her, knowing she wanted the truth. "It's pretty bad. The first and second floors are completely gone. Up to the fourth floor, only the west side of the building burned. Everything else is smoke damaged."

"That's not so bad," she wheezed, lying back against the pillows.

"Thank you for bringing my baby out," Mary said with moisture in her eyes. She sat on the bed beside Lisa.

"You'll do anything to get attention, won't you?" Kevin asked Lisa, bringing up their usual accusations toward one another.

He was relieved when she responded to his teasing in her usual manner. "Jealous," Lisa returned and moved her mask to stick out her tongue.

"Don't try to talk," Melvin said. "You sound horrible. I didn't think your voice could get any deeper but I believe it has."

"That's a rotten thing to say," Cara said from the perch she'd taken on the sink. Jet stood in front of Cara, allowing her to lean on his back.

"Cut it out. My poor baby is suffering," Mary said, putting an arm around Lisa.

"Are you using your inhalers the way you're supposed to?" Louise, who had been a nurse, sat at the foot of the bed.

"I forget," Lisa answered honestly and rested her head on her mother's shoulder.

"I don't think an inhaler would have helped today. Are you in pain?" Mary asked.

"Maybe we should stop talking so she can rest her voice. It must hurt for her to talk," Jonathan suggested.

Lisa removed the oxygen mask again. "There's no way any of these people will ever be able to stop talking, so don't even get your hope up," she said. Everyone laughed at the unexpected remark from the patient.

"That's right. Now hush before they put all of us out," Mary said.

"You know they've already told us that all of us couldn't come in," Louise said.

"Where—Oscar?" Lisa asked, opening her eyes.

"He's in the waiting room. You know he's a stickler for following rules," Mary said with fondness in her voice.

"Would either of you like my seat?" Jonathan asked the two older women.

"No, you look like you've been beaten up yourself. You stay there," Louise said. "Has anyone taken a look at you?"

"They tried," Jonathan replied.

"You don't sound well at all. You should be lying in a bed somewhere," Louise insisted.

"Maybe later," Jonathan said dismissively.

"You're risking pneumonia and permanent damage to your lungs," Louise persisted.

"Jonathan, you can go. I'm okay," Lisa said quietly.

"Maybe later. Look, the news is on. Do you want me to turn it up?" Jonathan was relieved to find a diversion as all eyes turned upward to the TV.

The camera was focused on the worst part of the building. A reporter stood in front of the smoldering ashes and said:

"Shortly after noon today, eleven hundred workers poured out of the Broadway Boulevard building, owned by Sand Castles Corporation of Miami, Florida. The thirty-one-story tower broke into flames while many of its employees were out to lunch. Some employees complained they never heard a fire alarm.

"Fire officials are investigating the fire's cause. Anonymous sources have told News Channel Five that the fire appears to be the result of arson.

"The first firefighters on the scene were from the historic Engine Company Number Two that covers downtown Nashville. The captain on duty, Jonathan Hill, immediately called for assistance, resulting in a five-alarm fire.

"The evacuation appeared to go smoothly and fire officials have said there were few injuries, but nothing life-threatening. Many of the injured were taken to Vanderbilt Medical Center and treated for smoke inhalation.

"In this video footage shot by an amateur, we see

Captain Hill in a heroic rescue of a woman who was overcome by smoke. She is identified as Lisa Stevens of the Sand Castles Corporation. The firm's regional office is housed in that building."

"Three cheers for Jonathan!" Kevin yelled.

"Way to go, Jonathan," the brothers said together.

"Jet, what are we going to do?" Lisa asked, trying to be sparse with words because talking was so painful.

"About what, baby?" Jet asked, moving to the other side of the bed.

"The people—our building," she managed to ask before the burning in her lungs and throat became so intense she had to put the mask back in place.

"Don't worry about that," Jet said soothingly. "You just get better."

"But I do," Lisa insisted.

"We're going to have a press conference this evening. It will be on the ten o'clock news," Mary explained. She also had recently resumed her role as the company's vice president for communications.

Jet added, "We'll let our employees know that we're there for them and they can take as much time off as they need."

"In the morning Louise and I will go visit all the employees who are hospitalized and let them know we'll take care of everything," Cara reported from her perch on the sink.

Their discussion was interrupted by the arrival of Dr. Faulkner, who entered the room on a breeze. A medium-brown, fatherly looking man with graying hair, he wore a white lab coat and a stethoscope around his neck and looked like a TV physician. He was followed by a young woman in bright blue and yellow scrubs with her hair pulled back. "Hello, everyone," the cheerful doctor said. "The nurse told me you're having a party in here. Am I too late?"

"No, you're right on time," Mary said, approaching the doctor. "I'm her mother, Mary Hawkins." She then introduced the others.

"Visitors do help patients, but you've got to let this young lady rest. After I examine her, you may come back to say good night. Go to the waiting room down the hall and I'll send a nurse for you when I'm finished," the doctor ordered.

Quickly and efficiently he examined his usually energetic patient. He was concerned with the fatigue he saw on her face and the whistling he heard in her chest. But that was to be expected, considering her accident.

"You're going to be just fine," Dr. Faulkner assured Lisa. "I've viewed your X-rays and frankly I'm surprised the damage to your lungs is not any worse than it is. You'll have a sore throat for a few days and your bronchials are inflamed, but the prednisone will take care of that. You could have been so much worse," he said seriously.

"I know," Lisa replied solemnly. "I am fortunate that Jonathan found me in time."

"Yes, you are. And that he gave you air immediately," the doctor added. "That's why you're pretty good."

"Yes, I feel real good. Why can't I go home?"

"Stay tonight so that we can keep an eye on you. If you do all right tonight, we'll discuss our next step. Let's just take this one day at a time." The doctor gave Lisa a paternal pat on the shoulder.

He turned to the nurse and asked her to retrieve the family. When they returned he said, "She's pretty exhausted. The mere act of breathing is a major task for her. I'll check her again in the morning. Now only one of you may stay the night." He left just as quickly as he'd entered.

"He said we can't stay the night. He didn't say we have to leave right now," Mary said wisely.

A nurse interrupted her. "Dr. Faulkner ordered this prednisone injection." She pulled a cart with medical instruments on it. She closed the curtain around the bed and then paused to say, "Okay, gang. I've got to clear the room. I need everyone to leave now. You can check on her in the morning. She needs her rest."

"I'm sorry, Lisa. We've got to go," Jet said.

"I'll see you in the morning, Big Head," Lisa said, using her nickname for him.

"It's time for the press conference," Mary said, reluctant to leave. "Do you want me to come back later?"

"I can stay," Louise offered.

"No, I need you to come with me. Lisa will be cared for," Cara said quickly.

The family kissed Lisa one by one and filed out. "What about you?" the nurse asked when only Jonathan remained.

"I'm staying," he said matter-of-factly.

She raised one eyebrow but said no more. After Lisa was given the injection, she fell asleep immediately. In a few minutes, the nurse came back with pillows and a blanket for Jonathan. She showed him how to let the chair out to make a bed.

Still coated in smoke and soot from the fire, Jonathan wanted to take a shower, but had no clothes to put on. He was surprised to look up to see Melvin come through the door. He wondered if he'd come back for the beat-down he'd missed earlier when he had accused Jonathan of not getting to Lisa quickly enough.

"What brings you back?" Jonathan asked, not bothering to stand as Melvin approached.

"Look here, we know Lisa's crazy about you. Every conversation we have with her, she manages to work your name into it somehow. I'm glad you're taking care of her," Melvin said.

Jonathan assumed this was some kind of apology for his earlier remarks. "No harm done. I guess I would be the same way if I had a sister," Jonathan said easily. He was actually too exhausted to be having that conversation.

"Mother wanted me to give you our cell phone numbers in case Lisa needs anything." He gave a list of numbers to Jonathan. "And we picked up a little something for you."

Jonathan had expected dinner. He knew the Styrofoam take-out carton was for him, but he was surprised the shopping bag was too. Looking inside the huge bag, he found a jogging suit, underclothes, socks, sneakers—everything he needed to change clothes.

"Kevin and I figured you're about our size. Not as big as Jet but not as slim as Kevin and me. I hope it fits," Melvin said.

"Thanks. I appreciate this," Jonathan said. That simple gesture meant so much to him. Her family obviously approved of their relationship. They weren't concerned about her being with a poor fireman.

"Don't get all excited," Melvin said as if reading his mind. "With you sitting here reeking of smoke, she'll never get better. Take a shower and change your clothes."

"Yeah, okay," Jonathan said, not quite knowing how to take Melvin.

"You hate for people to see your soft side," Lisa

whispered to Melvin. Both men turned toward her, startled. "Don't let his bark bother you," she added to Jonathan.

After Melvin left, Jonathan hurried through the shower, thoroughly washing the remains of the fire from his body.

When he returned, Lisa was sound asleep. She didn't wake up again until four o'clock the next morning. She walked over to the big chair where Jonathan slept under a sheet and blanket and crawled in next to him.

"What's wrong, baby? Are you okay?" he asked, alarmed.

"I'm okay, but you have some talking to do," she said through the mask on her face.

CHAPTER 8

"You sound so serious, Lisa. Can't anything we need to discuss wait until you're better?" Jonathan asked, feeling desperate. Before the fire, before he'd known what it felt like to lose her, he'd been prepared to tell her the story of his sordid past—a past that included murder and a drug-addicted mother. That was before he'd found her in between life and death in the stairwell. Now he knew what it would be like to no longer have her in his life, because for a fleeting moment he'd thought she was gone.

Now more than ever he wanted to see their relationship in full bloom, to see what it could grow into. If he told her about his past, that would never happen. He had no time to wonder how she had found out, but without a doubt, she had. He'd never heard such a serious note in her voice before.

"No, we've already put this conversation off long enough. Talk now," she wheezed, and quickly replaced the oxygen mask, dragging the long hose from the wall unit to her new bed next to him.

"Everything," she added, not bothering to remove the oxygen mask.

He dropped his head, unable to meet her clear, direct gaze. "I have served time in the state penitentiary," he finally said.

"Why? Joyriding?" she said, hoping it was a youthful indiscretion. Her sentences were now short and choppy.

"No, I killed a man." He plunged right in, not bothering to sugarcoat the truth. There was no way he could. His voice was stark, hard. The horror in her eyes was real, just as he had imagined. It was quickly followed by looks of pain and panic. He watched stoically as the emotions washed over her face, one followed by another. She was silent so long, he wondered if she was having some kind of attack.

She lay in stunned silence. That was the last thing she had expected to hear. She had convinced herself that he'd probably served time for something very innocuous. Never in a million years would she have guessed murder. Not Jonathan. He was the most compassionate, gentle person she knew.

"Lisa, your asthma. Maybe we shouldn't do this until you're better," he said, fearing she would stop breathing at any moment.

"Stress is not a trigger for my asthma—smoke and pollen induced. Tell—tell everything," she demanded.

"I can't justify it and I'm very sorry. I have been every day since I committed—my—my crime," he said miserably. He slowly got up and walked away from Lisa, who watched his dejected posture, the ache in her heart now for him.

"Don't want justification. Want to understand.

Who did you—k-kill?" Lisa stuttered just trying to say the word. A chill went down her spine.

"Lawrence T. Hudson." Jonathan turned around and looked at her, saying the name slowly, pronouncing each syllable with emphasis. The name, the person, his face were forever a part of his life. That one simple act had changed him forever.

"Why?" With her recovering from her initial shock, the dazed look had been replaced by one of pure curiosity.

"He was my mother's drug dealer," Jonathan said bluntly. Miraculously, a feeling of relief washed over him. Now he'd have nothing to hide from. The last person he wanted to know about his criminal past would finally know. If it was over between them, at least he didn't have to be afraid anymore. He'd no longer have to feel so guilty every time he was around her.

Anxious to get it all out, he continued, "The man sold drugs to my mother and was destroying her."

Jonathan returned to his place next to Lisa on the chair. He put his feet up and his hands behind his head as he talked. Lisa closed her eyes, but he didn't doubt she was listening. With her eyes closed, he felt less exposed as he revealed the details of a past he'd tried to keep hidden from the woman whose respect he craved.

Memory of that time, when he'd been fourteen years old, returned to him. It had been so long since he'd thought of that day. He'd tried to erase it from his memory. Tonight it played like an old movie in his mind. Slowly he related the story to Lisa, his voice without emotion, yet somehow she knew his lingering pain. He began with the day his life had changed.

"My mother had an unusual opportunity to take

a promotion, but she had to relocate to Nashville. She felt she needed to network more, and in the course of networking, she was introduced to illegal drugs. My father was angry, but I wanted to take care of her."

Lisa's breathing became less of a struggle. Jonathan turned to see if she was still awake. She opened her arms to him and he leaned in to her. Hugging him tightly, she crooned, "You poor baby. You've always wanted to rescue people, haven't you?"

"After her drug use became so bad, my parents split up. He, my brother and I returned to Detroit. The year I finished the eleventh grade, Dad sent me to Nashville for the summer and I refused to return home that fall.

"Things were bad here, but I thought I could make them better. I went from living in a nice middle-class neighborhood on Lake St. Clair to living in a one-bedroom walk-up with a broken window air conditioner and a flimsy front door for security. Half of the time, my mother didn't know I was with her.

"I had been in Nashville for about a year when I came home from school one day and our raggedy furniture was in front of the apartment building. We had been evicted because we'd fallen so far behind on our rent."

Afraid that he was crushing her, Jonathan reversed their positions, taking Lisa into his arms. She rested her head on his chest and listened to his heavy sigh before he finished his story.

"My father had sent us money, but my mother had taken it all to her drug dealer. I wanted to find her to see if there was any money left because we had nowhere to stay. When I found her, she was with Lawrence Hudson. I tried to get her away from him, but she refused to leave." Jonathan was staring straight ahead again. He remained silent so long, Lisa didn't think he'd finish the story and she didn't have the heart to prod him. Finally he spoke again.

"Mr. Hudson pulled his gun out on me. I fought him and the gun went off. When I realized what had happened, he'd been shot. I was arrested for murder."

"Oh, baby, I'm sorry." Lisa reached up and hugged him. "Surely everyone knew it was self-defense. How could you be arrested?"

"The prosecutor convinced me to take a plea bargain. I pleaded guilty and my case never went to trial." Jonathan told the story without emotion, as if it had happened to someone other than him.

"I was serving time when Mr. Mueller came into my life. He read about my case in the newspaper and decided his law firm would win my release. In his opinion the courts had gotten too conservative when every juvenile that did anything was tried as an adult and given the maximum penalty. He wanted to use my case to put a face on that particular kind of injustice."

"Why did he choose you?" Lisa asked, moving away from his chest to look up at Jonathan's grim profile. The room was dark except for the soft glow of a light near the entrance.

"Alan had done his research. I'd been an honor student and had never been in trouble of any kind before. He knew my story would pull on the public's sympathy," Jonathan explained neutrally. "We went back to court and I was released. The judge said the evidence in my favor was blatant that my case should have been dismissed in the beginning."

"What kind of evidence?" Lisa asked curiously.

"Character witnesses who'd come forward on my

behalf, but had not been heard because my case never went to trial. An eyewitness who'd been looking out her window and seen the victim pull his gun on me and the whole struggle after that. People in the neighborhood gave statements that Mr. Hudson was seen regularly meeting with his clientele in his car." Jonathan did not seem triumphant or joyous as he told of his victory.

Lisa threw an arm over Jonathan's shoulders and drew him closer. They lay nose to nose. "You could have told me this story before," she whispered.

"I couldn't. I enjoyed seeing the light and pride in your eyes when you looked at me. I wanted you to see me as someone noble," he said, rising on one elbow and looking at her.

"I do see you as noble," she said. "When I first found out about your serving time, I was so upset. It wasn't about the serving time part—that doesn't change who you are. I was upset because it showed how far apart we are. It proved that you didn't trust me."

"It was my mistake. Can you forgive me?" he asked, rubbing a hand up and down her back.

"I have already. You took a life, but you've saved my life twice now. How can I feel anything but a deep gratitude for you?" she asked.

"I appreciate your gratitude, but I need your love," Jonathan said, seeking the truth in her eyes.

"You have that. I told you I love you once and I always will. That won't change. You just have to start trusting me."

"I'd give my life for you," Jonathan pledged.

"I know."

"I thought you'd be very upset—maybe even afraid of me—when you learned the truth," he said tightly.

"Jonathan, I'm no fool. I knew you were holding

something back. I've been complicit in my own deception. You talk very little about high school. You never visit your father and although you talk to your mother several times a day, I've never met her."

"Why didn't you ask to meet my mother?" Jonathan asked, surprised when she brought his mother up.

"Usually if a guy takes you to meet his mother, the relationship is very special. I just assumed I wasn't that special to you," Lisa confessed. She rose from the chair and walked across the room.

"Oh, baby, no. That's not it at all. I just figured Mom might blow my cover," Jonathan confided.

"So you admit, you're an undercover brother," Lisa teased.

"Don't even go there. Put your mask back on before you start wheezing again."

"I feel one hundred percent again. I don't need it."

"Use it anyway," Jonathan ordered.

Before she could return the mask to her face, Lisa was caught up in the throes of a coughing episode. Jonathan ran to her and rubbed her back, feeling helpless. He took her back to the bed. When the coughing ended, her face glazed over in pain. He rang for a nurse, who came immediately and started another breathing treatment for her. As the medicine filled her bronchial tubes and lungs, breathing became easier for her.

"What can I do for you?" Jonathan asked, feeling helpless when the treatment ended.

"My stomach hurts so much from coughing. Just hold me," she whispered. Jonathan lay on the bed next to her. Nestled in his powerful arms, she drifted off to sleep. He was amazed she'd stayed awake as long as she had, considering the massive dosages of medication she'd been given that day.

As he fell asleep, he felt lighter than he had in ages. The secrets of his past were no longer a heavy burden for him to bear alone. Moving forward was now a possibility. He could even ask Lisa to marry. He felt like anything was possible.

The next morning a cheerful nurse entered the room. "Okay, lovebirds. I need to check the patient's vitals. Give me some room."

Jonathan woke up groggily and rose from the narrow bed they had shared. This was a far cry from how he had expected his first time sleeping with Lisa to be.

While the nurse was with Lisa he took care of his morning toiletries. "You've done remarkably well," she said. "You don't need this oxygen anymore." She flipped a switch, cutting off the oxygen.

"Does this mean I can go home?" Lisa asked anxiously.

"You have to talk to Dr. Faulkner about that," the nurse said noncommittally, expertly making the bed. "If you don't go home, your brother has arranged for you to be moved to the VIP suite."

"I don't need it. I'm going home," Lisa resolved.

"Okay. Dr. Faulkner usually makes his rounds around seven-thirty. He'll let us know," the nurse said as she left the room.

When a breakfast tray for each of them arrived, Jonathan helped Lisa from the bed. They sat on either side of a small round table. He took the metal cover from the tray and stirred butter and sugar into her oatmeal.

"I don't want to be here all day, Jonathan," she announced, gingerly tasting her oatmeal, then taking another bite.

"Slow down, Lisa. There's no reason for you to go

home until we're sure you're okay," Jonathan warned her.

"I feel fine. I can do breathing treatments at home. Please take me home," she pleaded, looking at him with big, innocent eyes.

"Wait until the doctor sees you. We'll see what kind of care you need," Jonathan argued.

"Somebody will take care of me," Lisa replied, swallowing a spoonful of applesauce. It felt good on her raw throat.

"Come to my house. I'll take care of you," Jonathan offered, noting that the events of the previous day had weakened her appetite.

Surprised by his offer, she had no immediate response. "I wasn't trying to get you to take care of me. My mother is here," she finally said.

"She's staying at a hotel. And you only have one bed at your house. Did you forget Oscar is with her?" Jonathan asked, referring to Mary's husband. He took another bite of the bland hospital fare.

"I can go to the hotel with her. She has a suite," Lisa said stubbornly.

"I want to take care of you, and your mother can come to my house," he decided.

"What about Oscar?" Lisa asked.

"He can come too," Jonathan volunteered.

Just then Dr. Faulkner entered the room. "Good morning. I see you're up already. A little breathing problem can't keep a good woman like you down, can it?" he asked cheerfully.

She turned toward the door to greet the kind physician. "No way. I'm ready to go home. I was just about to call you," she responded.

"How are you doing?" Dr. Faulkner asked.

"I'm just fine," she said. "In fact, I'm doing so well I should be at home."

"I heard you've been making all kinds of fuss about being kept here against your will. Let me take a look at you. Excuse us," the good-natured doctor said as he pushed buttons on the computerized patient chart hooked to the foot of the bed.

Jonathan left the room and strolled the hallways. Hospital personnel were rushing here and there with carts—computers on carts, medicine carts, and carts of equipment.

The doctor found him drifting about. "She's doing very well," the doctor began. "But I want her to stay here another day. We need to see if the bronchial inflammation responds to medication I've prescribed."

After leaving the doctor, Jonathan returned to Lisa's room. She was in a full depression. He suggested she call her family and she responded, "They're too busy for me. They have things to do." He smiled at the way she pouted with her bottom lip stuck out just like a little child's.

Jonathan picked up the card Melvin had delivered the night before. Dialing the number for the Loews Hotel, he asked for the room for Mrs. Mary Hawkins.

"Good morning, Mrs. Hawkins," Jonathan said when she picked up.

"Is Lisa okay?" Mary asked immediately.

"She's just fine physically. I'm concerned for her emotional state. She doesn't want to be in the hospital anymore and she's giving everyone here a hard time. Can you get the party started up here again?" Jonathan asked, looking at a big smile spread across Lisa's face as he talked.

Within an hour, the whole family had returned to the hospital. Cara had even located a beautician who came with everything needed to do Lisa's hair.

Oscar, who arrived with the group, excused himself when the beautician began washing Lisa's hair. He wanted no part of such activity in a hospital room.

Lisa was in her element, surrounded by family. She was used to being the center of their attention and it showed. In fact, one of the things Jonathan admired most about the Stevens family was their effusive affection for one another. He had been surprised and pleased when that affection flowed over to include him.

After Lisa's hair was washed and blow-dried, the beautician bumped it with a jumbo curling iron. She was only halfway finished when a nurse came in to give Lisa a prednisone injection. Lisa protested, "I don't need that intravenously today. Please get the pill for me."

The nurse replied, "Dr. Faulkner ordered an injection."

"Yes, I'm sure he did. He also wouldn't sign my discharge papers today. Do I look like I need to be here another day? Perhaps Dr. Faulkner can be wrong," she suggested.

The nurse looked from the tall, slender patient with bright eyes, glowing skin, and a beautician hovering over her, to the many people scattered around the room: the three tall, good-looking men lounging on chairs and the one on the bed watching a college football game on television, the two tall women and one petite woman who were playing a card game. "I guess not," she replied.

"Then call Dr. Faulkner and tell him to change that order to a pill, please. I'll be here," Lisa said imperiously as she dismissed the nurse.

The nurse gave her a final glance before leaving the room. Seeing that Lisa had everything under control, Jonathan called Artis to pick him up. He wanted to go by the fire hall to get his car.

With his arrangement made, Jonathan went to Lisa. Kneeling before the chair where she sat, he whispered, "I'm going to the firehouse for a while. I'll be back in time for dinner."

"You're going to miss the best part of the party," she teased.

"I'll hurry," he promised.

When Jonathan entered the station, the men gathered around to ask about his hero status. He brushed past them to get to his bunk where he hoped his gear had been taken. It wasn't there.

He rushed out to the garage and saw the pile of turnouts. He hurried through the pile of coats, searching the pockets as quickly as possible. Finally, when exhaustion was about to overtake him, he came to the last coat. Still, there was no bracelet. He was so certain that it would be in his pocket that he stood in confusion trying to figure what to do next.

His friend's voice startled him. "What are you doing out here?" Jonathan asked.

"Captain, are you really all right?" Foster asked.

"Yeah, I am," Jonathan said absently. "I think I'll go on back up to the hospital now."

Jonathan realized he'd have to tell Lisa he'd found the bracelet and lost it again. Hopefully she would have a logical explanation for how it got into the middle of the room where the fire started.

CHAPTER 9

Jonathan left the fire hall and went to the Broadway Boulevard building. "What do you want?" the foreman asked.

It was Saturday afternoon. He had not expected to find anyone around. Quickly he thought up a response. Flashing his ID, he said, "I'm with the Metro Fire Department. I need to take a look around." Authoritatively he walked around the yellow tape protecting the disaster scene.

"Aren't you guys finished here yet? We're trying to clean up. Everything you could possibly want is out," the rugged-looking construction worker said, following the tall, intense-looking young man.

"I just want to look at the first floor again. I won't get in your way," Jonathan called as he hurried away.

Debris was being scraped up and taken out to waiting dump trucks. He realized if he'd dropped the bracelet, it had already been found again. With no hope of recovering the bracelet, he concentrated on the fire investigation. He had not wanted to scare Lisa, but he knew she'd be a prime suspect.

He wanted to move ahead of the investigators and come up with a feasible alternative suspect.

He walked across the first floor, which was now an empty shell, trying to imagine how it had looked before the fire. Hadn't Lisa mentioned that the mail room was also on the first floor? And shipping and receiving was down here somewhere. Some of the employees had been evacuated from the loading dock.

Everyone who worked in the building had reason to use the first-floor facilities. Anyone could have had access to the alarm system. All employees or former employees could walk through without drawing attention. Even a former employee—maybe an employee who had been fired. Someone had set the fire—that was no longer the question. But who? Who could have seen what happened immediately before the fire? Jonathan walked through the building, floor by floor, noticing every little thing. It was like collecting puzzle pieces. He didn't know where everything fit, but everything would be needed.

By the time he walked outside the building, the construction crew had abandoned their heavy equipment and left for the day. He had stayed later than he planned and felt guilty for leaving Lisa so long. But he had one more stop to make. He went to see his friend Alan Mueller.

"Hey, boy, I've seen you all over the news. How are you holding up?" Alan greeted Jonathan after answering his doorbell. "Come on in."

"I'm doing pretty well, all things considered," Jonathan replied, following Alan into his den. "How is Mrs. Mueller?"

"She's fine. She's gone to one of her meetings. Would you like to have a beer or something else?" Alan asked before they were seated.

"No, sir. I'm fine," Jonathan replied.

"How's Lisa?" Alan asked, dropping onto the long, brown worn leather sofa.

"She's doing a lot better. The fire was extra hard on her because she was exposed to the smoke for so long and she has asthma," Jonathan explained, knowing that Alan truly wanted to know about her. He'd met Lisa several times since she was always with Jonathan and he held her in high regard. If he could have chosen a young woman for Jonathan, she would have been the one.

"What's on your mind, son?" Alan asked, noting that Jonathan had not accepted the offered seat, but was pacing the room instead.

He plunged right in, certain of his decision. "I came over on business. I'm thinking about selling Zora."

"You're selling Zora? Why the sudden change of mind?" Alan asked, concern clear in his eyes.

"Zora represents a time in my life that I'm ready to leave behind. I don't need anything else from my mother or father and I'm not upset over what they didn't do for me. I need to move on. My father gave her to me to take my mind off my mother's absence in my life. I've finally gotten over that hurt. I can move on." Jonathan knew that Alan would understand.

Alan moved back in his seat and crossed his legs, contemplating the young man's explanation. "I guess you've told Lisa everything."

"Yes, I have and she didn't even blink. Of course, she was upset with me for hiding that part of myself from her. But she accepted it. It's a part of me. It's not desirable or even pleasant, but it happened. She's in love with me, Mr. Mueller," Jonathan said in wonder.

A wide smile had spread across the young man's face. In that moment, Alan received the return on his investment of long hours and hard work in winning Jonathan's freedom. This was the normalcy he'd always wanted for the boy.

"How much do you want for Zora?" Alan asked.

"I figure I can get at least fifty for her. What do you think? What do you want to pay?" Jonathan asked hesitantly.

"Way more than that. I know what you've put into her over the years. She's truly one of a kind with custom everything. Honestly, I can't pay you what she's worth," Alan said, uncrossing his legs and leaning toward Jonathan. "Are you in some kind of financial bind?"

"No, nothing like that." Jonathan sat down in the chair directly across from the sofa where Alan sat. "I want to buy a diamond. An engagement ring for Lisa. Her mother and sister-in-law are here and I've never seen such beautiful stones outside a museum in my life. I know I can't compete with them, but I don't want Lisa to be ashamed of her ring."

"I don't know Lisa as well as you do, but I don't think the ring matters that much to her. Just get her the best diamond you can for your money. Focus on the cut and clarity. You can always trade up later," the older man advised.

"Thanks, I'll do that," Jonathan said, about to rise from his seat.

"I said I can't buy the car," Alan continued. Jonathan paused and looked at him. "But that doesn't mean I can't get the car sold for you. I have a friend who has been bugging me about my car. Every time we go to lunch, he wants me to drive just so he can get in my car. He's offered me double what I paid you for it. Would you like me to broker a deal for you?"

"Yes, yes, that would be great," Jonathan said. He was smiling again and looked relaxed.

"When can I bring him out to see it? I want him to see your garage and your whole setup before we tell him what the car's going to cost him. I think he'll be impressed by your level of professionalism."

"Lisa's still in the hospital and I've been staying with her as much as I can. She should be home in the next day or so. What about Tuesday afternoon?"

"That sounds good. I'll call and let you know for sure." Alan stood with his young friend and walked him to the door.

Slapping Jonathan on the shoulder, Alan said, "You're about to take a big step, son. But I know you've given it a lot of thought and know what you're doing. Lisa is a good girl. I wish you the best."

Jonathan turned and impulsively gave Alan a quick man-type hug. That demonstrative act took Alan by surprise. He hid his face in the shadows as he watched Jonathan walk to his car. He didn't want the young man to see the tears in his eyes.

When Jonathan returned to the hospital, Mary and Oscar were there alone with Lisa. Cara, Jet, and Louise had gone shopping for groceries. They wanted to have a feast for Sunday's dinner, either at the hospital or at Jonathan's house, wherever Lisa would be the next day. They'd all agreed that it was best for Lisa to go to Jonathan's when she was discharged. His large house would accommodate the whole family easily.

Shortly after he returned, Mary and Oscar left. They needed to go by Lisa's house to pack up more clothes and personal items for her to have at Jonathan's. A nurse came to settle Lisa for the night and Jonathan pulled out the sleeper. After barely sleeping the previous night, both slept soundly throughout the night.

Dr. Faulkner arrived early the next morning, sending Jonathan to the waiting room. After examining Lisa, he found Jonathan there. "She's convinced me to release her. I understand she's going home with you?" the doctor asked.

"That's right," Jonathan confirmed, nodding.

"Okay, I've written a prescription for prednisone and albuterol. Get these filled. Also, she'll need her nebulizer. Use that only when she is having trouble breathing. It's for backup only. She's actually doing much better than anyone would have predicted. I've told her to play it by ear. I haven't put any restrictions on her activities. She can do whatever she feels like doing. In fact, she could go to work tomorrow if she wanted. Do you have any questions?"

"No, sir," Jonathan replied, ready to go get Lisa. He turned to leave the room.

"Why don't you go downstairs for her discharge papers? She's packing her things and should be ready to go by the time you get back," Dr. Faulkner suggested, leaving the room with Jonathan.

"I'll do just that," Jonathan said, walking with the doctor to the elevator. They boarded, chatting until Dr. Faulkner exited at the next floor. Jonathan stayed on until he reached the first floor and followed the signs to the admissions department.

Lisa changed into the cute little off-the-shoulder red T-shirt and flared denim miniskirt her mother had brought her to wear home. She put on the socks and sneakers that had been included and was ready to go. She called her mother to meet her at Jonathan's.

She was surprised when a young African-American woman about her age entered the room. The honey-brown woman's hair was styled neatly in a tapered cut. She was dressed stylishly in a tailored business pantsuit and heels and carried a portfolio under one arm. A Louis Vuitton purse was under the other. Lisa quickly dismissed the thought that she might be hospital personnel. No, not with the designer purse and expensive attire.

The woman introduced herself, offering a card to Lisa when she was close enough. "Hello, I'm Janice McKee, an investigator for the Nashville Fire Department. I have a few questions to ask about the fire in your building on Friday."

"Sure. Have a seat," Lisa said.

Pulling one of the sturdy chairs around so that she could face Lisa, Janice studied the other woman for a moment. As a firefighter and emergency medical technician, she could tell the patient was having trouble breathing. Otherwise there were no signs of illness. In fact, she looked very young and pretty. Her attire was casual and trendy. She looked like someone waiting to go out shopping or to the movies. "Are you doing okay?" Janice felt compelled to ask, though she was focused on the business at hand.

"I'm okay. I'm just waiting to check out," Lisa replied, returning the woman's thoughtful gaze.

"I wish I could wait before I begin my investigation, but I can't. Your fire was arson," Janice said point-blank.

"Why do you say that?" Lisa asked, her voice filled with apprehension.

"The fire started in a closet. No combustibles

were stored there, no wiring problems or anything else we could determine spontaneously ignited the fire. It had to have been set," Janice said forcefully as if daring Lisa to argue.

"I would think our system would have prevented anything like that," Lisa said, suddenly feeling drained. The thought that they'd been the victim of arson was devastating. She felt angry, frightened, and perplexed.

"The employees that I talked with yesterday told me that the smoke was everywhere suddenly. They had no warning," Janice said, relaxing in her seat and crossing one leg over the other.

"As soon as smoke was detected our state-of-the-art system should have alerted the fire department and sent a warning to our security staff."

"Do you know why that didn't happen?" Janice inquired. She looked expectantly at Lisa as if she should have the answer.

"I have no idea," Lisa said, not wanting to play games by daring a guess.

"The system had been disengaged," Janice said, moving forward in her seat to watch Lisa's reaction. She relaxed somewhat when the other woman's face registered shock.

"How? That can't be. Even if it was accidentally knocked off-line, we have an instantaneous backup system with an alternative power source," Lisa explained.

"The electricity to the system was interrupted and the telephone lines were cut," Janice announced. She loved tossing out unknown tidbits like that. Innocent folks usually displayed their honest emotions when they were surprised by the information she threw at them. The guilty never showed any reaction.

"What are you talking about?" Lisa asked incredulously. For a moment she had trouble pulling in air. All of this was distressing to her.

"Someone intentionally went under the console and pulled out the lines for the system," Janice clarified patiently.

"Why would anyone do that?" Lisa was having trouble comprehending the significance of the investigator's news.

"Perhaps they wanted to start a fire without being detected," Janice offered sarcastically. *Why* was so obvious to her. "Whoever did it knew exactly what they were doing."

"No, that doesn't make sense. Who would deliberately start a fire? What would they have to gain?" Lisa asked. Now she was becoming angry. Not at Janice, but at the fact that someone would dare violate her property that way.

"More often than not, we find that it is for the insurance money. We understand that the building was scheduled for massive renovations in the coming year." Janice decided to ditch the subtleties and be up front with the suspect. She couldn't tell if Lisa was as innocent as she appeared or a really good actress.

"Yes, it is. But we have budgeted for them. It's no biggie," Lisa said quickly.

Janice leafed through the notes in her portfolio. She looked up after finding the page she'd searched for. "Last year there was a fire in your Church Street building."

Not sure if that was a question, Lisa nodded anyway. Disbelief was growing within her. She didn't know where the questions were going, but she didn't like them.

"We just closed our investigation of that fire."

"I know," Lisa replied.

"Yes, we kept it open and continued our investigation as long as the insurance company asked us to work with them. We weren't sure the first building was an arson. By the time we began our investigation, our leads were contaminated. That won't happen this time," Janice warned.

"I see," Lisa said, rubbing her hands up and down her arms. She was suddenly chilled. The thought that this had happened twice in her company alarmed her.

"I have a copy of the check the insurance company sent you." Janice held out the photocopy for Lisa to see.

"So do I," Lisa replied, ignoring the proffered copy.

"That was a major fire," Janice stated.

Lisa smiled at the woman's grand announcement of the obvious, wanting to return her earlier sarcasm, but thought better of it. Instead she planted an angelic smile on her face and said, "I'm most grateful that one was at night and no employees were endangered."

Janice watched Lisa in amazement. How could this clearly ill woman sit there smiling at her as if she didn't have a care in the world? Didn't she realize she was the palpable suspect for the fire? Who else would gain so much? Remembering the photocopy of the check that Lisa had not bothered to look at, Janice stuck it back in her portfolio.

"That was a generous settlement from your insurance company," Janice noted, her eyes downcast as she focused on putting the photocopy away. She listened intently for the woman's reaction.

"You should see our monthly premium," Lisa shot back. She was growing impatient with the investigator's implications. Did the woman think she was too stupid to understand she was the prime suspect until they found someone better?

"Did you think the premiums were too expensive? Did you feel you deserved to get some of your money back?" Janice asked. Her voice held a confrontational edge that instantly irritated Lisa.

"We get the best coverage we can afford, praying we never have to use it," Lisa explained calmly, although her annoyance was growing.

"The Church Street building had *also* been scheduled for renovation before it burned. I guess you got enough money from your insurance company to finance the cost of the renovations already scheduled," Janice tossed out.

Lisa replied stiffly, "The fire cost us so much more than that settlement. Instead of shopping for temporary relocation space at a leisurely pace, we had to pay a premium price for whatever we could get. We couldn't negotiate with our contractors or suppliers because we'd gone from making scheduled repairs to reacting to an emergency. And now we've been put in that position again."

"Ladies, good morning," Jonathan said from the doorway. He'd heard enough to know that Lisa's anger was growing and he didn't want her to alienate Janice. Joining them, he kissed Lisa on the cheek before dropping into the recliner.

"Jonathan, I'd like to introduce Ms. Janice McKee," Lisa said, smiling up at him.

"We know each other," Jonathan said dryly. "We were in the same graduating class at the Nashville Fire Training Academy."

"Jonathan and I are old friends," Janice said with a disturbing familiarity. "I'm so proud of his rapid rise through the ranks."

"Mine hasn't been as rapid as yours," Jonathan

returned. "I'm just a captain and you're an investigator. What's so important that you're here on a Sunday morning, Ms. Janice?"

Gag me and save me from this mutual admiration society, Lisa thought. She caught the fleeting look that flashed across Janice's face. Was this another secret Jonathan hadn't told her about?

"I've worked night and day since the fire. We want to have answers by the time reporters come calling tomorrow. Why are you here? Do you visit all of your rescue victims?" Janice asked, bantering with Jonathan.

"This is my lady. I'm taking care of her," Jonathan explained clearly, looking directly at Janice.

"Was she your lady before you rescued her or is that how you're meeting women these days?" Janice gave Jonathan a challenging look.

"Is that question part of your investigation?" Jonathan asked.

At least she had the decency to blush. "So what I heard is true. Is this the lady who gave you what-for to your face at the fire hall?"

Jonathan ignored the question. "Can't your interrogation wait until I get Lisa home? She's just been released and I told her family to meet me out at my place," he said, trying unsuccessfully to hide his irritation.

"No, it can't wait," Janice said, opening her portfolio to a clean sheet of paper. "I have a question or two for you too."

Jonathan leaned back in his chair. He didn't have any choice. "Okay, I'm ready."

"Let me finish with Ms. Stevens first," she said crisply. "Ms. Stevens, why didn't you evacuate the building with all the other employees?"

Jonathan and Lisa exchanged a glance that Janice

didn't miss. "I have asthma and smoke is one of my triggers. I had gone to my private restroom to use my inhaler."

"Why is that such a big deal? I saw the look you and Captain Hill exchanged. Is there more you need to tell me?" Janice asked.

"No, that's it. Jonathan looked at me because he knows that I don't like to confess to my weakness. I used to say I had been cured of asthma, so I guess he was wondering what I would say."

"So asthma kept you from evacuating the building with one thousand other people?" Janice asked, sarcasm evident in her voice.

"That's right," Lisa replied and said nothing more.

After several moments of silence, Janice asked, "Is there anything else you'd like to tell me?"

"No," Lisa said, sitting erectly on the bed although fatigue showed on her face. She looked as if she'd droop at any moment.

"That's all for now, but I'll be back to you later today. Okay?"

"Sure," Lisa said, giving up the pretense of being okay and stretching out on the bed.

Turning her attention to Jonathan, Janice began a new round of questions. "You were the first on the scene. Did you see anything suspicious when you arrived?"

"Other than a building cloaked in smoke, I didn't see a thing."

Janice allowed a faint smile and continued, "You also found the room where the fire originated. What did you see in there?"

"You must have that report by now," Jonathan said tiredly. "I told the chief about everything as they put me in the ambulance."

"What did you find?" Janice repeated, fixing Jonathan with a direct gaze.

"As we advanced through the building extinguishing flames they became most intense in the first-floor janitor's closet. The only things not destroyed in the closet were the faucets and copper plumbing," he said sarcastically.

"Jonathan Hill, don't mess with me. I'm here on official business," she said, reprimanding him. Her tone was not as severe as her words.

"And I commend you for your professionalism. I like the way you carry your authority," he returned gallantly.

"I liked you better when you were the no-nonsense Jonathan. I'm not sure if I like your sense of humor," Janice retorted.

"You have this lady to thank for bringing out the wittiness in me." Jonathan nodded toward Lisa.

Janice ignored Jonathan's comment and continued, "Now, back to business. Captain Hill, what did you see when you got to the source of the fire?"

Patiently Jonathan described the scene again.

"Is that all?" Janice asked when he stopped talking. As she looked up from the scribbled notes, her eyes penetrated his.

"Yes, ma'am," he said, meeting her gaze.

"Do you mind excusing us for a moment?" Janice requested, turning her attention to Lisa.

"No, not at all," Lisa said, watching as they walked into the hallway. She'd had the feeling that she was missing something in the exchange between the two coworkers.

"Jonathan, if you're trying to cover for your *lady*, you'd better tell me now," Janice warned.

"You've been an investigator too long. You've become a suspicious old woman," Jonathan teased.

"If you have left anything out, your ass is mine," Janice shot back. With that she walked away.

By the time they made it to the farm, two long limousines were in front of the house waiting for Lisa and Jonathan. As soon as the little red Corvette stopped, all the Stevenses jumped out of their vehicles to surround Lisa and Jonathan. Fatigue was in Lisa's every motion. Quickly explaining why they were late, Jonathan lifted Lisa into his arms and carried her upstairs.

Everyone followed, wanting to know more about the investigation. "Why did she have to question Lisa while she was still in the hospital?" Mary demanded, following Jonathan up the steps. With her shorter legs, she strained to keep up.

"That's standard procedure, Mary. If she waits, important information will be forgotten," Jonathan explained, taking the steps two at a time.

"How can she question Lisa without her lawyer present?" Jet called around Mary as he trailed her impatiently.

"We didn't think she needed an attorney," Jonathan replied. "They were standard questions that needed to be answered."

Once in his bedroom, Jonathan placed Lisa on the bed. "Is this okay?" he asked her softly, trying to protect her from her concerned family members.

"Yes. Thank you," she wheezed, leaning against the pillows.

"What do you need?" Mary asked, walking around Jonathan's large body.

"Sleep," Lisa whispered. She was indeed tired. The morning had been full with the doctor's probing examination, nurses performing final treatments, and then Janice's intrusion.

"I've got this," Jonathan whispered, as he smoothed the covers over her. He kissed her temple before turning around. "Okay, everyone—out. Let's let her rest."

Mary opened her mouth and closed it. Instead of asking Jonathan where he had gotten his authority, she reached up and pulled him down to her petite level to give him a hug. "That's right. Take care of my baby," she whispered in his ear.

Lisa slept through most of her family's visit. She didn't wake up until dinnertime. She found Cara, Mary, and Louise working together in the kitchen. They were preparing the evening meal when Lisa appeared in the doorway. "Do you need help?" she asked.

"No, we don't. How are you feeling, baby?" Louise asked, pausing in opening the oven door.

"I feel so much better. I think I tried to take on too much too quickly this morning, but I really am better now. Do you guys need any help?" Lisa had showered and dressed in jeans and a T-shirt.

"Jet and Jonathan are out on the screened porch. Go out and enjoy the beautiful weather," Mary replied, shooing Lisa away.

"Where are Melvin and Kevin?" Lisa asked, looking around.

"They flew back home with Oscar after lunch," Mary replied, looking up from the potatoes she was peeling.

"When are they coming back?" Lisa asked, crushed. She had wanted more time with her family.

Now that they were gone it was a reminder that the others would be gone soon too.

"They didn't say. The semester has just started for Melvin and he needed to get back to his class. You know they don't have substitute teachers for professors," Louise replied, setting a large ham on the countertop.

"We thought you had too much company," Cara commented.

"I thought they would have at least told me good-bye," Lisa said, yawning.

"Kevin is right, you are spoiled," Cara teased.

"Yes, she is. She's my only girl. What was I supposed to do?" Mary asked, lightly shrugging a shoulder. "I'm guilty but I confess."

"I think I'll go outside now. My character is being impugned," Lisa said, raising her head haughtily and moving toward the door. She staggered slightly and Cara rushed over to Lisa's side to offer her help, but she said, "I can make it. I'm not as weak as I look."

Lisa joined the men on the screened porch, where they sat looking at the river below. The native Floridians enjoyed the bite of the crisp fall day. Frost had painted the trees brilliant hues of orange and yellow overnight. For a while, the scenery was enough. Jonathan and Jet inquired about her health and scurried to make her comfortable. At last they settled into a peaceful silence. After a quiet interval, Lisa asked, "Do you have a dollar amount yet?"

Jet immediately knew what she was talking about. "It's pretty bad. We haven't finished, but the first floor had to be gutted."

"The investigator says they're certain this was no accident. My biggest question is why us?" Lisa asked, propping her feet up on the half wall before her. The rest of the wall was a screen that allowed them to see the river below them and the trees surrounding them.

"We don't have a clue yet," Jet replied solemnly, still focused on the brilliant water before him. "I asked for tape from the first-floor camera, but it had been turned off early in the day."

Lisa sighed. "So much for our state-of-the-art security system."

"The security system can only work if it is in use," Jet noted. "This one had been totally disengaged."

"Who would know how to do that?" Jonathan asked.

"Someone who worked for us or a professional who was around that kind of equipment all the time. It was computer based," Lisa explained.

"Did the investigator that came to see you this morning have any leads?" Jet asked.

"She's so certain that I did it that I doubt she'll look elsewhere," Lisa replied heavily.

"You should have called our attorney before speaking with her," Jet remarked.

"If I'd known she was coming, I would have thought of that. She caught me by surprise."

"I don't think she's convinced you did it. You are just the starting point. I'm sure she'll widen her scope," Jonathan explained.

"You seem to know her pretty well," Lisa accused him.

"Yes, I do," Jonathan responded quickly.

"Oh yes, I guess your class at the fire academy was pretty intimate," Lisa said and waited.

"I wouldn't say intimate, but we were close," Jonathan replied evenly.

"Excuse me. I'll go check on dinner," Jet said, standing. He sensed the couple needed to clear the air and he didn't want to hear the details.

"Lisa, please ask me what you want to know," Jonathan said as soon as the screen door slammed.

"Come on, Jonathan, don't play dumb. We've been through this before. I shouldn't have to ask you things you ought to tell me," Lisa said impatiently.

Jonathan moved to Lisa's chair and lifted her from it. Taking her seat, he placed her on his lap. "Okay, I'll tell you what I think you want to know. Janice and I dated a few years ago—I think it was five. Does that meet the statute of limitations?"

"For what?" Lisa asked, puzzled.

"For the number of years between dating someone and being their friend?" he replied. "Is it okay with you if Janice and I are friends?"

"Don't be silly. There was no statute of limitations for us. We went from dating to being friends in the same day," she said, punching him lightly on the arm. "If you don't make Janice feel the way you make me feel, you can be friends. Otherwise—"

"I assure you, nothing is there. I like where we are now," he said, wrapping his arms tightly around her.

"Yes, where are we?" she asked, looking up at him.

Cara stuck her head out the door. "Come on in, you two. That's enough love talk for the invalid. Dinner's ready."

Jonathan and Lisa walked into the kitchen hand in hand. "Oh, I forgot, while you were sleeping I went to the pharmacy to get your prescriptions filled. You need to take a pill before you eat." He took a couple of brown bottles out of the bag. Curiously, he folded the sack neatly with a square package still in it and stuck it in a drawer. Perhaps it was a special tea that he didn't want anyone to get into.

Everyone was already settled around the long pine-wood table by the time Lisa had taken her pill. Jonathan helped her into a chair and took a seat at the other end. The conversation quickly returned to the fire.

"We have space for the branch office in the Church Street building. But what about the other tenants?" Lisa asked. "We need to find space for all of them in one of our properties so we won't have trouble renewing their leases." She buttered a roll and realized how hungry she'd become. She must be getting better.

"I'm glad you've already begun planning. Bryce Johnson will arrive tomorrow to help with the relocation, but he'll definitely need your input," Jet replied, speaking of the company's president.

"I don't think she should go in tomorrow," Mary said quickly.

"She doesn't have to. Bryce will spend tomorrow familiarizing himself with the territory. He doesn't know much about this region because Lisa is a control freak and won't let us visit." Jet took a bite of cheesy scalloped potatoes while he waited for Lisa's comeback. To his surprise, she let his remark about her control issue pass.

"Will you be ready to go in by Tuesday?" Jonathan asked, wanting the decision to return to work to be Lisa's.

"Oh yes, I feel fine today. But I think I'll take tomorrow just to increase my stamina," Lisa proclaimed, taking another bite of a roll. "And yes, Jet, I am a control freak. You taught me everything I know in business."

"I think you should have another press conference so our clients will know we're not losing any ground," Mary suggested, ignoring the banter between the siblings.

"I don't think this is a good time for me to go before the media. They may ask me questions more difficult than the ones posed by the fire department's investigator. I'm not going out front to incriminate myself," Lisa said soberly.

"That's a good point. Do you think you're really considered a suspect?"

"I could be by tomorrow," Lisa said.

"Then you need to have your attorney with you any time you speak to the investigator," Jet said quickly.

"I think Janice—the investigator—was just gathering information," Jonathan said, hoping to alleviate Lisa's concern. "What about all of those people who were treated for smoke inhalation? Do you think you'll be sued?"

"I don't think our employees will sue," Cara replied.

"Why is that?" Jonathan asked.

"Because it will cost them in the end. They own part of the company through the employee stock option program," Lisa explained.

"People usually sue when they're angry," Louise added. "And all the people we visited were pleased that we had come to check on them while they were still in the hospital. They know we care about them."

"But the tenants and their employees will have no reservations about suing. We should be ready for lawsuits from them," Lisa warned.

"We are. Our liability is covered by insurance," Jet explained.

When dinner was over, Jonathan and Jet were on cleanup duty. Accustomed to working that detail, they developed a system. Jet made short work of the pots and pans the cooks had left while Jonathan loaded the dishwasher and wiped off the countertops. After the kitchen was clean, all the Stevenses except Lisa prepared to return to their hotel.

"I thought you were going to stay here, Mama,"

Lisa complained as her mother gave her a kiss on her cheek.

"I don't need to. I see you're in very good hands. We're going to leave for Miami very early in the morning and I don't want to disturb you," Mary explained, reaching up to hug her tall daughter.

"You all are welcome to stay. We have plenty of room," Jonathan said. Lisa noted that he said *we*, but didn't dare comment.

"It looks like you have things under control here," Cara said. "Jet is going to be in the city a few more days. But Louise and I have a board meeting tomorrow afternoon at the Liberty City Center."

"I know that project needs you," Lisa said, pulling herself together, "so I'll let you go." She gave each of them a hug and a kiss on a cheek.

Jonathan and Lisa stood out on the graveled drive until the limousines were out of sight. Back inside, Jonathan said, "You need to go back to bed. We're not going to stay up all night talking again. You'll never recuperate that way."

They walked upstairs arm in arm. Jonathan was feeling protective and put an arm around her to help her up the steps. At the top she was again breathing heavily.

They parted when she entered the master bedroom, which Jonathan had given up for her. After changing into a pajama bottom and a white T-shirt, he decided to go to Lisa's room to check on her.

Knocking on the door, he got no answer. He knocked again, thinking she might be back in the bathroom. Still no answer. He opened the door a crack and peeked inside. He saw that she was in bed. Entering the room, he inched closer. He was surprised to find that she was asleep already.

As quietly as he could, he brought a large overstuffed chair from the other side of the room to her bedside. With the lamp off, the moonlight flooding through the large windows filled the room with a surreal glow. For the first time since the fire had almost claimed her life, her beautiful face showed no signs of pain. Her heavy, long eyelashes lay against her high cheekbones and her full lips looked ripe and ready to be kissed. Something deep within him began to throb. Feeling guilty for wanting to make love to her in her weakened condition, he tried to push all such thoughts from his mind.

Had it been only Thursday night that he'd had the opportunity to make love to her and had let it slip away? He'd have to add that to his list of bad decisions. Who could have guessed what the next day would bring?

She turned and her hair fell across her face. He wanted desperately to move it back, but he wouldn't dare disturb her sleep. Tossing and turning as frequently as she was, her sleep was no longer peaceful. He wondered if he should wake her after all. He decided to stay and watch over her. Obviously, she was in some kind of distress.

When she awakened, Jonathan was sitting in the chair, watching her sleep. At first she was confused in the unfamiliar, dimly lit room. Seeing only the soft glow of his dark eyes, she remembered where she was.

"Are you all right?" he whispered.

"Yes," she answered, lying still, not quite ready to move.

"Were you having a nightmare?" he asked, leaning closer to look at her.

"Yes," she said, turning to her side and propping up on one elbow so that she could see him better.

"I dreamed that I was in the building again and you couldn't find me."

"Baby, you don't ever have to worry about that. There's no way I would have left that building without you," he said, rising from the chair and gathering her in his arms.

"What are you doing sitting in here?" she asked.

"I was just admiring a very gorgeous woman. You are absolutely beautiful in moonlight," he said softly.

"Thank you," she replied humbly.

"It's about time for another dose of medicine. I'll get water for you." He rose and lifted his arms above his head to loosen the kinks from sitting so long. Her eyes were drawn to his lean, well-sculpted midsection. She gazed at his long, muscular body until he caught her looking. The pure lust in her eyes stirred him, reigniting the desire he'd had such a difficult time extinguishing earlier. Embarrassed that he couldn't control his arousal, he left the room quickly.

He returned shortly with a fresh pitcher of ice water and poured it into the glass that was on the stand next to the bed. Sitting on the side of the bed, he held the drink to her lips. She put her hands over his to keep him from removing the glass, but her soft touch sent tremors of desire through him. He had to get away before he gave in to his baser instincts.

"Are you okay now?" he asked tenderly.

"No, I'm not okay. I'm afraid to go back to sleep. Will you stay with me?" she asked, still holding his hands.

"Yes, Lisa. I'll always take care of you," he promised.

She lifted the covers and he slid into bed next to her. Moving closer to her, he lay on his side and dropped his arm across her midsection. "Are you comfortable?" he asked.

Lying on her back, she turned to look at him briefly. "Yes, this mattress makes me feel like I could just sink into it. I guess that's why I slept so long earlier today. Are you glad to be back in your own bed?"

"With you in it, I certainly am," he said, rising on an elbow to look at her. He wondered what it would do to her breathing if he kissed her.

"I like your house, Jonathan. It's come a long way," she said, looking around the room. "Do you know I've never seen your bedroom?"

"Yes, I know. I was afraid to be in any room with a bed in it around you," he confessed, only half joking. Leaning toward her, he looked into her eyes and gently stroked her cheek as he drank in her beauty.

"You don't seem to be afraid tonight," she said softly, moved by his tenderness. Her heart was racing and she knew it wasn't from the medication. She wanted this man in the worst way. But tonight was not the night; she was still rather tired from her recent ordeal.

"Yes, I'm afraid—I'm very afraid," he said with a fake accent like a character in a horror movie. "I just hope you're too ill to take advantage of me."

"You're safe for now," she said, snuggling against him. "But watch out for the sunrise. That's when I gain my strength," she teased. The truth was, she didn't feel well enough for hanky-panky that night. For now it was enough to be held in his arms.

CHAPTER 10

The sun streaming through the nylon curtains woke Lisa early the next morning. She stretched and realized she was in bed alone. Forgetting her robe, she went looking for Jonathan. She had gone to sleep with the intention of making love to him the first thing that morning. Before he'd gotten out of bed, before he knew what had hit him. So much for her plans to jump his bones.

After checking the adjoining bathroom and the rooms upstairs, she dashed down the steps. She found him flipping pancakes at the stove. His back was to her and he was intent on his work. His white T-shirt highlighted the strength of his broad shoulders and back. With his jeans hanging low without a belt, she admired his slim waist and firm buttocks. He was all man and soon to be all hers.

"Good morning," she called out when she'd gotten an eyeful.

Jonathan greeted her, turning from the skillet. "Hey, baby, what are you doing down here? I was going to bring you breakfast in bed."

"I couldn't believe you left me in bed all alone,"

she said, pouting. Leaning on the doorjamb, she put one hand on her hip.

Jonathan turned around completely and looked at her. She wore a soft cotton nightgown that clearly revealed the outline of her slim dark body. Her breasts stood high with the nipples visible through the diaphanous fabric. He moved from drinking in the splendor of her soft curves to look into her dark, intense eyes. He saw the desire there and it was his undoing. At that moment he knew he'd do anything for her.

He turned to move the skillet from the hot eyes of the stove top. Opening a drawer, he took out the bag from the pharmacy he'd hidden from view the night before. With his back still to her, he lifted out the small box. Turning around, he clutched it in his hand. "Lisa, are you ready to make love to me?"

She was surprised by the slight catch in his voice. "You know I am."

He tossed the box to her and she caught it with sure hands. She looked at it and a slow smile spread across her face. "You got the economy box. How long do you think it'll take us to use all of these?"

"Wanna find out?" he asked, giving her a leering smile.

She didn't respond. He was different today—confident, alive, sexy. Yet he was still the most handsome man she'd ever seen. Wanting him more than ever, she held out her arms and he walked to her. Pulling her to his chest, he bent his head to kiss her soft, ripe lips. They were so sweet. One hand was buried deeply into her soft hair, the other gently stroked her back.

His hard manhood pressed against her stomach, driving her to try to make her pelvis level with his. She stood on her toes, straining to get closer. Realizing her need, he lifted her up. She wrapped her arms around his neck and her legs around his waist. Her gown rose up, exposing her round, brown thighs.

"Lisa, how do you feel this morning?" he asked, his hoarse voice deeper. Although he thought he'd go crazy if he couldn't have her right away, he was willing to restrain himself if she needed him to do so.

"I'll feel a lot better after you make love to me," she said into his ear.

That was the green light he needed. Even her warm breath in his ear aroused him. "I'm thinking we could spend the day together—in bed."

"That's right. I need bed rest," she said, exploring his ear with her tongue. A tremor ran through him so strong that he almost dropped to his knees.

"Am I too heavy for you?" she asked.

"No, but I've got to have you now. Forget the bed. I want to make love to you right now," he repeated, to be sure she understood as he lowered her to the long pine table.

He looked at her lovingly, worshipfully. Glorying in his lustful gaze, she pulled her gown over her head and let him have his fill. He moved back to her, wrapping her in his arms and letting his tongue tease her mouth. When his hand found her hard nipple, heat surged through her body like hot lava.

She threw her head back and his lips moved to her neck, tasting her salty skin. If he didn't make love to her soon, she thought she'd implode. He stepped back, assessing her health again. His concern for her was the only thing that slowed him. Breathlessly she held his gaze, breaking it only when he bent his head to plant a hard, demanding kiss on her lips. It was as if he wanted to possess her from the inside out.

She let her tongue play around with his, savoring his taste. She nibbled gently on his lower lip.

What did she have to do that for? He lost all self-control. He kissed her again, a kiss born of his desperate pent-up need for her. The kiss intensified as wave after wave of passion swept over him. Just when she thought she couldn't take any more, he knelt before her and suckled at her breasts, first one, and then the other. He licked between them, his tongue trailing down to her navel. She'd never known her navel to be an erogenous zone. But his tongue licking around and across it was deeply sensual. She was quivering and wiggling so much, she wondered if she could have an orgasm from that stimulation.

Jonathan stood up again and pulled her to the edge of the table. She quickly reached for the box next to her and broke into a small foil packet. He looked at her with passion-filled eyes as she took out the contents and smoothed it over his turgid manhood. When she was finished he carefully put his hands beneath her hips, raising her to meet him. As he entered her, she wrapped her long legs around his waist. She bit her bottom lip to keep from yelling. The pleasure was so intense as he found his way to her center. The heat built within her with such power that she thought she would surely pass out. On the verge of losing control, he waited for a moment before movement began again. The last thing in the world he wanted to do was to leave her wanting.

The heat between them grew as he moved in and out rhythmically. She found his rhythm and rocked with him. Heat surrounded them, building like the hot air before a tornado. She felt it escalating in the pit of her stomach and spiraling outward. Then she erupted with such force that her writhing and rolling would have thrown her from the table if he hadn't had a firm grip on her buttocks. As his passion unleashed and roared through him, he released a loud cry of joy.

Lisa and Jonathan were surprised by the force of their first union. They looked at one another in awe. "Did you feel that?" he asked, looking into her flushed face.

"Yes, do you mean you felt it too?" Her voice was filled with wonder. She still clung to him. The sporadic tremors rippling through her were like electrical undercurrents after an electrical storm.

"I sure did. That was incredible. Do you want to do it again?" he asked with a boyish enthusiasm. He gathered her in his arms.

"Yes, in the bedroom. Wait a sec," she exclaimed as he lifted her from the table. She grabbed their treasure chest to take to the bedroom with them.

After Jonathan placed Lisa in the center of the bed, he stood back and admired her nakedness. Shamelessly she let him. When he would have lain next to her, she opened her legs to invite him to lie between them. He positioned himself, rising on his elbows so that he could see her face clearly.

She remained silent as he studied her. Moving his gaze from her face, he palmed her breasts. Putting them together, he buried his face in them, inhaling her fragrance. Backing away, he looked at her soft, round breasts and raspberry-brown nipples that stared back at him. They still protruded from being sucked so vigorously moments before.

"These sure are some pretty girls," he said into her breasts. "Would you like me to lick them for you?"

"If you do that, you can't stop there," she answered, putting her hands lightly on his shoulders. He licked around one nipple several times before he popped it into his mouth. She moaned with pleasure. Being careful not to put his weight on her, he settled there for several moments, enjoying the feel of the tender bud against his tongue.

Reveling in the intense pleasure assaulting every pore in her body, she closed her eyes and lay perfectly still. She didn't want to prod him to hurry, nor did she want to slow him. The moment was perfect and she focused on enjoying it.

Rising over her, he stroked a nipple with his thumb while he admired the rest of her body. It was so perfectly chiseled that it could have been carved from a piece of brown marble.

Watching his careful appraisal, Lisa felt pride in a body that she usually critiqued harshly. As an athlete, she knew her body performed well for her, but she'd never felt particularly feminine. Not until she saw herself reflected in his eyes.

Kneeling over her, he stroked the curved outline of her body and caressed her hard abdomen and soft belly before allowing his fingers to trace a pattern around her navel. Bending down, he touched his tongue to her navel and noted her fiery response.

His fingers trailed down to the coarse hair between her legs. He stroked the soft mound tenderly, enjoying the rich texture of the natural hair there. She moaned and sighed, her senses under assault from his careful ministrations.

"What's wrong, baby?" he asked, lifting his head to look at her.

"That feels so good," she moaned.

"How does this feel?" he asked, inserting a finger inside her. He became further aroused by the hot, slick interior that folded around his finger. With the heel of his hand gently pressing against her mound, he moved his long, thick finger in and out of her.

She didn't answer but gyrated against his hand. Awash in the sensations flowing through her, she closed her eyes in abandonment. When her movements became jerky, he knew she was right on the precipice. Taking another packet from the box, he sheathed himself before moving over her again. As he sank into her hot tightness, he kissed her deeply, slowing to enjoy her soft lips, the texture of her tongue, and the warmth of her body against his.

She jerked with spasms as he buried himself deeper and deeper into her warm, welcoming chamber. Their lovemaking was slow and exquisite. Waves of heat flowed through her and over her. Every time she thought she couldn't take any more, he stopped and changed the rhythm. Their passion heightened until there was no turning back. The intensity of their release rocked the bed and left them panting. He collapsed, allowing himself to sprawl across her. Unable to speak or move, he remained motionless for several moments. Slowly he removed himself from her body and rolled over to lie next to her.

Jonathan looked at Lisa anxiously when his ability to think returned. "Are you okay?" he asked.

"I'll never be the same again." She laughed. Lying on her side, she reached out to stroke his cheek. "Jonathan, my inability to breathe has nothing to do with asthma. You were pretty out of breath yourself."

"I know. That's why I was worried about you," he conceded. "I figured if it was that bad for me, it could have been worse for you."

"Was it bad?" she teased, pretending to be hurt.

"No, it was very good, but it was breathtaking. How are you?" he asked, laying a hand on her chest.

"I told you before, my asthma is not exercise- or stress-induced. This is just what the doctor ordered," she said, closing her eyes tiredly.

"I must have missed that prescription," he said, rolling to his back and looking up at the ceiling. His body was hot and he needed to look away from her to cool off.

In a few minutes, he heard Lisa's steady breathing. Knowing that she'd fallen asleep, he relaxed and fell asleep too.

When Lisa awakened, she felt refreshed—renewed. She stretched and went to take a shower, expecting to find Jonathan awake when she returned. Surprisingly he slept through the shower and even as she dressed.

Poor baby, she thought, he should have been nursed after the fire too. Instead, his only concern had been for her. He'd never gotten the care that he needed. She marveled at the remarkable stamina and willpower that had kept him going over the past few days.

After she dressed, she headed downstairs. Her appetite had returned with a vengeance. Opening the refrigerator, she found the ham from Sunday's dinner. Her mouth watered just thinking about it. To be honest, Louise cooked a better ham than anyone in the family.

Lisa set the ham out on the counter and sliced up a platterful. Intent on making a couple of sandwiches, she was digging through the refrigerator when she felt Jonathan press against her upturned hips. She straightened and turned around with a jar of mayonnaise in one hand and a tomato in the other.

"Are you trying to tell me you're ready for more?" she said with a challenge in her voice.

"No, not at all," he said, backing away with his arms

up in surrender. "I just couldn't resist trying, though. Your hips were the first things I saw when I walked into the room."

She walked over to the counter and sliced the tomatoes into a dish. "Would you like one of my HLTs?" she asked.

"What is an HLT?" He took a seat on a stool on the opposite side of the counter.

"That's an HLT," she said, setting a sandwich on a small plate before him.

"Oh, this ham, lettuce, tomato," he said, chuckling before taking a big bite from the sandwich. After putting it down and chewing for a moment, he asked, "What would you like to drink?"

"I'll have lemonade. Don't we have some left from last night?" she asked.

"I'll check," he replied, rising from the stool. Going to the cabinet, he took down two tall glasses and filled them with lemonade before setting them on the counter next to their sandwiches.

"Thanks, Jonathan," Lisa said, taking the stool next to his at the counter.

"Are you sure you're ready to go back to work?" he asked, his face full of concern.

"Jonathan, come on, think about it. I just spent the day making love to you. My job is a lot less strenuous than that," she said with laughter in her voice.

"You've come a long way fast," he commented, standing to make another sandwich.

"In what way?" She set her half-eaten sandwich on the plate to listen to him.

"I'm referring to your health, Lisa," Jonathan said, noting the mischief in her eyes. "What other way could I have meant it?"

"Our relationship perhaps," she said bluntly. "After

Thursday night when you asked me to wait, I wondered how long you had in mind."

He looked at her and, knowing she really wanted an answer, he gave careful consideration to what he was about to say. "Subconsciously I made up reasons to keep us apart. If you had accused me of doing that, I would have disagreed with you. But after I told you about my past I felt totally free to let my guard down. I don't have to hold anything back. I couldn't make love to you one day and have you look at me with disgust the next. I didn't know how you'd feel about me if you knew my background—that I'd served time."

"Jonathan, my feelings for you could never change," Lisa assured him, jumping from her stool to stand between his long legs as he sat on the stool.

"I just didn't know. Your world is so different from mine. I bet you don't know anyone who has served time," he challenged her.

"I don't. But who knows? Maybe the people who have just don't want to share that information with me," she said, shrugging.

"Maybe not," he agreed, pulling her closer.

"Everyone has something in their past they don't want everyone to know," she suggested thoughtfully.

"I can't believe you do, Ms. Stevens. Your world is so clean—so—so—aboveboard. What secrets are you keeping?" he teased.

She shrugged after thinking for a moment. "I can't think of anything right now. Maybe it would be my insecurities," she finally admitted.

"You, insecure? The woman who has everything?" he asked with exaggerated disbelief.

"Why is that so hard to believe? I worry—that I'm not pretty enough—that I'm not feminine enough.

Louise nearly blew a gasket when I was in college and still hadn't changed. She said I was supposed to get a husband while I was in college. Every time I was home for any length of time, she made appointments for us to get manicures because I always had grease under my nails," she said, leaning against his leg.

"You were a mechanical engineer major. You were *supposed* to have grease under your nails. That doesn't make you any less feminine. Today should have gotten rid of any lingering insecurities. I'll call Louise and tell her you're all woman," he quipped.

"I knew there was a reason I love you so much," she said, wrapping her arms around his waist and resting her head on his shoulder.

He held her tightly in his arms before letting her go. "Do you want to finish eating?" he asked hoarsely. "Or would you rather do something else?"

"Let's take this upstairs," she said happily, eager to follow him. He carried the pitcher of lemonade and platter of ham. She grabbed the mayonnaise, tomatoes, and a loaf of bread.

In between making love, they fortified themselves with the repast. They knew that their interlude would be over soon, with the intrusion of their problems rushing in on them. But for that night, with the moonlight streaming through the window, everything was perfect.

The next morning, Lisa awakened to a ringing phone. Refusing to open her eyes, she listened as Jonathan talked. "Yes, she's fine. No, she's still asleep. Okay, ten o'clock. Sure, I'll tell her."

"What was that all about?" Lisa asked, still not bothering to open her eyes.

"That was Jet. Your security specialist is in town and he needs to talk with you. They need you at the Church Street building by ten o'clock," he reported.

Lisa sat up and stretched. "Well, it's back to work I go, hi-ho, hi-ho," she sang.

Jonathan watched her as she padded to the restroom in a terry cloth robe that hung open loosely. Her breasts bounced slightly as she moved around. The wonderful thing about Lisa was he had not found her inhibitions, if she had any. For the past twenty-four hours he'd had the pleasure of looking at her long, lithe body without any encumbrances.

When she returned, she asked, "Can you take me home? I don't have anything to wear to work."

"Sure, I'll be ready in a sec," Jonathan replied. He began dressing quickly. As casually as he could, he asked, "Is your security specialist Rodney Grimes?"

"Yes," she replied. The concern in his voice caused her to slow down and pay attention to the meaning beneath his words. "But there was never anything between Rodney and me."

He raised an eyebrow as if to imply she was lying. She quickly clarified, "Not like there is between you and me. He was never in love with me."

"I'm not concerned about how he feels about you. No man could be around you without feeling something. How do you feel about him?"

Lisa stepped to him and wrapped her arms around his waist. "Look at where I am right now," she said, standing on tiptoe to punctuate her words with a kiss in between each.

"He asked you to marry him. That's hard on a man. He wouldn't expose himself that way unless he thought he had a strong possibility of getting a *yes*,"

Jonathan insisted, wanting to purge himself of the old jealousies he'd kept hidden so long. "Your rejection must have been real hard on his ego."

"His proposal is a testament to the man's arrogance. He thought all he had to do was ask and I'd fall to my knees in gratitude," she explained, walking to lean against the solid wooden dresser.

"Why did he think you'd be grateful?" he asked, standing where she'd left him.

"Because he doesn't know me well. Women chased him for years and he couldn't believe I'd be any different. He never took the time to know *me*," she said, pointing at her chest. "The only reason he proposed was that he thought I'd be able to help him build his business," she said.

"I can't believe that's the only reason he wanted to marry you," he said, still clearly skeptical. He went to where she stood and placed both hands on her shoulders.

"And I wouldn't mess with his bank balance," she said, looking Jonathan straight in the eye. "Because I have my own money."

Jonathan gave her a wry smile and put a finger under her chin, lifting her eyes to his. "I want to go on record saying that if he makes a move on you, I'll come down there and give him the worst beat-down of his life."

"So noted. But it's not going to come to that. I'm telling you the truth when I say Rodney was always a good friend, nothing more," she declared.

He dropped his head to kiss her and said, "That's what worries me. I know what happens between you and your good friends. I don't see how any man can be around you without romantic, lustful, and lewd thoughts."

"I'm glad you feel that way," she said, giggling. She moved away from him to finish dressing.

When Lisa entered her new office in the Church Street building, she was pleased to see Kita had already made herself at home. The assistant rose from behind her newly acquired desk to welcome her boss. "Oh, I'm so glad to see you. How are you?"

"I'm just great. How about you?" Lisa said, giving Kita a big hug.

"I'm okay. Lisa, I'm so sorry we left without you. I had no idea you were still there. I thought maybe you'd run an errand on one of the lower floors. I'm so sorry," Kita repeated. The young woman's face was full of sincere regret.

"You had no way of knowing I was holed up in the restroom. But I'm okay now. I'm thankful we had no fatalities," Lisa said, trying to remove the attention from herself. She didn't want to discuss her frailties. "I didn't think you'd be here today. Employees aren't due to return until tomorrow."

"I wanted to be sure things were ready for you when you returned. I'm having our files copied to new paper because they absorbed so much smoke. We don't want to trigger your asthma again. Also, we've ordered new reference books to replace the ones with smoke damage," Kita explained.

"Save all those receipts. We'll turn them over to the insurance company," Lisa requested.

"I sure will. Here are your messages. Your brother and Mr. Johnson want to meet with you. They asked me to call as soon as you arrive. Are you ready?" Kita asked.

"Yes, let's get this ball rolling," Lisa said, putting on her game face.

Ten minutes later she was reading her mail when Bryce Johnson and Jet arrived.

"We must be in pretty bad shape if both my CEO and my president have to work my territory. What did you find out about me while I was out yesterday?" she inquired.

"That you work too hard. The first thing we'll do is change your organizational structure. You'll never make it if we don't—" Jet began.

"What do you mean by that? Do you think I can't handle my job?" Lisa interrupted, rising to her feet. "Hold on a minute," Jet said. "Let's settle down; maybe we jumped into this too quickly, but we thought you'd be relieved." He knew his sister well and should have realized she'd be defensive. She'd spent most of her life proving herself, even to her father and him. No one would ever say she had a job because of nepotism.

"I should be relieved that you're reducing my responsibilities?" Lisa asked, putting a hand on her hip.

"Yes," Jet answered. "Rebuilding after this fire and the already scheduled renovations will keep you busier than ever."

"Where were you when I had to deal with a fire last year?" she challenged. "I managed to survive that and open up several new buildings too."

"That's just it," Bryce interjected. "Your territory has grown tremendously in five years. You have more direct reports than any one manager should have."

"Is this because of the fire?" Lisa asked suspiciously. "Regardless of how we're structured, it would not have prevented that fire."

"This is a positive reflection of your ability," Jet explained hastily.

"I sure hope you're not discriminating against me because I'm a woman," Lisa threatened, returning to her seat but not relaxing. She made direct eye contact with each of the men without smiling.

"Stop being defensive and listen," Jet responded patiently. Of course, he should have asked Lisa for her input before now. Always needing to be in control, she hated to be told what she was going to do.

"We looked at how the region has grown since you've been here. It's seriously in need of restructuring so that you can pay attention to the big picture. We'd like to see you focus on acquiring existing properties and new developments," Bryce explained.

"With your degree in mechanical engineering, your talents are best used on new projects. We want you to continue in this area," Jet added.

When they'd finished their proposal, Lisa said, "So you're not going to take any of my properties?"

"No, we just want to free you up to do what you do best," Bryce replied.

"Your new title will be regional vice president. You'll have three regional managers under you. The property managers will be divided into three groups reporting to one of those managers. Is that all right?" Jet asked, leaning back in his chair and taking an audible breath.

"What is all that huffing about? You know I'm not that difficult to deal with," Lisa said, chastising Jet. She looked more relaxed now, but still sat on the edge of her seat as if she might leap from it at any moment.

"No, you're not. You're just as easy as eating peas with a knife," Jet returned. "It's going to be up to you to choose your managers. Do you have anyone in mind?" Now was their opportunity to get out from under the gun. The ball was back in her court.

"Bruce from Brentwood, of course. He's a stickler

for details and makes his decisions based on what's best for the company," she replied immediately.

"Anyone else?" Jet prodded. "Name them now. We thought we'd bring them in right away to free you up for the rebuilding of your headquarters."

"Let me think about it. It may not be one of my property managers. I have a few people in other positions I may want to move up," Lisa said, resting her head on the back of her high-back executive chair.

"I thought you would have chosen Jennifer," Bryce remarked.

"Jennifer? You mean the Jennifer who manages this building?" Lisa asked, surprised.

"Yes, she's been very helpful while you were out," Bryce stated.

"How could she be helpful? That woman is barely doing her own job. Right now she's on probation because of her inability to perform up to standard. Didn't you see my files?" Lisa asked, wondering how they could miss the woman's apparent ineptitude.

"She came in Saturday to help employees from headquarters get set up. And she has a wealth of information on various procedures. In fact, she even showed us how to network the computers to the finance department at corporate. Without her we would not have been able to get a link to import payroll information from each of your property managers," Jet expounded.

"She's obviously been hiding her talent under a bushel because I had no idea that she had any abilities, not to mention technical skills," Lisa said dryly.

"She has hidden talents all right," Bryce said, not picking up on her sarcasm, though her brother did.

Jet tried to convince Lisa. "We brought someone from information technology in, but Jennifer ended up helping him."

"Let's get back to my new management team later," Lisa said, rising from her seat to look out the window. "Could you give me an update on the Broadway building?"

"The first floor has been gutted. The other floors only need to be treated for smoke damage and we'll make the scheduled renovations in the process. Of course, we'll have to replace all carpets and drapes," Bryce reported.

"I need to go over there to see what's going on," Lisa decided.

"No, I don't think that's a good idea. Believe it or not, after all that's been done, smoke is still lingering in the air. We'll take care of that building for you," Jet advised.

To his amazement, his sister didn't argue. She must have been frightened by her near miss.

Jet's thoughts were interrupted by Kita, who announced Rodney's arrival. "Take him to the conference room," Lisa responded. "We'll be there shortly."

She gathered a legal tablet and led the men to the conference room. "Hello, Lisa, are you doing any better?" Rodney asked, rising from his seat and taking both her hands into his and looking her over carefully.

"Yes, I'm one hundred percent," she replied cheerfully, returning his smile.

"You don't look like you've been ill at all. You're actually glowing. What's new in your life?" he asked.

She let go of his hand and moved to the head of the table. "Let's have a seat," she said to Jet and Bryce, who had followed her into the room.

"Good morning, Rodney," Jet said, reaching across the table for Rodney's hand after they were seated.

Bryce's greeting followed and the four executives were totally engrossed in business within moments.

Just after twelve o'clock Jet glanced at his watch. "The morning has flown and I'm starving. Could we continue this over lunch?" He stood and stretched, waiting for the others to answer.

"Dang, Jet, can't you focus for another hour without eating?" Lisa complained. "We're almost finished."

"I'm with brother man," Rodney said. "Is it your treat?"

"Sure it is, if you let me order for you. When I pay you buy the most expensive food on the menu," Jet said, ribbing his old friend.

Bryce stood with the men and they moved toward the door. "Lisa, aren't you coming?" he asked when he noticed Lisa hadn't budged from her seat.

"Yes, I guess I have to. Give me a couple of minutes to make a phone call. I'll meet you out at the parking lot in a few."

As she dashed to her office, Kita passed her a handful of messages. Lisa flipped through the pink notes until she found the one for Jonathan. Good, he was at home. She dropped into her plush leather chair and quickly dialed his number. After their concentrated time together over the past few days, her thoughts had drifted to him continually all morning.

"How is your first day without your patient?" she asked, leaning back in her chair and spinning around.

"Lonely," he complained, holding the phone with his shoulder while he wiped grease from his hands.

"What are you doing today?" she asked, playing with the cord.

"Nothing much. I'm working on the pewter car

today. But I think my smoke inhalation problem is catching up to me. I think I need someone to come nurse me back to health." He faked a couple of coughs.

"I'll be there as soon as I can," she promised. "We're going to meet over lunch. After that I'll cut out. Do you want me to bring anything?" She spun her chair around to face the window.

"Just your long, gorgeous legs. I can't wait to have them wrapped around me," he teased.

"Jonathan, I'm in the office. Please don't tease me like this," she whispered with longing in her voice.

"I can't think about anything else," he said. "I can't wait until you get home. I love you so much."

"I love you too. I've got to go. The others are waiting to go to lunch," she said, eyeing her watch.

When she turned around, she was surprised to see Rodney waiting for her. "I volunteered to escort you to the limousine. It's not on the parking lot. Matt's pulled it out front."

"Thank you," she said, wondering how much of her conversation Rodney had heard. She didn't have to wonder for long.

Rodney said, "You didn't waste any time hooking up with him after you left me, did you?"

"You know efficiency is my middle name. I try not to waste time on anything I do," Lisa quipped, not believing Rodney would dare pretend he was hurt. There was no way he'd ever had any deep feelings for her.

"You don't have to be flippant about it. In fact, I thought maybe you'd be sorry that you'd broken my heart by now," Rodney said, trying to match her light tone.

"I'm not sorry and neither are you. Why are you

putting on this act?" Lisa asked, continuing to walk down the long corridor.

"This is no act, Lisa. I see why you never gave our relationship a chance. It was always about that fireman, wasn't it?" Rodney accused her.

"The fireman has a name. His name is Jonathan," she said, turning to look Rodney in the eyes.

"So it's like that, is it?" He stuck his hands in his pockets.

"Yes," she said and couldn't contain her big smile. "Let's go before Jet and Bryce come looking for us." She walked past Rodney and out the door.

"Damn, you never smiled like that around me," Rodney said, trying to match her long-legged stride. As they approached the waiting limousine, Jet looked at them thoughtfully.

They worked through lunch and returned to the conference room. By the end of the day, a security plan had been established for all the Sand Castles properties in middle Tennessee. The team worked without debate until Jet insisted on assigning a bodyguard to Lisa. She rejected his suggestion, advice, or whatever he wanted to call it. She totally refused to see his point of view.

To her relief, Rodney agreed with her. He offered to have one of his workers go to her house and to Jonathan's to evaluate their security systems. Based on what they had in place, they would enhance it in light of their present situation. "After all, someone has torched two of your buildings. You could be in danger," Rodney warned.

"Okay, we'll enhance our current alarm systems. That's all," she agreed.

As they were leaving, Lisa felt that the day had been productive. She was meticulously putting away her notes when Jet joined her at the back of the conference room.

"Are you having any doubts about rejecting Rodney?" he asked.

"No, big brother," she replied quietly. She didn't care for the others to hear them.

However, Rodney sidled up to them as if he belonged and injected his thoughts into their conversation. "She would be marrying me right now if you'd given us any encouragement." He took Lisa's trench coat from her hands and helped her into it.

"No, I wouldn't," Lisa said firmly. "My career is enough for me. This is what I've always wanted." She turned off the conference room lights and they headed out of the building.

"I can vouch for that," Jet said. "When she was a little girl, she never played dolls with the other girls. When our female cousins came over and wanted to play house, she told them she'd build a house for them."

It had grown cooler outside since lunchtime. Streetlights illuminated the parking lot where they stood near Lisa's pickup truck. Bright orange and gold leaves shimmered briefly in the light as they drifted to the ground.

"I could make her change her mind," Rodney insisted.

"Rodney, we have a lot of business ahead of us. I'm sorry if I hurt you. Can we be friends again?" Lisa's patience was growing thin with his same old song. She knew she didn't matter to him, but she had wounded his pride and wanted to help him save face.

When Rodney didn't answer, Jet asked, "Do you have plans for dinner? I'm a bachelor this week and I thought I'd stop for a bite on my way to the hotel."

"Well—uh—yeah," he stammered.

"What are you going to do? Surely you don't know anyone in Nashville," Lisa asked with exaggerated concern in her voice. She knew Rodney had met some woman. He'd done that even when they were dating.

"I—um—met this honey on the plane," Rodney explained, kicking at the fallen leaves.

"What were you going to do if I wanted to spend the evening with you?" Lisa asked.

"Cancel her, of course. She's not a class act like you, Ms. Stevens," Rodney said sweetly.

"Tell me anything," Lisa joked.

"That's why I told you to leave my little sister alone. You're a womanizer and can't help yourself," Jet reminded Rodney.

"I would have been good to her. I *was* good to you, wasn't I, Lisa?" Rodney pled his defense.

"Yes, Rodney, you are a very good *friend*." Lisa patted his arm and climbed into the truck.

CHAPTER 11

While Lisa had spent her day with Jet, Bryce, and Rodney, Jonathan had spent his making plans to sell his Corvette. Wanting Alan Mueller's friend, Dr. Frederick Freeman, to see the car in the best light possible, Jonathan had spent the morning revamping the barn. Rigging together two ramps and a steel platform, he set up a stage in the center of the cavernous space. After a quick trip to the hardware store, he returned to hang spotlights from the fluorescent tubes in the ceiling.

All in all, the staging made the car look spectacular. Alan Mueller and Dr. Freeman arrived at the barn promptly at two o'clock that day. When the two men walked into the room, the little red Corvette was center stage with two spotlights shining on it.

"Wow! This is sweet. This is your nicest work yet and I like it," Mr. Mueller exclaimed. Dr. Freeman made no comment, but he couldn't keep his eyes off the car.

"How much are you asking?" Dr. Freeman asked after walking around the stage twice.

"Eighty thousand dollars?" Jonathan asked, not

certain if he was too high. Mr. Mueller had told him
to expect Dr. Freeman to haggle over the price.

"Is that all?" Mr. Mueller said. "You know how
long I've wanted that car. I'll give you eighty-five."

"You've been talking about it for ages and haven't
been able to get it yet," Dr. Freeman argued. "The
car would still be off-limits if I hadn't made an offer.
I'll give you ninety thousand."

"Ninety-five," Alan said quickly.

"One hundred ten," Dr. Freeman countered.

The two men continued to battle for the little
red Corvette and Jonathan didn't open his mouth.
He couldn't believe what was happening.

"One hundred fifty thousand!" Dr. Freeman
shouted, hoping to shut Alan up once and for all.

"That's too rich for my blood. I've got to let her
go," Mr. Mueller said sadly.

"May I write a personal check?" Dr. Freeman
asked, about to pop with pride. Not only had he
gotten the car he wanted, but he'd bested Alan
Mueller, his poker buddy, in the process.

"Absolutely. I know you're an honest man. I'll
take this right up the street to your bank. Do you
have the funds on deposit now?" Jonathan asked.

"I most certainly do," Dr. Freeman replied, insulted.

"Great. I'll roll her off the platform for a test
drive," Jonathan offered, walking toward the car.

"That won't be necessary. I've ridden in the car you
refurbished for Alan. I know your work. Thanks," Dr.
Freeman said gleefully, taking the keys from
Jonathan's hand and jumping into the car.

"Be careful on the gravel road," Jonathan called
as the joyful middle-aged man sped away like a
teenager with a new driver's license.

"I didn't know you'd changed your mind about
buying the car," Jonathan said apologetically.

"I didn't." Alan Mueller smiled and popped his collar twice, to signify his status as a major player.

"Go on with your bad self." Jonathan grinned at his friend. "You know you're too fresh for an old man like me."

After Alan left, Lisa called to invite Jonathan to meet her and Jet for dinner. He readily agreed. Showered and shaved, Jonathan looked and smelled good when he joined the siblings, who were having drinks while they waited for him.

They had a relaxing conversation as they ate their meal. Jonathan again enjoyed the easy camaraderie between the brother and sister. He had never experienced anything like that with his family.

When dinner was over the conversation took a serious turn. Jonathan was surprised when Jet asked, "Have you thought about leaving public service?"

"No," Jonathan replied succinctly.

"If you come to work for Sand Castles, we could offer you a competitive salary, plus bonuses." Jet talked casually, but he'd thought about offering Jonathan a position in their facilities management department for several days.

"You would, no doubt, increase my pay," Jonathan said thoughtfully with his hands steepled before him. "But I don't believe you can top my current job satisfaction. I enjoy what I do for a living and am immensely gratified by my work."

"Jonathan is a firefighter, Jet. I didn't know you had any positions open for firefighters," Lisa said to her brother.

"We don't. But I believe Jonathan has an engineering degree. I could use a good man to head up our facilities management department." Jet looked from Lisa to Jonathan expectantly.

"You should have discussed this with me," Lisa scolded. "Are you trying to take Jonathan from me?"

"He wouldn't have to move to Miami," Jet said easily. "He could work out of the Nashville office."

"Look, we don't need to spend a lot of time painting this picture. It's all a moot point. I'm not interested in doing anything but what I do. Is that all right with you, Lisa?" He flashed his devastating smile at her as he took her hand in his and raised it to his lips. When he brushed her knuckles with a light kiss, heat flushed to the soles of her feet. She couldn't contain her smile.

Jet looked at them and relaxed. He didn't have to worry about his little sister anymore.

The following day, Janice McKee caught up with Jonathan at Engine Company 2. She'd heard that Jonathan would return to work that day. Not certain she'd get the information she wanted if his girlfriend was present, she'd come out to talk to him alone. This was all about business anyway.

"You look much better than the last time I saw you," she said as they sat across from each other at the kitchen table. "Have you recovered completely? You know you didn't have to return yet."

"I know, but I'm ready."

"Jonathan, I have to ask you some tough questions today. Please remember it's my job and I have to get at the truth. I know I owe you a lot. You always looked after me when we were at the academy. The other men tried to give me a rough time because I'm female. They thought I couldn't carry my weight and they were always testing me or playing gags. But you always had my back. I haven't forgotten." She looked at him so earnestly that he dreaded what would come next.

He nodded and joined her in a sentimental moment. "No, it wasn't that long ago, but we've both come a long way. You were such a star firefighter that you quickly moved into training and now you're a big-time arson investigator."

"I remember when you were wondering if you should take the lieutenant's exam, but when the captain's exam came up, you were full of confidence. You went at it without talking to anyone. Who would have thought you could become a captain in just five years?" Janice reminisced.

"Yeah, who would have thought?" Jonathan repeated as if he was just as amazed as anyone else by his good fortune. After he'd thought about it, a smile slowly swept across his face, transforming his stern features to lighthearted boyishness.

Janice wondered why she hadn't noticed how devastating his smile was when he'd shown interest in her. Back then he'd seemed too young to her and she'd brushed him off. Realizing she'd blown her chance, she pushed that thought aside and turned to business.

Seeing the change in her demeanor, he figuratively opened the door for her. "Now you're here to investigate me. What've you got?"

She graciously accepted the opening. "Jonathan, have you been looking for this?" She took the tennis bracelet from a small brown envelope that had been secured only with a brass clasp.

"Yes." He nodded, staring at the magnificent diamonds that managed to sparkle in spite of the dirt that still lined their settings.

"We wondered how it got out of a burning building to a pawnshop on Gallatin Road. Do you know?" Janice asked.

"Diamond is one of the hardest substances known to man," Jonathan replied. "It could easily survive a fire."

"You're being glib and you know this is serious. I'm not sure if I like the new, lighter Jonathan at all," she said, reprimanding him.

"Janice, you're being entirely too serious about this bracelet. It has nothing to do with your arson investigation," Jonathan argued, casually sprawling out in his chair with his long legs before him.

"Let's try again. This bracelet is all I have for now. The owner of a pawnshop on Gallatin Road called me to report that he suspected it was somehow connected to the big fire downtown. Someone attempted to clean it, but the soot is evident in all the crevices. The person who tried to pawn it was one of the EMTs on the ambulance that took you to the hospital. He took it out of the pocket of your turnout coat. My question is, how did it get into your pocket?" Jonathan noted the pen that lay relaxed between her fingers. Whatever he said would become a part of her official investigation.

"I found it in the janitor's closet. It was too valuable to leave there. I was going to turn it in, but I got distracted by saving a life," he said sardonically.

"Were you *really* going to turn it in?" Janice asked, looking at him closely. Before he could answer, she added, "Jonathan, I know about your incarceration. Please don't try to cover for someone else. Your record will be unsealed in a heartbeat and you'll be investigated as the guilty party. The best thing you can do to help is be honest," she said in a tone tinged with authority.

"I was cleared of all charges."

"Of course you were. And your previous conviction is not supposed to count against you, but we know it will. Those things have a way of getting out into the open. You'll look very suspicious," Janice warned.

"I frankly don't care how I look," Jonathan said evenly, glaring at Janice.

"But you do care how Lisa looks. Why are you trying to cover for her? Do you think she had something to hide?"

"What are you talking about?" he asked, keeping his eyes steadily on her face.

"This bracelet has to be Lisa Stevens's. What other woman in that building could wear a thirty-thousand-dollar bracelet to work? I've shown it to one or two people who work with her and they recognize it. She wore it to work the day of the fire," Janice reported.

"So, you're here to bait me. What kind of friend are you?" He said it with humor in his voice, but she knew he was serious.

"On this job I get that friendship thing every day. It doesn't work. I certainly don't expect it from you. You know better," Janice said firmly.

Taking a deep breath, Jonathan continued looking at her warily. "It's obvious to us that you suspect Lisa, so I wonder why you're here talking to me. Shouldn't you be having this conversation with her? Do you think I'll give her up to you?"

"The bracelet is not enough to prove she set the fire. Getting a big insurance check won't even prove it. But I knew you were hiding something when I interviewed you Sunday. My hunch has proved right so far," Janice said, relaxing in her seat and taking in the full length of the man before her.

"You're not making sense. There's no way Lisa set that fire. Why would she end up passed out, almost dead, if she'd set it?"

"Maybe because she was exposed to the smoke before anyone else and it got out of hand. Who knows but Ms. Stevens if she was trying to go up the stairs or come down the stairs? We don't know what she was burning yet, but you turned in the fibers from the ashes yourself. I'll have it all together once we get the report from the lab." Janice tossed out her allegations and watched to see what Jonathan would do with the information.

"It sounds like you've already made up your mind," he declared, returning her gaze with a scowl. The hard, angular planes of his face gave him a harsh, threatening look.

Janice was unmoved by his scowl. "Show me someone else with access and motive."

Jonathan's face softened a little. "If our friendship means anything to you, do me one favor."

"Your friendship means a lot to me. If I can do a *legal* favor for you, I will," Janice said, relenting.

"Try, just try, to find another suspect."

"At this point she's not a suspect, she's labeled a *person of interest*," Janice corrected.

"Okay, have you looked around to see if there is another *person of interest*?" Jonathan suggested.

"Now you're going to tell me how to run my investigation," Janice said, but her tone was much lighter.

"If you knew Lisa, you'd know that she's incapable of a crime this evil. There is nothing in the world that would make her put other people in harm's way like that. Please be open-minded," Jonathan pleaded.

"The pressure is on for us to solve this crime. The papers call every day, the mayor calls every hour, and the chief is on my back. I don't have a lot of choice," Janice said, preparing to leave.

"And one more thing," Jonathan said as she stood.

"What is that?" Janice asked, puzzled.

"Take good care of that bracelet. She's crazy about it."

"But she hasn't mentioned to you that she lost it and swears she was never in the janitor's closet." Janice put her file of notes into her briefcase.

"And I believe her."

Jonathan touched Janice with his sincerity. "I don't know her the way you do. I can't share your blind faith," she said. "But I will talk with her again."

Jonathan walked Janice to the front of the building and watched her drive away.

Jonathan decided it was now time to tell Lisa about the bracelet. He had to know why she hadn't mentioned losing it. As soon as Janice left, he called Lisa.

"Hey, babe," he said as soon as he heard her whiskey-toned voice on the other end of the line.

"Hey yourself. I was just about to call to let you know I'm working with Jet through dinner. I should be home by ten if you want to call me to say good night," she said suggestively. She was balanced on the edge of the credenza in her office.

"I wanted to be sure you don't have plans for early in the morning. May I stop by when I get off in the morning?" he asked, not wanting to get into why he needed to see her.

"Sure, you know you don't have to make an appointment with me," Lisa said, frowning and beginning to pace.

To lighten the tone of their conversation, he said, "And you don't have to stay up all night making rolls for me."

"Good. I didn't plan on it," she replied, the smile back in her voice.

When their call ended, Lisa couldn't quite put her finger on the energy that she picked up in his tone.

He seemed nervous; maybe it was anxiety. She wondered if something was wrong. Why had he felt like he needed to call to make a date with her? What could be so important?

Jonathan hadn't called her that night. She figured he'd gotten busy. Sometimes they were called to one alarm after another. It was hard to tell how busy he would be on any given night. That was the nature of emergencies. She had no way of knowing that Jonathan did not call because he had to prepare himself for their discussion.

The next morning, Jonathan left the fire hall in downtown Nashville and headed straight for Lisa's small bungalow just east of the Cumberland River. When she greeted him at the door, he almost changed his mind about having that serious conversation with her. She was wearing a short, pale pink kimono that hung open to reveal a lacy camisole that stopped just at the tip of her ribs, and matching boy shorts that began below her navel. Her exposed midsection set him on fire.

He accepted her quick kiss before spinning her away so that he could get a better view. "Girl, let me get a look at what you have on. What are you trying to do to me?"

"I'm trying to keep you interested, perhaps?" she replied, posing with one hand on her hip and the other in the air.

"You've met your goal. I'm very interested," Jonathan said, pulling her back into his arms and wrapping them around her inside the kimono. The soft skin of her torso set him to craving her. "You smell so good," he moaned.

"You could be smelling breakfast. I decided to cook for you, although you won't get the fire this time," she said, leading him through the dining room into the kitchen.

"No, it's definitely you," he said, inhaling the fragrance of her neck before nibbling it. His kisses went from the tender flesh just below her earlobe to her collarbone.

As his lips moved lower, she warned, "If you want to eat breakfast, you'd better stop now."

"I'm not hungry for breakfast," he growled. His lips singed her torrid flesh. He was heating her up big time and she liked it. She had no desire to ask him to stop and was almost frantic when he said, "Stay right here." He moved to the stove and turned off everything.

He returned to her and they stoked the flame between them again. The heat was so intense that she dropped the kimono from her shoulders and let it fall to the floor. That was all the invitation he needed. He grasped the soft flesh of her buttocks and rotated against her. She wrapped her arms around his shoulders and stroked the back of his neck as he bent over her, nibbling the tender flesh of her throat.

Without knowing how, she found herself under him on the living room sofa. He gripped the stretchy fabric of her camisole and lifted it over her head. Tossing it away from them without looking to see where it landed, he turned his attention immediately to removing the boy shorts. They followed the camisole.

Desperate to be close to him, she wrapped her legs around his waist. He melted into her warm embrace, planting random kisses over her body.

"Come here, sweetheart," Lisa said, lifting her head and propping up on her elbows.

He rose on his knees to look at her inquiringly. What could be so important that she'd stop him now? he wondered.

She answered his unasked question. "You have on entirely too many clothes." Leaning forward, she pulled his navy T-shirt over his head. Getting the idea, he unzipped his pants and took out a foil packet before he kicked them off at the same time he stepped out of his shoes.

Within seconds he'd returned to his spot between her legs. "Do you feel better now?" he asked, grinning at her and caressing her soft hips.

"I could feel better." She stroked a small bud on his chest with one hand and held on to his shoulder with the other. When his mouth closed around her ripened nipple, the heat that coursed through her almost melted her from the inside out.

"That feels so good," she whispered before surrendering completely to the waves of passion engulfing her. His entry was slow and tantalizing. Inch by inch he found his way as she folded around him, enticing him with her erotic movements. When she thought she could not stand his teasing a moment longer, he seated himself to the hilt and stayed. Trying to stall his impending release, he didn't move for several moments.

At last they surrendered to the scorching eruptions roiling from their point of contact and spreading throughout their bodies. Following the impulses building in his groin, Jonathan began a rhythm that Lisa instinctively matched. As they stoked the heat each found in the other, their passion erupted, leaving them limp and breathless.

They lay entwined for several moments. Feeling as winded as when he ran a marathon, Jonathan enjoyed the comfort of Lisa's arms around him. After several moments, he lifted his head from her shoulder. "Oh, baby, I'm sorry. Am I too heavy for you?" He searched her face to see if she was okay.

"It's too late to ask about that now. I think I've lost the use of this leg," she said, pointing to her left leg that she'd let fall from the sofa.

He jumped up immediately, pulling her up as he rose. "Let's go to bed and get under the covers."

"I need to find my clothes." Lisa began gathering her scattered things. She put on the kimono and tucked the lace shorts set under her arm for the short dash to her bedroom.

Jonathan raced her to the bed. Just as her knee hit the mattress, she saw the time. "I can't believe it's already seven-thirty. I've got to get to the office."

"What's going on that you can't call in sick?" he said, only half joking.

"I'm the boss, remember? I have no one to call in to. Do you want to stay here?" she asked, sitting on the bed next to him and stroking his arm.

"No, I'll leave when you leave. Don't you have time for breakfast?" he asked, hoping to get more time with her. He'd never talked to her about the bracelet. He had momentarily forgotten the purpose for his visit.

"Go ahead and eat. I'll join you as soon as I'm dressed." She jumped off the bed and headed toward the bathroom before he could respond. He thought about joining her there, but decided to stay put. Maybe they could talk while she dressed. He was running out of time to discuss her missing bracelet with her. It wouldn't be long before the opportunity was taken from him entirely.

When she came out of the shower, she was surprised that he was still sitting on her bed in the exact spot where she'd left him. As she walked to her closet to pull out a pair of jeans and a shirt, she asked, "Did you want to take a shower?"

"No, Lisa, I thought we'd talk while you dress," he

suggested, trying to sound casual. But his serious tone caught her attention.

"What's on your mind?" She laid the clothes on back of a big upholstered chair and moved to her desk to check her Blackberry calendar.

"Where is your diamond tennis bracelet? I haven't seen it since the fire," he said, deciding to plunge right in. He sat up on the bed, wearing only his navy uniform pants. He'd left his shoes and shirt on the living room floor.

"I don't know," she answered honestly. "I remember putting it on the day of the fire and I haven't seen it since." She scrolled the Blackberry to check her schedule for the day.

"Did you list it as a loss on your insurance claim?" he asked, putting his hands behind his head and resting his back on the headboard of her big bed.

"We haven't finished the claim yet. I wouldn't consider it a loss from the fire at any rate. I could have lost it when I took my jacket off in the office that morning. Or it could have fallen off on my way to work. I just can't imagine where it is." She tried to concentrate on the events of last Friday morning, but so much had happened since then, she could barely remember the details of the day.

"Do you have any idea who could have set the fire?" he asked, keeping his gaze on her.

His abrupt change of topic didn't fluster her at all. To him it was probably all related since she'd lost it on the day of the fire. "No, I don't. I truly wish I did." She shook her head to match the words.

"Janice McKee came to see me yesterday. She insists the fire had to have been started by the person who had the most to gain," he threw out, watching to see her reaction.

He had her complete attention now. She put the

Blackberry back in its base and rested her hands on her knees. "Would you try to protect me if you thought I was guilty?" she asked.

Her question caught him off guard. He looked at her for a long moment before answering, "Yes, Lisa. I would do anything in the world for you."

"But would you cover for me? Would you hide evidence or destroy evidence for me?" she persisted.

"Yes," he answered flatly without any embellishment. She had to know that he would. Didn't she know how much he loved her?

"You don't have to do that. I assure you, I'm not guilty," she said in her straightforward manner. "Can you tell me what Janice said when she asked to speak to you alone at the hospital?"

"She wanted to know if I'd told her everything," Jonathan admitted uncomfortably.

"Why would she think you were holding back? She's known you for a long time. Both of you made that clear. Is she accustomed to your withholding information during an investigation?" Lisa asked, not really looking at Jonathan anymore. She seemed to be focused on something outside the room.

"No," he answered, fascinated with her agile mind. She'd caught on too quickly for him. He anticipated her next question. "This one is different because I'm in love with the woman who owns the building. The one who can presumably gain from the insurance settlement."

"What does my bracelet have to do with your cover-up? If you know something, tell me so that I can appreciate your gallantry." Lisa waited for Jonathan's response.

"I found your bracelet in the janitor's closet on the first floor after the fire," he confessed.

She stared at him, stunned, her face distorted

with confusion. "What are you talking about?" was all she managed to ask.

"As soon as I saw it, I thought something had happened to you. It's so seldom that you go anywhere without it. I rushed up to your office and when you weren't there, I panicked. I went crazy trying to figure out where you'd be. My mind was completely on trying to find you. I forgot all about the bracelet until I turned in the evidence bag. I had to leave it in my turnout and hope no one would find it. When I went looking for it the next day, it was no longer in my pocket." He looked at her earnestly, hoping she would understand.

"What were you going to do with it?" she asked, becoming distraught with the implication of what he was saying.

"I knew it could be evidence." His discomfort was also increasing by the minute, but he was trying to be objective. He needed to lay everything out for her, to help her see things the way Janice or any other investigator would see them.

"Evidence?" she asked.

"Yes, it was clear that the fire was no accident," he replied without thinking. She glared at him so defiantly, he felt a need to defend himself. "Don't look at me like that."

She stood up, still glaring at him. All the color had drained from her face. "You really don't know me." She grabbed her clothes and headed back to the adjoining bathroom, slamming the door as he approached it.

"When I was thinking clearly again I knew you had nothing to do with it. But it was *your* bracelet," he said, standing outside the closed door to talk to her. He heard movement on the other side, but she didn't acknowledge his presence.

After a while he tried again. "I know it sounds as if I'm accusing you, but I'm not. I swear I'm not. It's just that when I saw your bracelet, I wondered how on earth it had ended up hidden away in a janitor's closet on the day of a catastrophic fire. How could it have gotten there if you had not worn it down there?"

"And if I had gone to that closet on the day in question, would that automatically make me guilty of arson?" she cried out, throwing the door open and walking out fully dressed.

"No, no, that's not it." He sat on the foot of the bed facing her as she put on her socks and work boots. She didn't respond. When she was finished, she picked up her cell phone and purse and rushed from the room. "Slow down. Let's talk," he pleaded, racing through the house behind her.

She reached the back door and with one hand on the knob, she turned to face him. "I don't need the man I love to doubt my integrity. I can take it from the public and from the investigators. I can even take it from the insurance company. I can take it from them because they don't know me intimately. You're supposed to know me, Jonathan. When we made love, we became one."

"Baby, please don't be so angry." His gaze drifted from her shiny hair that she'd pulled into a ponytail to her tear-filled eyes. His eyes settled on her beautiful plump lips that tempted him, begging for his kiss. He pulled her to him and held her in his arms, not daring to kiss her. She stood stiffly in his embrace, not responding in any way. He released her and stepped back, stunned.

"How do you want me to lock your doors?" He thought he had her there. She'd have to wait for him. Instead she pulled a key off her key ring and put it in his hand.

"I told you I'm running late." She didn't look at him as she walked away.

"Are you going to be okay driving?" he called to her back.

"I'm just fine," she said dully. She walked the short path from her house to the garage. Moments later her big truck rolled in reverse down the driveway and out into the street. She switched gears and pressed the accelerator, roaring around the corner. Jonathan watched from her doorway. He went back into the house to get his things and left immediately.

He had gone to her house with the intention of helping her. Leaving, he felt like he'd made everything a bigger mess.

CHAPTER 12

When Lisa walked into her office an hour later than her expected arrival time, Kita looked up to ask her what had happened to her. But one look at her boss told Kita to keep her mouth shut. She'd be better off left alone to cool off. Kita returned her attention to her computer screen and Lisa closed the door to her office.

On the other side of the door Lisa was so angry that she couldn't stay in her seat. She paced around trying to figure out where Jonathan got the nerve to accuse her of torching her own building. He was so sure she'd done it, he didn't even tell her about the bracelet. He'd decided to cover for her.

Kita had to make a quick decision. She was in a catch-22 situation. She knew that someone had riled Lisa's temper, but she also knew Lisa would be upset with her if she wasn't reminded about her meeting. So Kita took a chance and tapped on the door. "Lisa, your project manager just called. Is there a reason you're not answering your direct line?"

Lisa looked at her assistant with a clear *none of your business* expression on her face.

Kita decided to go for broke. "He's waiting on you at the Murfreesboro construction site. Are you still going out today or do you want me to cancel? We need to let him know something. I promised I'd call him back." Kita looked at Lisa expectantly.

"I'm going," Lisa replied with a sigh. She no longer had the desire to look at the building. She wanted to go home and tell Jonathan a few more things that were on her mind. "Duty calls," she muttered to herself as she grabbed her hard hat and a tube with blueprints in it.

As she was driving south on I-24, her cell phone rang. "Lisa, I hate to bother you again, but there's a Janice McKee on the line. She needs to see you today. When I told her you'd be out all day, she asked me 'out where?'" Kita's voice was full of attitude.

"Is she on the line now?" Lisa asked, pulling over to the right lane and slowing her usual above-the-speed-limit pace.

"I need to see you as soon as possible," Janice snapped, her voice full of urgency.

"I'm on my way to Murfreesboro," Lisa replied, hoping that was explanation enough to delay the meeting.

"I can come there to meet you," Janice offered.

"Has something new happened?" Lisa asked, trying to understand if meeting her today was really a necessity. She surely didn't feel like meeting anyone.

"Yes," Janice replied. "I could be there in about an hour. I'll be right behind you." *I'm trying to do you a favor by coming to you and you're telling me what time you can meet. If that's not a lot of nerve.*

"Would it be okay if we meet over lunch? I'll come back to the city by twelve and we could meet at the Midtown Café," Lisa suggested, picking up speed again.

That clinched it for Janice. "Okay, I'll see you at twelve." The Midtown was one of her favorite eating establishments and one she didn't visit frequently because it was so expensive.

Lisa finished her meeting with the project manager by 11:15 and headed back into Nashville. Janice's opinion of Lisa changed slightly when she arrived at the Midtown Café and the young executive was waiting for her. At least she had enough class not to keep her waiting. Apparently this was a regular spot for Lisa. The service staff knew her by name. As soon as Janice mentioned who she was to meet, the maitre d' led her to Lisa's booth.

"Order anything you like, this is on me," Lisa told the investigator, after Janice had settled in her seat and picked up the menu.

After Janice had placed her order, Lisa told the server that she'd have the usual.

When the server brought Janice's house salad, he also brought a large bowl of lemon artichoke soup for Lisa. Unconsciously, the women eased into an animated conversation as they began their meal.

"How do you like Nashville?" Janice asked to break the ice.

Lisa explained, "I've been here five years, but I've worked too hard to relax and enjoy myself. From what I know about Nashville, I like it."

"You can always move back to Miami," Janice ventured, taking a bite of the salad the server had just placed on the table.

"I could, but I like my independence. My family loves to tell me what to do and meddle in my business. It's bad enough from a distance, but I can't imagine what it would be like if I were there."

"You don't seem like you'd need a lot of help from your family. Why would they treat you that way?" Janice asked, taking another bite of her salad but eyeing Lisa's bowl. She wished she'd tried the artichoke soup. Unfortunately the name hadn't sounded as good as the soup looked and she hadn't ordered it.

"My family is pretty traditional. I have three brothers and they think they're supposed to take care of me. That's the way our father raised them. Unfortunately, I'm my mother's daughter. I don't have a submissive gene. When they're around, I have to constantly remind them that I can take care of myself. They should know better by now, but they don't. To prove that I'm just as tough as they are, I have beaten all of them racing, playing tennis, or swimming." Lisa paused to take another spoonful of the delicious soup.

"And that doesn't settle it for them?" Janice asked, looking at the woman she had assumed was a spoiled rich girl in a new light. Maybe there was more to her.

"No." Lisa laughed. "They always used the excuse that they let me win because I'm a girl and they didn't want me to strain too much." She rested her spoon on the saucer beneath her plate.

As soon as she set the spoon down, the bowl was whisked away and Lisa's entrée of veal piccata in a white wine sauce, fresh herbed angel-hair pasta, and baby peas was served.

"I would think Jonathan would be pretty protective of you too," Janice ventured. Waiting for a reply, she tasted her slow-roasted, apple-crusted salmon wrapped in apple-smoked bacon. It was so good that she followed it with a bite of the creamed savoy cabbage and was instantly transported to tastebud heaven.

Lisa pondered Janice's question, giving it serious consideration. "Jonathan is different from my brothers. He doesn't automatically assume that because I'm a woman I'm not as capable as he is. He recognizes my strength, but he also helps me when necessary. We all need help sometimes, even men. Don't you think?" she asked Janice.

"Yes, you're right about Jonathan. When we were new recruits at the fire department's training academy, he didn't rush over to do things for me, but he was there to help out where needed. The other men in our class stood back and hoped I'd fail. As if my failure would add to their success. But Jonathan wasn't like that. He always tried to make things a little easier for everyone, even me. We had one drill where we had to lift a one-hundred-pound bag of grain and carry it down a ladder over one shoulder. Well, I could lift the bag, but I couldn't get it positioned properly and it would throw me off balance. The men would laugh each time I fell. Jonathan would laugh too, but then he'd come over to help me get the weight balanced on my shoulder. He got me to the point where I could laugh at myself and I was less angry with my classmates. After I got to that point, the rest of the training was a breeze."

"Jonathan told me you dated for a while. Why did you stop?" Lisa asked, inquisitive and blunt as usual.

"What did Jonathan tell you?" Janice asked, looking across the delicate purple iris that sat on the table between them.

"That he'd liked you a lot and suddenly you started finding excuses not to go out with him anymore," Lisa said. "He never knew why you stopped seeing him."

"And now you want to know if I'm going to try to

make a play for him since he's with someone else?" Janice asked, resuming her consumption of the delicious meal before her.

"No, not really. If he wanted to be with you there's nothing I could do to stop him. To be honest I sensed some hostility in you the first time we met and again when we spoke on the phone this morning. Since I don't know you, I thought maybe you were resentful of my relationship with Jonathan. And that scares the heck out of me because you hold my life in your hands." Lisa was glad to finally be able to say what was uppermost on her mind. Waiting for Janice's reply, she continued eating.

Lisa had spoken in such a matter-of-fact manner that Janice took a moment to decide if she should be insulted. Deciding that Lisa was simply being true to her nature, she answered in like manner.

"I don't like the implication that I would let a personal bias affect my investigation," Janice began, leaning back in the booth. She looked around and wished she could have a glass of the apple-laced port that was served with her dish. This conversation was getting pretty heavy. But she had to deny herself since she was on duty.

"So is your personal bias against me?" Lisa asked, watching the woman's eyes scroll around the room. "It looks like you still have feelings for Jonathan."

"You're right. I care for Jonathan. He's always been there for me. I'll have less of his attention with you in the picture. But I had my chance with him and let him slip out of my hands. Back in the day, I liked men who spent money extravagantly and appeared to be making it, even if they weren't. When Jonathan would pick me up in one of his old Corvettes he was working on, I would cringe from embarrassment. Does that make me sound superficial?"

"In a way it does. Did you know how valuable his vintage cars are?" Lisa asked, trying to be more tactful.

"I didn't know then and now that I know, it doesn't matter. They look like junk to me. But I bet you appreciate them, don't you?" Janice asked, leaning against the cushion of the booth as the server cleared the table.

"Yes, I like all things mechanical. But I like working with cars most of all. Their designs are so intricate. It takes a lot of moving parts to keep them running. The faster they go, the more I like them," she said, her eyes becoming animated at the thought of speeding in a Corvette with the top down.

"See, that's something he and I never shared. I didn't even like riding to an emergency on the truck. I hate speed. But aside from the things you have in common, you two have a special chemistry. Those looks he gives you make me envious. I don't want the looks from Jonathan, but I want a man who looks at me that way."

A big smile spread across Lisa's face as she acknowledged Janice's observation for the truth. "I'm so crazy about him, I don't know what to do."

"Does it scare you?" Janice asked, questioning the bemused look on Lisa's face.

"Yes, it does," she said honestly. "My feelings for him are so powerful, I'm doing things I never thought I'd do, like cooking at six o'clock in the morning."

"He's doing some things I never thought he'd do too," Janice said and shrugged a shoulder to indicate she didn't really mean anything by the remark.

Lisa let it pass. They would get to the reason for their meeting soon enough. The investigator had become more erect in her seat and she was no longer talking to a girlfriend, but to a suspect.

Their server had long since cleared the table. He returned to discreetly leave their check in a black leather folder. Opening it, Lisa glanced over the bill and quickly stuck her American Express card in the folds.

"Let's get to the investigation before your time is up. I know how busy you are," Janice said more abrasively than she'd intended. Her heavy belly full of some of the finest food in town and Lisa's grimace made her instantly regret her curt words.

"I didn't mean that I didn't have time to talk with you," Lisa began to explain immediately. "The problem is this fire has added so much to my workload. Our CEO and president were in town most of the week and I didn't get to item one on my things-to-do list. Now all new things have been added. My priorities are all topsy-turvy."

Janice commiserated, but she had a job to do. Taking the brown envelope from her briefcase, she released the clasp and took out the evidence bag that contained the bracelet. "Does this belong to you?"

"Yes, I've looked high and low for it. Jonathan told me he'd found it, but lost it again. Where did you find it?" Lisa asked, stretching out an open palm.

Janice put it away quickly. Picking up a pen and notepad, she said kindly, "I have to keep it until after the investigation. When did you know it was missing?"

"The day of the fire. I stopped to look for it, but couldn't figure out when or where I had lost it," she said thoughtfully.

"Are you sure you didn't go into the janitor's closet on the first floor at any time before the fire?"

"No, I would remember if I went into the janitor's

closet for anything. I have absolutely no need to hang out on the first floor."

Janice sat assessing her *person of interest* quietly for several moments. Lisa didn't flinch under her intense gaze, but did have trouble staying quiet. Finally Janice made a decision and said, "I guess you were asking me to be objective. So did Jonathan. But I have to tell you, it would be easier to prove that you did it."

"Maybe in proving that I didn't commit the arson, you'll find out who actually did it," Lisa suggested.

"The facts tell me that you're my best bet. You have the three things we look at first." Janice held up three fingers. She touched each finger with the forefinger of her other hand as she spoke. "First, you have the opportunity. After all, it is your building. You have access to the security equipment. Second, we have evidence linking you to the crime scene." To remind Lisa about the bracelet, Janice briefly touched her wrist with the finger doing the ticking. "And of course there's the motive—your hefty insurance policy."

Lisa laughed heartily. "Our insurance settlement would hardly motivate me. After we make repairs, there will be nothing left. We're just hoping the payment will cover the repairs."

"But you are going to file a claim? You will get money to pay for the repairs, which means you can save the money in your renovation budget," Janice said, raising one eyebrow to be sure Lisa understood her point.

"Yes, we'll file a claim. All those people who had to be treated at the hospital will have unexpected medical bills. They shouldn't have to bear the burden of those expenses alone. I understand they'll be paid regardless of the outcome of your investigation. Is that right?" Lisa asked.

"Yes, your insurance company will process that paperwork and begin payments immediately. In most cases, though, won't the medical insurance pay first?" Janice asked.

"No, they'll expect our fire insurance to pay. Then medical will pick up the balance. I know our employees are taken care of, but I'm concerned about our tenants and their employees. They may not have insurance," Lisa explained.

"Don't worry about that. I'll do what I can to be sure payments begin without a hitch," Janice promised.

The two women parted, with Janice finding herself making a promise to Lisa. "I'll keep you updated on our status." That was a promise Janice almost never made. They had found kindred spirits. Both women were close to the same age and Janice had found Lisa to be unpretentious. Both women were trying to make it in male-dominated professions. Each could see a little of herself in the other.

Back in her office, Lisa couldn't focus on her work. She'd started the morning with Jonathan suggesting that she'd torched her building, and now Janice had done the same. The only positive thing in the matter was they'd told her what they thought to her face. She didn't have to wonder.

Looking at the pile of work around her, she tried to figure out what to do next. She unrolled her blueprints to compare them to the change order the project manager had given her that morning. She needed to be sure the changes were necessary, because at this stage in construction, they were extremely expensive. She looked at the project manager's change order and couldn't remember what she was doing.

It was time to go home. After she rerolled the blueprints and placed them in their tube, she stuck the change order in a folder. Lifting the receiver on her phone, she spoke to Kita. "I'm not feeling well. If anyone looks for me, I'm at home."

At home she sat at the desk in her bedroom and made a time line of the morning of the fire. As an engineer, she was used to having designs to help focus her thoughts. Two things were unusual about that morning. Jennifer had brought doughnuts to the meeting and Artis had been in her office when she returned from the meeting. In between those two events, her bracelet had made it to the janitor's closet. The only logical person to go to the janitor's closet was, of course, the janitor. That would be Artis.

Lisa's head began to hurt. No new thoughts entered her mind. The same old ones kept recycling. Around and around they went as she walked around and around her room. Sick with the throbbing pain in her head and worn out from pacing, she took two pain relievers and fell asleep.

When she woke up, the room had grown dark. She felt like someone was in the house with her. Just as she rose up in bed to listen for another sound, Jonathan called out to her, "Lisa, Lisa, are you here?"

"I'm in bed," she replied, relief flooding her.

He stopped at the threshold and stood silent, as if waiting for permission to enter. She patted the mattress next to her and he stepped forward, smiling.

"How was your day?" he asked.

"Pretty rough," she replied, resting her forehead on her raised knees. "I had an interview with your *girlfriend* today."

"I know," Jonathan said solemnly.

"Did she call you and tell you about it?" she asked, looking at him, amazed. She'd known the fire department's grapevine was awesome, but she had no idea it was that rapid.

"No, the investigative reporter on channel five got wind of you two having lunch together and it was on the five o'clock news," Jonathan said reluctantly, as if he wanted to spare her the bad news.

Lisa glanced at her watch. "I've been asleep a long time. What did he say about our having lunch together?" she asked, turning her attention to Jonathan.

"He suggested that you're getting preferential treatment."

"I don't feel that way," Lisa said sadly.

"He made some good points. The first fireman on the scene, who handled vitally important evidence, is dating the prime suspect in the case. The person investigating the case is apparently good friends with the suspect. They were seen having lunch and a very good time at the Midtown Café today," Jonathan quoted almost verbatim.

"I see. Janice is going to have to settle this case soon, isn't she?" Lisa asked, concerned about how much time she had left.

"Yeah, she will. The chief is under a lot of pressure on this case. It's a big downtown fire that shut down several businesses that were in your building and cost the city tons of money to fight," he said thoughtfully.

"I'm sorry I got so upset with you this morning. Now I can understand why you would want to protect me. I just wish you'd told me about the bracelet in the beginning. Then we would have had time to figure things out together," she said, looking at him to see if he understood.

"I guess you were pretty shocked this morning

with everything I told you," he said, joining her on the bed.

"Yeah, I was shocked and angry. I appreciate your trying to protect me, I really do, but if we could work this out together—well, I think it would be better for both of us."

He put his arms around her shoulders. "Okay, woman, we're in this together. Now what do you want me to do?"

She rested her head on his shoulder. "I don't know. What should we do?"

"Find out who torched the building," Jonathan suggested. "If we deliver the flamethrower, your problems will be solved."

"That's what I was thinking. I started this time line about the day of the fire." She jumped from the bed and got her drawing for him. "See, two things were different that morning. Jennifer—that's her coming to the meeting early with doughnuts—and Artis working in my office to shred paper."

Jonathan studied her drawing. "What was out of the ordinary—Jennifer coming in early or bringing doughnuts?"

"I've told you about Jennifer." Lisa sat on her desk chair and turned to face him. "She's always late, for everything. She was even late for her performance evaluation."

"So did she have access to your bracelet?" Jonathan continued studying the time line.

"No, it wasn't on my arm when I went to the meeting. I wanted to fidget with it when Florence's presentation became boring and it wasn't there."

"That means you didn't have it when Artis was in your office shredding paper," he concluded.

She rose from the chair to stand behind Jonathan, looking at the drawing over his shoulder. "I had lost the bracelet before the meeting. It could have been in my office and—see here," she said, pointing to a sketch on the line. "That's Artis in my office with the shredder before I returned. He could have seen the bracelet on the floor or on my desk. Kita wasn't paying any attention to him. My office was completely accessible to him."

"You sound like you're convinced Artis took your bracelet," Jonathan said, laying the chart on his legs and looking straight ahead.

"I have an open mind," she said, folding her arms and walking around so she could face him. "But when Artis worked at the Church Street building, we had a major fire. We bring him to the Broadway Boulevard building and we have another fire. Do you call that a mere coincidence?"

"I know that Artis is not dishonest," Jonathan declared with conviction.

"What did he serve time for?" Lisa asked.

"Embezzlement," he replied, clenching his jaw tightly. She saw the tension, but felt compelled to state her case. This was worse than she'd imagined, but not as bad as the day she'd found out about Jonathan's criminal past.

Jonathan watched her, willing her not to say any more. "Embezzlement," she repeated. "He has taken something that wasn't his before."

"I've killed a man, but I'd never kill again," Jonathan said in a deadly soft voice.

"Your crime was accidental. Embezzlement is never an accident. Why are you so close to Artis anyway?" It had dawned on her that she would not be able to convince Jonathan that his best friend was a possible suspect.

"When I was thrown into the pen, I wasn't downtown at the comfortable new Criminal Justice Center.

I was in the big house with hard-core killers and rapists—the worst elements of our society. I was barely seventeen years old and scared witless. Artis was much smaller than me, but he had his bluff in on our cohabitants. He protected me, showed me how to swagger and look mean so I never had to fight. I looked tough even if I was too scared to go to the bathroom."

"I see." Lisa sat down in the chair again. "I know he's your friend, but what if he wanted my bracelet? What if he wanted it to give to Raquel? Remember how she went on and on about it at the race?"

"She didn't go on and on about your bracelet. If I remember correctly, she asked you if she could see it and said it was nice or something like that," Jonathan argued.

"Yeah, okay. I see now. You believe I can set a building full of people on fire, but you can't believe Artis would steal my bracelet." Lisa stared at him.

They sat silently for several moments. Jonathan was lost in his thoughts about Artis. His faith in his friend was unshakable, but so was his belief in his woman. Should he have to choose between them?

Looking at Lisa, he felt terrible. She looked so lost and miserable. Hadn't he said he'd do anything in the world to protect her? Maybe he should go have a talk with Artis. If he did that much, at least she would know he believed her. But tonight he would focus on making her feel better.

"Have you eaten anything since lunch?" he asked. She was caught off guard by his question. Before he'd spoken, she had been gearing up for another round of arguments.

"No. When I fell asleep it was only four o'clock," she replied, clearing her desk.

"Why don't you take a shower and I'll whip up something for dinner?" he suggested.

"That sounds good to me. Especially since I fell asleep in my clothes. I'll be right out." The big smile she gave him was worth putting aside his doubts. He'd do anything for her.

Lisa felt refreshed after a quick shower. She walked into the kitchen wearing a white terry cloth bathrobe and matching slippers to find Jonathan standing over the stove.

"What are we having?" she asked, trying to identify the assortment of vegetables on the chopping block.

"I was trying to think of something quick," Jonathan said, not turning around. "Will an everything-but-the-kitchen-sink omelet do?"

"Yeah, that should be interesting," Lisa said cautiously, finding a perch on the counter behind him.

"Don't worry," Jonathan said, hearing the uneasiness in her voice. "I'm not putting but a few jalapeños in it. I've also chopped up fresh green onions, tomatoes, black olives, ham, and cheese."

"That sounds good. What do you need me to do?" she asked, hopping down to stand next to him.

"Put bread in the toaster and I'll do the rest," he replied, turning to smile at her. Her hair was pinned up haphazardly and all she was wearing was a bathrobe, but she looked absolutely irresistible. Putting one arm around her shoulders, he pulled her to him and kissed her gently on the neck. "You smell good enough to eat," he whispered.

"Would you like to?" she asked.

"Lisa, you're a naughty girl. I'm going to tell your mother about you the next time she's in town," he said, turning back to the skillet. He slowly added the ingredients to the egg mixture.

"My mother taught me everything I know. She'd be proud of me," Lisa said shamelessly.

"Oh, really?" Jonathan asked, giving her a sidelong glance. "I'll verify that with her too."

"Don't you dare," she said, punching his hard biceps.

"Ouch, that hurt. You don't hit like a girl," he complained, still teasing her.

"You don't know much about girls then," she replied, turning away to get the bread.

He quickly swatted her bottom and said, "I'm willing to learn. Do you want to teach me?"

"Yeah, I've got some things I can show you." She walked toward him with a seductive look in her eyes.

"If you're hungry, you'd better stop messing with the cook," he replied, eyeing her hungrily.

"I'm hungry," she admitted. "We can pick this up after dinner." She put bread in the toaster and took out eating utensils and plates, setting the plates next to the stove top. As Jonathan finished the omelets, he tossed them onto the plates.

By that time, she'd buttered the hot toast and put juice and silverware on the table. "You're a creative genius," she said, taking a first bite when they were in their seats at the table.

"Yeah, I know," he agreed audaciously, his bright smile easing the hard planes of his face.

"Who taught you how to cook? Your mother?" She took a long swallow of orange juice.

"No, not really. Even when she was with my dad, my mother was not very domestic. She made dinner for us every night, but it was never anything elaborate, just the basics," he replied easily. Since he'd told Lisa about his family, their conversations had become more relaxed. He didn't have to worry about revealing too much.

"How is your mother doing? Have you seen her lately?" she inquired.

"I haven't had much time for my mother lately. I've been all caught up in my love life. Would you like to meet her?" Jonathan asked the question very casually, but Lisa caught the tension in his face when he asked.

"Sure. If you're ready for me to," she replied. In her opinion, meeting a man's mother was a big step. Of course, she'd met Rodney's mother, but that was because of his longtime relationship with Jet.

He touched her hand and looked at her tentatively. "My mother is not nurturing like yours. Our relationship is hard to describe," he tried to explain.

"Is she more like a big sister?" Lisa offered, trying to help him find a description.

"No, it's not that warm either. More like an older woman with a young male acquaintance. You'll see," Jonathan said. "I'm off again Sunday. Would you like to go over there?"

"We could do that. Or I could cook dinner at your place and have her come out. Would you like that?"

"That's a good idea. It's been a while since she's been out to the farm. She says she's not comfortable with all that fresh air and open space." Jonathan chuckled, having long ago accepted his mother's eccentricities.

"Do you have to go in tomorrow?" Lisa asked, having gotten confused about his schedule with so many other things going on in their lives.

"No. Why do you ask?"

"Would you be up for a little after-dinner diversion then?" she asked suggestively. She stood and waited for his response.

"I could be. What do you have in mind?" He rose from his seat and stepped to her.

She untied the belt around her waist and let the ends fall to either side. The robe gaped open, revealing a glimpse of her dark skin. That was all the invitation he needed.

CHAPTER 13

After Lisa left for work the next morning, Jonathan called Alan Mueller. "Would you go with me to pick out a ring for Lisa?" Jonathan was leaning over the counter in Lisa's kitchen.

"I'd be honored to, but don't you want to take her with you?" Alan asked cautiously.

"No, I want to surprise her," Jonathan announced happily.

"Well, okay. If you think so." Alan was still skeptical. He rested an arm on his large maple and walnut desk, giving his complete attention to their conversation.

"I'm sure. I know just what I want her to wear and she'll tell me I'm being too extravagant if she sees if before I buy it." Jonathan stood up and began pacing the kitchen.

"What do you want her to have?" Alan asked, setting aside the contract he'd been reviewing.

"The biggest diamond I can afford," Jonathan replied unabashedly.

"Well, I guess that's natural for a man in love.

But don't forget you have to live after the wedding," Alan advised.

"I'm not spending more than I can afford. Fortunately, my house is paid for since I bought it on the auction block and I either did all the renovations myself or bartered with contractors to get it done. Mr. Mueller, I honestly don't have any expenses. I can splurge and give my girl a ring she'll be proud to show off." Jonathan fiddled with the phone cord, wondering at his friend's warning.

"Are you trying to impress her or her family?" Mr. Mueller asked. "I have only seen Lisa a few times and the only jewelry I've seen her wear is that bracelet and diamond stud earrings."

"If she can buy a thirty-thousand-dollar bracelet for herself, I surely don't want to give her less. A small two-thousand-dollar diamond ring will look out of proportion next to that bracelet when she gets it back," Jonathan said with certainty in his voice.

"Okay, you have me convinced. I know you had concerns about her wealth at one time and I don't want you to enter a long-term relationship until you have those resolved." Jonathan heard the gravity and sincerity in his friend's voice.

"I know where you're coming from and I appreciate your concern. We've worked through all that. If she can accept me the way I am—prison record and all—I have to accept her the way she is—wealth and all." Jonathan gave the older man more explanation than he gave most people because he owed the man so much.

"I guess it's time for me to let go. My young protégé is a man now." Alan Mueller was impressed with the progress Jonathan seemed to have made in the past few months. He'd been angry and guilty for so long.

"No, Mr. Mueller. I'll never be so much a man that I don't need to run things by you. That's why I called you this morning. Will you help me select a diamond for Lisa?" Jonathan's voice was still solemn, but now contained a hint of glee.

"Yes, you know I will," Alan replied without hesitation. "Marrying Lisa will prove to be the best move you've ever made. She's a real sensible girl and will help keep you out of trouble," Alan said easily.

"What time can you leave your office?" Jonathan asked, taking a seat at the kitchen table now that the serious part of the conversation had ended.

"I'm in court all morning. Let's plan on getting together late this afternoon," Alan suggested, looking at his watch.

"What time? About three o'clock?" the young man asked.

"No. Let's make it two o'clock. This may take longer than you think," Alan warned.

Jonathan locked up Lisa's house and headed to the shop that was painting his pewter Corvette. That would be his principal car now that he no longer had Zora. The only good thing about the fire investigation was that Lisa had too much on her mind to question him about Zora. She knew that he drove other cars from time to time, but he'd been without Zora for a while now.

He left the old Corvette he was driving at the shop for a paint job and drove the beautiful, fully restored pewter-gray car home. Just as Lisa had predicted, the black velour and houndstooth upholstery gave the car a distinctive, distinguished look.

By the time he'd put the finishing touches on the car and dressed, it was time to pick up Mr. Mueller. The older man was standing out in front of the office building on Commerce Street in downtown Nashville, which housed his prosperous law firm.

As soon as he was seated, he whistled. "You've done it again, young man. This is a talent not to be taken lightly. When I first saw this wreck, I had no hope for it."

"I can't believe the two people I'm closest to doubted me," Jonathan said, looking in his side mirror before pulling away from the curb, into the steady stream of traffic.

"Did Lisa have doubts too?" Alan asked, fiddling with the switches on the dashboard.

"Initially she did, but after a few minutes of walking around the car and touching it, she gave me her vision for it. She's the one that suggested this fabric for the interior," Jonathan explained.

"It's nice. I like the headliner, but it's a shame that this is not a convertible," Alan said.

"Yeah, it is. But this is a one-of-a-kind car. It will be easy to sell," Jonathan said easily, breaking free of the inner-city traffic and heading south on the interstate.

Nearing the exit off I-65, he asked, "Where do I go from here?" Conversation between the men ceased as Alan gave Jonathan directions to a diamond distributor. He'd called immediately after talking with Jonathan that morning to make arrangements for the visit.

Jonathan could see a short, gray-haired man wearing a beanie through the window of the jewelry store. The elderly gentleman pressed a buzzer in response to Alan ringing the doorbell. The buzzer gave the men fifteen seconds to enter the store.

"Hello, Mr. Goldbaum," Alan rang out. The older man shuffled from behind the counter to shake Alan's hand. "This is my friend Jonathan, whom I told you about this morning." Jonathan held out a hand for the elderly man, who ignored it.

He took a step back so that he could see Jonathan better. "So you're the young man in need of a big diamond, eh?"

"Yes, sir." Jonathan stood still to let Mr. Goldbaum finish assessing him.

"I wouldn't let you in if you weren't with my friend Mr. Mueller." Then he surprised Jonathan by taking his hand and shaking it vigorously. "You know, you can't be too careful anymore. People would rather steal than work," the old man muttered, moving back behind the counter.

"Ira, please get the tray I prepared for Mr. Mueller."

A young man came from behind swinging half doors with a tray of large glittering diamonds. Jonathan was mesmerized, just staring at the brilliant stones.

"Go ahead, pick one up," Mr. Goldbaum urged. "Do you know what you're looking for?"

"I know that I'm supposed to look for clarity, color, and cut. Of course, I want as many carats as I can afford in a quality diamond. I'd like for it to be flawless though. I guess if I could accept a few flaws, the diamond could be larger?" Jonathan paused and the older men nodded approvingly.

"That's right," the old jeweler said with respect. "And what shape do you want?"

"I know she'll like the heart-shaped diamond. I don't think she'd care for a yellow diamond. Let's stick with the clear ones," Jonathan decided, looking at the diamonds on the tray before him.

"Have a seat," Mr. Goldbaum ordered. The two men sat on stools at the counter. The jeweler picked up an instrument that looked like tweezers and held up a large heart-shaped stone. "What do you think?"

"Yes, that's it," Jonathan said, becoming excited.

"Take a closer look." Mr. Goldbaum gave Jonathan a magnifier.

"This is perfect," Jonathan announced.

"No, it's not, son." The old man smiled, showing slightly beige teeth. "Its imperfections are hidden because of the many facets cut into it. But it's nearly perfect."

"In other words, you have a good diamond there," Alan interjected.

"How much does it weigh?" Jonathan asked.

Mr. Goldbaum held the diamond up for inspection again. "It's five carats," he said as Jonathan looked at the stone as if hypnotized.

"I'd like that one in a platinum setting with an amethyst on either side," Jonathan said firmly.

"Do you think you should look at others?" Alan suggested gently.

"No, I know what she likes. I'm fairly certain this will make her happy," Jonathan said, not bothering to look at any other diamond.

"I've been in this business a long time," Mr. Goldbaum said, putting the diamond Jonathan had selected into a small, brown envelope. "This young man knows what he wants because he's done his homework. Now let's settle on details for the setting and the amethysts."

With the help of Mr. Mueller and Mr. Goldbaum, Jonathan decided to put three small deep purple amethysts on either side and at the point of the diamond. Satisfied, Jonathan stood to leave. "When can I pick it up?"

"When do you plan to propose?" Mr. Goldbaum asked in return.

"Next Saturday morning," Jonathan replied.

"I'll have it ready this time next week," Mr. Goldbaum promised.

After Jonathan and Alan were on the highway again, the middle-aged man asked, "How is the investigation into the fire going?"

"It's pretty rough for Lisa. She's the prime suspect and she's never so much as had a speeding ticket before. Only the Lord knows how she's gotten by so long without one." The two men shared a good-natured laugh. Lisa was well known for the lead in her foot as she flew around town in her big, wide pickup truck.

"I'm surprised you're going to propose while she's under so much pressure," Alan ventured, knowing Jonathan wouldn't want to hear his caution this time either.

"You're right. I could be putting her under more pressure, but I think we need each other now more than ever. I want her to know I'm there for her in good times as well as bad. Besides, this investigation could go on for another year or so. I don't want to wait that long," Jonathan said calmly, keeping his eyes on the road.

"These investigations usually get worse before they get better," Mr. Mueller agreed. "If either of you need me, call me."

"You know we will. Thank you," Jonathan said sincerely.

As they approached the exit to Mr. Mueller's house he turned to Jonathan. "Won't you come in for dinner?"

"I don't know. Mrs. Mueller's not expecting me." Jonathan turned down the beautiful tree-lined street where his friend's home had been for the past twenty-five years.

"She'll be glad to see you. Of course, she's a little upset over the toy you sold me. She thinks you should be ashamed of yourself for encouraging me in my midlife crisis." Alan laughed and Jonathan gave him a quick smile.

"In that case, are you sure it's safe for me to go in?" Jonathan asked.

"You might just as well come in and get it over with. Whenever she sees you, she'll tell you what she thinks about my new toy."

Mrs. Mueller was effusive in her affection toward Jonathan. Her adult children lived in other cities. She enjoyed fussing over the young man who always seemed to be so much more grateful for her attention than her own children.

She placed platters and bowls on the dining room table. After everyone was served, she asked the men what they'd been up to that day. "I hope it didn't have anything to do with a car," she said with a threat clear in her voice.

"No, Phyllis, we did a different kind of shopping today," Alan began and paused dramatically.

"What does that mean? What kind of shopping did you do?" she asked suspiciously. He had stoked her curiosity.

"You tell her, Jonathan." Alan grinned big in expectation of his wife's reaction.

"We shopped for diamonds," Jonathan said matter-of-factly, reaching for the bowl of mashed potatoes. He didn't think anyone would care but him and Lisa.

She surprised him by swatting his hand. "Put that bowl down and don't take another bite until you tell me everything."

Startled, Jonathan looked from Mr. to Mrs. Mueller, trying to figure out what he'd done wrong. Alan prompted him. "Son, this is where you give her the details. Women love to hear about romance and proposals and stuff."

Jonathan gave her a big smile then. "I'm going to ask Lisa to marry me, but I need a ring before I do. So we're having one made up." He reached for the bowl of potatoes again and she let him get it this time. She had jumped out of her seat and was coming around the table to hug his neck.

"Jonathan, congratulations! I'm so happy for you. She's such a pretty girl and so kind. Lisa is just right for you. Oh, this is such a good thing. After all you've been through, you deserve this," Phyllis Mueller went on and on with tears in her eyes. Jonathan wanted to eat, but her off-target hug had him in sort of a headlock.

After allowing her time to celebrate, Alan cleared his throat and asked, "Uhhh, Phyllis, could we eat now?"

She wiped her eyes with a napkin. "Sure." She returned to her seat, but reached across the table for Jonathan's hand. "You're about to enter the best part of your life."

That same day, Lisa had awakened bright and re- freshed. In spite of her late night, she felt no ill ef- fects. When she walked through the office, Kita was relieved to see the spring back in her step.

"Good morning," they greeted each other. "Has the new finance printout come in yet?" Lisa asked, pausing at Kita's desk to glance through her mes- sages.

"No, not yet. It should be in today. Your variance report is due in next Tuesday," Kita reminded her.

"Well, I'll need the finance data before I can do the variance report."

"If it's not in today's mail I'll check to see where it is." Kita made a note as she spoke.

"Okay. Remind me about that due date again if we get it. I still haven't signed off on the change order. I'll be in my office working on that this morning." Lisa moved on into her office and quickly became engrossed in her work.

While she was sitting at her desk, Jennifer stuck her head in the door. "I picked up your finance report from the mail room for you," she said. "I was coming this way anyway," she added when Lisa looked at her blankly.

"Thanks. I appreciate your help."

Jennifer shrugged her shoulders and left. Lisa set the big green binder aside, deciding to wait until she had time to focus on it. It would help if she had last month's report as she reviewed it. Searching her office to see if she could find the last report had been to no avail. She had hoped it had reappeared among the things that had been moved in, but it was still missing. She put in the three digits to Kita's extension. "Have you run across my last finance printout?"

"No, I haven't. I don't know why you told them to stop e-mailing it to you. When it came as an e-mail attachment, we could print it out as needed," Kita complained.

"I never told them to stop e-mailing it," Lisa said incredulously. "What gave you that idea?"

"I assumed you'd made the change," the other woman said.

"Get the finance director on the phone. This doesn't make sense," Lisa insisted.

In a few minutes Kita came into Lisa's office. "I talked with Glenn. He is going to send the reports to you in an electronic format. But he says he stopped sending them because of your e-mail request several months ago. Perhaps you forgot."

"I would remember something like that. Ask him if he has a copy of that request. If he does, tell him to forward it to me," Lisa directed.

"Sure thing," Kita said, turning to leave the office.

That evening, Lisa was surprised that she didn't hear from Jonathan. While she was preparing a light evening meal, he called to say he was having dinner with Alan Mueller and his family.

Missing Jonathan's company, she decided to keep busy. After eating, she opened up the green binder and pored over the data. First she looked at the figures to get in mind how the fire would affect their expenses. However, somehow the salary expenditures did not quite line up. Something was out of order. It was close to midnight and she knew she should get to bed. She hadn't gotten much sleep the night before.

Saturday she had little time to spend on work. She went shopping for groceries to cook dinner for Jonathan's mother.

Sunday morning, immediately after early morning service at church, she drove out to Jonathan's place to begin preparations for the dinner.

Jonathan was on his riding mower far away from the house, but saw her as she approached the road leading to his property. He hurried across the field to help unload her shopping bags. When everything was on the kitchen counter, he wrapped his long arms around her and gave her a long, leisurely kiss. "It's been a long time, hasn't it?"

"Yes, it has. I hope you missed me." She leaned against his chest and put her arms around his waist, enjoying his solid strength.

"You know I did." He gently stroked her back. "Are you sure you don't mind cooking?"

"I'm sure. I started the rolls yesterday. They're already on pans. Will you get them out of the truck for me?"

"Okay." He accepted her keys and headed out the back door.

Once she was started, he went out to finish his yard work. She looked up when a shadow came across the area of the kitchen table where she was working. Turning swiftly toward the door, she saw a woman enter the room from the back porch.

Her appearance shocked Lisa initially. The woman had a scar that ran from high on her right cheek to low on her chin. Her dark hair, liberally sprinkled with gray, was dry and lifeless.

"You must be Lisa," the older woman said, approaching her. The screen door slammed behind the woman.

"Yes, yes, I am," Lisa replied, hoping the shock she felt didn't register on her face.

"I'm Barbara Hill, Jonathan's mother." Her voice had a challenge to it as if waiting for Lisa's negative response to her.

"Hello, I'm so glad to finally meet you," Lisa said, quickly recovering from her initial shock. She hurriedly dried her hands on the towel she'd placed over one shoulder and walked toward Mrs. Hill expecting to hug her.

Barbara took a quick step back. "I'm sorry." She took a seat at the table across from where a bowl and a bag of green beans sat.

Lisa was thrown off balance and couldn't think of what to say. Finally she said, "Jonathan's out back on his riding mower. He'll be in shortly."

"I'm a little early. I figure it's better to be early than to be late," Barbara said lightly.

Lisa eased back into her seat and continued snapping the beans.

"I hope you haven't gone through too much trouble for dinner." Barbara watched Lisa's hands as they methodically picked up a long bean from the bag, snapped the ends off, and then broke the bean three more times. She dropped the end pieces back into the bag and the other three into the bowl. Repeating the process over and over, she had a certain rhythm to her work.

"I'll wash my hands and help you. Or is there something else you prefer I do?"

"No, there's not. I saved the beans for last. Everything else is ready. I'd appreciate your help though."

Barbara went to the powder room and washed her hands. Taking her seat again, she said, "I was just looking at the way the sun is beaming in here on your hair. It's so nice and shiny. Is all that your hair?"

"Yes, ma'am." Lisa looked at her in surprise.

"It's so thick and pretty, I just wondered. Mine is absolutely lifeless. It won't hold a curl or anything." She touched the brittle ends of her hair.

"It looks neat," Lisa said, dropping a bean into the bag.

"I used to wear my hair long like yours. How do you keep it up?"

"I go to the beauty shop every week," Lisa confessed.

Barbara still had not picked up a bean. "Jonathan told me he's finally told you about his past and my drug addiction."

Lisa looked at the woman and replied honestly, "Yes, he has."

"I don't have any excuse for the way I treated my

family. I'm sorry, but I can't undo anything," she said with a doomed finality that pained Lisa's heart.

"Your problem is in the past," Lisa said, trying to take a positive view.

"No, it's not. My addiction is something I live with every day. Each morning when I wake up I crave that high. It's on my mind all day. Over and over again, I have to make a commitment not to go looking for that euphoric high again. I miss it," Barbara declared.

"Even after all the consequences you've suffered?"

"Yes. I know what I've endured," Barbara said, running a finger along the scar on her cheek. "But that high is something else. It's better than anything I've ever experienced. I'm not an ignorant woman. Intellectually I know better, but physiologically I want to get high." She laid the statement on the table between them, daring Lisa to pick it up.

"I'm so sorry," Lisa said sincerely.

"So am I. Mostly I'm sorry for my baby son who loves me unconditionally. He's seen me at my worst and he loves me still. Regardless of what I do, he still feels it's his calling to save me." Barbara picked up a bean and broke it in half. She took a bite of a broken end and chewed slowly as if exploring the taste.

"You deserve to be saved," Lisa said, resting her arms on the table before her. "He thinks the best of you."

"Yes, he does, poor boy. He thinks I'm better than I am. I don't want to hurt him anymore, so each day I get up and resolve to become the person he thinks I am. But the addiction is always waiting for a weak moment to take over." Barbara studied Lisa's face, looking for the disgust she expected to find. Instead all she saw was compassion.

"We'll help you," Lisa promised.

"You're as sweet and innocent as my son. This is

something I have to do alone. No one can help me," Barbara said with conviction.

Lisa reached for the woman's hand, but she jerked away. "I'm sorry, I don't like to be touched."

"I see," Lisa said, deciding one would have to be licensed to explore that statement. "No one should ever be alone. In my family we believe in sticking together. Regardless of what we go through, we can count on each other." She said it with such conviction that it forced an involuntary smile from Barbara.

"Good. Jonathan told me about your whole family coming to your bedside. He deserves a family like yours. I hope he stays with you a long time."

"I do too," Lisa said with such a big smile that the doom-and-gloom Barbara smiled again.

Barbara appeared to have said what she came to say. She remained silent for a long time. Lisa checked on the pot roast and then put the green beans on the stove top. When she returned to the table, she told Barbara the menu. "I hope those are things you like."

"They are. I'm glad to finally get a chance to taste your rolls. Jonathan was raving about them when you cooked for him."

"I have to admit, they're pretty good," Lisa agreed immodestly. "Jonathan told me that you work for the Nightingale Center. What do you do there?" she asked.

"I'm a drug counselor."

"Oh." Lisa was caught by surprise again.

"It's not as unusual as you might think. Addicts most often counsel addicts because we can be non-judgmental while offering guidance," Barbara explained.

When Jonathan came in, he was relieved to see the two most important people in his life talking.

"I hope you're going to take a shower," Lisa said, grimacing at the sweat and grime that covered him.

"Yes, dear," Jonathan said.

"That's right, son. Those are the two most important words for you to learn. You need to learn them early," Barbara teased.

CHAPTER 14

The next morning was a typical Monday. Lisa accidentally knocked over her coffee, obliterating the blueprints that were spread before her. She turned quickly in her chair to grab the phone, which was on its third ring. When she did, the phone line became twisted in the wheels of the chair and Lisa was thrown to the floor. She tried to answer the phone professionally, not conveying to the caller that she was sitting on the floor.

"Lisa, this is Janice McKee," an authoritative voice informed her. "I need to see you now." The woman's demand was direct and impersonal.

"Sure, come on over," Lisa replied, wondering at the woman's urgency.

When Janice arrived, Kita escorted her to Lisa's office. The young executive had moved to a small table near the window and invited the investigator to sit across from her. "What's going on?" Lisa asked with no small degree of trepidation.

"Did you see yesterday's newspaper?" Janice asked, taking a folded newspaper from her briefcase.

"No, I was pretty busy this weekend," Lisa explained.

"The chief didn't like this," Janice said, laying the paper on the table before her.

NO PROGRESS IN FIRE INVESTIGATION, the headline read.

Millionaire real estate developer Lisa Stevens of the Sand Castles family is still listed as a suspect in the fire, but no arrest has been made. When contacted, a fire department representative said that the investigation is ongoing. However, an unknown source has divulged that there is evidence linking Stevens to the fire.

Councilwoman Winifred Brown is calling for a look into the fire department's handling of the disaster. "This was a major fire event and the cost to this city has been tremendous. We need to know if the fire department is dragging its feet on the investigation because the main suspect has connections," Brown said at a meeting last week.

"We'll look into the councilwoman's allegations. If someone is getting preferential treatment, we'll move the investigation to the Tennessee Bureau of Investigation," Mayor Adams said in response to Brown's allegations.

The story also included a picture of Lisa from the newspaper's file.

Lisa finished reading the article and laid the paper on the table. "It looks like my time is up," she said almost to herself, resignation clear in her voice. She sighed deeply and rested her head on her hands.

"I've stalled long enough," Janice agreed, nodding. "Things look pretty dismal. I stand to lose my job, but worse than that, you stand to lose your freedom."

Lisa read the entire article again. "When did I cease being a *person of interest* and become your *suspect?*" she asked.

"The councilwoman was just talking, she doesn't know the difference. You're still officially a person of interest. When I report the new evidence, you'll become a suspect and your arrest will be imminent," Janice explained.

"The bracelet?"

Janice nodded her head. "Yes, the reporters don't know we have it yet. The chief wants me to announce that we have the bracelet today to show that we're making progress. I'll have to say that because of the investigation, we've had to play our hand close to the vest. Withholding the evidence was part of our strategy to bring out the culprit or something like that, you know?" Janice looked at Lisa sympathetically. Lisa's face was ashen and she looked to be barely breathing.

"I can't answer any more questions without my attorney. I have the number over here somewhere," Lisa said, rising. Her hands were shaking and her voice was raspy.

Seeing the other woman's nervousness, Janice said, "Hold on. Why don't you come to my office with your attorney this afternoon? I'll tell the chief you refused to talk. Is that okay?"

"Yes, you'll be telling him the truth. I do refuse to talk. I understand this is an official investigation and my freedom is at stake. I can't say any more," Lisa answered.

Janice accepted Lisa's decision and left. Lisa immediately called Jonathan with the latest development.

"I'll call Mr. Mueller now," Jonathan answered, trying to conceal his anxiety. She didn't sound well and he wanted to be with her right away. "We'll come get you."

"Okay, I've got to call headquarters and let Jet and Bryce know about this latest development. If you don't reach me when you call back, leave a message."

When she talked with Jet, he also wanted to be with her. "I can be there in a couple of hours," he offered.

"You can come if you want, but it may be too early. I'll probably need you more later. If things get any worse, I'll let you know." She tried to be stoic but felt like crying. Fear was in her voice.

"Then I'll send Vincent," Jet insisted, referring to his corporate attorney. He was angry that the situation had come to that point. He was ready to take matters in hand now.

"Jonathan is bringing his friend Alan Mueller to me. He's a big-shot criminal attorney in town. Vincent's expertise is in mergers and acquisitions," Lisa responded, trying to remain calm and think. It was hard for her to grasp the fact that she'd simply run out of time.

"I'll send Vincent to be sure that your criminal attorney knows that you're priority one," Jet responded.

Lisa was pacing nervously around her office when Jonathan and Mr. Mueller arrived in less than twenty minutes. Mr. Mueller gave Lisa a quick hug before saying, "This kind of situation is always upsetting. But you may relax now. We need you to keep your wits. You are the key to your own defense. You have to tell us what we need to know to win this case."

"Do you think it'll go to court?" Jonathan asked,

putting an arm around Lisa. Alan Mueller looked at the poor young man who was beside himself with worry. He didn't know who needed the most comforting, Lisa or Jonathan. She was afraid, but was being analytical and practical. Jonathan was so beside himself with worry that he was on the verge of losing his rationality.

"I'm always prepared to go to trial. I won't settle when I'm sure my client is innocent," Mr. Mueller said with conviction.

"Thank you. You're a good friend," Lisa said, grateful for that vote of confidence.

"I'm more than that. You only know me as Jonathan's friend, but I'm a very competitive attorney. I've tried more than a hundred cases before a jury and have won all but one. That one was lost because my client withheld vital information from me. I'm not bragging. These are facts you need so that you can relax and trust me. Now do you think you can work with me?" Mr. Mueller's voice was brusque, but his eyes held a kind twinkle. Lisa knew beyond a doubt he'd do his best for her.

"Yes." She smiled at last.

Vincent Walker arrived while Alan was still gathering information from Lisa. He had knowledge about the company's safety policies and procedures that would affect the case that Mr. Mueller had not known to ask about and Lisa had not offered. After the two compared notes, it was time to go to the fire department for Lisa's interrogation.

Jonathan stood with them as the attorneys stuffed their long yellow tablets into their briefcases. "Son, I know you want to give Lisa your support, but I don't think it's wise for you to come to this interrogation. Enough has been said about your relationship with Janice."

"You're probably right," Jonathan agreed reluctantly. He walked to the garage with them and headed on an errand of his own.

Janice was completely professional, all familiarity absent. She was not adversarial, but neither was she sympathetic. She held up a small bag.

"These are the remains of a ledger binder. I'm told your financial reports were sent to you in ledger binders. The ashes were found in the janitor's closet," Janice said. "The one where the fire started," she added with emphasis. "Why would your binder have been in there?"

"I don't know," Lisa replied. Her answers were unadorned as the attorneys had instructed.

"Did you know that similar fragments were found at the Church Street fire?"

"No," Lisa answered.

"That fire began in the mail room. Otherwise the fires are very similar," Janice noted. She browsed through her legal pad slowly without saying a word. Several moments passed.

"Do you know who disengaged the company's state-of-the-art alarm system?"

"No."

"When Captain Hill found you passed out on the steps, were you trying to get out of the building or back to your office?" Janice looked at Lisa and waited for her response.

"I was trying to get out," Lisa said, barely breathing at the memory of the day.

"Why did everyone evacuate but you?"

"I told you, I was in my private restroom," Lisa said impatiently.

"What were you doing in there?" Janice was

unfazed by Lisa's growing impatience. The men looked at each other but didn't say anything.

"I was using my inhaler."

"What is your inhaler for?"

"Asthma." Lisa knew she'd been through that before.

"This is a matter of record now," Janice said, interpreting Lisa's annoyance. "What triggers your asthma?"

"Smoke, pollen, things in the air," Lisa replied tiredly.

"How long were you in the restroom?" The questions were coming faster and faster.

Lisa had not been asked that question before and looked at Alan Mueller before she answered. He nodded. "About fifteen or twenty minutes."

"So you had a reaction to smoke before anyone else knew to evacuate the building." Janice paused.

"Is there a question in that statement?" Mr. Mueller asked Janice.

"Yes. How is it that you were affected by the smoke five minutes before anyone else knew the building was on fire?" Janice asked and sat back waiting. She hoped Lisa had a good answer.

"It came through the ventilation system. If the alarm had worked, our ventilation system would have shut down and not circulated the smoke, but it came to me that way," Lisa explained.

"No one else has complained about smoke coming through the ventilation system," Janice said.

The room remained silent.

"Do you have any other questions for our client?" Attorney Mueller asked.

"Yes. Have you figured out how your bracelet made it to the janitor's closet?"

"No."

"Then I'll figure it out and give all of you a call," Janice replied. "I'll let you know when I have more questions." She stood and showed the *suspect* and her two attorneys to the door.

While Lisa was in her interrogation, Jonathan was in a meeting of another kind. He had gone to confront his friend about Lisa's bracelet.

Raquel answered the door to the apartment on the first knock. "Artis, your friend is here to see you!" she yelled as she headed back into the kitchen. She left Jonathan standing at the door, but after a moment he found his way to the living room.

"What up, dog? What brings you to this neck of the woods?" Artis asked.

"I need to talk with you. Got a minute?"

"Sure. We were about to eat dinner. Do you want something?" Artis offered.

"No, I don't have much time. Look here, Lisa told me you had been up to see her on the day of the fire," Jonathan started. He circled the familiar room, looking at but not seeing the objects that decorated it.

"That's right," Artis replied, looking at his old friend carefully and rubbing his chin. Jonathan had a strange energy today. Artis could feel the man's barely leashed anger.

"Did you happen to see that bracelet she wears all the time? She lost it that day," Jonathan said, stopping to pin his friend with a cold stare.

"If this don't beat all. I wondered when someone would come knocking on my door about that fire. It's always easy to blame it on the ex-con. But I expected better from you. This is like the pot calling the kettle black." Artis's hands were fisted at his side. His anger had risen as soon as he heard the accusation implied in Jonathan's words.

"I'm just asking a question. They're trying to pin this on her."

"Do you think I'd be a better suspect?" Artis asked.

"No, man, it's not like that. I just need to know how that bracelet got down there. I found it in the same room that the fire started in," Jonathan explained quickly. "Did you see the bracelet?"

Artis burst out laughing. "That's for me to know and you to find out."

"Don't be childish. Just answer the question," Jonathan said, moving to stand over the shorter man. He had him by a good six or seven inches.

Artis wouldn't step back. He'd taught Jonathan that intimidation technique back in the joint. And now he was going to try it on the master. "Why do you think I took the bracelet? Because I'm not living high and mighty like you? No, I still live in this same stinking apartment I moved into when I first got out of the joint. And my woman may not have a fifty-thousand-dollar diamond bracelet." Artis wasn't sure about the value of the bracelet, but made a good guess. "Everything I have is mine! I got it for myself!" He yelled the last few words.

"Did you want her to have a fifty-thousand-dollar bracelet? You know she admired Lisa's. You wanted her to have it, didn't you?" Jonathan was circling Artis now, bent over toward him.

"Just because my lady likes nice things doesn't mean I'd steal them for her." Artis was puffing with belligerence. His fists remained knotted at his side and he was ready to come to blows with his friend.

"You *have* stolen before," Jonathan said. He stopped pacing and glared at Artis.

"Yeah, I live with my mistake every day. I'm not

trying to perpetrate like some folks. You must think you're rich like your woman. You've forgotten all about serving time or just pretend you have." The shorter man was practically on his toes yelling back at Jonathan.

"What're you talking about? Nobody's perpetrating around here but you if you have that bracelet."

"You not perpetrating, huh? Then why is it Miss Lisa didn't know about your time in the joint? I wondered why you broke out in a sweat and changed the subject every time I brought up our past. Then when I mentioned it to Lisa she almost passed out. That's when I knew you'd been hiding from her." Artis released a dry, humorless snigger.

Jonathan took a breath before speaking. "So you're the one who told her. Why did you have to tell her that?"

"I did it for her own good," Artis said. "I'm like you. You broke her heart for her own good. I was just looking out for her, man." Sarcasm dripped from every word Artis spoke. Jonathan had to remind himself that he never wanted to hurt another human. He desperately wanted to smash the little man's face in.

Artis became emboldened by Jonathan's silence. "She needed to see that you're just like me. I was afraid she'd find out about my criminal record and get me fired. She questioned me just because I knew what financial statements look like. If she found out I had worked as a staff accountant, she'd find out I'd gotten into a little trouble for misdirecting funds. I had to let her see your crime was worse than mine. She loves you. I couldn't be that bad. It was perfect." Artis was grinning slyly, feeling very pleased with his shrewdness. "After all, you're no better than me."

"Maybe not. My only problem is messing around with you," Jonathan snapped. "All I want to know is how that bracelet got down to the fire. You took it, didn't you?"

"How're you going to come up in here, to my own home with my wife and kids, and accuse me of stealing a damn bracelet we can't even use? I think you'd better get your ass out of my house," Artis ordered, getting in Jonathan's space.

"Put me out. I'm not leaving until you tell me about the bracelet," Jonathan said, folding his arms across his chest.

"You think I'm not man enough to throw you out?" Artis pushed up against Jonathan's shoulder.

"Keep your hands off me. All that is not necessary," Jonathan said in a steely, quiet voice.

"Keep my hands off or what? I had to take care of your punk ass when we were locked up. Now all of a sudden you're going to take me on?" Artis challenged.

"That's right. I've never had anything to fight for before," Jonathan returned.

Artis shoved Jonathan again, first one shoulder, then the other. Anger flared up in Jonathan, driving him to grab Artis by the collar and push him against the wall. When Raquel came into the room, she started hitting Jonathan on the back with one of her bedroom slippers. "Let him go! Let him go before I call the police!" she yelled.

"That's right, call the police. Tell them where Lisa's bracelet is," Jonathan responded, looking over his shoulder and sliding Artis up the wall until his feet dangled inches from the floor.

"Man, I don't have the damn bracelet. I didn't see it that day and I haven't seen it since. I don't know why ya'll think I have it," Artis said.

Jonathan looked into his eyes and believed him. He dropped Artis to the floor.

"Get out of here!" Raquel yelled over and over. "I wouldn't want anything that big and gaudy if you gave it to me."

Jonathan looked down at Artis, seeing the fear in his friend's eyes, and suddenly realized what he had done. "Hey, I'm sorry," he said, looking at his hands.

"You my boy and I don't want to hurt you. Why don't you get out before I get real mad?" Artis said in a voice hoarse with anger.

When Lisa's meeting with Janice ended, Vincent headed for the airport. Mr. Mueller was concerned for his young client. "You seem so distraught, would you like for me to take you home?"

"No, I'll be all right," she said, feeling as if she'd fall apart at any moment and not wanting the older man to see her weakness.

"Do I need to drop you somewhere?" he asked solicitously, concern etched in the lines of his face.

"Yes, sir, I was going to call for a company car, but if you don't mind, I need a ride back to the building to get my truck."

She looked so worn out from the hours of questioning that his heart went out to her. "When you get home call Jonathan and tell him to come take care of you." He held the door open to his little red Corvette and headed uptown with her.

They drove in silence, winding their way through one-way streets. In less than five minutes, they were in front of the Church Street building. "Get some rest. We don't know what the future holds, but we need you at your best," he advised her.

"I'll be okay," she said quietly.

She called Jonathan, but he didn't answer his phone. Too keyed up to rest, she decided to drive out to his place. She pulled up in front of the house, but stayed in the truck because she didn't see a car out front. Closing her eyes, she rested until she heard a knock on the window.

"Hey, what are you doing here?" Jonathan asked. His face was all angles and attitude.

"I wanted to be with you," she said, opening the door. He stepped back to help her without uttering a word. He walked up on the porch and unlocked the door. She followed him as he entered the house.

He moved through the house without turning on lights.

"What wrong with you?" she asked to his back.

"Nothing," he muttered.

"Where have you been?" He stopped in his tracks and turned to look at her. The cold, angry mask that met her froze her in place.

"I've been to Artis's house," was all he said. She didn't ask more. Something was definitely wrong and she wasn't sure she could take more that night.

Jonathan walked into the kitchen and flipped on a light. He sat at the table and put his head on his hands. She stood in the doorway trying to decide if she wanted to join him or leave.

Jonathan lifted his head and looked at her miserably. "He didn't take your bracelet."

"How do you know?" Lisa asked.

"Because I went to his place and promised him a beat-down if he didn't come up with the truth. He admitted to a lot of things, but not to taking your bracelet." Jonathan looked at her and she recognized the misery in his eyes.

"Well, what did he admit to?"

"He told you about my prison sentence." Jonathan stared at her desolately.

She remained standing straight on the threshold. "Yes, he did."

"Did you get upset?" He looked at her expectantly.

"Yes, I was shocked. I was devastated. I couldn't believe I was in love with a man who'd done—whatever. I didn't know what you'd done. That's why I waited to talk with you."

"I knew you'd trip. That's why I'd kept it from you so long." She could tell he was cruising for an argument.

"Who wouldn't after finding out something like that from an acquaintance? Artis is your friend, not mine. That's something you should have told me a long time ago."

"Don't try to put that on me. You were the one who couldn't take the truth about me. You almost died locking yourself up in the bathroom like that."

"I was having an asthma attack. That had nothing to do with finding out about your prison record. It was coincidental," she said softly from her station at the threshold.

"No, you're afraid of people with a criminal history. You paint all of us with the same brush. When you found out about Artis's incarceration, you decided that he had to be the one that set the fire to your building," Jonathan accused.

"When he was at the Church Street building we had a fire and when he moved to the Broadway Boulevard building, we have a fire. Are we supposed to believe that those were mere coincidences?" Lisa asked in a huff.

"He didn't take your dang bracelet, Lisa. You had me go after my friend for nothing! he shouted.

"Don't yell at me. I didn't tell you to go after your friend! You did that on your own," she retorted.

"You went on and on about how he had been in your office all alone and you'd left the bracelet in there," he said.

"I told you I didn't know where the bracelet was. So now it's all my fault? You didn't tell me you were going to interrogate Artis." She put one hand on her hip and stepped into the room.

"So it's like that. I have to consult with you?" he snapped.

"If we're going to have a relationship we need to communicate. One person doesn't have all the answers or we wouldn't need each other," she said, her anger rising.

"Artis is the best friend I ever had and I was ready to beat him up," Jonathan said, looking at his hands. He wasn't ready to hear reason. He was more disgusted with himself than anything.

"Look, your friend divulged to your woman information you weren't ready for me to have. If that's what you call a friend, I don't need any. And I don't need this from you. I wish I could comfort you, but I've had a pretty rough day. I'm going on home now." She turned and fled from the house. He ran behind her.

He was close on her heels, but she was in an all-out sprint. He couldn't quite catch up with her. "Don't you walk away from me like that," he ordered.

Neither slowing her pace, nor looking back, she threw the door of the big truck open and climbed in. When he caught up with her, he tried the door. To his surprise it flew open.

"Don't leave this angry, Lisa. You could have an accident," he pleaded.

"Tell me why I should stay. I know you're angry

with me and you blame me for everything with your friend," she said, resting her head on the steering wheel.

"No, I don't. I'm very sorry. I didn't say the right things when you walked in. I was still kicking myself for what I said to Artis. It's all me. You're right, I should have talked to you first. I love you and I wanted to help you and it seems that each time I do, bad matters only get worse."

She turned in her seat and looked at him. Touched by the sincerity on his face, she stroked his cheek. "I accept your apology." She held out her arms for him to lift her down. He let her body slowly slide down his. When she was on the ground, he saw the tears in her eyes. "Baby, I'm so sorry. I never wanted to make you cry."

"You didn't make me cry. You made me angry and I always cry when I'm angry," she replied stubbornly.

"Let's go inside before you catch your death out here." He picked her up and carried her into the house.

"When have you eaten?" he asked as he set her on her feet in the kitchen.

"Not today. That's for certain," she replied.

"I have homemade soup we can warm up," he offered. "And we have homemade rolls left over from yesterday."

"That sounds delicious," she said. As they ate, he asked about her visit with Janice.

"Baby, I know you've been through a rough time today. I'm sorry I added to it," Jonathan said, taking her hand in his.

"It's frightening. I don't know what to do next. Janice suggested I retrace my steps, but that gets me nowhere," Lisa replied, setting her spoon in her bowl.

"You can't be finished already?" Jonathan asked in alarm.

"I'm not hungry."

"You have to eat," he insisted. "Going hungry won't solve your problems."

"What will?" she asked. Fear shone in her eyes and her breathing was shallow.

Jonathan had not realized before how afraid Lisa was. "It will work out all right," he assured her.

"I'm not so certain. If we can't find another suspect, it looks like I'm it," Lisa said, looking down at her bowl because she didn't want Jonathan to see her very real tears that were about to spill over.

He lifted her chin and studied her beautiful, tear-stained face. "Sweetheart, I'm not going to let anything happen to you," he promised. He stood and held out a hand for her.

Accepting his hand, she stood, but did not move from her spot. "Don't you want to finish eating?" she asked.

"I can eat anytime," he replied. "Right now, you need a little TLC."

They climbed the stairs silently together. "Sit here," he said, walking her to one of the chairs in the bedroom. When she was seated, he filled the deep bathtub with water and soothing bath salts.

She pinned up her hair and stripped out of her business attire, tossing it over the chair she'd just left. Jonathan tested the water for warmth before he called her into the bathroom. "Relax for a moment. I'll be right back." Resting her head against the back of the deep tub, she closed her eyes and tried to clear her mind of the day's events.

Before leaving the room, he poured massage oil into a small warming pot, and setting it on the bedside table, he plugged it in. Going to the living room, he dropped her John Legend CD into the player. When the singer's voice filled the house, she smiled for the first time that day. In a few minutes Jonathan returned with a glass of chilled zinfandel.

"Take a sip of this," he directed as he kneeled beside the tub.

"This is just what the doctor ordered." She sighed, setting the glass on the ledge.

"Are you ready for me to bathe you?"

"That's not necessary," she replied.

"Yes, it is. You've had a very rough day and I didn't help any by adding my problems to yours. This is your time to relax." He sponged her gently before helping her from the big tub. After drying her with an oversize towel, he wrapped her in it and took her to his bed.

"What is that?" she asked.

"Massage oil." He gently rubbed the warm liquid into her skin from her head to each of her toes. When she was glowing with his touch, he lay on the bed beside her. "Thank you, Jon. I feel so much better," she whispered, stroking his lean face.

"Tell me when you've had enough," he said before kissing her deeply. His tongue enjoyed the sensuous texture of hers. He stroked her smooth, satiny shoulder, then her soft breasts. His lips moved from her mouth to follow the trail his hands blazed from her shoulder to her torso. He stopped only long enough to plant tiny, fluttering kisses around her navel and the sensitive skin of her abdomen. His tongue blazed a trail from her flat abdomen to the throbbing moistness between her legs. Gently licking the swollen bud, he savored her sweet juices. He covered the area with his lips and greedily kissed it just as he had her mouth.

She moaned and writhed beneath him. Opening

her legs wider, she invited him to have his fill of her. Passion roiled throughout her body, coiling into a tight knot in the pit of her stomach. When she was so tense she couldn't move or breathe, the tightness unwound suddenly. A powerful force spiraled outward, causing her body to jerk convulsively.

Jonathan gave her full rein, but did not remove his mouth. He gripped her buttocks and deepened his kiss, intensifying the searing sensations surging through her veins. Writhing and squirming from his touch, she was overcome with pleasure. The powerful force that had overtaken her receded slowly, allowing her tense muscles to relax.

Depleted, all she could do was moan his name. He took a moment to take care of protection. While she was still wet and warm, he covered her body with his and entered her. His rock-hard member created powerful sensations that began building up again immediately. Wrapping her legs around his waist, she rose off the mattress, meeting him halfway. Already aroused beyond his control, he sank deeply into her. He rocked and pushed higher and higher toward his summit. Calling out her name, he yielded to the power of their connection, allowing himself to luxuriate in the force of their union. Momentarily exhausted and completely fulfilled, he dropped next to her and wrapped his arms around her waist. Neither uttered another word until morning.

CHAPTER 15

Toward the middle of the week Jonathan was off duty again and wanted to make good use of his time. He had to find some way to help Lisa, if for no other reason than to relieve her anxiety. He started with Janice, who refused to talk with him. "Anything we discuss will become a matter of record," she informed him.

"But I just have a couple of questions to ask you," he insisted.

"Jonathan, don't do this. I can't help if you have me removed from the case, and I will be if anyone thinks I've given you protected information. Don't compromise my case."

He told her he understood and ended the call.

He had another brainstorm and called Lisa. "Have you fired anyone who may hold a grudge against you?" he asked.

"No, we're very careful about how we let people go. We usually write them up and give them several warnings. Why do you ask?"

"I'm trying to figure this thing out. It shouldn't

be this difficult. I'm sure it's someone right under our noses."

"That's what I've been thinking, but I don't know where to look," she responded.

"Maybe it's something in an employee record or a file that will trigger an idea," he suggested.

"Could be. I'll stay a little later this evening to see what I can come up with."

"I don't want you up there alone at night. I'll bring your dinner and keep you company," Jonathan protested.

"It's okay. We have so much security around here now, I can hardly get in and out," Lisa replied.

Jonathan went home and tried to work on a car that was due to be finished soon. He'd already put off the owner a couple of times. Yet, even now, he found it difficult to focus. Inspiration just would not come to him.

Going back into the house, Jonathan replaced his coveralls with shorts and a T-shirt. He put sweats over them. Grabbing his basketball, he headed to the community center near Artis's house. He knew his friend sometimes played ball there after work.

He spotted Artis dribbling and running up and down the court alone as soon as he entered the gymnasium. "Hey, man, want to shoot some hoops?" Jonathan called.

By way of an answer, Artis passed him the ball with unnecessary force. Jonathan caught it easily and made a layup shot. The two played one-on-one until both were covered with perspiration. Neither could best the other. When Jonathan scored two points, Artis would score two more. They played like that for nearly an hour when, huffing and puffing, both called a time-out. Jonathan was leaned over at the waist trying to catch his breath, when Artis walked over and bumped into him on purpose.

Jonathan looked up and laughed. "Did that make you feel more like a man? You wanted to get close to me, didn't you, punk?"

"I don't need any more of your shit," Artis said, walking around Jonathan, trying to loosen his tightening calf muscles.

"About the other night—" Jonathan began.

"I know. You're upset your old lady might be going down for something she didn't do," Artis said. "I might be a little crazy too if it was Raquie."

"Thanks," Jonathan said, no longer gasping for air.

"What are you doing over here anyway?" Artis asked.

"Looking for you. I need to ask you something."

"I should have known. No, I don't have the bracelet and I don't know anything about it," Artis said with emphasis on each word. He turned to walk away.

"Wait up, man. I have another question," Jonathan called, easily trotting to catch up with Artis.

"Back to ol' Artis for help?" He stopped his exit to turn and look at his friend, waiting for him to speak. "You owe me, man. I thought you were my friend and you sold me out for a job. You owe me."

"I don't owe you nothing." He didn't walk away, but waited for Jonathan to speak.

"I spent a lot of time looking at the site today. Do you use that closet throughout the day?"

Artis nodded his head.

"Did you see anybody down there that day that shouldn't have been down there?" Jonathan continued.

"No, can't say I did," Artis answered after frowning and thinking a moment. "But you know what, Karl

Kemp plays ball over here sometimes. Hang around and see if he shows up."

"Who is Karl Kemp?"

"He's one of the janitors. I'm sure he's already been questioned, everyone has. Maybe he hasn't been asked the right questions yet."

The two men played basketball another hour, but Karl Kemp never showed up. Artis saw a friend of Karl's and spoke to him briefly.

"Karl lives a couple of streets over," Artis said when he returned. "Want to ride?"

"Sure, what can it hurt?"

Karl invited Artis in right away. When Artis explained who Jonathan was, the janitor was more than cordial. "Oh, you're the one they say she's hooked up with. You lucky dog. That woman's got it going on."

"That's the truth," Jonathan agreed.

"Look, if there's anything I can do to help, I will. She's been good to us. You know the janitorial service is contracted out, but she tips each of us at Christmas. I mean, really big," Karl related.

"Do you remember the day of the fire?" Jonathan asked, getting right to the point. He wanted to ask his questions while he had the chance.

"Yes. You know, since that fire, she's arranged for us to work at some of the other buildings. She didn't have to do that. But yes, I was around the day of the fire," Karl added, eager to help.

"Did you see anything out of place in the janitorial closet on the first floor?" Jonathan asked.

"No, I didn't. We're in and out of there all day. But you know there's more than one closet on each floor," Karl replied.

"I didn't know that. Did you use the one that the fire started in?" Jonathan asked.

"No, but I went down to the mail room to get some money my friend Rick owed me and I stopped to talk with one of the other custodians near the closet." Karl looked around as if he was thinking.

"What did you see?" Artis prompted him.

"This girl that runs the Church Street building rushed into the closet. It stands out in my mind because me and Rick spotted her at the same time and couldn't stop looking at her," Karl said.

"Because it's unusual to see a manager in that area?" Jonathan asked.

"Well, yes, it is, but that wasn't it. She's got a big behind to be such a little bitty thing," Karl said and held out his hand for Jonathan to give him five.

Giving the hanging hand a halfhearted slap, Jonathan asked, "Did she say anything to you guys?"

"No, I don't think she even noticed us. She rushed in there and didn't come out while I was talking to my man. We couldn't figure out what she was doing in there. Then we decided she may have been hooking up with some dude. We sure didn't want to witness that," Karl remembered.

"Did she have anything with her when she went in the closet?" Jonathan tried to think of the questions the investigators might not have asked.

"Yes, she had a big book," Karl said.

"Maybe she was hiding Lisa's bracelet in it," Artis suggested facetiously.

Jonathan took him seriously. "That's right. That could be it."

"What are you guys talking about?" Karl asked.

"Never mind. We've got to go," Artis said, turning toward the door.

"Thanks, I appreciate your help," Jonathan added.

"I sure don't want to see Lisa behind bars." Karl

followed them to the front porch, ready to continue their visit. Artis and Jonathan rushed away.

After dropping Artis off, Jonathan called Lisa's office and got her voice mail. The same thing happened when he called her cell phone and house. He made a quick decision to go to her office anyway. He took the next exit off Ellington Parkway and turned around to head south, back toward downtown.

Lisa was tired of being afraid and crying over her situation. She'd come to the conclusion that she'd have to take matters into her own hands. Instinct told her to start with her financial reports. Unfortunately she'd already had the older ones shredded. She could only look at the first ten months of the current year. She wished she still had the older ones on the computer.

George in the finance department had never sent her a copy of the e-mail from her that supposedly asked for hard copies of the monthly finance reports. For the past few years, the reports had been e-mailed to her. When had they started sending hard copies?

Going back through her files, she found that the electronic transmissions had stopped in March, over a year ago. It was funny how one could get busy and accept changes without question. That was something she should have noticed if she wasn't going in so many directions at once. Maybe dividing up her duties wasn't such a bad idea. Now she would have time to pay more attention to details. Her new assistants should arrive within the next week. They were busy training their replacements.

She picked up her phone and called Kita. "Please

call George again and tell him to forward my message asking for the financials via e-mail."

"I did that already."

"I haven't received it," Lisa replied.

"I'll call him again," Kita volunteered.

In a few minutes she rang Lisa's line again. "George said he tried to forward the message to you and it keeps popping back. He cut and pasted it into another document and it still popped back 'undeliverable,' your e-mail can't be delivered.' I'll called IT to check it out."

"Don't bother," Lisa said contemplatively. "Please tell George to express it overnight."

"Sure thing. Do you want me to ask him about your monthly financial report? I haven't seen it yet."

"I have it. Jennifer brought it to me last Friday," Lisa replied.

"How did she get past me?"

"I guess you were on break."

"That woman is up to no good. I never leave my desk for more than five minutes at the most, unless it's for lunch. There's something funny about her," Kita noted.

"Why would you say that? I'm sure she was trying to be helpful. I think she feels like she's hosting us since we're on her property," Lisa said, hoping that she was right. But hadn't Bruce said the same thing about Jennifer? She trusted both Bruce's and Kita's judgment.

"I have come in and found her near our offices more than once. I'm going to have the locks changed on our doors." Kita's voice was brisk and full of decision.

Lisa didn't try to argue with her, nor did she want to add to Kita's paranoia. Trying to remain neutral, Lisa said, "I'm sure she's trying to help."

"Yeah, right. Like we need that kind of help."

When their conversation ended, Lisa's attention returned to the stacks of data surrounding her. As she was poring over the documents line by line, it finally hit her. All the property managers showed salary figures that fluctuated, but not Jennifer. The salaries for the Church Street building remained the same month after month. She really needed those older reports to compare year to year for the same property. With that comparison she'd be able to tell if Jennifer's employees had stayed for the past few years. Had no one resigned after the fire? If she had brought on new employees, wouldn't their salaries fluctuate based on their level of experience?

She called Kita's extension again. "Have you called George yet?"

"Yes, of course," Kita replied, wondering at her boss's persistence over that one little message.

"Please call him again. Tell him to send my financial reports for the past two years."

"Month by month?" Kita asked, doubt clear in her voice.

"Yes," Lisa said crisply. "And I need them overnight express also. And yes, I do know how much they'll weigh. But I need them." She did not want to argue with her assistant, but she wanted to be clear about what she needed.

Realizing she'd have to wait for what she needed, she decided she would try an alternative. She went to the human resource department to talk with Miss Florence Henry. "I'm a little curious about staffing in this building," Lisa said as she took a seat.

"Jennifer does a wonderful job of maintaining her employees. We have never gotten a request from her for a new hire. She's doing something right." The director sighed, thinking about the many requests she received from the other managers.

"But look at Brentwood. That's one of our best-run properties, yet it has a twenty-five percent attrition rate," Lisa pointed out.

"Yes, he's better than average, but Jennifer's rate is better than industry standard."

"Do you know how she does that?" Lisa asked.

"Until we moved over here, I seldom saw Jennifer. I haven't discussed it with her."

"I see." Lisa walked away with more questions than answers.

Back at her desk, she stared at the figures on her spreadsheets, trying to discern the secrets they held. Her statistics professors had told her that numbers won't lie to you. You can count on them.

Here she was, the woman's supervisor, and she was sitting around speculating about why her salary figures were unchanged. The best thing would be to just go up to her office and ask her.

She tapped once on Jennifer's closed office door and walked in without hesitating. After all, it was an office, not private quarters. Entering the room, she was slammed with a surprise. Her name was shining brightly on Jennifer's computer screen. It topped a memo set up for an Outlook e-mail.

"What are you looking at?" Lisa asked.

"I'm just browsing through old memos," the young woman answered, not bothering to look at Lisa.

"It looked like you were in my e-mail box," Lisa stated.

"Don't be ridiculous. That was an e-mail from you." Jennifer tried to block the screen by moving her chair in front of the computer monitor, but Lisa could still see over her head.

"When I walked in I could have sworn my Outlook heading was on your screen," Lisa persisted.

"Yes, I was just going over a policy you sent out a while back," Jennifer said, shrugging.

"It was a blank. It looked like you were about to send out a memo," Lisa replied, irritated by the other woman's witless attempts at deception.

Jennifer rose from her seat and stared at Lisa. "What can I do for you this evening? I would have thought you'd be at home warm and cozy by now."

"I was reviewing this month's finance report. How could you possibly have the same expenses for payroll month after month? That doesn't happen." Lisa was blunt, hoping that Jennifer would be caught off guard and give an honest answer.

"Perhaps I'm a better manager than you think," Jennifer suggested unapologetically.

"Or worse. Maybe these numbers are made up," Lisa said, hazarding a guess. She was losing patience because the other woman was being brazen as usual.

"No, they're not made up. That is what we pay the employees over here," Jennifer insisted.

"And no one left you during the period the building was being renovated after the fire?" Again Lisa made a guess. She didn't have the numbers before her, but if they had remained the same for ten months, she assumed they'd be the same for the previous fourteen.

"My employees are very loyal. They would never leave me," Jennifer replied boldly.

"I need a list of all your employees and their Social Security numbers," Lisa said.

Obviously that request caught Jennifer off guard. She stammered for several moments before she said, "I don't have them. You'll have to get that information from HR."

"What? You have to have them. How do you approve their time?"

"I send everything to HR. Shouldn't that information be in a central location?" Jennifer asked sweetly.

"I see." Lisa continued standing before Jennifer, not wanting to leave until she was sure all her questions were answered. She had a feeling she wouldn't get a second chance with this woman. As she looked her over, an eerie feeling came over Lisa. Something was not quite right about Jennifer. Maybe it was the bottomless look in her eyes or the insipid smirk on her lips. Lisa suddenly wanted to be far from her. "Well, take care of yourself." Lisa had had enough. The woman was making her crazy with her lies.

"Lisa," Jennifer called behind her.

"Yes?"

"I'll go to HR first thing in the morning and have the information you requested sent to you."

"Don't bother. I'll go now." Lisa tried to curb her desire to run away from Jennifer. She managed to maintain a moderate pace.

When she turned to leave the office, Joe the security guard was just entering. "Hi, Lisa. I was just coming to check on you night owls. How is everything this evening?"

"Oh, they're just fine." Lisa tried to conceal her uneasiness.

"Is your hand healing okay?" Joe asked Jennifer, looking around Lisa.

The other woman instantly dropped her right hand into her lap. "I'm okay. I barely have a scar," she called out lightly as if she dared him to come any closer.

"Were you injured during our fire?" Lisa asked

curiously. That was the first she'd heard of Jennifer receiving an injury. She thought she would have known about one of her property managers being hurt.

"This was way before the fire," Joe said talkatively. "She burned her hands on the copier that morning. We took her to the first-aid room so she could get some Neosporin on her hands," the security guard related proudly.

"You're always good to me, Joe, but I was in a meeting all Friday morning." Jennifer fixed Joe with a cold stare. Lisa made a mental note to talk to Joe later.

Joe opened his mouth and closed it. Lisa turned to the jovial guard. "Come on, Joe, you can walk me to my office."

CHAPTER 16

Lisa walked away from Jennifer's office calmly, not willing to let the other woman see her growing apprehension. After their conversation, Lisa had no doubt that Jennifer was the perpetrator.

Entering her own office, Lisa heard the ringing phone. She grabbed it in time to hear one of the night shift security officers. "Ms. Stevens—ah, Captain Hill is here to see you. Should I send him up?"

"Yes, certainly, please send him to my office," Lisa said breathlessly. The conversation with Jennifer had truly unnerved her. She was so glad he'd come to her.

Jonathan arrived shortly. "What's wrong?" Taking one look at her face, he knew she was deeply disturbed. Lisa was usually unshakable, but something had certainly rattled her this time.

Lisa told him about her conversation with Jennifer. "In that case, you shouldn't be here. Did you tell security?" Jonathan asked.

"And what shall I tell them? That one of my employees spooked me? That doesn't make sense. She just raised the hair on my neck. I'm not sure if she's done anything wrong." Lisa was trying to talk herself down from the fit of nerves that had seized her.

"Okay, let's call Mr. Mueller. He should know what we can do. Maybe you could get an order of protection to keep her away from you," Jonathan advised.

"We can call him, but let's not go overboard. She just made me uneasy. That's all," Lisa repeated.

Jonathan dialed the attorney's number and gave the phone to Lisa. Alan listened attentively, then said, "Call the security chief and tell him what you just told me. Have them put extra guards on tonight." Lisa had tried to convince herself that her concerns were silly, but the tone of his voice proved otherwise. "Have the head of your human resource department gather all files you may possibly need," Mr. Mueller added.

"Sure, I'll leave a note for her to do it first thing in the morning," Lisa replied.

"No, do it tonight," Mr. Mueller stressed, urgency in his voice.

"Can't this wait until morning?" Lisa returned. "It's after ten o'clock. I hate to disturb her this time of night."

"Disturb her. Since this Jennifer person refused to give you information she obviously has, get your HR documents tonight. Who knows what tomorrow may bring? Have someone from your security team stay with you," the attorney instructed further.

"Jonathan is here with me," Lisa countered.

"Good. Now call security. Who knows what this person is capable of? She may not be the arsonist, but something is clearly out of order with her. Don't take this lightly," he warned. "We have workplace violence cases that explode based on much less than what you've told me. Move quickly." He wanted to be sure she understood the real threat facing her.

"I will," she promised.

"Come to my office first thing in the morning," he instructed finally.

When the phone call ended, Lisa filled in the missing pieces of the conversation for Jonathan. He agreed with everything Alan had said. Lisa called security with a request to meet her in the HR department. Jonathan walked with her, taking a second to look at every shadow in the well-lighted hallways.

The security officer that Lisa had called waited for them at the entrance to the department and unlocked the door as they approached. When they entered the large cubicle-filled area, the room was completely dark except for a soft gray glow emanating from a far corner. "Someone's been here," Lisa whispered.

"How do you know?" Jonathan asked.

"That light is from a computer monitor. It is highly unlikely anyone in this department left their computer on. That would be cause for a serious reprimand," she explained. "It's one of our policies to prevent hackers."

The officer motioned for them to remain near the door while he made his way to the computer. "No one is here," he called out. "But the unit is warm. Someone was here recently."

"Is it okay if I turn on the lights?" Lisa asked.

"Sure, go ahead. I believe we are alone," the guard replied.

After switching on the lights, Lisa went to the central file cabinet where information for the Church Street building was maintained. Nothing was there, but papers littered the floor. It was as if someone had left in a hurry.

"The files are gone," Lisa gasped, staring into an empty file drawer.

"And I bet if you tried to access any information by computer, that would be gone also," Jonathan opined, joining her at the cabinet.

They were still standing in the file room trying to come to terms with what they were up against when the HR director arrived. Lisa introduced Florence Henry to Jonathan. Told of the missing files, Florence went to her office and logged on. Sure enough, most of the personnel files had been deleted. Not just for Church Street, but for the entire region.

"Thank God for backups," Florence Henry said. "All of this information is on a backup disk at the bank. I'll get it for you in the morning."

They agreed there was no more for them to do that evening. Lisa left, wondering what she should do next. She had the uneasy feeling that something was about to happen. Would there be another fire?

Fortunately the building and all concerned made it through the night safely. The next morning Jonathan refused to go to work. Lisa insisted that she would be okay, but he knew that anything could happen.

"Anything can happen whether I'm with you or alone," Lisa reasoned.

"I'll feel better if I'm with you. Can you give in to me on this?" Jonathan argued.

"Okay, if you insist." As they drove to the attorney's office, he could see that she was relieved to have him with her.

"It's not so great going it alone all the time, is it?" he remarked as they went down Clarksville Highway.

"I can do it alone. But it is nice to have help," she relented, accepting his warm hand over hers. The smile she threw his way was all the gratitude he needed.

After seeing that they had coffee, Alan Mueller's secretary took a seat with them at the small cherry-wood table in the center of the spacious office. They had a clear view of nearby office buildings.

"I'm glad you came along," Mr. Mueller said to Jonathan. "I have questions regarding your role in fighting the fire. Perhaps you can give us the inside scoop on some things that have me confused."

"Absolutely. I'm here to help," Jonathan assured the attorney.

"First, tell me about your encounter with Jennifer . . . what is her name?"

"Jennifer Malone," Lisa supplied.

"Yes, Ms. Malone. How long has she worked for you?"

"Almost two years now."

"How long was she with you before the Church Street fire?"

"Six months."

"Why does that answer come to you so easily?" Mr. Mueller asked.

"Because I had conducted her employee evaluation a day or two before the fire. We give three- and six-month evaluations for our new hires," Lisa explained.

"Oh, I see."

Alan Mueller fired off questions and Lisa shot back answers for more than an hour. The secretary flipped the tape in her small recorder and continued taking notes.

When he'd exhausted his list of questions, he turned to Jonathan. "The last time we met with Janice McKee, she showed Lisa brass binder slides and pieces of a green binder. Was that part of the evidence you turned in after the fire?"

"Yes, sir." Jonathan listened to Mr. Mueller's questions intently, realizing how important his answers would be to Lisa's future, their future.

"Were they in the same vicinity as the bracelet?" Mr. Mueller did not look at Jonathan, but focused on the legal pad before him. He didn't want his eyes to prompt Jonathan to give any answer but the truth. At this point, the truth was all they had on their side.

"Well, yes. I saw the brass slides lying in the midst of a thick pile of ashes. When I kicked them around, I uncovered the bracelet," Jonathan explained.

"What did you do?"

"I bent over and picked the bracelet up. It was hard to believe that it was in there. I had to be sure it was Lisa's. I held it in my hand and my mind went to at least a dozen possibilities. Foremost in my mind was that if her bracelet was there, she was around somewhere. She always wore the bracelet," Jonathan related and stopped to be sure he was giving Alan what he wanted.

"Keep that last piece of information to yourself. That will be the prosecutor's contention," Alan advised, adjusting his glasses to review his notes. "As this investigation is conducted, only answer the question that is asked, nothing more."

"Even if it's you doing the asking?" Jonathan asked for clarification.

"Yes. If I don't ask a question, it may be because I don't need to know the answer. Do you understand?" Mr. Mueller looked gravely from Jonathan to Lisa.

They both nodded and Mr. Mueller continued, "Janice McKee contends that they've examined the ashes and they have identified pieces from a ledger report cover, such as those used to bind Lisa's financial reports. Those are going to be key to the state's evidence. It further links Lisa to that room. The bracelet may not have been enough, but all that together will make jurors think, 'Okay, one coincidence is possible, but a second is stretching my belief,'" Alan Mueller explained.

"So what is our explanation?" Lisa asked, wanting to move on to discover how bad things were looking for her.

Jonathan had a ready answer. "I talked to a janitor in the building who saw Jennifer Malone go in that closet with something that could have been the ledger. What if her bracelet had dropped off Lisa's wrist and was concealed in the ledger? All Jennifer wanted was the ledger but ended up burning a diamond bracelet."

"My catch was broken. The bracelet had begun to fall frequently," Lisa explained.

"Could it have come off at your desk?" Mueller probed.

"Yes. It wasn't on my wrist when I got to the property managers' meeting. That was the first time I knew it was missing. Before the meeting, I had been working on the financial report. When I returned, Artis was in my office shredding old reports, but the new report was missing. We looked but couldn't find it." She could see that morning in her mind.

"So Jennifer came into your office, got the ledger, and burned it without realizing a diamond bracelet was in it," Jonathan quickly surmised.

"Why would Ms. Malone burn the ledger?" Mr. Mueller asked. "Is there a logical explanation?"

"It has something to do with her employee figures. Her salary dollars and employee base are too consistent. She's found a way to embezzle money and it's through salary dollars," Lisa posited.

"Good thinking!" Mr. Mueller surprised Lisa with his praise. "Now that's logical thinking and easy to prove. It'll take some time and it won't be easy, but we can do it. We'll have to do a major trace to find her bank. If she's clever enough to hide her theft this long, we'll have to conduct a pretty in-depth search for sure." Mr. Mueller seemed to relax now that he had something to sink his teeth into.

"What if she has offshore accounts? We may never find them," Lisa noted, not quite ready to celebrate with the others.

"They can look at her pattern of spending. Find out what she's purchased," Jonathan supplied. "She's bound to have slipped up somewhere."

Lisa gave him a questioning look and he explained, "That's how they caught Artis." He shrugged in nonchalance to let her know that discussing Artis no longer bothered him.

"We'll find it. I have a team of auditors that are experienced at tracking ill-gotten gains. Go home until I call you. This is all but over," Mr. Mueller assured the young couple.

They were preparing to leave when Florence Henry showed up with the backup disk. "I could have been here sooner, but I stopped by the office to make a copy of the disk. I was afraid to walk around with our only copy," she explained anxiously.

Lisa added, "Mrs. Henry's records will document what I said about Jennifer's employees. Mr. Mueller, do you have a computer Florence could use? It won't take but a moment for her to pull up the disk. It would help if she directs us to what's pertinent."

There it was right before their eyes. Lisa said, "Of the nineteen positions, only ten people actually have used vacation days or sick leave in two years. For the other nine employees, those days continue to accrue. That's what I saw on the monthly financial reports." Lisa turned to explain to the others staring at the screen over her shoulder. She continued to scroll the data.

"Jennifer's staff has an unusually high number of sick days and annual days. Half of them never take off. It is totally unrealistic."

"What about other benefits?" Jonathan asked.

Mrs. Henry leaned over Lisa and used the mouse to move the cursor to the next section of the data. "No, they haven't bought stock through the employee stock option program, nor have they used the credit union, been garnisheed, changed medical or dental benefits, or anything. Their accounts remained unchanged, but they continued receiving raises. Let's look at one more report," Mrs. Henry said.

Next Mrs. Henry went to the unemployment insurance claim report. Skimming to the Church Street section, she found one employee listed two years back. Noble Parker had filed for unemployment insurance.

"He's listed as one of her current employees," Lisa said. "Go back to her employee list."

There he was listed on the most recent payroll report. "When did you receive his request from the employment office?" Lisa asked.

"February twenty-fifth, 2003," Florence read from the top of the document.

"That was two days before the fire in the Church Street building," Jonathan said.

Lisa looked at him surprised and he replied, "I told you I'll always remember that date."

"So why did Jennifer need a fire?" Alan Mueller asked. "What was she burning? The human resource department had already received the unemployment compensation claim. What was she trying to destroy?"

"I don't know," Lisa said, puzzled. "Let's look at benefit claims a few days before the Broadway Boulevard building fire," Lisa suggested.

Sure enough, one of Jennifer's former employees had applied for COBRA, temporary health care coverage, after she'd quit working at Sand Castles.

"The information we have here is good evidence for an embezzlement case. It looks like she kept employees on payroll after they left the company in order to get their paychecks for herself. But what does all this have to do with the fire?" Alan Mueller asked.

"Give me time to look over this information and compare it to my monthly financial statements," Lisa said. "There is a definite connection and like you said before, I'm probably the only one who can find it."

Florence Henry printed out hard copies of the information for Lisa and the attorney. They parted feeling they'd made headway that morning.

When Lisa returned to her office, the overnight express bundle from the corporate office in Miami was on her desk. This was the final piece of the puzzle. Lisa tore into the package and barricaded herself behind the closed door. She cross-checked and rechecked data, trying to discover a pattern. What were they telling her? She was certain the answers were there, but she hadn't found the best way to pull them out yet.

Late in the evening, her cell phone rang while she was sitting at her desk. "Hello, Lisa, I have good news for you. At least it's the answer to one of your questions," Mr. Mueller said.

"What's that?" she asked.

"Seventy-five thousand dollars a month is the answer to *how much*. And to an account in her mother's name in Virginia is the answer to the question *where*. I'll turn everything over to the Metro Fire Department's arson investigator," Mr. Mueller said, sounding relieved. "You can go home now. Don't stay there all alone."

Lisa wanted to build an airtight case against Jennifer so that no one would dare consider her a suspect again. She called to check in with Jonathan and tell him about Alan Mueller's most recent discovery.

"I just got a call from Mr. Mueller. We have more evidence that it's Jennifer. Deposits to a bank account in her mother's name can be traced back to Jennifer," Lisa said after sliding down in her big comfortable chair. Her back had gotten tired from sitting still so long.

"Didn't you tell me her facility is the most poorly maintained of all Sand Castles properties?" Jonathan asked.

Lisa nodded, the light coming to her immediately. "Yes, she had to cut back somewhere. She also reduced the number of janitors under contract. She is still budgeting the same amount of dollars for employees and for that contract."

"And she knew that if you had accurate monthly reports, you would immediately know what she was doing. So she was intercepting your report every month to be sure you got the information she wanted you to have," Jonathan guessed.

"That's right. Except in the months where someone filed a claim. Those claims show up as budgetary items and it would lead me to cross-check to see who had left," Lisa supplied.

"And she didn't want you to know anyone had left. Thus the fire," Jonathan added.

"Why did she burn them? Why didn't she just shred the reports?" Lisa asked. "She put so many lives at risk with her fires."

"Shredded information can be put back together with the technology available now," Jonathan said. "Besides, she wasn't trying to burn the buildings. How was she to know the sink in the janitor's closet was flammable?"

"I guess she couldn't very easily have walked out with the reports either. She knew someone would notice them right away," Lisa surmised.

"Don't think about her anymore. Get your things together and come home," Jonathan ordered.

"Okay. I'll leave in a few minutes," Lisa agreed.

Lisa took another look at the human resource report. It proved that Jennifer's terminated employees remained on the payroll. When their paychecks were delivered from the home office in Miami, Jennifer accepted them and deposited them into an account in her mother's name.

Lisa ran a total of the paychecks for the nine former employees on Jennifer's payroll. The paychecks did not total seventy-five thousand dollars a month. But add to that the money she could skim from the janitorial contract and you did have the magic number, a nice monthly total of seventy-five thousand dollars. That was a bonus any employee would appreciate. And Jennifer could get it without much difficulty. Home office always sent paychecks directly to the properties to expedite their delivery. And each manager could write checks for regular expenses without approval, such as the janitorial service contract.

The phone rang again. She looked at her watch.

It was almost seven o'clock. She noticed that it was already dark outside her windows and she had not bothered to close the blinds. "Hello," she replied absently.

"Lisa, if you don't lock up and go home now, I'm coming to get you." Jonathan's voice rang through her preoccupied fog.

"Okay, okay. I'm leaving," she said, standing while she spoke as if he could see her.

"I'll call you again in fifteen minutes and you'd better be in your car," he threatened.

"Okay, I'm leaving," she promised, piling the precious documents into her briefcase.

Her door opened, startling her. "I thought you'd still be here," Jennifer said pleasantly.

"Why are you here so late?" Lisa asked. The hair stood up on her neck, but she tried not to show her alarm.

"I'm always here. This is my building and I take my responsibility very seriously, or hadn't you noticed?" Jennifer asked. She strolled into Lisa's office and took a seat at the desk.

"I'd say you do," Lisa agreed readily. "I was just about to go home. What do you want?"

"Don't be so snippy," Jennifer said smoothly. "I just wanted to give you my resignation letter."

She dropped a sheet of Sand Castles stationery before Lisa, who read it without picking it up.

"I'm sure your mother will be glad to have you back home," Lisa said, referring to the young woman's statement that she was leaving to go work for a company in Richmond.

"My mother is dead," Jennifer corrected. "I just have two sisters still living there. They're married with families, but we're real close."

"Oh, I see," Lisa said, suddenly feeling ill again.

"I've turned down many opportunities since I've worked for you because I'm loyal. But you never respected my abilities," Jennifer accused.

"I'm sure another company may be better suited for your abilities," Lisa said as neutrally as possible. "I'm about to call security to have a guard walk me out. Do you want me to wait for you?" Lisa wanted to run and leave Jennifer in her office, but she instinctively knew it would be a mistake to let the other woman see her fear. She wondered if she could smell it.

"I was just wondering if you found what you're looking for." Jennifer moved to stand closer to the desk.

"Yes." Lisa kept her eyes on the woman as she approached her.

"What are you trying to do?" Jennifer asked.

"Get enough evidence to prove you're behind all my troubles." Lisa watched for Jennifer's reaction to her words.

"You know I can't let you do that. I should have taken care of you last night," Jennifer said coldly.

"Take care of me?" Lisa asked, not wanting to decipher euphemisms. She wanted to be sure of what she was dealing with.

"Yes—take care of you. I don't want to have to. Murder has never been my forte. But I will if I have to."

"What do you plan to do?" Lisa asked, looking for a way to get around Jennifer.

Without any warning whatsoever, the computer hurled through the air at the same time Lisa slipped from the chair and rolled under her desk. Instinct had made her drop and roll just in the nick of time. The computer landed in the chair where she had been sitting.

"Come out, come out, wherever you are," Jennifer called, coming around the desk.

When she was within reach, Lisa clutched the petite woman's ankle and flipped her to the floor. Without a second thought, Lisa jumped on top of her and screamed for help. Jennifer was squirming, kicking, and yelling.

The door slammed open. "Are you ladies okay?" a security guard asked, distracting Lisa. The smaller woman surprised her, tossing her to the side. Before Lisa could react, Jennifer was on her feet and running out the door.

Lisa rose to her knees and yelled, "Stop her!"

"What's going on?" the guard asked.

"She's been burning our buildings," Lisa said, running around the guard and behind Jennifer.

Jennifer ran past the elevator and toward the stairwell. As she opened the door, she ran full force into Jonathan, who stumbled backward and almost tumbled into Janice, who followed him.

"What the hell! Let me go!" Jennifer yelled. Jonathan firmly gripped both of her arms as she struggled to get away.

"We can't do that, dear," Janice said kindly. "Calm down or I will have to put my nice silver bracelets on you. Do you want that?"

Janice now had a firm grip on the culprit and Jonathan gladly released his hold. When Jennifer didn't answer, Janice said, "No, I didn't think so."

"What's going on?" Jonathan asked, wrapping his arms around Lisa.

"Where did you guys come from? Why were you using the steps? What are you doing here?" she asked breathlessly.

"Take a deep breath. Now let it go," Jonathan instructed.

"Why are you here?" she asked again.

"I told you to go home or I was coming to get you. I saw there was no sense in calling you again," Jonathan explained, still holding Lisa close at his side.

"I was on my way to arrest Ms. Malone," Janice said. "I reviewed everything Mr. Mueller sent over and just received an arrest warrant. I have a couple of uniforms coming up the elevator. Oh, here they are now." She referred the two Metro Police officers who were coming down the hall toward them. They joined Janice as she walked with Jennifer. "Do you have somewhere we can sit for a moment or two?"

"Let's go back to my office. All my evidence is in there. Go down the hall and it's the first door to the right," Lisa replied. "I'm glad you guys were here. She could have gotten away."

After a couple of hours of questions, Janice was able to piece together Jennifer's story. Jennifer admitted that she had taken the paychecks from terminated employees. That was hard for her to deny since all the evidence was there.

Janice had all the particulars on the bank account that Jennifer had opened in her mother's name. When Lisa told Janice about the security guard from the night before, Janice called him in.

While they waited for Joe to arrive, Lisa explained her evidence. "I checked and rechecked the configurations to my e-mail. I had to figure out why I couldn't get certain reports. That's when I discovered any e-mail I received from finance was forwarded to Jennifer. Of course, she knew I'd look for my finance reports. So she decided to have hard copies sent to me and she could easily come by and fix them up."

When Joe arrived, all attention was turned to him.

"Tell me about Ms. Malone's burns on the day of the big fire at the Broadway Bouldevard building," Janice directed.

"I was sitting at my desk when Ms. Malone came running toward my desk. She said she'd burned her hand trying to clear the copier," he related.

"What did you do?" Janice asked.

"I went to look at her hands and she said she needed me to get her documents out of the copier. She said they were highly confidential and she didn't want anybody to see them. I wanted to help her but she said the papers were more important. All she needed me to do was unlock the first-aid room so that she could get some Neosporin."

"The first-aid room is also the room that houses the controls for our security system," Lisa explained to Janice.

"Was she burned badly?" Janice asked.

"I didn't actually see the burn, but I thought she was. She had tears in her eyes. She seemed to be in a great deal of pain. Now that I think about it, she had a white handkerchief or something around it." Joe was extremely nervous. "Have I done something wrong?"

"No, Joe, we just need you to help us," Lisa said.

"Ms. Malone is a manager. I didn't think anything about her going into the first-aid room," Joe offered apologetically.

"So you opened the first-aid room and went to clear the paper jam. What happened next?" Janice asked.

"I pulled out the paper and was about to bring it to her when she met me halfway across the lobby. She was a pitiful little thing. I mean, tears were running down her face, but she didn't really make a sound. I recommended she go to the doctor and she said she needed to go to a meeting." He looked around proudly to see how his story was being accepted.

"Why didn't you tell us about Ms. Malone when you were questioned before?" the investigator asked.

"Because all of that was early in the day. It had nothing to do with the fire," he explained, waving his hand.

Janice turned to Jennifer. "Did you send this guard away so that you could pull the wires to the alarm system?"

"I don't have to answer that without an attorney present," Jennifer replied.

"Joe, did you notice that the system wasn't working after Jennifer left?" Lisa couldn't help but ask.

"No, I went on my rounds, then went to lunch, and when I came back the building was burning."

"What time did Ms. Malone ask for your help?" Jennifer asked.

"It was around ten o'clock," Joe answered.

"She did all that in the middle of our ADA meeting!" Lisa exclaimed. "She went upstairs and got my financial report. You never knew you had my bracelet, did you?" Lisa asked.

"I will not answer any questions without my attorney," Jennifer repeated.

"In that case, I'll read you your rights and take you in. Have your attorney meet you up the street at the Criminal Justice Center."

CHAPTER 17

After everyone had left, Lisa closed her door and leaned against it. "Jonathan, thank you so much for believing in me and trusting me."

"You are a good, honest woman, Lisa. I have never had any reason to question your innocence."

"Come here," she said. He walked into her arms. "You saved my life again. That woman was determined to kill me tonight."

"That wasn't even a possibility. She would have had to come through me," he said, gently rubbing Lisa's tense back.

"I'm so glad you're always there for me." She rested her cheek against his chest, relaxing for the first time in what seemed like weeks.

"I will always take care of you," he promised. She felt soft and warm in his arms. He was instantly aroused by the feel of her body against his and tried to suppress his desire.

"You're my hero," she said teasingly, rising to her tiptoes to plant a kiss on his lips. When her firm breasts slid up his chest, he reminded himself that he was supposed to be comforting her, not thinking about his lust.

"I wish. You're the courageous one. I can't believe you stayed in here talking calmly to that woman you knew wanted to kill you." He smoothed the strands of hair away from her face and drank in her warm beauty. Remembering what she'd gone through that evening filled him with fear all over again. He had been beside himself as Lisa had given her account of her most recent episode with Jennifer.

"But I'm not the one who runs into burning buildings," she returned.

"I'm trained to run into burning buildings. I have on protection and it's a calculated risk. When you confronted that potential killer you had no such protection," he said, finally showing his fear for her safety.

"Well, you had my back." She tried to alleviate his concern.

"Please stop being such a daredevil," he pleaded.

"That means I'll get boring and you'll have to find an interesting woman. No, I think I'll go for adventure any day."

"I hope you've had enough for one day. Can we get out of here?" he asked, looking around at the shambles her office had been left in.

"Can you give me a few minutes to make a couple of phone calls? When I get home I don't want to have to deal with this mess anymore."

"Is there something I can do to help?"

"Yes, please call Mr. Mueller first and tell him about what's happened. I'll call Jet and the family."

Jonathan sat at the table to make his phone calls while Lisa moved to her desk. She gave Jet the play-by-play of Jennifer Malone's eventual arrest. They decided to downplay the fraud and embezzlement charges. Neither looked good for the company. They would simply send out a news release stating the arsonist had been found.

When Lisa called her mother, they cried with joy. Mary was so relieved that Lisa's ordeal was finally over. Lisa ended the call by promising her mother she'd be home soon.

When she finished, she noticed Jonathan was sitting watching her. The desire in his eyes called out to her. She moved to where he was and sat on his lap. The hem of her skirt rose and he reached under it to stroke the soft, warm flesh of her hips.

"What's on your mind?" she asked huskily.

"You—you are the most beautiful, sexy woman I've ever seen in my life. I just enjoy looking at you," he whispered into her neck.

"No, you are. I love everything about you." She took his lower lip between her teeth and teased it gently. Relaxing in his arms, she enjoyed the feel of his hot hand against her cool flesh. Each movement of his hand seared her, sending waves of heat through her body.

He continued to stroke her gently. "Ummm, baby, that feels so good," she whispered, holding on to him with her arms wrapped around his neck.

He slipped his fingers inside her panties and found the center of her heat. Rubbing the slick nub briskly with his forefinger, he nibbled her ears and licked her neck. She got caught up in the rhythm flowing through her and opened her legs to give him better access. Her hips rose and fell with the movement of his hand. Her skirt was now up around her waist.

Before she knew what was happening, she was rocked with a torrid explosion that left her senseless. He held on to her tightly, burying his face in her neck.

When her movements ceased, he said, "That was just a little something for the built-up tension. Do you feel better now?"

She nodded, surprised at what she'd just done. Jonathan continued holding on to her tightly. When her tremors had subsided, she rose to her feet and grabbed his hand. "Let's go home for the main course," she invited.

They were smiling and holding hands as they hurriedly left the building. "Do you want to go to your place or mine?" Jonathan asked.

"I want to go the farm. I don't want to talk with reporters for a while. As soon as the fire department makes its announcement, I'll start getting calls. Let's hide," Lisa decided.

The night had grown cold, but without the threat of a prison sentence hanging over her head, Lisa felt young and free for the first time in weeks. She looked around and saw things that she'd been too busy to notice since she'd first known she was a *person of interest* in the arson case.

"Jonathan, why do you drive this silver car all the time now?" Lisa asked when they entered the garage.

"She's one of a kind. I like her a lot," he replied, not daring to look at the lady eyeing him critically. He'd promised her no more dishonesty and he wondered if his response would count. To tell her that he'd sold Zora would lead her to ask why and he wasn't ready to tell that yet.

"I haven't seen Zora for a long time. Are you having something new done to her?" Lisa asked.

"No." Jonathan took Lisa by the elbow and helped her into her truck. "I'll see you at home."

Lisa wondered at his cryptic responses.

When they arrived at the farm, Jonathan said,

"Let's go to bed. We had a little appetizer. Are you ready for the main course?"

Their lovemaking was sweet and tender that night. Lisa clung to Jonathan, thankful that she was still alive. Jonathan cherished Lisa, grateful that he had another day with her.

After they were satisfied, Lisa asked, "What do you want to do now?"

"Go to sleep," Jonathan growled. "We have to get an early start tomorrow."

"An early start doing what?" Lisa asked curiously, following him through the house as he turned off lights.

"You'll see," was his only response

"But I'm not sleepy," she protested. "I'm still too wound up." She sat up in bed.

"Then lie in my arms and just let me hold you," he insisted, wrapping her in his arms again.

Saturday was usually the one day of the week that Lisa could count on for sleeping in. Needless to say, she was more than a little perturbed when Jonathan began singing "You Are My Sunshine" loud and off-key in her ear.

She tried to swat him away without opening her eyes, but he was persistent. "Jonathan, why are you waking me up this early? I just went to sleep. What's wrong with you?" She sat up in bed, his T-shirt she'd used as a gown slipping off her shoulder. Her hair was tousled all over her head. She was such a beautiful, disheveled mess, he was tempted to get back in bed. He dismissed the thought, reminding himself of the special day he had planned.

"Let's go, Ms. Lisa. We have things to do today." He tugged at her arm, pulling her from the bed.

"What do we have to do before sunrise?" she asked, sitting on the side of the bed.

"Go get dressed. It's cool out and we're going to be outside a long time," he said mysteriously.

By now she was intrigued by his secrecy. Something was definitely going on. She could feel excitement emanating from Jonathan's pores. Once they were in the car, he drove deeper into Cheatham County instead of back into the city.

When they stopped out on a grassy field she exclaimed, "Hot-air balloons? You want to go hot-air ballooning?"

He grinned and jumped out of the car. "Yes, Lisa. You and I are going up today."

"I thought you said you'd never ride in anything where you don't have control of the steering wheel."

"That's true. I did say that. But I reserve the right to change my mind today and forevermore," he said solemnly.

She laughed at his solemn attitude and from sheer excitement. By the time he'd opened the car door for her, she was bouncing with anticipation. The pilot met them halfway as Lisa, in her enthusiasm, pulled Jonathan across the field.

"Good morning, Jonathan. It looks like the lady is raring to go." Jonathan shook the man's hand. "Firmin, this is the lady I told you about, Lisa Stevens. She usually likes her rides fast and low, but I think she'll get a thrill out of going up high and slow today. Lisa, I'd like you to meet the pilot for our trip, Firmin Josten."

Lisa shook the pilot's hand and followed him toward his crew that was busy inflating the balloon. They arrived at the brilliantly colored raspberry, purple, gold, and red balloon as the crew was setting

the basket upright. "Step in, Firmin," one of the crew
members said.

He did as instructed and pulled a lever to shoot
a flame into the envelope. The balloon grew larger
as the air inside became warmer. When it was fully
inflated he signaled for Lisa and Jonathan to join
him in the basket.

They eagerly jumped in and held their breaths as
they rose slowly above the treetops. A gust of wind
took them south, over farms they had passed on the
way to the field. Firmin allowed the balloon to de-
scend, just above the treetops, to give them a better
look at the land they were passing over.

From their vantage point high above the clouds,
silence surrounded them except for the occasional
sound of the burner heating the air inside the balloon. Beneath them they could see fields, trees, and
a house or miniature car here and there. Looking
far beyond the river, they had an unobstructed view
of the tallest buildings downtown. That morning
everything was wrapped in an ethereal fog.

The balloon drifted with the wind. Lisa felt almost
no movement. The only way she could tell they
moved at all was by the change of scenery. It was a
welcome, soothing sensation after the weeks of tension she'd endured. Jonathan stood behind her and
wrapped his arms around her waist. She rested her
head against his chest and enjoyed the sight of the
rising sun over the Cumberland River. The whole
earth was bathed in shades of yellow and gold.

"It's amazing how much we can see from up here,
isn't it?" he asked in her ear.

Nodding her head, she kept her eyes on the magnificent scenery.

"If I could, I would give you everything you see,"
Jonathan said softly.

"I don't want all that. It's too much responsibility," she said, turning in his arms.

"What do you want, Lisa?" he asked, his voice becoming hoarse.

"I want you," she said, raising honest eyes to look into his.

"That's good to hear," he said, sounding relieved. He surprised her completely when he dropped to one knee. "Lisa Stevens, will you give me the honor of becoming my wife?" He took a small heart-shaped box from inside his jacket pocket.

She covered her mouth with both hands to keep from screaming *yes*. Tears streamed down both cheeks. He opened the box and, taking out the ring, put the box back in his pocket. Standing, he gently pried a hand from her face and placed the ring on her finger.

"It's a perfect fit," she said, amazed, holding her hand before her and staring at the ring.

"Yes, it is. Do you like it?" he asked nervously. He remembered Mr. Mueller's warning not to buy a ring without her.

"I love it. It's beautiful," she said, throwing her arms around his neck. "I love you so much. This is beautiful."

"Lisa," he said quietly, "will you marry me?"

"Yes, yes, yes!"

Wrapped in a bliss of their own, they were unaware the balloon had returned to earth until they heard Firmin's voice. Looking around, they saw the crew approaching them in the chase truck. Firmin and Jonathan jumped from the basket and then turned to offer a hand to Lisa.

After that the newly engaged couple had no more personal time. They were put to work milking the balloon, squeezing an armful of the balloon and stuffing it into a heavy storage bag.

When that job was done, Lisa noticed a table set in the near distance. The autumn day had become quite warm and as they walked to the table, she began shedding layers of clothes and stuffing them into her backpack.

The crew, gathered around the table, called out for Lisa and Jonathan to join them. The table was covered with a white Battenburg lace cloth, set with heavy silver, china, and crystal. A floral arrangement of mums and gladiolas sat in the center of the snow-white elegance. Chairs were covered in the same white cloth.

Firmin, who was seated at the head of the table, motioned for Lisa and Jonathan to join him. They sat side by side to Firmin's right. An oversize picnic basket sat next to the container and a member of the crew was busily removing containers from it and passing them to others at the table. They each took a portion of food from each container before passing it.

When all glasses and plates were filled, Firmin stood and said, "It is our tradition to drink a toast at the end of a flight. Today's flight was extra special. I witnessed Lisa and Jonathan make a lifelong commitment to each other. In honor of this occasion, we've prepared an extra-special champagne brunch. We want to be the first people on earth to congratulate you."

"Hear, hear!" the rowdy crew of six men and one woman shouted.

Captain Josten stood and raised his glass. His crew joined him. "May God, the best maker of all marriages, combine your hearts in one."

"Salute," rang out from the crew.

As the meal was enjoyed, Jonathan and Lisa were

roasted. Everyone had a bad joke about marriage. One man asked Jonathan, "Do you know what Groucho Marx said about marriage?"

"No," Jonathan replied, realizing he was the straight man for a joke.

"Marriage is a wonderful institution, but who wants to live in an institution?"

"Who was Groucho Marx?" Lisa asked, tongue in cheek.

The older man took her question seriously and answered, "He was a great comedian back in the—"

"I know, I know," Lisa interrupted. "I just wanted to take some wind out of your sails."

"Why do all the jokes about marriage make it seem that women want to be married more than men?"

"They don't," one of the women said. "These men just refuse to tell the truth on themselves. Have you ever heard that behind every great man is a surprised mother-in-law?"

"I hadn't heard that one," Lisa admitted.

"Actually, I believe marriage is wonderful if you can work through the difficult year," the cynical crew member said.

"Which year is that?" Jonathan asked.

"It's always the year you're in," was the answer.

"Don't listen to him. He's always bitter in between marriages. How many times have you been married now?" Firmin asked the weary-looking middle-aged man.

"Do you mean, how many houses do I have mortgages on?" the man bantered.

The crew joked back and forth throughout the meal. When the meal ended, the captain offered a prayer of thanksgiving for their safe return to earth before the crew parted. One of the crew members drove the couple back to Jonathan's car while the others packed up.

Lisa and Jonathan were driving down the highway, headed home, when Lisa asked, "Jonathan, when do you want to get married?"

"I don't know. I guess you want a wedding, and those things take a while to plan. But as far as I'm concerned, the sooner it is the better." He stole a glance at her to be sure he'd given her the answer she wanted.

"Good. I want to call my mother and get her started with the plans. Is that okay with you?" Lisa asked.

"Sure. Whatever you want to do. Just don't go overboard, please," he said.

"No, no way," she said, taking her cell phone from her backpack. She hit the one number needed to connect her to her mother.

"Mama, how are you doing this beautiful, glorious day?" Lisa asked when her mother answered the phone.

"I'm great and rejoicing because all that legal mess is behind you," Mary answered. "You must be very happy."

"I am, Mama."

"I figured you're ecstatic, considering you're up this early on a Saturday," Mary teased.

"It was a heavy burden and I am happier than I was yesterday. Do you want to know why?" Lisa was practically bouncing in her seat.

"Why?" Mary asked.

"Mama, Jonathan and I just came down from a hot-air balloon trip where he asked me to marry him." Lisa tried to keep her voice calm, but excitement was in every word.

"Oh my God, that's wonderful. When is the

wedding? What do I need to do? Do you want me to come there? Oscar, Oscar, Lisa just got engaged."

Lisa moved the phone away from her ear, waiting for her mother to calm down.

"Lisa, this is fantastic news," Oscar said.

"Oscar, good morning. I didn't wake you up, did I?" Lisa asked.

"No, you didn't, but your mother did. She's running around the bedroom praising God."

"Was she that afraid I'd never marry?" Lisa asked, laughing at the image of her mother shouting around the bedroom.

"No, she was a little worried about who you might marry. She's thanking God that he sent her baby a good man. Do you want to hold on until she finishes her praise service?" Oscar asked, only half joking.

"Give me that phone," Lisa heard her mother say in the background before Oscar said, "Bye, Lisa, we'll talk. Let me know what you want me to do for the wedding."

"Lisa, I don't want to talk about this over the phone. I'll call Louise and we'll be there Monday morning. By the time we get there you should have a date in mind and we'll discuss locations, and all the details. Good-bye, darling. I'm so happy for you."

"Whew! That wasn't the reaction I expected," Lisa said when her call to her mother ended.

"What did you expect?" Jonathan asked.

"My mother is usually cool, calm, and collected. She's never bugged me about getting married the way Louise does. But I get the feeling she doubted my ability to find the right man. She sounded more relieved than anything," Lisa said, wondering at her mother's reaction.

"She *is* pretty crazy about me," Jonathan answered arrogantly.

"Don't go getting conceited," Lisa said, punching his biceps.

"I'm just stating a fact," he teased. "Do you know why she never asked you what your answer was?"

"Tell me why, Jonathan," Lisa said with a threatening edge to her voice.

He looked at her and figured he'd teased her enough. "Ugh—maybe because you wouldn't have called sounding happy otherwise," he offered.

"You're a smart man, Jonathan. If you'd given the wrong answer that time, you would have found yourself walking home."

"Were you going to put me out of my own car?" he asked. Looking at her, he decided she would.

"Yes," she said and didn't elaborate.

As they approached the road to his house, Jonathan asked, "Do you want to go back to my place?"

"No, I'd better go on home and prepare for the mothers. I hope they bring Cara. She takes some of the pressure off me when they start double-teaming me." Lisa didn't sound miserable at all. In fact, she sounded as if she was looking forward to all the fuss.

"I thought you and I would have a little time to get used to the idea of being engaged," Jonathan said, wondering at the turn of events. He felt like he was about to lose his woman.

"We will. My mother's years of being in public relations have taken over now that she's about to plan a major event. Once I tell her what I want, I'll be out of the equation. She's just coming into town for a consultation. After that, she'll give me what I want and I won't have to do a thing."

Those were Lisa's famous last words. It would be two weeks before the couple had quality time alone again.

Mary and Louise flew up on the Gulfstream and went directly to the Loews Hotel where they rented the presidential suite. They called for Lisa and Jonathan to come to them immediately. Jonathan wanted to beg out of the consultation, but Lisa reminded him that her mother was crazy about him and he needed to at least go and say hello in person.

"When do you want the wedding to be?" Mary asked when they'd gathered around a table in the living room.

"Next week," Jonathan said at the same time Lisa said, "Next month."

"What's your hurry, girl?" Louise asked, tugging her Walgreens bifocals lower on her nose.

"We want to be together," Jonathan said.

Louise frowned. That answer wasn't good enough for her.

"We know what we're doing," Lisa added. "It's not like we have to get to know each other."

"Is there a reason to rush?" Louise asked, looking closely at her son's sister.

"No, ma'am," Lisa replied, feeling like a teenager again under the older woman's scrutiny. If a blush could have shown on Lisa's dark complexion, Louise would have been the cause of it.

"We need to know so we'll know what kind of time limitations we have," Mary explained, flipping a sheet of her notepad. She was no longer Lisa's mother but all business.

Jonathan took Lisa's hand in his and kissed the palm before saying, "Please hurry up. I'm crazy about this woman and I don't want her to change her mind."

"We could do wonders if you gave us a year," Mary said, waiting to see what kind of response she'd get.

"If you need one year, we'll go to the courthouse and save you all this trouble," Lisa threatened.

"Okay, six months," Louise bargained.

"No," Lisa replied, looking from her mother to her dear friend.

"When do you want the wedding?" Mary asked, tired of playing around.

"November twenty-fifth," Lisa and Jonathan said together.

"So you've already decided?" Mary asked, smiling at the young couple. She should have known that her daughter, the organizer, would have a plan. The girl always did. She was like her mother in that regard.

"Yes, that's the Saturday after Thanksgiving. Our guests will have a long weekend to travel," Jonathan explained, still holding Lisa's hand.

"Do you want to have it at your church?" Mary asked, still jotting notes.

"No, it's so beautiful out at the farm this time of year. We'll hardly need to decorate with all the beautiful fall foliage. I wish we could just open the windows and let everyone enjoy the gorgeous colors."

Mary ignored Lisa's gushing on about the colors. She said, "That severely limits your guest list."

"We don't want many people," Jonathan said.

"How many?" Mary asked, peering at Jonathan over her tablet.

"One hundred," Lisa replied.

"You can't get that many people in that house!" Jonathan exclaimed. He looked at Lisa as if she were nuts.

"My mother can make it happen," Lisa said, resting her arms on the table before her and looking at Mary.

Mary leaned back in her chair, crossing one short leg over the other. She tapped her pen on the table as she looked up in the air. Lisa had no doubt her mother was calculating the square footage necessary per person. Everyone remained silent.

"This is what we'll do." Mary turned to a fresh sheet of paper and drew diagrams. "Your wedding march will be down the stairs and across the foyer to the mantel in the living room. That mantel will be your altar. Guests can stand on either side of the stairwell and foyer and behind you in the living room."

"Can't they have seats" Lisa asked.

"We won't have room for them to sit during the wedding. But tables will be set throughout the house for the reception dinner." Mary drew a circle on the tablet in spaces she had marked *LR* for living room and *DR* for dining room.

"Don't forget about the sunroom. We can put diners out there," Jonathan suggested.

"And the den too," Lisa added. "Can we take the furniture out of the downstairs bedroom and put it in storage? That's a lot of space."

Jonathan nodded.

"Actually, we're going to take all of the downstairs furniture out of the house," Mary declared. "Is that all right with you?" She waited for Jonathan's response. Lisa sensed his hesitation and squeezed his hand. He smiled at her and nodded.

"That includes the pool table in your dining room," Mary clarified. She didn't want any problems later.

"You'll bring it back, won't you?" Jonathan couldn't contain his concern on that one.

"If we must," Louise said. "You need to consider a nice dining room table. You're about to become a married man."

"I enjoy playing pool as much as Jonathan does," Lisa insisted. "We'll bring the table back." Jonathan squeezed her hand back in appreciation.

"Your house is too nice for that big old—" Louise began.

"We're just planning the wedding, not the marriage," Mary said mildly.

Louise was about to argue, but could plainly see that Mary's thoughts had moved to other matters.

"How soon can we have the guest list?" Mary asked.

"I'll have Kita print mine out tomorrow," Lisa replied.

"I don't have a guest list." Jonathan had no idea where he was supposed to get a guest list from.

"Yes, you do. You just haven't seen it yet," Mary advised him. "Think about the people you've known over the years—college, jobs, family, friends, neighbors."

"We'll work on it together," Lisa offered, her hand still in his.

"Doesn't your mother live in Nashville?" Mary asked.

"Yes," Jonathan replied.

"I'm sure she'll have people she wants to invite. Bring her over to help with the planning," Mary suggested. She knew Jonathan's story, but she wanted him to know his mother was welcome.

"I don't think she'll be interested," he replied. "But I'll ask her," he added, seeing the look of reproach on Mary's face.

Before the end of the day, Mary had located an engraver for the invitations. The foursome went together to place the order. After they were back to the limousine, Mary marked invitations off her list. "Next we need to select your wedding dress. Can you go shopping with us tomorrow?"

"I'm sorry, Mama. I have to travel the rest of the week. I'd scheduled these days to work with Bruce and Eric, my new territory managers. We have so many appointments it would be impossible to reschedule all of them. Call me on my cell phone if you need me." She saw her mother's frown.

"I wish I'd known it was that easy. I would have called in my part too," Jonathan whispered in Lisa's ear when Mary and Louise became distracted by their debate about the best place to find Lisa's dress.

As they lumbered through the streets of the central business district in the big old limousine, Mary saw a restaurant she had wanted to try during a previous visit. She had the driver stop.

During dinner, Mary took the time to ask Jonathan the probing questions she had not asked before he was engaged to her daughter.

"Why don't you think your mother would want to be involved in planning your wedding?" Mary asked after they'd ordered dinner.

"She's very busy." Jonathan gave his generic response. He had never explained his mother's personality to anyone because he couldn't.

"Too busy for her son's wedding? What does she do that keeps her so busy?"

Lisa remained quiet. She had known her mother would have to do an inquisition at some point before the wedding.

"She's a counselor at a substance abuse rehab center. She's a former addict," he said and waited for the questions.

"Recovering addict," Louise corrected. "No one is ever a former addict. With addictions everyone is always in the process of recovering. It's something you don't get over."

"Louise is a former nurse. That is, recovering nurse," Lisa explained. "She hasn't worked in ages, but the medicine is still in her."

Jonathan chuckled, knowing that Lisa was trying to lighten the mood.

"Well, just tell your mother she's welcome to join us anytime," Mary said with finality as their meal arrived. She was ready to end her probe and return to plans for the wedding.

After dinner the car dropped Mary and Louise off at the hotel first. "Do you want to go home with me?" Lisa asked.

"You know I do," Jonathan said eagerly. Before they arrived at her place, he was sound asleep. She shook his shoulder and he awakened instantly, only to fall asleep again once they were inside. The next day she began her four-day jaunt through her region.

CHAPTER 18

Lisa returned to Nashville Friday afternoon and went straight to her office. She had planned to be there only a short time because Jonathan had asked her out for the evening. Of course, she got caught up in work that had piled up while she was away. As she was reading through a contract, Mary called.

"Hi, Lisa. Welcome home. Was your trip productive?"

"Yes, it was—very," Lisa said, holding the phone with her shoulder. She didn't focus on her mother's conversation until she heard, "We've hired two young ladies to help us with the wedding plans. One of them, Linda, does beautiful calligraphy. She has already addressed the invitations. But if we're going to have them in the mail by midnight, you and Jonathan need to come over to stuff them and put stamps on them."

"Yes, ma'am," Lisa responded. She had escaped *wedding central* long enough. That was Jonathan's term for Mary's and Louise's hotel room.

The evening turned out to be more fun than one would have imagined. Linda and Valerie, the two secretaries that Mary had hired, stayed to help. Not only did the crew work on the wedding invitations, but they finalized the seating chart, asking Lisa and Jonathan questions about the guests as they planned the seating. Linda calligraphied the place cards for the reception dinner. Valerie developed a spreadsheet for tracking responses and gifts.

Mary took care of a million other details while her crew handled the more mundane chores. Everyone was busy when a knock sounded at the door. Jonathan leaped to his feet to answer it. "Dinner is here," he called out.

"And right on time too," Mary said, looking at her watch. "I told them to have it here by seven-thirty and here they are. I took the liberty of ordering the same thing for everyone."

They shifted the work that was spread on the table to make a place for the meal. Mary uncovered dishes of baked chicken filets in an orange sauce, squash casserole, fresh steamed asparagus, and crescent rolls. As they ate, the plans continued.

"Oh, by the way, Jonathan, are you off duty tomorrow?" Mary asked.

"Yes, I am."

"We need you to get fitted for a tux. Have you thought of who you will ask to be your attendants?" She spread butter on a warm roll as she talked.

He looked at her with a bewildered expression. Before he could answer, Louise chimed in, "And, Lisa, you've got to make a decision about your outfit. Did you get the faxes of Vera's designs? She stopped everything she was doing to create them for you. We need to get back to her. It's going to be a rush as it is."

"I haven't decided yet." Lisa felt guilty that she hadn't looked at them after her mother and Louise had flown to Atlanta to get sketches from Vera Wang, her favorite designer. "They're all beautiful. Vera can't produce a bad design."

"We also need a color scheme. We have to order flowers Monday," Louise said, going down her list.

"Let's use peach, sage green, and gold," Lisa said, thinking of the colors of the leaves on the farm.

Shortly after dinner, Linda and Valerie left to take the invitations to the airport post office as Jonathan and Lisa headed home.

"Jonathan," Lisa began when they were in the car on the way to her place, "I see you invited your father. Don't you want to call him? A formal invitation to his son's wedding may seem a little impersonal."

"If I call, his wife will answer the phone. She may or may not let me talk with him," Jonathan replied with dejection lacing his tone.

"You know I don't ask for much, but please do this. If she doesn't let you talk with him, at least you've tried." Lisa's throaty voice had a soft, pleading quality that would have made Jonathan say yes to anything she suggested.

"Okay, I'll do it for you," he said, moving the gearshift to fourth. "Will you do something for me?"

"Sure, what is it?" she asked.

"Give me a little of your time," he replied.

"You have all my time you want," she said seductively, laying her hand over his.

"Is that right?" he asked, leaning over to kiss her cheek.

"You know it is." She stroked his leg as she said the words softly in his ear.

"Let's hurry and get home," he said, flooring the accelerator.

"Do you realize you're doing more than one hundred?" she asked, looking at the speedometer with excitement. The car moved smoothly, the big, super-charged engine roaring with power.

"I know," he said. "I want to be in bed before one of us falls asleep."

"We don't always have to make love in the bed," she said, stroking his inner thigh suggestively. Her hand moved slowly toward his crotch, and she was gratified to find a bulge there.

"What do you have in mind, Ms. Lisa?" he asked, tremors of pleasure flowing through him.

"I want a lifetime of adventure," she replied. "I don't want our lovemaking to ever become predictable."

"I'll see what I can do about that," was his short reply.

Jonathan was pulling into the driveway behind Lisa's bungalow when his cell phone rang. He was tempted to ignore it, but felt compelled to pull it from his pocket to check. "It's my mother, Lisa. I have to see what's wrong."

"I know," she replied, gently stroking his shoulder.

"Okay, I'll be right there," he said after a brief conversation. "I've got to go."

"I'll be right here." Lisa gave him a long, leisurely kiss, sucking lightly on his upper lip. "Hurry back," she said, jumping lithely from the little car.

When Jonathan arrived at his mother's house, she was in a state he hadn't seen in a long time. He wasn't sure what she was high on. "What happened, Mom? Do you need more time from me?" he asked.

"No, Jonathan. This has nothing to do with you. I called you because I don't want to go back out there. Can you stay with me tonight? I'm so glad I made it home," she said as she passed out.

Jonathan sat in a chair and watched with disappointment as his mother lay on her back, snoring loudly with her mouth open. He'd thought those days of his caring for her as she came down from a high were behind him. Leaning forward with his forearms resting on his upper thighs and his head hanging low, he wondered what had precipitated her binge. Had he driven her to it by talking about his wedding too much? Was the thought of the social event too stressful for her? Or was it that he didn't have enough time to spend with her anymore? He had thought the normalcy of his relationship with Lisa would make his mother happy.

Still wearing her street clothes, Barbara Hill lay sprawled out on top of the bedspread. After removing her shoes, he covered her with a blanket from the closet and tiptoed from the room. He chuckled at the irony of his trying to be quiet. He could blast a bomb next to her head and she'd never stir.

Stretching out on the sofa, Jonathan couldn't fall asleep. Not because the sofa was too short and narrow for him, but because he couldn't stop the thoughts spinning in his head. How would Mary and Louise react to his mother? They were dynamic, take-charge women. Over the years, his mother had lost much of the energy he admired in Lisa and the women who had reared her. In the wee hours of the morning, Jonathan fell asleep.

His cell phone, which he had lain within easy reach on the floor, rang twice before he was conscious enough to answer it.

"Good morning." Lisa's husky morning voice greeted him. She sat at her kitchen table and took another sip of strong coffee. "How is your mother? I stayed up waiting for you to call me last night." Her tone held no hint of an accusation, only deep concern.

"She was high on something when I got here. She passed out and we didn't get a chance to talk.

I don't know why she would do that after so long," he said, sounding hurt, bewildered, and disappointed all at once. He pulled his big, aching body up on the sofa to prepare for a conversation.

"Do you want me to cancel things at *wedding central* today?" she asked.

"I don't know. Maybe I should, but if I don't show up today it could throw things off schedule. I don't want to postpone our wedding under any circumstances," Jonathan said, rubbing his head with his free hand.

"We can always cancel the wedding, but not the marriage," Lisa said firmly. "When your mother wakes up, why don't you bring her with you?"

"I don't know," Jonathan said, uncertainty strong in his voice.

"Mama and Louise already know about the struggles you and your mother have been through. Believe me, they're not judgmental. They take people as they come. Besides, your mother may enjoy the diversion," Lisa coaxed.

Listening to her deep, warm voice lifted his spirits immensely. Her persuasive words required consideration. Suddenly, he was looking forward to the day ahead. "After Mother wakes up I'll see how she is and we'll take it from there," was all he allowed himself to promise. His mother had disappointed him many times in the past.

"That's good enough for me. I'm going over to have breakfast with the *girls* and we'll take care of my *grand ensemble* first," Lisa said, purposely forcing a snooty air to her voice.

"I only hope I can come up to your standards." Jonathan's voice was lightly teasing. "What does your mother have in mind for me to wear?"

"She's going to leave that up to you. Have you

decided on your attendants?" Lisa took another sip of her coffee as they spoke.

"I definitely want Mr. Mueller for my best man. He's been with me through thick and thin. Beyond him, I guess—"

"Jonathan, that's enough. We don't have that much room at the altar to have a whole slew of people. I want only Cara to stand with me. She's been my best friend for the past couple of years. I can talk to her about anything."

"I guess I should have asked Jet to be one of my attendants."

"No, we don't have to have a matching set. Mr. Mueller is your choice and Cara is mine. Let's leave it at that."

"Good, I'll give him a quick call before he goes out for the day." Jonathan had stood and was already in motion as he said the words.

After their conversation, he headed toward the kitchen and almost bumped into Barbara. "Hey, Mom. I didn't know you were up yet."

"I've been up for a while. I heard your conversation. There's no need for you to continue babysitting me," she said, her words thick and slow.

"You called *me*. Why did you call me last night?" he asked tightly.

"I was high. How am I supposed to know what I did or why I did it?" Barbara said lightly. "Go on with your new family. Don't let me hold you back."

"I'm not going anywhere until you tell me what's going on with you," Jonathan insisted.

"Nothing. Absolutely nothing." She walked past Jonathan into the kitchen. He followed her.

"Wait a second. We need to talk." She turned to face him and he was hurt by the blank look she gave him. It was completely devoid of expression or recognition.

"What good will talking do?" she asked.

"You're the counselor. Why don't you tell me? You deal with this mess every day," Jonathan answered, not moving an inch.

"It's no big deal. I had a little slip. For the first time in five years I decided to party a little. I've got it under control," she snapped.

"You nearly died out there on the streets before," Jonathan said patiently, tracing the scar on her face with his fingertip. "Did you have your addiction under control then?"

"What do you want from me?" she asked, giving him a look that clearly said she wished he'd disappear. She was sick of his pity and gentleness.

"I think you should go to a twelve-step meeting today," Jonathan suggested.

"I don't need that." She moved to her kitchen cabinet and took out a can of coffee.

"You don't need to be alone. Come help us plan the wedding." Jonathan appealed to his mother, thinking that it would do her good to be around "normal" people. She dealt with substance abusers every day and was never too far from her demons.

"I can't," Barbara began.

"Please, Mom. I don't ask for much, but this means a lot to me," he pled.

"I don't know why it's so important," she replied, scooping coffee out of a nearly full can.

"Getting married is a special time and it's all about family—the one you're joining, the one you came from, and the one you're building," Jonathan explained.

"If it means that much to you, I'll go," she relented, not looking at him.

"Good, I'll be back for you in an hour. I'll go home and change clothes."

While at home, Jonathan called Alan and asked him to be his best man. Jonathan had been hesitant about asking, not wanting to be presumptuous about their relationship. "I'd be delighted," Alan said instantly. "How could you think I'd be anything but honored?"

"I know you're a busy person and we're not exactly in the same social circle—" Jonathan began.

"I thought we were," Alan interrupted. "I spend as much time with you as I do anyone. Don't even think those boring old men I play poker with are any closer to me than you are."

"Thanks, Mr. Mueller," Jonathan replied. "Lisa's mother, Mrs. Hawkins, wants me to come to their hotel suite to get fitted for a tux today. Do you have time to come with me? I know this is last minute and you might have other plans."

"I can change my plans. In fact, I'll bring Phyllis. She'll have fun meeting Lisa's family too. This is just great. Where is Mrs. Hawkins getting the tuxes?"

"I don't know. She just said she'd have some brought over for me to try." Jonathan had not even thought to ask where they were coming from. His goal throughout all the planning was to see Lisa smile. He knew the wedding meant more to her than she'd ever admit.

"I have a tailor who has been making my suits for years. Do you think she'd mind if I bring him along?" Alan asked, wanting his young friend to have the best for the biggest day of his life.

Several hours later, *wedding central* at the Loews Hotel looked like a live-action demonstration of the chaos theory. The whole room was a mass of confusion, but order reigned supreme. In spite of the various activities and people spread throughout, everyone moved about in quiet productivity. Mary was a kind and gentle ruler from her throne in the living room, keeping her chart of activities close by. If anyone lost focus, she reminded them of their task. Louise circulated from group to group, directing activities.

Oscar, Jet, and Cara had arrived that morning with plans to stay for the weekend. They were there when Jonathan and Barbara arrived. Alan and Phyllis Mueller had just entered the suite when Joseph, Alan's tailor, knocked on the door. Introductions were made all around.

Oscar and Alan took over one bedroom for the tux fitting. They paired up to help Jonathan with his tuxedo selection. "Do you think this is okay?" Jonathan turned to Jet after listening to the older men's advice.

"What's wrong with us?" Alan asked. "Do you think we're too old to guide you in looking stylish and debonair?" Oscar held his hand up for Alan to give him five.

Jet laughed at them. "Don't stress Jon. He's afraid he won't look good enough for my sister."

"So true," Jonathan agreed. "I've got to get this right."

"If things work out, this will be your only chance," Oscar joked.

"I'll definitely only do this once," Jonathan assured everyone.

In the other bedroom, Lisa was going over her final selection for an outfit with Cara, who agreed that her choice would make her look absolutely enchanting. They decided to meet in Atlanta when Lisa went to Vera for a fitting.

Louise, Barbara, and Phyllis joined Mary in the living room. All of the middle-aged women but Barbara were chatting like old friends.

"When we were planning my daughter's wedding, we had a terrible time getting the number down to three hundred," Phyllis said. "We felt obligated to invite everyone we knew."

"If it were left up to me, we'd do the same," Mary said, "but unfortunately, once my daughter makes up her mind, there's no changing it. She wants a small wedding and she's managed to keep the number to one hundred."

"Won't your business associates feel slighted?" Phyllis asked.

"Maybe, but when I married Oscar we invited business associates and anyone else we thought might be interested in seeing two old folks wed," Mary joked.

"So you were married recently?" Phyllis asked.

"We've been married two years," Mary said. "And for my wedding I pulled out all the stops."

"So she doesn't have to force her daughter to have the wedding she always wanted," Louise added.

"That's the way to do it," Phyllis said, cheering her on. "What color are you wearing?"

"My dress will be gold," Mary said. "It's a floor-length silk."

"And I'm wearing a sage-green crepe suit," Louise volunteered.

"What about you, Barbara? Have you decided what color to wear?" Mary asked, turning to include their silent member.

"I haven't decided," she said and let the conversation drop.

"We're going shopping in Atlanta Tuesday. Do you want to fly down with us? We'll use the corporate jet," Mary offered.

"I don't know. I'll have to check my calendar at work," Barbara replied.

"Let us know. Jonathan has our numbers," Louise said.

"You're about to run out of time," Mary couldn't help adding. "The wedding is a week from Friday."

"That's practically two weeks," Louise corrected.

When the men had returned to the living room to have a drink, Joseph, the tailor, managed to have a conversation with Louise. He had been eyeing her all day. The tall, big-boned, gray-haired woman with the sharp tongue was just the kind of woman he liked.

As the day wore on, the group decided to go to dinner together. Joseph made sure he was squeezed in next to Louise.

After dinner, Jonathan excused himself because he had to report for duty at six o'clock the next morning. Lisa rose to leave with him.

"Don't leave your family. I'll see you Monday evening," he promised, kissing her lightly on the lips.

"I'm looking forward to it," she said, putting her arms around his neck and kissing him again. Warmth surged through his body as he reluctantly pulled himself away. He was torn. He wanted to be with Lisa but decided to sacrifice his pleasure.

"Call me on my cell phone. I'm going to stay with Mother when I take her home," Jonathan said casually.

"Is something wrong?" Lisa asked, instantly concerned.

"No, I just don't want to leave her alone yet. This is Saturday night and, well, it might be tempting for her to go find old friends." Jonathan finished up hesitantly, not wanting to go into much more detail than necessary.

"I see," Lisa said, realizing that being with his mother was why he had suggested that she stay and visit with her family longer. She decided not to launch that discussion in a room that gave them little privacy. She watched Barbara and Jonathan walk out the door.

The weekend passed in a flurry of activity and Monday came too soon. Lisa spent the day at her desk and ended up working later than intended. Things continued to pile up on her desk in spite of having two new area managers. She needed time to reorganize enough to shift more work to them. Piling work into her briefcase, she decided to take it home in case she had an idle moment.

Taking the elevator to the first floor, she crossed the lobby to the parking garage. The building was isolated. She wondered where the security guards were.

She stepped into the dim parking garage and had a strange feeling that someone was close by. She shrugged the feeling away. She was still jumpy from the Jennifer Malone episode. She opened her truck door and with one foot on the truck's running board, hands gripped her around the waist, lifting her off her feet. The attacker was about to be given a maiming blow when he whispered, "Can you help me find the woman I'm in love with? She disappeared after I gave her an engagement ring."

Lisa wanted to turn around, but he pushed her against the truck and pressed his body against her back. At that point she let her head roll against his chest and her body relaxed into his.

When she rubbed her hips against his lower extremities, he lowered himself a little so that his groin was level with her buttocks. She gyrated her backside against him until she was satisfied with his arousal.

In spite of his resolve to tease her a moment and then finish at home, he succumbed to her antics. Feeling her softness was driving him crazy. He put his hands inside her jacket and found the opening to her blouse. Tugging at it, he got it open with only a few buttons being lost along the way. With one hand, he stroked her breasts through the soft fabric of her bra.

By now, he was no longer the aggressor, but following her lead. With one hand, she reached up and brought his head down to her neck. He lifted her hair so that he could sprinkle the tender skin of her neck with light, spine-tingling kisses. When he moved to her earlobe, she couldn't contain her moans. Her other hand reached between them and unzipped his pants. He understood what she wanted and quickly unsnapped his jeans and pulled out a foil packet before letting them fall.

Pulling up her skirt and reaching into her thin bikini panties, he was delighted to find silky smooth moisture within the tender folds of her flesh. Wiggling against his groin, she leaned forward to offer him easy access into her. Beside himself with desire, he accepted her offer.

"Baby, that feels so good," she said as he slid up and into her like a hot knife into butter. Wave after wave of heat rushed through her.

"Hm-m-m," he replied, not able to say more. Pulling her hips toward him, he thrust forward.

She was so hot inside he hoped he could satisfy her before he was too gone to care. It had been so long since they had been together—too long.

"Oh, Jon, Jon, Jon, oh-h-h," she moaned. Planting her hands low on the side of the truck for balance, she rolled her hips and moved with him. It was so good, she didn't want to, but she had to. She gave in to a sweet release when his hot liquid pushed her over the edge, bringing on her orgasm.

She remained motionless a moment before she turned and wrapped her arms around his neck. "Oh, my goodness, what is your name, sir?" she whispered. "If you don't find the woman you gave the ring to, would I do?"

"Lisa, you're a naughty girl," he replied, leaning his forehead against hers.

"Don't you know it? You bring out the nasty in me," she confessed.

He couldn't let her go. He kissed her face, her lips, and her ears. "I've missed you so much."

"Me too, Jonathan," she answered, enjoying his rain of kisses. "Let's go home and do this again."

They were at her house in record time. Lisa rushed into the house and headed for the shower. Jonathan came in behind her. "All I want to do is take a shower, nothing more," he promised as he stepped in.

Of course, he couldn't keep that promise. Lisa had other ideas. "Baby, can you soap me right here?" she asked. He stroked where she pointed, enjoying the feel of her soft skin with the liquid soap on his hands. Becoming more aroused as he went, he tried hard to keep his promise to shower and nothing else. But she enjoyed tempting him. With the water beating down on his head, he lowered himself to suck the water off her breasts. She threw her head back and giggled.

"What's so funny?" he asked, looking up at her.

"Nothing is funny. I'm happy, that's all. You make me so happy," she explained.

"I'm going to keep you happy," he pledged.

"Just keep doing what you're doing," she returned, putting a hand on each of his shoulders. When she was ready for him again, he unwrapped a condom and lifted her up so that he could enter her.

She wrapped her long legs around his waist as he moved her hips up and down on his thickened shaft. Each motion sent scorching pleasure through their bodies. As the heat rose, she pressed her face against his neck and whispered, "Jon, Jon, Jon, I love you so."

Ecstasy enveloped them and shuddered through their bodies before they realized the water had grown cold. They finished their shower in cold water and raced to the bed to warm up. Lying in bed touching and enjoying one another, they talked about everything. It had been too long since they'd been alone.

"We're about to be married— can't we move in together now?" Jonathan asked, enjoying lying in bed next to her.

"I have to wait until after the wedding to move out to the farmhouse. You won't have any furniture," she reminded him, kissing his nose lightly.

"I didn't know you wanted to move out there," he replied. "But I'm glad you do. I thought since you'd put so much into renovating this house, you'd want to stay here."

"You've worked on your house just as much," she answered, rubbing her hand lightly over one of his muscled arms. "It's more practical to live on the farm. Where in the city could you keep all your cars?"

"That's a good point," he conceded.

"Speaking of cars," she said, holding up her hand and staring at her engagement ring, "thank you for your sacrifice."

"What are you talking about?"

"I know how much Zora meant to you. I can't believe you'd sell her to get me this ring, but I appreciate what you did. The ring is beautiful. It's exactly what I would have chosen and I'm proud to wear it every day."

"How did you know?" Jonathan asked, confounded.

"I didn't." She laughed lightly. "It was just a wild guess." She kissed him again. "You're so sweet."

The conversation went on that way for several hours. Toward midnight, they decided they wanted a large family and wanted to start right away. "But not tonight," Lisa added. As Jonathan moved toward her, she reached in the bedside table drawer for protection.

CHAPTER 19

Responses to the wedding invitation came in immediately with nearly everyone invited agreeing to come. On the Friday before the wedding, Alan and Phyllis Mueller invited family, friends, and out-of-town guests to their home for a rehearsal dinner. Lisa had decided that a rehearsal was unnecessary, but the Muellers wanted to have the dinner party anyway. Lisa figured she could manage to walk down the steps without practice.

The Muellers' large home in the ritzy Belle Meade neighborhood was filled with a broad cross section of people. Janice and other friends from the fire department were there, including Mia, Foster, and the men from Jonathan's crew. Kita and her new boyfriend came, along with the new territory managers, Bruce and Eric.

Beautiful flowers in rich hues of peach, gold, and green were in attractive bouquets throughout the house. Guests were greeted with a scrumptious buffet featuring pork tenderloin in an orange sauce, sesame chicken with a honey dip, artichoke dip with pita bread, stuffed new potatoes, asparagus roll-ups, and water chestnuts with bacon. For dessert the choices of coconut pecan squares, orange sugar cookies, and tiramisu were offered.

The crowd descended on the buffet tables as they wound their way through the rooms of the elegant older home. The music was mellow and conversation flowed easily with everyone clustered in small groups. The partygoers turned en masse when a late arrival entered the room. The woman swept through in a cloud of feathers and sequins and headed straight toward Lisa and Melvin, who were standing side by side.

"Who is that?" Melvin whispered in Lisa's ear.

Before Lisa could respond, the tall, majestic woman was standing too close for her to answer. Instead she greeted her guest. "Assouka, I am so glad you could come," Lisa said, hugging her friend.

"You naughty girl, how dare you think you could marry someone I have not met? I came to see if the wedding shall go on. Where is he?" she said dramatically, striking a pose as if she expected to be photographed.

After the second jab in the side from Melvin, Lisa said, "Assouka Yekka, I would like for you to meet my brother Melvin. Melvin, this is the international singing sensation whom we've told you so much about. She is now living in D.C. where she owns a nightclub."

"Why am I just meeting this man?" Assouka asked, eying Melvin closely. "He is too delectable."

"Thank you. I could say the same about you," Melvin replied, his voice lowering an octave.

"You look much like Jet, only, mmm, how do I say it—yes, you are so much less tame. You have a risky devil-may-care quality. Is that true? Do you have a wild streak?" Assouka asked, fixing Melvin with eyes made larger and darker with the aid of sparkling eye shadow and mascara.

"Let's discuss my qualities over a drink," Melvin said, taking her elbow and leading her away.

"We'll talk later," Lisa called facetiously to their backs. Several people around her laughed, because Assouka and Melvin ignored her completely. They'd already become engrossed in one another.

Bruce and his friend Dennis came to rescue the bride-to-be. "I'm so glad you could come," she said, giving Dennis a warm embrace.

"So am I," the tall, slender man replied emphatically. "Thank you for convincing Bruce that it's time that I'm no longer a nasty little secret to be kept away from family and friends."

"You were never a secret. We have a company policy to keep our private lives private, don't we, Lisa?" Bruce gave her an intense look as if to force her to say yes.

"Oh yes, that's right," Lisa said, nodding her head energetically.

"Be still, girl. Your curls are falling." Bruce reached up and tucked a curl back in place in her upsweep.

"It is such a pleasure to finally meet you. Bruce talks about you all the time," Dennis gushed.

"I hope he says nice things about me," Lisa quipped.

Dennis leaned forward to whisper confidentially, "He admires the way you never let yourself become defined by gender. You do what you want to do."

"I meant that in a nice way. I like the way you wear the plaid flannel shirts and work boots," Bruce said, as if he'd break out into a rash if he wore them himself.

Lisa threw her head back and laughed. She chatted a while, enjoying their lighthearted banter. As she looked around the room to be sure that their guests were entertained, she spotted Martin Hill, Jonathan's father, sitting with his second wife, Winnie. They were talking with Louise and Joseph.

Although Winnie and Martin had been in Nashville only twenty-four hours, it was plain to see that the woman had trust issues. Lisa laughed aloud when a voice in her ear said, "They are not actually attached at the hip. She just likes to keep him close."

"Now, Jonathan, be nice," Lisa said, turning to face her big, handsome fiancé.

"How can she be jealous of my father after all these years?" Jonathan asked.

"I hope that's a rhetorical question, because I honestly don't have a clue," Lisa replied. In fact, she'd wondered the same. Martin and his family had arrived in time for a big family Thanksgiving dinner that Louise and Mary had hosted out at the farm the day before. Winnie had refused to let either Louise or Mary talk to her husband unless she was present. If Winnie was not near Martin, she would race to his side as soon as one of the women engaged him in a conversation. In fact, she'd been so obvious that they'd actually tested her more than once to be sure their theory was correct.

"I don't think her jealousy has anything to do with your father. She's just a very insecure woman," Lisa observed.

"That's so true," Jonathan said, considering Lisa's words. "She's also jealous of me, Russell, and anything that Dad had in his life before she met him. When I see how close Jet is to you and your brothers, I wish we'd had adults who cared enough to give us that. I'm not sure if Marty and Marcia even know who I am." Jonathan was speaking of Martin Hill's two youngest children.

"They're here. That's a start," Lisa said, rubbing her hand up and down Jonathan's arm. "They're downstairs in the den. Mr. Mueller hooked up an old PlayStation Two for them. Let's go visit with them," Lisa suggested.

The two adolescents were staring glassy-eyed at the TV when Lisa and Jonathan entered the room. When they realized the two adults were watching them, the kids tried to ignore them, hoping they'd go away. After Lisa sat in a chair close to the sofa where they were sitting and Jonathan stood behind her, Marcia and Marty stopped the game.

"We're glad you came for our wedding," Lisa began.

"Thank you," Marcia replied, never looking at her.

"Who do those forty-five hundred points belong to?" Jonathan asked.

"They're mine," Marty said, darting a glance at Jonathan.

"What do you say I play the winner?" Jonathan challenged.

"You can start now," Marcia said, giving up the controller. "I can't beat him in this game because he likes race cars too much."

"So do I," Jonathan said, accepting the controller. "My top score for Death Race 2005 is ninety-eight hundred."

Marty looked at him skeptically, but was too well mannered to call an adult a liar. He couldn't control what his eyes said.

After the males had restarted the game, Marcia turned to Lisa. Curiosity had gotten the best of her. "There sure are a whole lot of people here. Do you know all of these folks?"

"Either I do or Jonathan does," Lisa answered.

"Have you known Jonathan a long time?" Marcia asked.

"About a year," Lisa answered, sitting relaxed in her chair, willing herself to answer whatever the girl might come up with.

"I've never been to an adult party before," Marcia said. "Mama thought about not letting us come, but Mrs. Mueller assured her we wouldn't be in the way. She's a nice lady. Is she your friend or Jonathan's?"

"She was Jonathan's friend first. But I like her a lot," Lisa replied.

"Do you think she'll be your friend because you're marrying Jonathan?" Marcia probed.

"I certainly hope so." Lisa looked at the young girl cautiously. She looked a lot like Jonathan. She was tall and skinny with a thin face.

The girl turned her questions on Jonathan. "Daddy told me that you're a fireman."

"Yes, I am," Jonathan replied, totally intent on not letting his younger brother beat him.

"You don't seem like you're our brother," Marty interjected.

"Why do you say that?" Jonathan asked. The remark caught him off guard. He paused the game to focus on what his brother was saying.

"Because you never come see us," Marty replied bluntly. "We don't know you at all."

"Daddy is always a little sad at Christmas because you aren't there," Marcia finished.

"Why did you pause the game?" Marty asked.

"I was thinking about what you said," Jonathan replied. He was startled to hear that his father missed him. Maybe he'd been too self-centered regarding his relationship with his father.

"Let's play. I'll beat you and then you can think," Marty challenged.

The room became silent as the game heated up. Both guys were intent on winning.

"Here she is," Kevin called over his shoulder as he entered the room.

"What's up?" Lisa asked when all three of her siblings stood before her.

"Jet told us that Oscar is walking you down the aisle," Kevin began.

"But when we asked Oscar he said Jet is," Melvin continued.

"Who is walking you down the aisle?" Kevin finished.

"I'm walking alone," Lisa stated and folded her arms before her. She'd been expecting this battle and wondered why it had taken the men in her family so long to figure it out.

"How can you make such a decision? That makes all of us look bad," Melvin protested.

"You're our sister. One of the men in the family should give you away," Kevin added.

"No, I don't want that," Lisa said succinctly. Then she made an attempt to change the subject. "Have you met Jonathan's brother and sister?" Lisa asked before introducing everyone.

But Melvin couldn't let it go. It must have been important for him if he'd walked away from Assouka. Lisa had assumed they would be together all night. "This is not the time to try to prove you're just as tough as we are."

"It has nothing to do with my toughness. I think I can make it down the steps alone. What is your problem?"

"We want you to let Oscar or Jet escort you to your groom," Kevin insisted.

"Kevin, how do you always get caught up in these things with Melvin?"

"He's right on this," Kevin said defensively. "Lisa, you're being stubborn. Jet, talk some sense into her," Kevin said, pleading to his oldest brother for help. Jet had always solved his problems.

"If I'd known this was why you told me to follow you, I would never have left my beautiful wife." Jet turned to walk away.

"So you're just going to let her do what she wants?" Melvin asked.

"Yes," Jonathan cut in. "It's our wedding, hers and mine. We've discussed this and know what we want." He pointed from Lisa's chest to his. "Tell them our plan," he prompted.

"I don't need their approval," Lisa snapped.

Seeking to soothe her brothers, Jonathan explained, "She feels that since she's lived on her own for several years—"

"Twelve years, to be exact," Lisa interrupted.

"She's an independent woman. As a metaphor for her independence, she'll come down the stairs alone. I'll meet her halfway and walk with her the rest of the way to the altar. That symbolizes our side-by-side walk the rest of our lives."

"But—" Kevin started.

"That's the way it's going to be," Lisa and Jonathan said together.

The brothers walked away without further argument.

"We'd better go mingle with the other guests," Jonathan said to Marcia and Marty as he and Lisa stood to leave, too.

"You're just going to up and leave? You're not going to give me a chance for a rematch?" Marty challenged.

"Come visit me and we'll have a tournament," Jonathan promised.

"We'll see you tomorrow," Marcia said.

"See you later," Marty called after them.

As they walked through the throng of people, Jonathan realized he hadn't seen his mother all night. She had assured him she'd come. He castigated himself, thinking he should have picked her up.

Jonathan asked Mary and Louise if they'd seen his mother yet. When he passed Alan and Phyllis, he asked them. He was certain his mother had not bothered to show up. Finding a quiet room, he stepped inside to call her and got no answer.

By then he was worried. He stayed until Alan had proposed a toast to them, but excused himself shortly afterward.

"Where are you going to look?" Lisa asked, concerned for his safety.

"Everywhere," he said, stepping into the cold midnight air.

"I should go with you and help," she offered.

"No, we don't want you to look tired and worn out on your wedding day. Go home and sleep well. I'll call you first thing in the morning."

Early on Saturday morning, his wedding day, he returned to his cold, dark house angry and frustrated. He had not found his mother and had run out of places to look. He called his contacts in the emergency rooms around town, asking his friends to be on the lookout for Barbara.

Upon his return, Jonathan slept four hours before getting up to resume his search for his mother. He called Lisa to let her know he'd be out of pocket for a while. Lisa doubted Barbara would be found before she was ready, but kept that thought to herself. She remembered the longing in Barbara's voice when she'd talked about her drug addiction. But, loving her fiancé as she did, Lisa only said, "Maybe you need help, Jonathan. Have you thought of hiring a private detective to locate her?"

"I can't," he answered honestly. "I could be getting her in worse trouble. What if she's involved in something illegal? Any ethical investigator would be duty-bound to report any such activity."

"I hadn't thought of that," Lisa confessed. Out of ideas on how she could help, she added, "Don't forget we're getting married today at seven o'clock. Will you be there?" She tried to make her voice sound casual, but she was truly concerned.

"I'll be there regardless," he promised. His tone was much less serious and had taken a husky, flirtatious tone. "I just want to know she's all right before we leave for our honeymoon."

"I understand," Lisa answered. They hung up and, unable to go back to sleep, she returned to her packing.

She was nearly finished when the phone rang again. She looked at her watch and saw that it was almost one o'clock. It couldn't be her mother, who had ordered her to sleep in. "Lisa, this is Barbara Hill."

"Where are you?" Lisa asked. "Jonathan has looked everywhere for you."

"I'm at a friend's house in Antioch. Can you come get me?" Barbara asked.

"Sure. I'll call Jonathan and we'll be there right away," Lisa said, slipping out of her robe and reaching for a pair of jeans. "Give me directions and the address."

"I want you to come without Jonathan. Please.

I'm not up to hearing one of his lectures and I'm sick of the way he looks at me," she said angrily.

"But he's worried sick about you," Lisa said. "The only way he looks at you is with tenderness."

"All I see in his eyes is disgust when he looks at me. If you don't come get me right now, I may not be here later," Barbara threatened.

"I'll just call to let him know you're okay." Lisa struggled to pull her jeans on and hold the phone.

Throwing on a T-shirt and an old jacket, Lisa dashed out of the house. Following Barbara's instructions, she easily found the address. The older woman was standing outside the well-kept house in a nice neighborhood. Lisa noticed that the lawn was neatly trimmed and the shrubbery surrounding the house had been pruned for the winter. The large, two-story house had been recently painted. This didn't look like the crack houses Jonathan had described as his mother's past hangouts.

As soon as Lisa slowed, Barbara walked to the curb and was ready to jump in almost before the big black truck had stopped.

"Thanks for coming. I know you have a million things to do today," Barbara began as Lisa wheeled back onto the main thoroughfare.

"To say the least," Lisa agreed dryly.

Barbara said, "I hope I didn't cause trouble between you two."

"This is our wedding day!" Lisa exclaimed, not able to contain her fury. "If you had waited one more day you could have done whatever you wanted for five days without Jonathan's interference. Did you consider that?"

"No, I didn't. This has nothing to do with Jonathan," Barbara said.

"I imagine to you it doesn't. It's all about you. You

missed our rehearsal dinner last night. Everyone was there. Jon's father drove his whole family down from Detroit, but you couldn't bother to put your youngest son first for even one night."

"I have a headache and you're talking too loud," Barbara said, relaxing against the headrest.

"Where do you want me to take you?" Lisa asked, fighting an impulse to put the selfish woman out on the street.

"I need to check into rehab. Take me out to the Fort Negley Rehabilitation Center. It's right off Eighth Avenue South. They're expecting me," Barbara said calmly.

"Do you mean you've already made arrangements to be admitted?" Lisa asked, keeping her eyes on the road.

"Yes. I'm sorry I have to miss your wedding," Barbara said easily. "But I don't think I'll be missed."

"Jonathan will miss you," Lisa reminded her. "Doesn't it matter to you how he feels?"

"When I became a mother, everyone told me my children would have to come first. I lost my figure because of them. I wasn't able to sleep straight through the night after they were born. It took me forever to get a promotion at work because of them. And having fun? It was out of the question. If we visited people, the children were the center of attention. All of our activities centered on the children for years. And when I thought I was free of all that, Jonathan decided to move down here to take care of me. I didn't need that. You should be asking if it matters how I feel," Barbara said, ending her tirade vehemently.

Lisa shuddered with the woman's last remark. There was no sense saying another word to her soon-to-be mother-in-law. Remaining silent, she moved into traffic on I-24. It was heavy for a Saturday afternoon. Then she remembered this was the big weekend for the UT–Vanderbilt football game. They could be stuck in traffic for hours.

Exasperated, she clenched the steering wheel, wishing she had brought her wedding attire along. She decided she'd better call Jonathan to let him know his mother was in her car. Keeping her eyes on the road, she dug around in her purse for her cell phone. It wasn't there. It was probably still in its base on her dresser.

Barbara broke into Lisa's thoughts when she said, "I've been walking the straight and narrow a long time. It was about time for me to party a little."

Lisa glanced at the woman, aghast with her reasoning. "Jonathan gave up going out with his friends after the rehearsal dinner last night when he realized you were missing. He looked for you all night long," she said, making a final effort to get through to Barbara.

"I knew he would look for me. He always does." She accepted his concern as her due.

"Do you plan to pull a disappearing act like this on a regular basis?" Lisa had to ask. "Because if you are, please be mature enough to call and let me know. That way I can tell Jonathan not to waste his time looking for you."

"Girl, don't try to chide me. I'm the mother here," Barbara said, raising her head enough to look over at Lisa. Then her tone changed and her voice sounded tired. "I might be getting a little too old for partying hard. This may be my last time going out on a binge like that. My crowd is getting old. Most of those old farts have to take medication just to keep their hearts ticking. One of those fools is going to die on me. The young crowd is too rough for me.

Yes, take me to rehab. I need to clean my system out and give this junk up."

"Did you try to call Jonathan?" Lisa asked. "You know he always has his cell phone on."

"No, I didn't try to call my warden," Barbara snapped. "I wanted to have this bit of fun without his making me feel guilty."

Lisa chastised her mother-in-law again. "You may not think about Jonathan or care that he'd risk his life going to crack houses and seedy neighborhoods looking for you, but he does. If something happens to him, I'll personally hold you responsible."

"You don't scare me, girl. I've faced the devil and won." Barbara stroked the scar on her face. "Yes, good old Jonathan, savior of mankind. I'm sure he went crazy looking for me, but he didn't need to do that. He can't save me. That's up to me. I can save myself."

Barbara seemed to be talking to herself. Lisa drove on silently, thinking of all the things she wanted to tell Mrs. Hill, but wondering if her words would make any difference. She held her peace.

When Lisa stopped the car in front of the rehabilitation hospital, Barbara said, "Don't think less of me. I'm the same wicked, selfish woman I always was. Jonathan wants to see me return to my former glory. But the truth is I'm the way I always was. I wasn't a drug addict before, but I liked to party and have fun. I'm selfish and that's all I am. Thanks for the ride," she said and walked away with her head held high.

Lisa hurried to her house and rushed in. She grabbed the bag containing her wedding ensemble and her toiletries. She'd have to finish packing later. When she pulled up the drive at the farm, Jonathan, Mary, Cara, Jet, and Louise rushed at her at once.

"Where have you been?" Jonathan asked, reaching her first.

"Let me out and I'll tell you everything," Lisa said, trying to open the door. Jonathan pulled it open and stepped back to let her out.

"Guests are already here. How are you going to get in?" Mary asked.

"We'll just walk with her through the kitchen, down the back hall, and up the stairs. No one will notice if we're all crowded around her," Cara suggested.

The family gathered around and Lisa walked in their midst.

"We thought something had happened to you," Mary said as they entered the house. "Where were you?"

"I need to talk to Jonathan alone first," she replied. She caught the look of dread on his face and clarified slightly, "I'm okay and I'm in love with you. We just need to talk."

He nodded and said nothing more, but Mary said, "You can talk all you want after you're dressed. The wedding is late. I've never coordinated a wedding that was late before."

"I'm sorry, Mama, but I need to talk with Jonathan before I dress," Lisa said as they climbed the steps.

"Then I hope you give him the abbreviated version of whatever you have to say." Mary breathed deeply and all the other family members remained silent. They were all curious about where Lisa had been, but realized that was one story they'd have to wait for.

CHAPTER 20

Lisa and Jonathan entered the master bedroom and closed the door tightly.

"Where have you been?" he asked again, as she took a seat on the bed.

"I picked your mother up and took her to Fort Negley Rehab."

He stood over her, staring in disbelief. "Where did you find her?"

"I didn't find her, she found me. I was packing when she called. She was at a residence in Antioch and called for a ride. She said she was fine, she just wants that mess out of her system," Lisa explained.

"Why didn't you call me? How is she?" he asked, agitated.

"Sit down," Lisa said, patting the seat next to her. He did as he was told. "She's okay. I didn't call because she asked me not to. Look, Jon, I understand—I even commend you for your concern for your mother. But I have to come first in your life. I don't intend to be in competition with my mother-in-law. Will I be the most important person in your life?"

"You shouldn't have to ask me that," he said,

pulling Lisa close and holding her in his arms. "You'll always be first in my life. But my mother warrants some attention. She needs it. When she goes on a binge, she gets in life-or-death situations," Jonathan explained. "She needs my help."

"She'll let you know when she needs you, believe me. You and I will go to her together when she asks for help. But don't force your good intentions on her. It's a waste of your time. You can't make her want what you want for her. This binge was a conscious decision for her, but I have a feeling it didn't live up to her expectations. I don't think she'll do it again."

Jonathan didn't hear the hope in Lisa's message. He was suffused in guilt. "I should have been there for her."

"Jonathan, your mother is a grown woman. We all make choices and live with the consequences. She chose what she wanted to do. You can't do it for her."

"I just want to keep her safe. Is that so bad?"

"I need you too." Lisa warned, "You left me all alone at our rehearsal dinner to go look for a grown woman. I needed you to be there for me. If you can't promise me that won't happen again, we can call the whole thing off right now." She looked at him expectantly.

"I'm so sorry, baby. That won't happen again." On impulse he dropped to his knees in front of her. "Lisa Stevens, I love you so much. Please marry me right now."

"I will," she said, putting her hands on his cheeks and leaning forward to give him a kiss.

Loud rapping sounded on the door. "Lisa, we're twenty-five minutes late. It's rude to keep your guests waiting any longer. What are you doing?"

"We're kissing," Jonathan called out and Lisa laughed.

"Get out of there. Both of you get dressed," Mary whispered loudly, to be heard through the thick oak door.

Jonathan went down the hall to another bedroom to dress and Louise, Mary, and Cara descended on Lisa in the master bedroom. A beautician trailed them.

They found Lisa leaning out the window, watching the beams dancing from headlights as a motorcade of guests slowly made their way up the graveled driveway from the highway.

"It's a good thing I'm late. It looks like a few folks would have missed the wedding if we'd started on time," Lisa said, turning toward the women.

"Girl, close that window. You're going to catch your death from pneumonia," Louise warned.

"She'll catch the rocking pneumonia and the boogie-woogie flu," Mary sang out gaily, dancing around the room. "Tracy is ready to salvage your hair. It's a good thing I asked her to come out here."

"It sure is," Lisa agreed. "I thought I could keep my hair up for two days, but today got the best of it."

"Where have you been today?" Louise asked.

"Don't tell us now," Mary interrupted. "Finish getting ready first."

"Are you ready for me to do your makeup now?" Cara asked, after Tracy left the room.

"Yes, I'm good and ready." Lisa sighed. "I'm ready to get this show on the road." She followed Cara to the vanity table she'd installed in the adjoining bathroom just a few days before.

After the makeup was applied, Mary carefully lifted her daughter's wedding attire from the padded hangers and handed it off to Louise. "Okay," Mary said, "the pants first." She held the pants low to the floor for Lisa to step into them. As they adjusted them at the waist, Louise gingerly held the top out, waiting for Mary to slip it over the bride's head.

The three women hovered over the bride-to-be until both pieces were adjusted properly. After they were sure everything was in place, they stood back to inspect their masterpiece. She was stunning in the two-piece, white lace pants ensemble that featured an A-line princess-cut tunic with an asymmetrical hip-length hemline. The only concession to tradition was the long train that flowed from the hem of the tunic.

"What do you think?" Louise asked, turning to Mary.

"We done good." The mother of the bride walked around her daughter slowly. "I have never seen you look lovelier." Tears formed in Mary's eyes as she hugged Lisa.

"Do you want us to stay with you until you're ready to come down?" Louise asked, dabbing her eyes.

"No, Cara and I have it. I want to see everyone important to me standing together as I come down the stairs. We'll be just fine." Lisa tried to sound brave, but the tears were about to flow.

The older women left the room, leaving Lisa and Cara behind. They stared at each other in silence for a moment. Lisa followed them to the door and peeked down the hall both ways to see who was lurking about.

"I guess the men are downstairs waiting," she commented.

"Do you hear our music yet?" Cara asked.

"Not yet." Lisa closed the door and walked toward Cara. "Well, sis, any final advice?"

"No advice. Just my best wishes. I hope your marriage is filled with as much joy and adventure as mine has been," Cara said softly, trying to contain the tears that threatened to overflow.

"Please don't make me cry," Lisa said. "You've spent too much time on this makeup."

"There's the music," Cara said, straining to hear the soft strains of harps. "Start walking and I'll adjust your train."

Lisa walked out the door and slowly down the hall. She stopped just before she reached the staircase so that she'd be hidden from the guests' view. Cara adjusted her train and then stood to adjust the top of her own pale green, two-piece lace outfit.

The strings of a violin and cello joined the harp in playing the first notes of "Ribbon in the Sky" by Stevie Wonder and Cara slowly descended the stairs. When she had taken her place opposite Alan Mueller and Jonathan, the music changed. The dramatic sounds of the "Wedding March" swelled and filled the air.

Lisa stood as still as a portrait at the top of the stairs. The guests turned toward her and a hush fell over the assembly. Jonathan looked up at her and was overwhelmed with her beauty. An upsweep hairstyle exposed her long, graceful neck. All he could do was grin when a smile as bright as the morning sun lit up her face. As she slowly descended the stairs, she kept her eyes on Jonathan as he approached her. They were spellbound, caught up in a world all their own.

By the time she reached the sixth step, he was at her side. She put one hand in the crook of his arm and they walked the rest of the way to the altar together. They stopped before the minister who stood in front of the fireplace.

"Dearly beloved, we are here today to witness and celebrate as these young folks make a lifelong commitment to each other. As friends and loved ones, do you promise to support them in their love for one another?" the minister asked.

"We do," the group proclaimed.

"Do you promise to encourage them to honor their vows?"

"We do," the participants pledged.

"Do you promise to help them to remember the good times when they come to you complaining about the bad times?"

"We do," the audience enthusiastically responded a third time.

"Then let us pay attention to the vows Lisa and Jonathan have written to each other." The minister nodded to Lisa, who spoke first. She took one of Jonathan's hands in both of hers as she looked into his eyes and said:

> "Jonathan, I met you when I felt so alone,
> Toiling each day all on my own,
> Never expecting or hoping for more.
> When my eyes met yours my spirits did soar.
>
> "'For you I'll walk through fire,' you did say.
> I thought those words were empty till the day
> You saved my life and swept me away.
> Now I vow by your side I'll stay.
>
> "You have become my confidant, friend, and lover.
> I'll make each passing day better than the others.
> When your days are tough and nothing goes right,
> Come to me, Jon. Shared burdens are light."

Tears were on the rims of Lisa's eyes, about to roll over. She dared not blink. As she said her heartfelt vows, she remembered all that Jonathan meant to her and all he had done for her.

Jonathan listened to Lisa's vows and his heart swelled with love. Walking through fire for her had been nothing that he wouldn't gladly do again. He loved this woman standing before him with all his heart. When she finished speaking, he bent his head and kissed her, only their lips touching, until the minister cleared his throat. Then Jonathan remembered it was time to recite his vows. He turned to her and, taking her hands in each of his, stood before her and promised:

"You know I'm a simple man,
So I have to talk straight from my heart.
For you, Lisa, I'll do the best I can.
I always have, right from the start.

"Once my days were shades of gray.
I can't believe you chose to stay.
A gift from God I never thought
to receive.

"Now my life is filled with pleasure.
Your love, girl, I truly treasure.
On this day you become my wife,
I promise to keep from you pain and strife.

"This I vow to you my bride,
I'll forever be at your side.
One thing I know to be true,
I'd give my very life for you."

By the time Jonathan finished, Lisa was sniffling loudly. He took a handkerchief from his pocket and gently wiped her tears away. The minister cleared his throat again, as if he were moved emotionally, before he led them in exchanging wedding rings.

The ceremony ended when the minister said, "By the power vested in me by the State of Tennessee, I now pronounce you husband and wife. Do you want to kiss again?"

When the minister asked the last question, everyone laughed, cheered, and applauded while Jonathan kissed Lisa lightly on her lips. When he lifted his head, he and Lisa turned to greet their guests. The minister announced, "I now present to you Jonathan and Lisa Hill."

The guests found their names on place cards on the tables placed throughout the first floor. Lisa and Jonathan sat at a large, round table with Oscar and Mary, Alan and Phyllis, Cara and Jet, and Louise and Joseph. Hors d'oeuvres of spicy stuffed snow peas, crab cakes, and caviar on toast points were already on the table. Guests munched the delicious appetizers and poured champagne from bottles in nearby chillers as Jonathan and Lisa made their way from table to table to thank their guests for coming.

By the time they'd made the rounds the main course of beef tenderloin with béarnaise sauce, baby rack of lamb with mint sauce, twice-baked potatoes, spicy spinach, and fresh steamed asparagus was served. While many of the diners were still eating, Alan stood and proposed a toast to Jonathan.

Holding his champagne glass high, Alan said, "I admire Jonathan Hill because he is a sincere young man with integrity, determination, and compassion. Many of us give our children everything and they expect it. Jonathan, on the other hand, has worked hard for what he has and is grateful. Jonathan, you are like one of my sons. I wish you and Lisa a world of happiness and joy."

After the toasts, it was time to cut the wedding cake. Mary led the couple over. "Come on, Jonathan. You have to cut the groom's cake first."

"What is a groom's cake?" Jonathan asked, puzzled.

"It's a Southern tradition to have a special cake that suits the groom," Lisa explained, walking him to the table. He was surprised and delighted when he saw a three-dimensional fire truck sitting on a table next to the five-tier wedding cake. When he cut through the red-colored cream cheese frosting, he discovered his favorite, red velvet cake, inside.

While guests gathered around to watch Lisa and Jonathan make the first slice on the wedding cake and feed each other, the catering crew folded up the tables. The floors were now cleared for dancing.

Lisa danced with Jonathan first and then with Oscar. Alan tapped him on the shoulder and he was Lisa's partner until their dance was cut short by Foster and then Artis. During the course of the evening Lisa danced with one firefighter after the other until she would have sworn she'd danced with the entire Nashville Fire Department.

When Jonathan was able to free himself from the line of ladies waiting to dance with him, he found Lisa. "Let's get out of here," he whispered. "The plane is waiting for us at the airport."

Her mother saw them and motioned for the stairs where she met Lisa. She followed her daughter to the master bedroom where she quickly helped her undress and change into her honeymoon attire.

"Thank you so much for everything, Mama. The wedding and dinner were beautiful."

"You're welcome. I like the way things turned out too. I would have planned a wedding that didn't suit you and Jonathan at all if you'd let me get carried away. I hope you were able to have a little fun too," Mary said, reaching up to put a strand of Lisa's hair back into the upsweep.

"I did. But most of all, I'm looking forward to my marriage," Lisa said sincerely with love shining in her eyes.

"I know you are, baby. Can you wait a minute before you get started?"

"Sure, is something wrong?" Lisa asked, sitting on a bench at the foot of the bed. Mary sat in the big armchair on the wall in front of the bench.

"I have a gift for you. I've wanted you to have it for a while, and when you announced your engagement I held off. I wasn't sure if it was appropriate, but now I'm certain it is."

Lisa eagerly tore into the small bundle. Inside was a velvet jewelry box. When she saw the pendant inside, her eyes filled with tears again. "I'm bound and determined to cry today," she said, sniffing and holding her head down.

"Do you like it?" Mary asked anxiously. She leaned forward in her chair to get a good look at her daughter's face.

"I love it. It is so dainty. You've never given me anything so delicate before," Lisa said.

"I didn't think you'd appreciate anything like that before," Mary admitted. "The diamond in the pendant is from the engagement ring your father gave me."

"Oh, Mama, thank you. I must be getting old because I do like sentimental things now." Lisa jumped from the bench and kneeled before her mother, giving her a warm hug. "That is so thoughtful. I love it and I love you for knowing me so well. Yes, I'm ready for this gift now."

"Don't think that I've forgotten your father just because I'm giving you that diamond or because I've married again. Eddie will always have a special place in my heart. He gave me three wonderful children. Your father was a fantastic man with an extraordinary vision. A hardworking man who was willing to do what it took to provide for his family. Not just tangible things but comfort, security—everything. Lisa, you've married a man just like your father. I hope you are as happy as we were for twenty-two years."

Lisa didn't try to stop the tears that rolled down her cheeks. "Mama, you're right. Jonathan is wonderful and he does make me feel all those things. And I love him so much."

"Then don't sit here talking to me. Get ready to go with your man," Mary said, gently pushing Lisa away and laughing. Lisa reached up and hugged her mother one last time before she and Jonathan slipped away.

Jonathan had taken care of their honeymoon arrangements and it was a surprise to Lisa. All she knew was that they were going to Phoenix. The Gulfstream arrived at Phoenix Sky Harbor International Airport at midnight where they were met by a limousine that promptly delivered them to the Royal Palms Resort and Spa. "This place is absolutely enchanting," Lisa gushed as they pulled up to the Mediterranean-style estate with Camelback Mountain as its backdrop. "We could be in another country or another century."

Jonathan looked at his wife's flushed face and was pleased that she liked his selection for their honeymoon hotel. He'd taken the advice of friends and kept his fingers crossed that she would like it.

They were met at the hotel entrance and escorted through revolving doors to a concierge who was apparently awaiting their arrival. He whisked them away to a private casita on the other side of the Valencia Gardens.

The luxurious suite was decorated with Spanish Colonial furnishings, including an oversize canopy bed curtained with white netting. After showing the newlyweds through the suite, the concierge opened the French doors that led to a private patio and an awe-inspiring view of the mountains. They followed him onto the patio where he pointed out a nearby orange grove and a croquet lawn.

They returned to the living room where the concierge offered to start a fire in the fireplace. "No, thank you," Jonathan said. "We'll be going to bed shortly. I don't want to leave the fire burning while we sleep."

Lisa stood beside Jonathan and wrapped an arm around his waist. Looking up at him, she said, "It sounds like you are as tired as I am."

"Yes, this has been a long day. Let's go to bed." They went to the bedroom arm in arm. Lisa took a negligee from her suitcase and went into the bathroom to change. Jonathan remained in the room and slipped into black silk boxers.

While Lisa changed, Jonathan was sitting in a chair, afraid he'd fall asleep if he lay in the bed. After all, he'd slept little the night before. He'd spent all but four hours of it looking for his mother. He knew Lisa must be tired too. They could wait and consummate their marriage the next morning.

After all, why would one night be more important than another?

The bathroom door opened and Lisa stood before him wearing black-mesh baby doll pajamas that consisted of a sheer tank top with deep splits on both sides and a thong. His breath caught in his throat and his eyes ravished her, filling her with warmth. As if mesmerized, he met her halfway as he had earlier that day. He led her back to the bed where he took a seat and looked up at her worshipfully. Of their own volition, his hands slid under the sheer top and stroked her tender sides.

She massaged his broad shoulders and luxuriated in the feel of his large hands on her. He licked her nipples through the fabric, first one, then the other. When they were as firm as pebbles, he stood and lifted the top over her head. Tossing it aside, he pulled her close. He looked into her eyes and seeing the passion there, he kissed her ardently.

Again, she felt her legs weakening as the passion rose inside. He held her tightly and laid her back on the bed. "Lisa Stevens, you're too much for me."

"That would be Lisa Hill," she corrected saucily as she folded him in her arms.

"Ah yes, Mrs. Hill. What is this power you have over me?" he asked, lying between her legs and looking up into her face.

"It's got to be love," she said. "That's all I have over you—a powerful love."

They made love then, sweetly, tenderly, all through the night, and just when they thought they had no more energy, it was restored by love.

The next morning Lisa woke up before Jonathan. She went into the bathroom and returned to find him sitting up in bed. "Where is that flimsy little thing you had on last night?" he asked.

"I put it away. Don't you like this one?" she asked. She wore a long-sleeve opaque robe.

"Let me guess. The one you wore last night was a gift from your mother. This is a gift from Louise."

Lisa didn't answer but released her throaty, mirthful laughter.

"I can tell by your laughter I got it right." He stood and released the belt on the robe. Letting it slide from her shoulders, he tossed it to a chair. "Tell Louise not to buy any more lingerie for you."

"I can't do that. She'll be hurt," Lisa protested. "And she may not give me any more gifts at all."

"And I know how much you like giving and getting gifts. Do you want to see your surprise now?" Jonathan asked, reaching into a table beside the bed.

"Sure I do," Lisa said expectantly.

Jonathan gave her a large, square envelope. "You told me that you want to see how fast you can go. Now here's your chance. You'll learn how to drive like a professional race car driver in the next three days."

Lisa opened the envelope and then jumped off the bed. Forgetting her nudity, she jumped up and down. "You got me a gift certificate to Racing Legends driving school. Thank you! Thank you! Thank you!"

Instantly aroused looking at her, he wished he'd let her keep her robe. "You may not thank me when you're finished. It's a pretty strenuous program. But you'll be behind the wheel of a race car on the first day and you'll be able to get up to real race car speeds."

She sat down on the bed again and read through the brochure. "I'll get a helmet and racing uniform too. You won't be able to touch me," she joked.

"I'm married to a true gearhead," Jonathan marveled.

"Don't hate on me because I like grease and engines. This is going to be so fun. Thank you," she said again, bouncing across the bed to hug him.

"You don't have to go three days if you don't want. I just thought that by the third day, you should really have some skills to take home with you. But we can do something else," he said, reconsidering his gift to his wife.

"This gift is perfect. It's just what I wanted, but I never would have thought to get it for myself. You know me so well." She hugged him again, causing a big grin to spread across his face.

"I don't know you as well as I'm going to know you." He laid her down in bed and covered her with his body.

"Do you know what the wonderful thing about that is?" she asked.

"I think I can figure out several wonderful things, but tell me what you're thinking," he said, lightly kissing her temples.

"We have a lifetime to get to know each other." Her light strokes on his back were stoking a flame in his groin.

"We'll share all our little idiosyncrasies," he murmured, nibbling her ear.

"And fantasies," she added, giving in to the desire swirling from deep inside her core.

"This is going to be a wonderful lifetime," he said, kissing her deeply.

CHAPTER 21

Five years later

Lisa waddled across the long expanse between the back door of the farmhouse and the nearest picnic table. Jonathan met her before she was halfway to her destination and took the large yellow bowl containing potato salad from her hands.

"I told you that you couldn't have this party if you tired yourself out," he scolded lightly.

"Yes, you did," she agreed. "But I can't think of a better way to celebrate the first NASCAR victory for the Sand Castles team."

"Are you all right, sis?" Jet asked, coming to take her elbow.

"I've been pregnant three times. Why do you guys always get so nervous?" Lisa asked.

"Could it be because you get so big?" Melvin asked, joining them.

"Or because you won't slow down?" Kevin offered.

They reached the picnic table where Phyllis Mueller and Cara were laying out food. "You guys need to stop fussing over Lisa. It's not many women in their ninth month who move as well as she does. Jet, please take Jeff and Nia inside to wash their hands. We'll eat shortly." Cara referred to the couple's five-year-old son and three-year-old daughter.

Louise and Mary were at the other end of the table. "Jonathan, you should take Joanie and Jason in too," Louise instructed. "They need to wash up."

"I'll take care of Joanie," Barbara Hill offered. She held her two-year-old granddaughter on her lap and wasn't ready to give her up. It was so seldom the child would let anyone hold her.

Four-year-old Jason looked at his father coming toward him and took off in a full gallop. Marty, Jonathan's brother, blocked Jason. "That's why I'm glad you're in school here, man. This boy needs two fast runners to catch him," Jonathan said. Marty was in Nashville attending Tennessee State University. The farmhouse had become a second home for him during breaks and weekends.

As Jonathan was thanking Marty, Jason dipped between Marty's legs and took off running again. The two men chased the preschooler. The child never looked back, but laughed as he ran.

"The Sand Castles race team should be here any minute and with them will come the news reporters," Mary warned. "We should look like a family that supports the winning team."

"I can't believe we have our own race team," Mia said from a nearby chaise longue. She was as big as Lisa and was having trouble with her second pregnancy.

"We had to do it," Lisa explained. "There were no African-American race car drivers in NASCAR."

"Who would have thought you'd have a winning team your first year out?" Foster asked.

"I would have. Sand Castles had my man to

direct them on all the right things to do," Artis bragged loyally.

"It's a shame Jonathan wouldn't leave the fire department and manage the race team full-time," Alan said. "But I understand his loyalty."

"He's done his part. He knew all the right people to hire," Oscar added. "That Tuck Lane is a real coup and our secret weapon. We have the best pit crew in the circuit."

"Tuck and his ability to recruit interns from North Carolina AT&T. They bring a lot of innovation to our team," Joseph noted. "I'm glad we've got my little investment in there."

"Who would have thought I'd be down here in Tennessee watching people race cars and enjoying it?" Assouka said in her delightful British accent. She stroked the back of Melvin's neck and he relished it.

"Who would have thought you'd be married to the dean of a prestigious business school and living the life of a faculty wife on a historically black college campus?" Lisa asked, smiling at her friend.

"I'm not just a faculty wife. I have the best traveling dancing and singing troupe of any HBCU," Assouka asserted.

"Whatever you do, I'm glad you're doing it with me," Melvin said, taking her hand. He kissed the palm before kissing her wrist.

"Okay, Melvin, that's as far as you go," Louise said from the other side of the table. "The children are returning."

"This is my wife," Melvin argued.

"It's good for the children to see genuine affection," Mary advised.

"You're right," Louise agreed. "I just love to tease Melvin. He's never been so caught up with any woman in his life. This is fun to watch."

"Woman, I'll give you something to watch," Joseph said, coming behind Louise and wrapping his arms around her waist. She turned to her husband of five years and forgot about the others.

Jason returned from the house and ran toward his mother. "Here's my little man," Lisa said, trying to lift her son to her lap and giving up. She wrapped an arm around his chubby shoulders. "Did Daddy buy you another Corvette?" She took the car from her son's hand.

"Yes, this is Daddy's Zora," the child said.

"Don't let some girl talk you into selling it," Alan teased.

"Not unless you want to spend the rest of your life with her," Jonathan added. He bent over and placed the boy on Lisa's lap. She smiled at him and he knew he'd do anything in the world she wanted the rest of his life.

Dear Readers,

Plenty More Love is the last in the Stevens family trilogy. If you enjoyed this book, I'm sure you'd like to read *Passion's Promise,* the story of how Cara and Jet met, and *Love on Hold,* the story of how they stayed together.

In each of my novels the heroine has the personality traits of a member of my family. This is also true for Lisa Stevens, a young woman who grew up competing with her three brothers. My daughter, who was called a tomboy most of her life, came home one day with a T-shirt that said I'M NOT A TOMBOY, I'M AN ATHLETE. Since that time, she has continued to excel in many male-dominant roles while maintaining her femininity. These are the qualities I tried to portray in Lisa.

I truly enjoy hearing from each of you. Write to: christinetownsend615@yahoo.com or to P.O. Box 330555, Nashville, TN 37203. Please make my Web site a regular stop. It is updated monthly: www.christinetownsend.com.

Warmest regards,

Christine Townsend

More Sizzling Romance From
Candice Poarch

__Bargain Of The Heart	1-58314-222-3	$6.99US/$9.99CAN
__The Last Dance	1-58314-221-5	$5.99US/$7.99CAN
__Shattered Illusions	1-58314-122-7	$5.99US/$7.99CAN
__Tender Escape	1-58314-082-4	$5.99US/$7.99CAN
__Intimate Secrets	1-58314-033-6	$4.99US/$6.50CAN
__The Essence of Love	0-7860-0567-X	$4.99US/$6.50CAN
__White Lightning	0-7860-0365-0	$4.99US/$6.50CAN
__With This Kiss	0-7860-0474-6	$4.99US/$6.50CAN
__Lighthouse Magic	1-58314-349-1	$6.99US/$9.99CAN
__Courage Under Fire	1-58314-350-5	$6.99US/$9.99CAN

Available Wherever Books Are Sold!

Visit our website at www.BET.com.